PERM

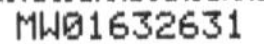

PERMUTED PRESS

NEEDS **YOU** TO HELP

SPREAD THE INFECTION

FOLLOW US!

FACEBOOK.COM/PERMUTEDPRESS

TWITTER.COM/PERMUTEDPRESS

REVIEW US!

WHEREVER YOU BUY OUR BOOKS, THEY CAN BE REVIEWED! **WE WANT TO KNOW WHAT YOU LIKE!**

GET INFECTED!

SIGN UP FOR OUR MAILING LIST AT **PERMUTEDPRESS.COM**

PERMUTED PRESS

SLOW BURN 2

MIKE FOSEN
HOLLIS WELLER

A PERMUTED PRESS book

ISBN (trade paperback): 978-1-61868-2-826
ISBN (eBook): 978-1-61868-2-833

Cover art by Roy Migabon

This book is a work of fiction. People, places, events, and situations are the product of the author's imagination. Any resemblance to actual persons, living or dead, or historical events, is purely coincidental.

You can take it from my cold, undead hands...

PROLOGUE

October 26
Dallas, Texas

The impact slammed Matvei hard, knocking him momentarily unconscious. The helicopter hit the ground with a deafening crash on its left side, killing the pilot instantly, his body pinned between his crumpled seat and the ground. The instrument panel showered Matvei with sparks and began to smoke heavily.

Matvei's vision swam as he regained consciousness, and for a moment he did not know where he was. He gasped for clean air, his mind flashing back to the past. His childhood in Russia, his military career, and being forced into mercenary work. The mercenary calling had caused him to work for the highest bidder, ultimately working for Mexico's most ruthless and powerful drug cartels. With the lure of power and money, Matvei had delivered a lethal biological weapon into the hands of his employers. It was then ruthlessly released into the unsuspecting world. The biological agent had worked beautifully at first, but then went horribly wrong. The weaponized virus had mutated once deployed, and instead of killing off the population, turned them into contagious killing machines. The horrific images of grotesque undead, snarling and clawing, prompted Matvei to get moving. Blinded by the thickening smoke, he felt for the instrument panel and was dismayed to find the radio destroyed. Hearing cries from the back, he knew that someone else was still alive. After struggling to get his seatbelt off, Matvei crawled back into the main cabin, trying to clear his head. He found that the two men sitting on the left side of the helicopter were also dead. The other two were alive, but one of them had a broken leg, his shattered femur sticking through the flesh of his thigh. The other survivor seemed stunned just like Matvei but otherwise uninjured. He didn't know their names and didn't really care. As Matvei and the uninjured man struggled to get the wounded guy out of the helicopter, an ominous sound soon rose above the injured man's screams.

"We have company," Matvei stated. "How long was I out?"

"Not long," the man replied. "Those bastards sure found us fast."

Dropping the injured man, Matvei pulled his USP .45 and fired at an infected man that suddenly appeared in the open doorway. When the infected snapped back from a .45 slug to the forehead, another took his place. Matvei soon emptied his magazine into three different targets. Reloading, he wondered how the infected had gotten there so quickly. The golf course was well north of the city. Matvei figured they must be on the move, perhaps chasing the remnants of his command as they fled north. The other uninjured man was now firing a rifle, and Matvei's ears rang loudly, adding to his sensory deprivation. Thankfully, no more grotesque figures appeared in the opening, allowing Matvei to gather his thoughts. He crawled back into the cockpit of the helicopter and retrieved his assault rifle from the floor. Examining the rifle, it appeared undamaged by the crash. He retrieved his backpack from under a seat in the main cabin and tossed it outside. He next hoisted himself out of the cabin and jumped down to the ground. The other man was already outside and was firing an AK-74 at several more shambling figures that were steadily advancing in the distance. Matvei glanced around and discovered that they had indeed crashed in the middle of the golf course green on the thirteenth hole. Even here the infected managed to be on them almost immediately.

Matvei opened his bag to retrieve a magazine for his rifle right as a grotesque infected woman appeared from behind the downed chopper. She set upon the other mercenary before either he or Matvei could react. The woman sank her teeth into the man's neck and ripped free a mouthful of flesh before being shot in the back of the head by Matvei. The round also passed through his comrade's head, and both fell limp to the ground. A quick double tap assured the kill. Clearing the rest of the ground around the chopper, Matvei found no other immediate threats, and from the shambling horde approaching, judged that he had a few minutes before becoming in danger of being surrounded. He climbed back into the Huey and looked around the cabin for anything else useful that may be inside. He had to crawl over the injured man to reach an ammo can containing extra magazines for his weapons. He grabbed the can and also a canteen full of water lying nearby. The injured man, now sweaty and pale-faced with shock, weakly asked Matvei for help.

"I'm sorry," Matvei replied while offering the man a drink of water. "The infected are almost here. Your leg's broken, and you'll be unable to move. There's nothing more I can do for you."

Matvei reached over and grabbed a pistol that was lying on the floor of the helicopter, dropped the magazine and handed it to the man. Clearing the chambered round from the weapon, Matvei climbed out of the chopper, tossing the handgun to the doomed mercenary.

"You know what you need to do," Matvei stated flatly and disappeared from sight before finishing his sentence, "and so do I."

Grabbing his bag, Matvei threw in the extra magazines and water, shouldered it, and picked up his rifle. Some of the newly infected were faster and beginning to close in, so he set off at a fast pace to the north. Determination was etched into his face as he raised his rifle in his hands and cleared a path through the infected. Before leaving the golf course, he heard a single shot from the crash site.

Matvei, once the commander of an entire mercenary army, was now alone. Alone to face the army of undead that he helped create.

1

October 26
Day 62
Joliet, Illinois

Bob Malkin crouched in the shadows of a row of bushes that lined the yard of an abandoned home. He nervously scanned the immediate area for those disgusting creatures that Father Kettle referred to as "Satan's Soldiers", but he knew better. They were fucking zombies. Bob had little knowledge of what had happened to the world as he knew it. He'd spent the last several months prior to the outbreak shacked up with his brother drinking heavily, getting high, and committing the random robbery to sustain said lifestyle. When society broke down, he was knee deep in some fine prostitute's fun box and missed the first days of chaos. When he had awoken from his drug and booze induced haze, he discovered that neither his brother, nor the hooker, were anywhere to be found.

The next month was spent running and hiding from the roaming bands of infected corpses until he had come across Father Kettle's camp. Even though he was not a religious man and did not believe the things that Father Kettle preached about, neither was he stupid. He knew that Kettle's camp was a perfect match. Booze and random types of drugs were commonplace. The women were nothing to brag about though, except for the ones that Kettle kept for himself. But beggars couldn't be choosers, and these days he was just happy to get a piece of ass. And a piece of ass for the good Father was what brought him and his buddies outside the safety of Kettle's camp. He glanced back towards the other men and waited for the last to catch up to the group.

"Let's hurry the fuck up, guys!" Bob growled at the others. "We've gotta get this set up before those assholes from the prison show up!"

The tattoo-covered men grunted and continued their brisk pace. They were not used to being up that early in the day, and had partied a little too late. Bob and his crew of four hardened criminals had been shadowing the prison crew's founding group and were now ordered by Father Kettle to move on them. They passed through a couple of neighborhoods until they came to a house that was well suited for their purpose. Jonas, a devoted follower of the good Father, was now inside the prison and confirmed what Father Kettle had been told. Mattie, the woman he desired, was going to be out on a supply raid in the Ridgewood neighborhood, orchestrated by the men Father Kettle despised.

"They're cops, don't forget," Bob reminded his crew. "Payback's gonna be a bitch."

Their top priority was to abduct that woman Mattie, whom Father Kettle insisted be delivered alive and unharmed. The others were to be killed if possible. The plan was to pick a house on the street near where their targets were hitting and to make sure the house that they chose for the ambush would be reached towards the end of the day, when they would be tired from the day's work. They would ambush the entry team, who would not be expecting anyone to be shooting back, grab Mattie as a hostage, and get safely out of the area.

Bob kicked open the rear door and sent the other men inside to clear it. Scanning the area, Bob had the feeling he was being watched and it didn't feel good. Adjusting his grip on the shotgun he held, Bob spat onto the rear steps and entered the residence. Inside the red brick two-story home, Bob saw that his men had finished checking out the house. Two men stood in the front room peering out the windows for movement, and two others were currently raiding the pantry for something to eat. After finding a few bags of pretzels the men settled in for a long wait.

"Remember fellas, if we get the chance, we snatch that Mattie whore and split," Bob reminded. "We don't have the firepower for a drawn out battle with the others if we can help it. If we don't see her we play nice and walk away."

"I'm gonna kill me a cop today," a hefty man with a rifle said. "Gonna cap his ass just like I always wanted."

"Do we get ta sample her before we get back?" one of them asked.

"Father Kettle says he wants her unharmed," Bob ordered. "And he would have our asses for it. But if she tries anything stupid I'll have that fine ass, we're all sinners after all."

The men laughed at Bob's joke, all eagerly looking forward to having a shot at the young woman. Inside the musty odor-filled home, Bob and his men sat waiting for the time to strike. Hours passed and the boredom began to take its toll. Bob alternated between pacing and smoking.

"Shouldn't have drank that last bottle last night," one of the men breathed between yawns. "I'm fucking beat."

This only drew a fraction of the response as Bob's joke had, as the others nodded tiredly. The men were not known for their work ethic or patience, so when nothing happened to keep their short attention span focused, one by one they began to drift off to sleep.

*

Chris made his way over to where I was resting with Mattie and sat down, opened his water bottle and took a long drink.

"That's the fifth house we've cleared and cleaned since lunch, Mike," he said between gulps. "How many more you plan on hitting? The men doing the grunt work are getting tired."

I looked over at his sweat stained-shirt and replied, "I wanna hit one more and call it a day. We got some good stuff the last few houses, and if the next one pans out, we can head back."

"Good, I'm sick of room clearing already," Chris said with a look of relief.

"Everyone's counting on us, Chris," Mattie said. "Think how grateful those kids are when they see you come back every night."

Chris didn't reply. He knew Mattie was right that the house to house raiding must be done. The small community at the prison counted on the resources gathered on these raids for their survival.

I scooted away from Chris during his silence and moved closer to Mattie. When Chris gave me a dirty look I just shrugged.

"She smells better," I said with a laugh. "You stink!"

"Yeah, I guess I do," Chris sighed.

I left Chris to his thoughts and headed over to where our entry team was taking their break. Catching the water bottle one of the guys tossed me, I chugged most of it down in one gulp.

"Any idea how many more targets we're hitting today, boss?" one of them asked.

"Probably just one or two more," I replied. "The last few houses hit pay dirt and if that trend continues, we're gonna be out of room in the trucks."

The rest of the team liked hearing that and let out a small cheer. Looking down the street, I visually inspected the remaining homes on the block that need to be cleared.

"Let's get this over with."

Grabbing the breaching ram, I got the men readied to hit the next house. It looked to be a promising building. It was a large two-story brick home; the structure looked intact and had no signs of being looted. The detached garage had already yielded quite a few gallons of gas and a pop up camper. Hopefully its former tenants were food hoarders and left all their shit behind, but I knew that was wishful thinking on my part. Hefting the breaching ram, I was about to assemble the team when my radio chirped to life.

"Mike, this is Chris, do you copy me?" the radio crackled.

"Go ahead Chris, what's up?"

"Listen up," Chris said. "We have a huge horde of undead heading our way from the east. They're two blocks away and coming right for us."

"How huge is huge? Is it something we can handle or no?" I asked.

"I'm guessing well over five hundred so far, and more are filtering in," Chris advised with his voice on edge. "That's way too many for my guys to take on."

"Roger that," I decided quickly. "Pull your men back and meet back here with us. We're out of here."

Grabbing everyone's attention around me, I notified them of what was closing in on us, that we were done for the day and pulling out.

"Looks like we've been spotted," I told the men as they mounted up. "We'll get to it another day."

Within minutes, my team was loaded up and ready to move out. When Chris finally made it to my truck and climbed in, an enormous chunk of the zombies spilled out onto the street a few houses away.

"Cutting it a bit close, aren't you?" I asked Chris while looking at their hungry eyes in my rear view mirror.

"I wanted to make sure everyone was accounted for," he replied quietly. "Don't want to leave a single one of my men behind."

I gave the signal and our little caravan pulled out for the prison, leaving a mass of frustrated undead in our wake.

*

The pitiful creature shuffled up to the rear door of the old brick home, pausing when it detected succulent fresh meat nearby. Approaching the rear door, it pushed against the damaged door. With the help of his comrades he forced it open and led the way inside. Many of his brethren flooded into the rear of the home, which was quickly filled with the sounds of screaming. Bob jerked his eyes open before the first scream had ended with a gurgling sound.

"Son of a bitch, when did I fall asleep?"

Stumbling to his feet, he turned to see what the problem was. His sleep fogged brain came instantly crystal clear as the first blood-covered man from his team came running into his room screaming, followed by a half dozen zombies.

Bob's shotgun roared in his hands as he blasted the disgusting creatures. Finishing them off, he already made out the terrifying low sound of a growling teammate. He struggled to feed fresh shells into the shotgun, and raised his gun just as the man attacked. Bob's weapon roared and the slug ripped most of the man's head clear off. With a wet, meaty splat, the former group member's corpse fell to the ground as more undead flooded into the room. Retreating, Bob ran up the nearby stairwell to the second floor. He grabbed nearby furniture and shoved it down the stairwell, creating a makeshift barrier for the encroaching zombies.

Howls of rage and hunger filled the home as more and more jammed into the small bottleneck. Standing there entranced at the scene before him, Bob could see the three other teammates at the foot of the stairs screaming for his blood.

He swore, reloading his shotgun, "Well, if this all just didn't go to shit!"

What the fuck had happened? He knew he'd told Harry to keep watch.

Below him the pieces of furniture began to fracture and break under the weight of the zombies. Frantically, he looked around and entered what was most likely the master bedroom of the home and barricaded the door. Glancing out the window, he saw the backyard was filled with more of the hideous creatures, but realized that he could climb out onto the roof from the window. Pushing it open, Bob carefully clambered out onto the roof as the horde below him sensed the nearness of a warm meal and erupted into fresh moans.

Navigating the steep angle of the roof, he saw that the house next door to him was about fifteen feet away. With a running jump, he barely cleared the gap and skidded to a stop on the neighboring rooftop.

Cursing at the large amount of skin he lost on the abrasive roof shingles, Bob got to his feet, breathing hard. Quickly running to the far side of the house, he scampered down an attached antenna tower to ground level. Now running like the wind, he was barely able to evade the pursuing undead until he reached his truck parked two blocks over. Cranking the engine over, he stomped on the accelerator, steering the truck back to the safety of the church.

Bob didn't know what scared him more, the zombies or telling Father Kettle that he had failed.

*

Walking to my quarters to unload my gear, I was flagged down by a little man yelling my name.

"Hey there, Mike isn't it?" the man asked.

"Yes it is. What can I do for you?"

"I was told you guys are making supply runs and was wondering if the provisions scavenged will be passed out evenly among the people here," he asked.

"The food and supplies are all sent to the gymnasium for processing and storage. Everything will be handed out as needed."

"Why would you hoard everything for yourselves? The people deserve to have what they want," the man replied testily.

"Look here, I'm not hoarding anything. The food is prepared by the cooks and we *all* line up for our meals." I was getting angry with this little fucker. "Nobody gets shafted. If you want anything extra, go get it on your own time. You can walk out of here whenever you damn well please!"

"You also have a much nicer RV than anyone here," he pointed out. "It's not fair that one person has that monstrosity while others are crammed in a smaller camper."

Was this guy's nose actually pointing up in the air at me? Dropping my bags in the dirt, I stepped close to the man and leaned down to look him in the eye.

"Listen, Comrade, I'm not sure what you are trying to say, but I don't like what I'm hearing," I barked. "You don't like my bus? Too fucking bad, go get your own. You don't like how the food is distributed? Again, too fucking bad, go get your own damned food. I haven't seen you on a single raid yet, so until I do and see you fight tooth and nail against dozens of undead, shut the fuck up."

The little pansy looked like he was going to say something while his hand drifted to his beltline, but when I started twisting my head from side to side cracking it, he made a very wise decision to be silent, did an about-face and stomped away. I really wasn't in the mood to beat the skinny man. I just wanted to get out of these nasty clothes and cleaned up. Grabbing my gear, I trudged to my bus, unlocked it and climbed aboard. I went to the refrigerator for a bottle of water and chugged it down before plopping my tired ass onto the couch. I turned on the stereo system and quietly listened to some old school Megadeth as I drifted off to sleep. The shower would have to wait.

*

Brother Jonas stomped away from Mike seething with rage. Now he knew exactly why Father Kettle hated these bastards. Fingering the hilt of the sheathed dagger under his long shirt in his beltline, he almost gave in to the urge to plant it in that big fucker's neck! The fact that Mike looked like he was about to snap his spine kept him from doing anything other than walking away.

"But only for the time being," he decided.

Jonas had been at the prison for only a short time, but couldn't help but be impressed with how things were run. It was true nobody went hungry, and everyone had ample shelter. He was only trying to feel out the former cop, looking for a weak spot. He had already felt out the others. The salty cigar smoker, Dan, was a dangerous one, not one to mess with. The only time he tried to approach Dan, he ended up staring down the barrel of the man's rifle, which was not a good place to be. Chris wasn't much better. He and Dan were almost inseparable, and he idolized Dan so much that he was becoming salty as well. Stephen was a weapons freak. Thinking back to when he saw Stephen walking his fat beagle around his RV last night in only his boxers, Jonas remembered him with a .45 tucked into his drawers.

No, he wouldn't be taken off guard either.

Mattie was an innocent at heart. However, he had strict orders to be hands off with her. Others were assigned the task of taking her alive, but after seeing her return with the supply team, he knew that those men had failed again.

That big bastard Mike was no pushover either. Built like a brick shithouse, the man would rather beat a zombie's head in by hand than shoot from a distance. He also seemed a bit on the crazy side.

Reaching his new home, Jonas climbed inside and began sharpening his dagger. Lulled by the hypnotic scratching sound of the stone scraping the razor sharp blade, he leaned back into his mattress.

It looked like he would just have to bide his time and wait for opportunity to knock.

"Something will present itself," he said aloud, staring at the razor edge of his blade. "It always does."

2

October 27
Day 63

Looking around the prison at the groups running errands not unlike an ant farm, I spotted Dan heading up to the second floor of the command center. He was probably going to make contact with his brother Dave and his former Sgt. from work, Tom Ogle. They were talking with each other over the radio every couple of days now, just to check in and see what has been going on at the different locations. Dave and Tom were always eager to hear Dan's stories about what we were going through. The stories from the hunting cabin down by Peoria were never as exciting. There were a couple of encounters with the infected that they had to deal with, but never to the level that we were experiencing. They had managed to help a few nearby families, and seemed to be in good shape themselves.

As Dan climbed up the stairs in the command tower, he ran into Chris, who was walking down with an updated list of needs given to him by a secretary. They needed to be made a priority on tomorrow's raids. At the top of the list was toilet paper, which up to now had been partially overlooked. Toilet paper was one of those things that you take for granted until you are out and your ass starts to hurt. The small TP fort that Stephen kept in his basement was now long used up.

"Are ya going to get on the radio?" Chris asked in passing.

"No," Dan replied, "I'm going to get on the satellite television and watch some porn."

"Smartass," Chris smirked, punching Dan in the arm. "Don't forget I found your stash of smutty DVD's, so the secret's out!"

Dan had a grin on his face but didn't let Chris see it. Dan didn't want anyone to know he was starting to look at everyone as family since they were forced together due to the outbreak. Flesh craving zombies had that effect on the living, bringing them closer. Dan knew deep down that he would probably see a lot of them die, and eventually he would meet his maker too.

"Do you mind if I listen in?" Chris asked. "I got nothing else going after I drop this list."

"Works for me," Dan replied.

Dan sat down at the base station and prepared to transmit, while Chris ran the list down to the command post's conference room and returned back upstairs as Dan began calling out his call sign. He was transmitting on the frequency used to talk to his brother in Peoria. There was no reply.

"This ever happened before?" Chris asked.

"Nope," Dan replied, with an edge to his voice. "They know our check-in times too. They also missed the one earlier."

After trying for about thirty minutes, Dan signed off in frustration, "Looks like the assholes fell asleep early tonight."

After writing down some instructions to the guys manning the radios later that night, he got up and headed down the stairs. Chris waited a minute and then went down to see what Dan was going to do. He knew that Dan was uneasy about what had just happened. The other group had never missed a meeting with Dan, and Chris could tell it wasn't sitting well with him.

He finally caught up with Dan in the camper they shared and noticed that he had his travel bags out and was checking their contents. Looking over the gear, Chris sighed. He'd spent enough time in the army to know when someone was packing for an extended patrol.

"What are you doing?" Chris asked.

"Nothing, kid," Dan replied. "Mind your own business."

"This is my business, what's going on?" Chris asked again after an awkward silence.

"Don't get involved," Dan replied.

"Fine, I'll let Mike and Stephen know what you are up to, and let them figure it out," Chris countered as he started to walk away.

"Alright!" Dan shouted. "I'm taking off tonight. My mind is made up."

"What do you got in mind?"

"I'll fill ya in, but don't say anything to the others," Dan said. "The last time I tried to go somewhere like this, they nearly broke my ribs. I'm going to Ogle's place outside Peoria to check on him and my brother Dave."

Chris's reply was short and sweet. "When do we leave?" Chris grabbed his backpack and checked the status of his rifle.

"Hey, kid, I'm not letting you come with," Dan said. "It's a long ways. I might not make it back and that's not a situation I'm going to let you get yourself into. I have to do this on my own."

They were nearly yelling at that point, with Chris demanding to come along and Dan threatening to cuff him to the toilet. They grew louder and louder, until they were able to be overheard by anyone walking outside.

*

Stephen and I opened the door to the trailer and found Chris and Dan squared off toe to toe over a pile of gear.

"Where are you two going?" I asked.

"Nowhere!" both Dan and Chris shouted at the same time.

The small room was quiet for what seemed like hours, and you could feel the tension building.

"Okay, everyone here needs to relax," Stephen interjected. "Chris, where are you guys going?"

Chris looked at Dan, who was gripping his AR-15 with a look in his eyes that made Chris pause. He didn't think Dan was really crazy, but some of the things he had seen him do were enough to make him wonder.

"We're going on a long ass supply run," he replied and turned to finish packing.

"When did we start planning runs on our own and not as a group?" Stephen asked with a bemused look on his face.

"This supply run is personal, and I'm going by myself!" Dan snapped.

"The fuck you are!" Chris yelled.

That's when I finally had enough.

"No one's going anywhere until someone tells me what the hell is going on," I demanded. "And I don't want any more pussyfooting around. How about giving us a straight answer?" Mattie must have been nearby and heard the commotion. She quietly slid in behind me and stood near the door to listen. I could feel the red coming up into my face, and everyone else could see it.

"You might as well tell them before Mike blows a gasket," Chris said to Dan with a smirk.

Dan was obviously not happy about everyone knowing his plan. I could tell he was hoping to slip out when no one was paying attention.

"I'm going to check on my brother and Ogle down in Peoria," Dan said defiantly, expecting an argument from me.

"That's fine with me. Just watch your six, and don't drop the soap around Chris," I responded and turned to walk out.

"Wait a minute!" Stephen asked. "You're going to leave it at that?"

"Do you think we should stop him?" I responded. "Remember what he said after Phil's group got taken over? And this's his family we're talking about. If he wants to leave, who are we to stop him? We're not talking about a suicide mission into Chicago here."

"Okay, that's fine, but everyone needs to slow it down a second," Stephen replied. "If Dan is going to check on his brother and Ogle, then we need to plan some stuff out."

"I don't have time to make a fucking plan," Dan snapped, picking up some of his bags and trying to walk out of the trailer. "May already be too late."

I knew Dan's stubbornness was starting to get under Stephen's skin but was still surprised when Stephen blocked Dan from leaving the doorway.

"I'm sick of you being so fucking stubborn!" Stephen snarled. "I understand why you want to go check on them, but to run off by yourself is just stupid. We haven't lived this long by being stupid. The idiots are all dead by now. We've made it because we use our heads. There's no reason we can't make this mission successful."

Dan wasn't sure how to respond. He knew Stephen was right, but he didn't want to risk anyone's life in something he knew he had to do.

"This is what we are going to do," Stephen said. "Chris and Dan, go find a vehicle in the yard to make the trip in. We have picked up a few new trucks this week. Find something rugged enough to make it there and back. Mattie, we know you are listening back there so go find the maps of LaSalle County and the other counties down to Peoria so we can plan a route. Mike and I will help the guys dig through the maintenance shop and look for stuff to help beef up your ride. We will meet in the shop in an hour and put a plan together that won't get your dumb ass killed. Oh, and one more thing Dan, you're taking someone with you, and that is not up for debate."

"And that would be me," Chris interjected. "No negotiating on that either."

*

Everyone completed their assignments in the allotted time. Chris and Dan settled on a green F350 Super Duty crew cab. Stephen and I also rounded up some bigger tires and extra material to up-armor it a bit more. After pulling the truck into the maintenance shop, everybody got busy. Before I became a cop I used to weld for a living, and was able to fabricate a simple steel brush guard for the grill. While I did that, our chief mechanic bolted some metal bars over the side windows and installed a trailer hitch. Others fabricated some reinforced skid plates to protect the truck's undercarriage. Stephen's idea to clean out the local auto parts stores while on a raid was a good one, allowing us to change out all the fluids and filters on the truck.

Stephen helped Dan equip the truck with an extra battery, along with a HAM radio and antenna. It wouldn't have the range to punch all the way back from Peoria, but it was better than nothing. In the back of the truck they mounted two heavy boxes to store gear in and two extra tires with rims. The guys in the shop went over every problem they could think of and added the tools and parts available to get them out of any jam. Chris and Dan finished getting together their personal gear and loaded up the truck. The best thing the truck had, according to Dan, was the gun rack in the back window. He made sure "Betty" had her spot in the gun rack. One final item that was hooked up to the truck was a small U-Haul trailer. It was loaded with some extra food, clothing, medical supplies, and other odds and ends that we thought Dave and Tom might need in Peoria. We stood back and admired our work, all hoping it would perform as well as it looked.

It was now late into the night. Mattie and I were going over the maps and picking out a good route down to Peoria. The trip from Joliet to Peoria could have been made in about three hours before the virus broke. The trip down there now was set up to take about two days. They would be taking smaller two-lane roads the whole way, and as many gravel roads as possible to avoid the small towns. The interstates most likely were parking lots if the ones around Joliet were any indication. Even though it was going to take longer, everyone was in agreement that this was the best plan. We laid out the route and went back over it several times. By the time we were done, Chris joked that he no longer even needed the map. Being that it was now nearly 0300 hours, Dan and Chris decided they would leave about 10:00 in the morning and drive three-quarters of the way there. They would find somewhere safe for the night and planned on finishing up the trip the next day. That way, they would arrive at Ogle's hunting cabin during the day, giving them better visibility.

*

Jonas made himself busy in the maintenance shop pretending to help outfit the truck. Overhearing Mike and Mattie go over Dan and Chris' route, he made a mental note of it and the time of their departure. Hearing this information was a stroke of good luck, and it was imperative that this bit of news got out in time for Father Kettle's men to react. His men had established a small camp at a lookout location near the prison, and could be reached via his small Motorola radio. It was different than the ones used by the prison, and it allowed Jonas to talk securely with those on the outside. Jonas slipped away to retrieve his radio and was finally able to reach them after numerous attempts. After a few minutes spent explaining the upcoming mission being planned by the unbelievers, Jonas returned his radio to its hidden charging station inside his small camper and reclined on his bed with a satisfied grin on his face.

*

The next morning as Dan and Chris prepared to head out, no one was eager to say goodbye. From Chris it was quick pats on the backs and handshakes. Dan, however, had different intentions. He gave out long hugs to Mattie and a number of women that stood waiting their turns with tears in their eyes.

"Sometimes I don't understand women at all," Stephen told his beagle, who wandered up to see what all the fuss was about.

Chris jumped in the driver's seat after Dan called shotgun. Chris started the large diesel and hit the horn as he headed for the doors. Casper, hearing the signal, opened the gate on cue. A few zombies that had wandered close were quickly taken out by Logan and Kleaner, who were manning the switch in the guard tower. There was a big raid planned to hit deep into the south end of town today, and they would be traveling south out of town with the convoy.

After the escorts turned off towards their target area for the day, Dan and Chris were quiet, listening to the rest of the Waylon Jennings greatest hits CD that had been in the player. When they got out near the edge of town and eventually settled in, thinking they were off to a smooth start, gunfire exploded from both sides of the highway. Chris almost lost control of the truck as both tires on the U-Haul disintegrated. One of the truck's dually tires came apart, and the ass end of the truck started careening into the ditch. Chris jerked the wheel violently, keeping the truck on the road.

"We got incoming!" Dan screamed as a round of buckshot tore across the hood of the truck. "I don't think zombies can shoot! Don't stop or we're dead men!"

Several rounds now slammed into the body of the truck, smacking dangerously close to its occupants.

"Not my first ambush!" Chris screamed, hitting the gas.

Dan, riding shotgun with his rifle, switched to full auto and finally sent some suppressive fire in the other direction. Hot casings from Dan's rifle were bouncing all over the cab of the truck, and more than a few sizzled upon making contact with Chris's neck.

"Goddamn, do you mind? I'm trying to drive over here!"

He kept the damaged truck on the road however. Sparks were flying off from under the damaged U-Haul in tow, but that beautiful diesel engine had no problem dragging the trailer down the road. Soon the only incoming rounds were smacking harmlessly into the back of the damaged trailer. After limping over a small crest in the road, Dan yelled for Chris to stop the truck.

"Are you hit?" Dan asked, looking himself over.

"I'm fine," Chris replied, rubbing the fresh burns on his neck. "I'm just glad whoever it was didn't have an IED and can't shoot for shit!"

Dan seconded that as he jumped out with "Betty", the .375 H&H, in his hands.

"Get that damn trailer unhooked and throw as much shit as you can in the back of the truck," Dan told Chris. "Then I'll help you with the truck tire. I'm going to buy us some time."

Dan lowered himself to the ground and crawled to the top of the hill, and peered through his rifle scope. He scanned the area near the ambush site, wishing he would see movement. Anyone dumb enough to show themselves so he could return the favor.

It wasn't long before Chris shouted back to Dan, "Hey, let's move out before they start shooting at us again."

Right as Dan was about to get up and stow away his sniper rifle, he saw something that made his mouth do something it rarely did these days.

Smile.

Down from where they were ambushed, Dan observed faint movement. After a moment, he saw the head of a man peek out from a burnt out shell of a pick-up truck.

"There you are, you little fuck," he mumbled.

Judging from the mill dots on his scope he did the quick math in his head and guessed the target to be right at 600 yards, give or take.

"Now where are your friends at, hmm?" Dan whispered to his target.

The figure in his crosshairs appeared to be speaking with someone, but he couldn't tell where the other man was.

After dialing in his scope to the approximate range Dan lined up his target.

"So are you going to help me with this tire or what?" Chris asked again from behind him.

Dan's reply was to slowly let his breath out, pause, and squeeze the trigger.

The huge rifle bucked mightily in his hands and he was rewarded a second later with the target's head exploding in a cloud of red mist. The man was dead before the sound of Dan's gun reached him.

"Hoorah bitches!" Dan whooped.

"Did you get one?" Chris asked.

"You could say that!" Dan replied. He crept backwards out of sight of the former ambush area. "I gave them something to think about at least. Come on, let's go."

After Dan pulled one of their spare tires from the back of the truck, he noticed that there were a couple of holes dangerously close to all four wheel wells.

"If a couple more of their rounds had connected, I'm not sure we would still be breathing," Dan remarked after a whistle.

"That was a well laid out ambush," Chris admitted. "But not perfect. They didn't start shooting till we were passing them."

"Yeah. Now we know that we have more to worry about out here than just zombies," Dan remarked. "We got outlaws to deal with too." After switching out the tire and climbing into their enormous truck, they were on the road again. They had to leave the trailer and some supplies, which was a disappointment, but better than being dead.

Dan fired up the HAM radio and made contact with the prison. He gave the information to Eddie's son Tyler and told him to get it to Mike and Stephen right away, then spent the next two hours dodging obstacles on the roadway, and making sure that they were not being followed. After fifty or sixty miles they were confident that they were not. Only after stopping for a piss break at the top of a hill and seeing no vehicles approaching did they finally relax. One of the pre-approved stops on the trip was to a rock quarry mining pit that was along the way. Dan told Chris that he knew a guy that worked there, and he wanted to stop to see if he could pick up some useful items. They rolled into the mining pits, and ran across a few zombies that Chris took care of with the steel ram on the front of the truck. As they drove around the pits, Dan explained what they were looking for. It would be a shack out by itself with a lot of warning signs on it. When they came around a corner, it stood out like a sore thumb. It was painted red and had a lot of signs on it that said "High Explosives."

The grins on both Dan and Chris' faces were uncontrollable.

Chris looked at Dan, "You are the man!"

"I know," Dan replied with a grin.

They unwound the cable from the front winch and pulled the door off the small building. Both of them stood in the opening and whistled at what their eyes beheld. Cases of mining explosives were stacked up in the building.

"We don't have enough room," Dan sighed.

"What a problem to have," Chris answered. They restacked the back of the truck, discarded more gear, and filled it up with crates of explosives. The stuff that wouldn't fit on the truck was moved to a large sand pile and hid for later pickup, if possible. They found another building labeled the same way that was a little smaller, which housed the blasting caps and other pieces of equipment to make everything work. It was secured with a lock that Dan made easy work of with a set of bolt cutters.

"I wish we still had that U-Haul trailer with us," Chris lamented. "We would have no problem taking all of this shit with us, and anything else useful we find along the way."

"Wish in one hand, shit in the other," Dan joked. "We can keep an eye out for a new trailer though. Just don't hold your breath."

They got back out on the road, both feeling pretty good about their chances. They had lived through the ambush that some asshole laid out for them, and they found a great score that would be a giant force multiplier. Traveling down a narrow gravel road in the middle of Nowhere, Illinois, the sun was starting to creep towards the horizon. This time of year the days were getting shorter and shorter.

"We better start looking for somewhere to crash for the night," Dan stated, nodding at the setting sun. "It'll be dark soon."

"No problem," Chris replied. "I see a hill coming up that would give us a pretty good view of the surroundings." He pulled up to the top of the hill, and both men jumped out with their binoculars, spending a few minutes scanning in all directions. They observed nothing in the distance but corn fields in need of harvesting, some trees, and a few dark farmhouses. Picking one that was set well off the road, they cautiously approached. They found an abandoned old farmhouse with a barn nearby. The house was empty prior to the outbreak, and the barn was actually in better shape than the house. Chris also discovered the barn had a huge hay loft that was a good fifteen feet off the ground. It would get them safely out of reach of any random zombie that might happen by overnight. They agreed it would be a good place to spend the night, and after searching the area and finding nothing of value, they settled in the loft with their sleeping bags, trying to get comfortable as the sun was sinking behind the horizon. Dan was unable to reach either Peoria or the prison on the radio, which was expected.

They decided on MREs for dinner and drank five cans of soda between them. It wasn't the greatest, but the food filled their bellies. They decided against a fire for security reasons and the fact that zombies seemed to have a fantastic sense of smell. Besides, they were in a hay loft, which was a tad bit flammable. The pair cleaned their weapons and called it a night. After the sun disappeared for a couple of hours, Dan asked Chris if he was asleep.

"No not yet, and I can't figure out what that glow is to the south of us," Chris replied.

"I was looking at that also," Dan mentioned. "It's in the direction of Pontiac or Bloomington, can't tell which. But it's definitely burning down."

"That's for sure," Chris noted. "We've been lucky not to have more fires in Joliet so far."

"Hey, take a look at that farmhouse way over there," Dan said, pointing to the southwest. "Somebody still has power."

"Why would they have a light on with nothing covering the windows?" Chris asked, not expecting an answer. "It stands out big time."

Dan tried to bring the farm into focus with his binoculars, but it was too far out.

"Opsec is the term son," Dan mused. "And they're lacking it. I wonder how many people are holed up over there."

"In the morning we'll go over there and find out. Maybe let them know the dangers of that and anything else we see that's ass backward," Chris replied. "Let's try and get some sleep for now though, we got a big day tomorrow."

Finally both drifted off to sleep. Neither one slept very well, as they both kept waking up thinking they would be surrounded by howling undead in the barnyard at dawn.

*

Stephen sat alone on top of the wall facing west from the prison. Well, not completely alone; his dog sat loyally by his side. Drinking a cold Coors Light, he watched both the sunset and the dozen or so approaching zombies shamble towards the prison with no real plan other than to stand at the wall and try climbing it in vain before eventually being shot. It was an endless, steady stream and Stephen wondered how long this would go on.

"There's no end in sight, Buddy," he sighed. "And it's about time I get to it."

Finishing his beer and climbing off the wall, he found Mike and Mattie sitting around the campfire and headed their way.

After talking to Eddie and learning of the vast number of refugees that descended on his family's hometown in Wisconsin, he knew he had a duty to go check up on his family. The fact that Dan left this morning to check on his own brother just cemented the deal for him taking off as well. Initially, he wanted to wait until Dan and Chris returned to make his trip, but he was growing anxious and decided he would leave in the morning. It was roughly 250 miles to his family's property and he wanted to swing by and check on his house on the west side of town first, dropping off some equipment for his bug out vehicle hopefully still parked in his garage. He figured he could manage it all round trip in two or three days. If his family was okay, he would leave them in the safety of the countryside or bring them back to the prison, if necessary.

He had acquired an interesting mode of transportation for his upcoming trip. He wasn't sure if it was feasible, but Mike thought so, and a side trip today to the railroad yard, the same one in which he had fought his way through at the start of the outbreak, yielded a

Chevrolet 2500 truck called a "High-Railer". Basically, it was truck with a chassis for driving on the railroad tracks. He would be able to follow rail lines all the way to Wisconsin. A simple pull of a lever would drop down a set of train wheels on the front and back of the truck. This would allow him to drive on the actual railroad itself. If he happened to come along a stalled train or other obstacle, that same lever would lift the train wheels and using the truck's regular wheels, and he could bypass the obstruction. Before climbing the wall to consider his plan, Stephen took some cans of spray paint and camouflaged the bright white and yellow truck so it would not stand out as much. He bolted a brush guard to the front, and a fabricated rear ram that slipped into the Reese hitch. The truck had a 75 gallon Transfer Flow cross-the-bed fuel tank system that would give him plenty of range to make the trip. He made sure it was topped off, and added a week's worth of food and water in the bed along with camping gear. There were no extra HAM radios available with the kind of range he needed, so he would have to do without.

He walked up as Mike was telling Mattie how badly he needed a neck massage. Stephen quickly changed the subject to his leaving, and repeated the security concerns over the attempted ambush of Dan and Chris that morning. They both agreed that bandits were going to be a real concern going forward. However, with him leaving via a different route and on railroad tracks, he should not have a problem.

"Well you can't go by yourself," Mattie said. "So who are you going to take with you?"

"I thought about that," Stephen replied and nodded towards the other side of the fire where Amber, Stephen's favorite bartender, sat. "I'm going to ask her."

"I'm sure that decision was made purely on a professional merit basis," Mike joked. "You guys have been hanging out more at night lately."

"She's good company," Stephen grinned, "and has been offering to help out. We can't afford to have either of you two gone with Dan and Chris already on the road. Plus, I'll need you guys to look after Buddy for me while I'm gone."

"You have plenty of excuses for taking a good looking woman along for the ride," Mike chuckled. "Sounds like your mind is made up, so have at it."

While Stephen arranged his trip with Amber on the other side of the campfire, Mike and Mattie plotted out Stephen's route on a map.

He was to take the rail line north through Plainfield and connect to the tracks that ran west along Route 30 near Sugar Grove. This rail line would take him northwest, crossing the Rock River near Oregon and up into Savanna. Traveling north along the Mississippi he would need to backtrack a little west on the tracks near Galena, so as to avoid Dubuque, Iowa. A smaller set of tracks would allow him to rejoin the main rail line near Cassville, Wisconsin and up into Prairie-du-Chien where his family was located.

Stephen was actually a little bit surprised when Amber agreed to go with little convincing needed.

"I've wanted to do something more proactive," Amber added with a look of relief. "Just doing inventory of the supplies you guys bring in is getting old. This will be something exciting for a change, and I'll be able to spend some time with you."

"Outstanding!" Stephen answered with a grin. "We have been so busy, and I have been trying to run into you a little more often as of late."

"Yeah, I know," Amber teased. "You're not as smooth as you think."

"It's not going to be all fun and games out there," Stephen said, blushing. "Wait here a minute."

He excitedly ran to his RV and quickly returned with a holster containing his Sig 9mm.

"I've never fired a gun before Stephen," Amber said hesitantly. "I wouldn't know where to start."

"I've taught more than a few people how to shoot. And there's no way that you could be worse than some of the guys at the FEMA camp. One dude shot off his own thumb. Idiot!"

Amber laughed and then apologized for it. "That's terrible."

"I'm sure you'll be the model student," Stephen said. "We'll start with the basics for now."

Stephen ran over the pistol's controls and had her fire a couple of loaded magazines over the wall to get the feel for the recoil and handling of the gun.

"It fits you," Stephen remarked. "You may end up liking it."

"I do like it," Amber replied with a grin. "I should've done this a while ago. I feel empowered already."

Stephen also told her to practice removing the gun from the holster, dry firing, and performing mag changes while the gun was empty. He hoped to give her some target practice at a later date, as she was a quick learner. Driving the tracks to Wisconsin, Stephen didn't think he would need her gun and was more or less counting on the extra set of eyes. He told her to be packed and ready in the morning, walked her to her uncle's camper and told her goodnight.

"I'll see you in the morning," Amber said as she turned and closed the door. "Now don't forget me!"

3

October 29
Day 65

At first light Amber was patiently waiting by the truck with her travel bags. Stephen arrived a short time later, Buddy in tow, muttering how he hated mornings and wondering aloud how Amber could look so happy to be up with the sunrise.

"I hated working nights at the bar," she admitted. "That's one thing I haven't missed. I always loved the sunrise and never got to enjoy as many as I would have liked."

Stephen scowled, heaved up his bags, and threw them in the extended cab of the truck. His mood lightened when he noticed his traveling companion was wearing a form fitting pair of jeans and a flattering auburn fleece. Staring at her dark brown hair pulled back into a ponytail and piercing green eyes, Stephen again recalled how she made so much money off him and everyone else while bartending.

"You seem happy this morning," Stephen conceded.

"This should be an exciting trip! I'm looking forward to it!" Amber replied. "It'll be nice to get out of here for a while."

"Shouldn't you be scared?" Stephen asked, shooting her a wary glance.

"I have full faith that you'll get us back home in one piece. Look at all we have made it through so far," she said, smiling. "What could go wrong?"

"Lots, but I like your attitude," Stephen teased. "And your company Thanks again for coming with. You remembered the pistol I gave you last night, right?"

Amber lifted her fleece and showed Stephen the holstered pistol on her right hip.

With a nod of approval, Stephen threw Amber's bags in the back of the cab before they both climbed in, and he started the truck. Buddy was now sitting on the seat wanting to go for a ride, and Stephen had to hand him out to Mattie, who had walked up to say goodbye.

"I'll be back in a couple days, big guy," Stephen said, scratching the beagle behind the ears. "Now go on and take this."

Stephen pulled out a rawhide from his pocket and handed it to Buddy, who suddenly acted like everyone wanted to steal his new trophy. In an instant, he was greedily hiding under Stephen's RV. Stephen laughed and settled in behind the wheel. Judging from the sounds around him, the prison was beginning to wake up. Several vehicles were assembled near the gate since yet another supply run was going out today. Due to the attack on Dan's truck yesterday, Stephen was going to have the raid escort them safely out of town.

"Thanks again for watching Buddy for me," Stephen said to Mattie. "I really appreciate it."

"Oh, it's no problem," Mattie replied. "Just be careful and get back safe. I hope you find your family safe too."

"That makes two of us," Stephen answered. "Where's Mike?"

"He's in the dump truck at the front of the column," Mattie stated, looking at the prison doors that were slowly opening. "He's leading the raid today. Since they're following you out of town, they're going to hit your neighborhood while they are out that way, so you'll see him out there."

The convoy moved out to a chorus of suppressive fire and made quick time to Stephen's house on the west side of town. He had not been there since they'd left for the safe zone quite a few weeks ago and was relieved to see the neighborhood had not burned down and his house was still intact. The rest of the convoy secured the area and got to work while Stephen checked his residence on the outside to make sure no person or zombie had gotten in and would be lying in wait. Finding everything intact, he unlocked the front door and waved Amber out of the truck then walked to the garage to check on his old truck. He brought out the brush guard and Reese hitch attachment and set them in the garage next to the truck for later installment. Stephen still wanted to leave the truck there for a backup, just in case.

After finishing up and again securing his residence, Stephen and

Amber watched the raiding party finish clearing their current target. During a break, they said their goodbyes to Mike and the others, climbed into their "High-Railer" railroad truck, and drove to the nearest set of tracks to begin their journey northwest. They made good time at first, traveling parallel to Route 30, and were soon well west of Joliet. There was a nervous excitement in the truck as they left town, but after a while they settled into small talk about the old times back at the bar and the way things used to be. It had been nearly two months since everything got turned upside down.

"I think you secretly like it," Amber remarked after Stephen got done explaining his plans for the coming months.

"What do you mean by like it?" Stephen asked defensively.

"Don't get me wrong," Amber replied, "I know you've lost a lot of friends. We all have, but you seem to be thriving on this. No more bills or worrying about money. You're always finding new toys on your raids and asking me about any fancy clothes or accessories you should be keeping an eye out for me."

There was a long pause before Stephen replied. "Yeah I suppose so," he finally conceded with a chuckle, "but I *am* worried. If things don't get back to normal, and I don't think they will, we will eventually run low on food, ammo and fuel, and things will get a lot harder. And just wait until we start to get sick. Things will get pretty rough without state of the art medical care. We'll be thrown back in time a hundred years or more."

As they debated the future of humanity, Amber looked on in amazement at the never ending wave of destruction that had rolled over every village and town they passed.

"Do you think things will ever get back to normal?" she finally asked with a hint of sadness in her voice.

"Yes, to an extent," Stephen replied. "The government has a shit ton of resources at their disposal, and I think that order will be restored to certain areas of the country at some point. They will have to start small and expand out like the early settlers did. Five years from now, I expect there to be a few fairly large cities, most likely on the coasts, with all the modern amenities you are used to. We just need to stay alive to see it."

The conversation turned back to their current surroundings. They had not seen a living soul, and Amber remarked how eerie it made things look. She pointed out a few zombies now and then, but they were too far away to worry about. The truck made very little noise, and the zombies had no time to react before Stephen and

Amber were safely past.

Amber was going through Stephen's iPod and remarked how, with no radio stations, the little broadcaster was playing music crystal clear over the truck's radio.

"We should try to get a radio station up and running," Amber mentioned after turning down the volume on Johnny Cash singing "When the Man Comes Around". "People might hear it, and it could give them some kind of useful information and the knowledge that they are not alone. We could also give them directions to the prison if they want to come help us."

"That's not a bad idea," Stephen replied, turning up the volume. "I like this song! I have wondered myself if that would be possible. We will have to look into that when we get back. I wouldn't know where to start, but someone else might."

Their discussion then turned to what kind of music the station should play between broadcasts with Stephen and Amber having vastly different ideas.

"You have enough to worry about," she said with a laugh. "Let me handle the music. Besides, your choice of music is depressing me right now."

With a town coming into view, Amber checked the map and announced that they were near Rochelle, Illinois. Soon a train appeared on the tracks, and Stephen had to pull off and drive around it. It was a BNSF locomotive with three engines and about sixty box cars. Stephen and Amber both wondered what was stacked in the box cars. It could have been anything.

"We should send somebody to drive it back to Joliet," Amber decided.

"Once again, I would have no idea where to begin," Stephen said. "We've had to get off the tracks at a couple of points already, and I wouldn't have a clue on how or even if we could get that beast rolling. But I'm sure it's packed with stuff we could use."

"Guess I'm a glass half full kinda girl," Amber replied with a wink. "That needs to rub off on you a bit."

Stephen was stuck on the part about "rubbing on Amber", but needed to focus on the task at hand. The train continued into a small downtown business district, and Stephen was forced to drive directly down Main Street. Smoke was seen a few blocks north, along with dozens of burned out buildings. Stalled cars littered the streets, slowing their progress. Of course, the pesky zombies were milling about, and Stephen hit a few of them with the truck, the reinforced bumper easily pushing them clear with a sickening thud.

"I've forgotten how gruesome these things are up close," Amber whispered when a ghoulish man walked directly into the path of the truck, and was rewarded by having his head caved in like a watermelon.

Stephen seemed oblivious to the carnage, and commented on how this was a fairly small, isolate town, with a population around 10,000. If it was that bad here, that did not bode well for the rest of the country.

"I'm sure there are places in Montana that haven't seen a single zombie though," he concluded.

Amber, not paying attention to a word he was saying, looked a little nervous about being off the tracks and no longer in the safety of the countryside. She clutched Stephen's leg and moved closer to him on the seat.

"This place gives me the creeps," she said, looking around. "I don't like it at all. It makes me wanna start smoking again."

"After three years?" Stephen tapped the brakes near a repugnant zombie who was standing by the road. "Not on my watch. If you want, I can slow down and you can get some target practice in. That should be a stress reliever."

The subsequent punch to his arm relayed her intentions, but she still looked at the creature with a morbid curiosity. The previously male zombie had clearly been dead for a while, and the flesh was hanging off his face, exposing his teeth under his cheeks. He was wearing clothes that now hung loosely from his gaunt frame; he had clearly lost a lot of weight since "dying". Amber squeezed Stephen's leg as he slowed.

"Roll down the window and take that fucker out!" he said.

Amber flat out refused, and soon the skulking creature was clawing at the glass. Stephen hit the gas, earning him another punch to the shoulder.

"Well if you can't smoke and won't shoot zombies," Stephen said with a straight face, "we do have one other option to relieve stress."

"Ouch, that hurt!" Stephen admitted while rubbing his shoulder after yet another punch.

"Play nice and you won't have anything to worry about," Amber snapped. "Now get me outta here before I really hurt you."

4

October 29
Day 65

When the sun came up on Dan and Chris' second day of their trip, they gave the barnyard they had called home for the night a good once over. After confirming that they were still alone, they jumped in the truck and headed towards the distant farmhouse that stood as a glimmering light in the darkness the night before. After several wrong turns on unmarked gravel roads, they stopped in front of a rusty old mailbox with the name "Harden" etched in faded red paint.

"Want to bring them up their mail?" Chris joked, staring at the mailbox. "Hell, maybe they have a Victoria's Secret catalog or something. I could use some new reading material."

"I'd rather not," Dan replied drily. "That's a Federal offense, and they probably still hang people for that down here."

They started up the long lane towards the house. The driveway had a steady uphill grade and then made a sharp right turn. The house itself was concealed behind a row of pine trees, designed as a barrier against the steady winds of the open prairie. It was evident from the design of the house and the age of the pines that the farm had been in place for quite some time. The old red barn itself looked like it had seen better days. A newer metal machine shed could also be seen in the distance. Neither man spoke as they drew close, both silently hoping that a trigger happy farmer didn't own an old hunting rifle. Dan stopped about fifty yards from the house and killed the engine.

"Hello! Is anyone there?" Dan yelled out the window.

For a few seconds there was no response, just total silence.

Then, "What do you fellows want here?" a suspicious sounding male voice shouted back.

"We saw your house all lit up like a Christmas tree last night and wanted to tell you that having a light on at night will bring the zombies like a moth to a flame," Dan replied. "We could give you some ideas about how to secure your property against attacks from both living and dead."

Shortly after that, a middle-aged man stepped out of the front door holding an old double barrel shotgun.

"Step out of that truck real slow, son," the man said flatly.

"He called you son, that's funny!" Chris whispered Dan. "You're not going out there, are you?"

"I don't think he'll be a problem," Dan replied. "Looks like a decent guy. Just cover me, kid."

"Already on it," Chris replied, giving his rifle a press check, making sure a round was chambered.

Dan exited the truck, and the man motioned for him to walk towards the front porch. It was one of those large wooden covered porches so common on turn of the century homes. Perfect for summer nights, drinking lemonade and watching the crops grow. The man was now standing just off of one of the porch's hefty wooden pillars.

He realized the man was using it as cover, so he wasn't a complete idiot.

Dan hoped Chris was covering him discreetly, so as to not spook the man into sending him to meet his maker prematurely. Dan walked up to the farmer with his arms raised, holding a cigar in one hand and a lighter in the other. He stopped about twenty feet away from the porch steps and lit his cigar.

"You really shouldn't leave your windows uncovered at night with the lights on, you know," Dan offered. "Your place looked like a lighthouse on the ocean last night and it might invite trouble."

"You already said that," the man replied, pausing to spit a big mouthful of chew. "What business is it of yours?"

"I was in law enforcement before this shit storm started," Dan explained. "Let's say that I know what kind of people are running around out there. It always pays to be careful."

"So you were a cop?" the man asked, his eyes shifting between Dan and Chris back in the truck. "Are you guys traveling alone way out here?"

"It's a long story, but yes were," Dan replied. "Just passing through and thought I'd offer up some friendly advice. We haven't seen many people alive as of late."

The man rubbed his chin, deep in thought. "Looks like you could use a hot cup of coffee and breakfast. Come on in. And tell that young fella in your truck he can take his finger off the trigger and come in for some food. Just watch the language please, we got kids'n all."

He then turned and walked back into the house, motioning them to follow with his hand.

Dan turned back to Chris, waving for him to follow. Chris exited the truck and continued after making sure his pistol was still holstered on his hip. Walking up to the door, Chris's mouth began to water at the scent of sausage. Inside, he was greeted by a simple yet clean country kitchen. Once seated, they introduced themselves and sat down to some hot coffee and some delicious sausage, biscuits and gravy. The man, Gary, and his wife Ann had two kids, Matt and Sara. Gary mentioned they were down to their last few brews of coffee and while saying grace asked the good Lord to provide if it was His will.

As they sat around the kitchen table talking, Dan and Chris were able to answer a few questions about how things were looking elsewhere around the country. Gary and Ann sent the kids out to play while Dan shared some of the horrors taking place in the cities. Ann told of going into town shortly after seeing the stories coming over the news broadcast, only to find the grocery store looted and people killing one another in the street.

"I'm talking about people who sat together in the same church on Sunday morning," Gary remarked, "in small town America."

After finishing his food, Chris said he needed some air and wanted to step outside to make sure the kids were okay. Gary said they hadn't seen any of the infected in a while and not to worry.

"There's no point in taking any chances," Chris replied. "I'll keep an eye on them for you."

Everyone agreed, and soon they saw Chris playing catch with a football with the duo in the front yard. Ann mentioned it was the first time she had seen her children smile in weeks.

"These biscuits are outstanding, Ann," Dan said happily, filling his plate again. "And this sausage gravy is delicious!"

"Why thank you, Dan," Ann gushed. "I'm glad you like it, eat up!"

Dan asked them if they needed anything in the way of supplies, and Gary informed him that they were getting along pretty good considering.

"We are low on a few things but we have plenty of meat," Ann added. “My husband has seen to that.”

Dan was kind of surprised at that, and quickly glanced down at his plate. Gary didn't appear to live on a working farm, and there weren’t any big patches of woods nearby that would hold deer or other animals.

Gary then steered the conversation back towards Dan’s truck, what they were hauling and where they were headed.

Dan started by telling his hosts about the prison and all that was being accomplished, about the cabin near Peoria where his brother and a few friends were, and how he was bringing a load of supplies to help out. Gary informed Dan that his place was near Manville close to Highway 17, and that they were indeed headed in the right direction.

"We had better be, or my navigator Chris is going to have a lot of explaining to do!" Dan said with a laugh.

After they finished breakfast, Dan stepped outside, relit his cigar, and walked out to talk to Chris in private.

“Keep your eye out. Something is a little weird here,” Dan said in a low voice. “I can feel it in my gut.”

Just then Gary came out of the house and asked if Dan had anything he wanted to trade for some diesel fuel, which he had plenty of. Dan walked over to their truck and told Chris to grab some sugar, coffee and a few canned goods from the back and trade it for the fuel.

"Go with Gary to fill up the truck," Dan said. “I have a few more questions for Ann."

“I think you want some more of her cooking,” Chris replied. “We are guests, try and show some restraint.”

“I won’t lie to ya, that shit was awesome!” Dan teased.

He then walked back up onto the porch, and struck up a conversation with Gary.

“So does you generator run on diesel?”

“Nope, propane,” he replied. I have a big tank behind my machine shed, and there is plenty more sitting in tanks around the county.”

“Did you already have the generator installed?” Dan asked.

“No again. Had it installed just over a month ago.”

“That must have been a big job,” Dan replied with a low whistle.

Chris returned with a box containing the supplies, handed it to Dan, and left with Gary to fill up the truck. Dan went back into the house and set the heavy box on the counter where Ann was cleaning up. He sheepishly asked her if she cared if he had another plate of food.

"Not at all young man, grab a plate," she replied happily.

"Where do you folks get this delicious meat from?" Dan asked, grabbing a clean plate.

"I don't know, my husband goes out and gets it," Ann replied.

Dan was slightly confused, looking around the kitchen and eyeing the nearly empty pantry in the corner.

"How often do you have meat?" Dan asked.

"Oh just about every meal," Ann replied. "Gary makes sausage, steaks and ground out of the animals he hunts."

"And you say he just brings it home?" Dan asked while spooning more of the tasty gravy into his mouth. "Where does he butcher the animals?"

"He prepares the meat out in the barn," she answered. "Why do you ask?"

"Out of habit, a cop thing," Dan remarked and finished wiping his plate clean with a fresh biscuit. "Do you share it with any of your neighbors?"

Ann frowned. "No, we haven't heard from our neighbors in a while now. Before all this Gary never really got along with them. We moved in after Gary's father died, but he was never much of a farmer. We sold the livestock and machinery, and lived of off the rent money we got from leasing the fields. Mr. Burns from the next farm over helped us put in our generator a few weeks back though, let us use his tractor and everything. I haven't seen him again since that day. In fact, you two are the first people I have seen alive since then. A few of those sick people have wandered by; Gary kills them and burns them in the ditch."

"I'm sorry to hear that, ma'am," Dan said.

"Things got real bad after the outbreak," she went on. "People in town got sick, and everyone was scared. Scared and hungry that is. The food shipments all stopped you know. The trucks just quit rolling. After a few weeks we were on the verge of starvation. The livestock dried up faster than you could have imagined, and a lot of it rotted in the open fields. We tried making it to a few of the safe places they listed on the radio, but after we found the first couple destroyed we just came back home. Besides, the sick people in the towns would always follow us, and it got real dangerous to move. Gary was down to our last box of shotgun shells and the kids were crying they were so hungry. We were desperate. Then my husband's luck started to change with hunting, and things have gotten better. I don't think many others have fared as well."

"I'm glad to see you and your family are doing better, ma'am," Dan said. "Let us know how we can help repay you for the meal and make sure your kids are safe."

"You're such a nice young man, handsome even with that horrible scar you have there," she replied. "We're fine for now. Thanks for the box of food and such. Would you like to take some of the summer sausage Gary made for the road?"

"Yes please," Dan answered. "That'd be great."

Dan thanked Ann again for breakfast and walked back outside, munching on the summer sausage he pulled from the large sack she had given him.

"Wow, this is fantastic!" he remarked. "I'll have to ask him what he seasoned it with."

Not seeing Chris or Gary returning yet with the truck, or the kids for that matter, Dan decided to have a quick look around. He walked out to the barn and entered through the gap between the large wooden doors. Finding nothing that would lead Dan to believe Gary was operating a working farm, he opened a door to a back room in the barn. He pulled his flashlight out of his pocket and lit up the room. Inside the room was equipment to butcher animals laying on a long sturdy-looking wooden bench. There were numerous big chest coolers at the end of the room and many heavy bags of rock salt on a pallet.

"He must salt down some of his meat for jerky," Dan said out loud and took another big bite of the sausage. "Good idea."

Just as he was about to leave the room, he noticed a mound of bloody clothing in the corner and shined his light on it. Thinking it was merely a pile of rags used for cleanup duty, he rummaged through it and found various clothing belonging to men, women and even some children. Some of it was blood-stained, and cut up into rags.

Why would he take the clothes of off the zombies before he burned them? Dan frowned. He looked at the bloody clothing, back to the summer sausage he was still eating, and then turned his head and looked over to one of the large chest freezers. He didn't want to look inside but was unable to resist not knowing what he was beginning to suspect. He marched over and opened the freezer door. Peering into the freezer, he saw a piece of bone connected to some meat buried in ice cubes. When Dan lifted the piece of meat out of the ice, he noticed something that confirmed what he dreaded. It was a human arm complete with fingers. Dan also remembered he was still chewing the sausage.

He promptly spit out his snack and tossed the arm and sausage to the floor. He thought he was going to vomit for a few seconds, but somehow kept his breakfast down.

"Shit!" he cursed. "That cannibal fuck is with Chris!"

Dan ran out of the room to find Chris, wishing again that he hadn't left his rifle in the truck.

"Son-of-a-bitch, I will never learn!" Dan snarled under his breath.

He pulled his 1911 out of its holster as he ran out of the barn and back around the smaller machine shed to where he thought he saw Chris take the truck. When he came around the corner he saw Gary, who had a shovel in his hands, standing over Chris' unconscious form on the ground on the far side of the building. From the looks of things, Chris had been pumping diesel from a gravity tank into the truck when he was hit from behind. Gary held up the shovel again to give Chris a final blow. It was going to be a tough shot, at a minimum twenty-five yards, and with his target at an angle. Everything went in slow motion for Dan as he raised his .45 and clicked off the thumb safety. He had a momentary flashback to the intruder he had shot in his house months ago, at the start of this terrible nightmare. Then his training took over.

Dan wasted no time in sending four 230 grain hollow points at Gary's torso. One or two of the slugs found their mark as his target flinched in pain and gasped for air. Gary fell to the ground, dropped the shovel, and then spun back behind the far side of the building out of sight. Dan had no idea if his adversary was armed or even still in the fight, and he really didn't want to stick around and find out. He ran up to Chris and checked for a pulse with his left hand while he covered his blind corner. Relieved to find a pulse, he dragged Chris to the truck and threw him into the front passenger seat. Chris was knocked out cold, but Dan was more than eager to get the hell out of there and apply first aid later. He fired up the truck and put it into drive. He put the hammer down and roared past the house, where he saw Ann coming out with a puzzled look on her face and the shotgun in her hand. She had undoubtedly heard the gunshots and feared the worst. Dan watched her silhouette fade away in his rearview mirror.

Boy did she have a surprise coming when she found out where her husband had been getting their meat!

Out on the highway, Dan pulled over and checked Chris' condition. His breathing and heartbeat seemed about normal to Dan, so he let him lay reclined in the front seat and sleep. As they were traveling down a gravel road an hour later, Chris started to come to and gingerly placed his hand on his head where he had a large, throbbing lump.

"What the hell happened?" Chris asked, wincing from his gentle touch of his wound.

Dan told Chris about what he found, and how he discovered it in the nick of time, adding, "I think Gary was going to add us to his meat collection."

Chris covered his mouth when he thought about the sausage he had eaten earlier that day.

"I don't feel so good," Chris remarked.

"I wondered why that sausage was so tender," Dan responded. "It must have been made from a hairy ass cheek!"

Chris looked at Dan with wide eyes, and then proceeded to empty his former meal forcefully out the window.

"I was wondering why I found a fingernail in my biscuits and gravy," Dan joked. "I thought it was Ann's and was going to let it go. She was kinda hot."

Chris looked at him with a greenish face and stuck his head back out the window for a second vomit session.

The rest of the trip to Peoria was filled with sick jokes and the sound of puking.

All around them the trees were dropping their leaves and Mother Nature was getting ready to take her long winter nap. The scenery became more pleasant, and you could almost forget the nature of their trip. The property was close now and quite remote, bordering the Woodford County Conservation Area. Crossing Highway 89, Chris unsuccessfully tried to reach the guys at the cabin on the radio one last time. Dan was again wondering what had happened to everyone at the cabin. They'd never missed a radio meeting prior to this trip, and now that he was here, he worried at what he might find. As the cabin's location got closer, their stomachs began to tighten up in anticipation. They arrived at the property a little later in the day than they had planned. It was shortly after three p.m., which still gave them plenty of time to investigate the property.

"All we can do is hope for the best."

5

October 29
Day 65

Wanting to steer clear of the nuclear power plant in Byron, Stephen chose to cross the Rock River well to the south near the town of Oregon. Although confident that the power plant's safeguards had overridden the reactor and shut it down, he did not want to get any closer to it than he had to. Amber agreed and asked what else Stephen knew about the area.

"Not much," he responded. "I mostly passed through here on my way back home. It gets more isolated the farther west you get. There are bound to be survivors out this way."

When they crossed the river using the railroad bridge located to the south, they could see down into the small town. A good-sized dam created a natural water barrier to their east, and the highway bridge was barricaded in the middle by several stacked cars and cement highway dividers. The barricade appeared to be unmanned but thousands of undead were bottled up in front of it.

"Oh my God!" Amber gasped. "Look at 'em all crammed together like that."

"Definitely a meal or two on the other side," Stephen remarked, drifting to a stop.

He retrieved his set of binoculars and surveyed the bridge and accompanying town for a few minutes.

A defensive ring of abandoned vehicles and makeshift watchtowers formed a perimeter around the town to the west, but it appeared for now that most of the zombie pressure was coming from the other side of the river. He spotted a number of men standing guard, their body language giving no indication that their truck had been spotted. He handed the binoculars to Amber, and she noted additional groups of people moving about in the town.

"I wonder how many people are living there," Amber asked. "Do you think we should go talk to them?"

"I don't see why not," Stephen said after mulling their options. "They might have information or something useful to pass along."

"Or they might kill us for our truck," Amber reminded him.

"If the town is intact then I'm gonna guess they are mostly local and decent people," Stephen said. "The bad guys can't stay in big groups like that. They use up the resources, turn on one another, and are forced to split up or die."

"I hope you're right," Amber replied as Stephen hit the gas.

They neared the fortification, he gave the horn a couple of honks and came in slow. Amber called out two men on top of a platform near the gate with rifles trained at them. Stephen stopped well short of the gate and put the truck in park. Slowly exiting his truck, he told Amber to slide over to the driver's seat and stay low behind the engine block, just in case. He was wearing his body armor, but it was useless against rifle rounds.

"Hello!" he called up. "I'm a former police officer passing through and was looking for word on survivors and to see if any news was coming in from the west."

A large man who seemed neither overly friendly nor hostile asked Stephen his name, where he was from, and who he had with him in the truck. They exchanged small talk, and Stephen mentioned a guy he went to the police academy with who worked in the area.

Eventually the pair seemed convinced that Stephen wasn't some advanced scout for a biker gang or something. The man informed Stephen that the town had roughly 4,500 residents prior to the outbreak and now had only 700. His buddy remained silent, but raised his rifle so it was no longer directly aimed at Stephen.

The man sounded defeated as he spoke. "Some took off, headed for FEMA camps I guess, but we still had to put down so many of our own. We burnt piles of bodies on the high school football field."

"How did you get hit out here so fast?" Stephen asked.

"Nobody knows for sure," the man replied. "We had a couple of car accidents involving out-of-towners at the grocery store and gas station. Next thing we know, everyone's running around biting and shooting one another. The town was almost done for until Colonel Finley took over. He served in Vietnam and ran the VFW in town, and now he runs the show here."

Stephen mentioned how they looked pretty well set up, all things considered, and inquired on the current zombie threat. The man told him how they had been able to use the lake created by the dam as a barrier from the zombies and had sufficient time to wall off a twelve square block section of town. The zombies hit in waves, but they were experiencing a lull at this time.

"Well, that's good for me I guess," Stephen laughed. "How are you making out on supplies?"

"Not enough to share if that's what you're asking," the man replied. "If you're looking for sanctuary you will have to be interviewed by our town board and quarantined to make sure you are not sick. Doc Krump at the clinic says he can take some blood samples and look at them under a microscope to see if you're infected. If we take you in, all your supplies become community property. We're getting by for now but need to store up provisions to make it through the winter."

"We're not looking for any help, but thanks anyway," Stephen said. "Just curious is all. We need as many people as possible to survive this."

Stephen informed the man of the stalled train in Rochelle and the possibility that it could hold valuable supplies. The man thanked him for the information, mentioning that the last man they sent out that direction to take a look around had never returned. He also warned Stephen that bandits were reported to be operating to the west and that no refugees had shown up from that direction for quite some time.

"We hung a couple guys last week," the man who had up to now remained silent added. "Raped and killed a girl on a farm outside of town. Found 'em both drunk in her bed while on a supply run. We're not tolerating any of that shit at all. The Colonel held a trial in the morning and hung 'em at noon."

"I would have done the same," Stephen conceded.

After giving the men radio frequencies that could be used to reach the prison, Stephen excused himself, stating he needed to get farther west before dark. They wished each other luck, and Stephen turned the truck around toward the tracks, heading west again. After they were safely on their way, he asked Amber how she thought the encounter went.

"I was scared the entire time," Amber admitted. "I don't think talking to that man was worth the risk. If they wanted to, they could've killed us both."

"In hindsight I think you're right," Stephen said. "We were sitting ducks but got lucky in meeting good people this time. Let's try to avoid getting into any more sticky situations and just steer clear of everybody for this trip."

"Agreed," Amber replied with a sigh of relief.

"Unless it's a bunch of co-eds trapped in a bus or something," Stephen said while grinning ear to ear, "then I'm stopping for sure."

Even Amber chuckled, "Sure thing there, hero."

They reached and passed through Savanna, located on the banks of the Mississippi River. The entire town looked like a war zone. Retail stores were nothing but charred piles of ash, some still sending faint trails of smoke into the air. Most had the windows smashed completely out. Debris and paper blew across the deserted streets. Here and there they could see vehicles that had been set ablaze and now were burnt out shells of twisted metal, many with scorched victims still in the seats.

"Phew...what is that smell?" Amber said scrunching up her face in disgust. "I think I am going to be sick."

A second later, the smell of death and rot assailed Stephen. He had an idea what was giving off the stench. Dead bodies...a *lot* of dead bodies.

Passing yet another burnt vehicle, they observed dozens of corpses lined up along the roadside. Many were being devoured by a flock of carrion birds that took wing as they passed. It looked as though this crossing point of the Mississippi had been flooded with refugees. With that many people filling the town with and little food available, it wasn't a stretch to believe that violence had erupted. Remembering what Eddie told him, Stephen worried that he would find the same back home in Wisconsin, the site of another river crossing. Amber tried to stay positive, but Stephen couldn't shake the feeling that he was not going to like what he found when he arrived. The bridge itself was littered with abandoned vehicles. The remnants of a National Guard roadblock was visible, which had clearly been overrun by either zombies or refugees. Stephen checked the bodies of some of the soldiers for weapons but found none.

"Wow," he said with a stunned look on his face. "It was a damn massacre. Let's get going. This place is giving me the creeps!"

Garbage and debris littered the roadway, and even the railroad tracks held evidence that a large group of refugees had traversed it on foot. Twice Stephen had to exit the truck to clear bodies that he thought might hang up their railroad truck. Gradually the wake of devastation ebbed, replaced by the tranquil countryside.

They continued north through the beautiful bluffs of the Mississippi River Valley following the river and the train tracks. The view reminded Stephen of his youth, growing up in a similar small river town. Back out in the peace and quiet they could almost forget how the world had gone to shit except for the horrors of the last hour that were still fresh in their minds. They snacked on beef jerky, washing it down with cans of Coca-Cola. Amber spotted a few bald eagles and snapped pictures with her digital camera. South of Galena, Illinois, with its historic downtown district, Stephen cut back on a set of tracks that ran northwest through town. A railroad bridge crossed the river due south of the highway bridge. It was getting dark and Stephen had a bad vibe. He shut off the truck a few hundred yards from the bridge.

"Wait in the truck," he ordered Amber. "It's getting dark, and I want to do a little scouting up ahead to find a place to sleep. Just stay put, and I'll be right back."

Stephen grabbed his assault rifle from the back seat, exiting the truck, shutting the door quietly. He moved up the tracks, making sure to keep along the trees on the west edge of the tracks until the bridge, and reached the bridge as darkness set in.

After he got eyes on the highway bridge, he went prone and found that his instincts had proven to be correct. A roadblock had been set up using the bridge as a choke point. Cars had been placed in such a way that a vehicle would have to slow considerably to weave around them before being ambushed from all sides. A large conversion van could then be rolled into the only path of escape, sealing the fate of any unsuspecting travelers. From what he could see, the trap was manned by four individuals. Due to the quiet night, Stephen was able to lay quietly on the tracks and hear the men's conversation clearly. They didn't seem overly bright and were not expecting anyone to approach from the railroad bridge to their south. A short, fat guy with long hair and a beard was bitching how no cars had tried to cross the river today, and he was tired of having to watch for and kill the occasional zombie that wandered up to them. He wanted to pull out. The leader, a guy they called Butch, told him to shut the fuck up and be quiet, and that if he ever wanted to find fresh pussy again he was going to have to be patient.

"It's your turn for watch and don't get fucking lazy on me. Remember what happened to Jake when he fell asleep on watch."

Nobody elaborated on the story so Stephen was unsure if a zombie or Butch had killed Jake. Butch had a shaved head and goatee, and was wearing a black leather biker jacket with patches on it that Stephen could not make out. There looked to be some sort of long gun next to where Butch was sitting, but Stephen couldn't make it out either.

A third man agreed, remarking how there were still survivors in the area and they were on the move due to the growing zombie population in the area.

"Just wait," he said. "They'll come right to us and we'll have them trapped like fish in a barrel. Ole Butch has this figured pretty good."

Stephen could clearly see the man, who was tall and slender in a black jacket, holding an AK-47 type rifle. The fourth was hunched over in a camp chair cooking some dinner over a 20lb propane tank with a burner and was mostly obscured from view. Stephen could smell pork & beans cooking even from the distance he was laying, and it made his stomach growl. The conversation turned towards their last few victims and how the driver never saw the roadblock until he was right on top of it. The tall guy, who they called "Slim", had killed the driver while the other male passenger begged for his life before Butch apparently shot him in the leg and fed him to a zombie that they had chained to a tree.

"Hey, where's that fucking bitch at?" Butch asked out of the blue.

"She's tied up in the back of the van," the guy cooking replied. "I think she's sleeping. We really wore her tight ass out today!"

"She resisted a little at first, but she loved it by the time we were through," the fat guy added. "I swore she begged me not to stop!"

This drew chuckles from the group, which irked Stephen. He settled into a proper shooting position and moved the selector on his rifle from SAFE to FIRE. He was grateful at how clear-cut it was that these were the bad guys, and they needed to be dealt with before they could hurt anyone else. Stephen had never killed a man while an officer but never doubted that he could do it if he needed to. Plus, he figured, all the killing of zombies had certainly desensitized him more than any video game ever could. It was growing darker by the minute, and he wanted to take the shot before visibility got much worse. The moon was offering decent visibility, but it looked like cloud cover was settling in quickly.

"Well, go get her. I'm dying for a blow job to go along with my supper," Butch ordered Slim. "I'll bet she will do about anything for a bowl of soup at this point. And, Fatty, keep watching the road or no sloppy seconds for you tonight. I don't want any surprises after dark."

The fat guy muttered something about always getting the worn out pussy while Slim walked towards the nearby conversion van.

Not having to make head shots was going to be easy. Stephen lined up his first target. He fired two rounds into the unsuspecting bandit's back, saw him crumple, and then quickly adjusted to fire on the fat man watching the road from behind the barricade. Stephen got two additional shots off before the man fell to the ground hard. Stephen was not sure if he scored a vital hit on the second man, but the first stayed down where he was, not moving. Stephen no longer could see the other two men, but one of them fired a weapon wildly into the air. Stephen simply adjusted his rifle again and sent six or seven rounds downrange to pin them down, and then a single round into the 20lb propane tank which exploded into a bright fireball. Less than a second later, the concussion reached Stephen.

He waited a full ten minutes for signs of movement and, seeing none, rose from his position cautiously. His heart was pumping from the one-sided firefight when he finally the crossed the bridge and crept up the east bank of the river to the barricade. Stephen passed it on the outside edge and circled in from the north. From this vantage point, he found that three of the men were dead, including Butch who, just like the man cooking, was lying right next to the propane tank looking for cover when it exploded. Both men sported severe skin burns and nasty wounds. Butch was nearly cut in half due to shrapnel from the exploding propane tank. The fourth man, the fat one, lay alive but wounded. He was shot in the shoulder and arm, and was propped up against the side of the barricade facing south, waiting for the unseen attacker to approach. He was clutching a shotgun, oblivious to Stephen's location. He, too, had been hurt in the explosion and judging from the blood and burns about his head, couldn't hear or see very well either. Stephen slung his rifle, quickly drew his pistol and without giving any warning put three rounds into the man's torso from his right flank.

It was over.

Stephen felt like a million bucks as a fresh wave of adrenaline coursed through his veins. He had successfully killed all four of the scumbags and wondered if it was normal to experience such joy in it. Not that there was anything normal anymore.

At least they wouldn't be able to cause any more suffering. And he could live with that.

6

October 29
Day 65

As Dan and Chris approached the entrance of the property, Dan had a growing knot in the pit of his stomach. Something seemed off already, but he couldn't put his finger on it. They carefully made the drive down the long lane to the cabin, and the structure finally came into view. Chris let out a gasp and Dan's heart sank. He had been right to be worried all along. The first thing they noticed was that the front door to the cabin was wide open, and there were a bunch of half-eaten corpses lying out in the yard. Dan stopped the truck suddenly, and both he and Chris jumped out and ran towards the cabin with their rifles at the ready.

"Check the outbuildings for survivors!" Dan shouted. "I'll check the cabin!"

"Roger!" Chris yelled back. "I know this doesn't look good, but stay focused and on point!"

They simultaneously started to clear the two buildings. Dan heard Chris fire off several rounds. All went quiet when Dan entered the kitchen and quickly put two rounds into the face of an infected subject from about a foot away. It popped up uncomfortably close, and as the back of the zombie's head exploded, its body dropped straight to the floor with a thud. Thankfully Dan didn't recognize his kill, and he continued after a short pause to gather his breath. He cleared the front room, coming across two other undead that he quickly dispatched.

Dan was in the zone.

Before moving down the hall to the back area of the cabin, he made a tactical reload and moved onward. At the end of the hall were doors to three bedrooms and two bathrooms. The bathrooms were first, and both were clear. Moving to the first bedroom, Dan opened the door and entered the room. At a moaning sound coming from the room, he whipped his rifle barrel up and cleared his blind side as he entered. The red dot of his reflex scope settled upon a disfigured being that was quickly closing the gap. Dan fired just as he recognized his target.

The creature crumpled to the floor missing a majority of its skull while Dan stood there in shock. Even with the head wound, the nasty bite wounds to its arms and neck area, Dan recognized his brother.

He stepped over the body and slowly sank down to sit on the edge of the nearby bed, tears filling his eyes as he stared at the corpse who used to be his brother Dave. From the hallway, a shuffling sound broke his trance, and his head snapped up in alarm. Knowing what awaited him out there, he now eagerly accepted it. He needed an outlet for the anger and despair that threatened to overcome him. Grabbing his rifle, he quickly moved to the hallway and was met by yet another handful of undead. Screaming his emotional pain, Dan fired again and again into the closely packed enemy. Chunks of rotting meat and bone fragments flew from the bodies of the doomed creatures. One after another, bloated, rotting bodies sank to the wood plank floor. All too soon his weapon ran dry, and Dan stood there, chest heaving and shaking with anger. Hoping that the remaining rooms held more of the bastards, Dan dropped the empty magazine from his rifle and slammed another home. Ready to unleash some hell, he stepped over the foul smelling lifeless corpses.

Unfortunately, the second bedroom presented no targets. The back bedroom brought Dan face to face with yet another horror. He could smell them before he opened the door. In the bedroom were his close friend Tom and his small children, who were found next to his body. It appeared that they had taken their own lives rather than be eaten alive. They had been eaten shortly after they killed themselves. Dan doubled over and vomited, adding to the stench. His stomach empty, he continued to dry heave until he pulled himself from the room and slammed the door shut. He closed his eyes as his head sank against the door, where he stood motionless for what felt like an eternity.

Footsteps behind him dragged his mind out of its funk, and he spun around to engage more of the hated enemy. Chris, who walked in behind Dan, quickly leaned to the side while batting the barrel of Dan's rifle out of his face.

"What the fuck is wrong with you?" Chris asked. "Have you lost your mind?"

As Chris said this, he was checking Dan for bite marks. He couldn't figure out why Dan was standing there not moving.

"We've gotta get the hell out of here!" Chris cried. "There are more bodies out back. They put up a fight but there is nothing left to see here, they are all gone. This area is crawling with zombies. Let's go!"

He shook Dan by his shoulder lightly, but Dan stood there staring at the closed door.

"Tom and his kids are in there."

Dan silently walked around Chris, stepped over the pile of zombie corpses in the hall and then entered the first bedroom and sat on the edge of the bed again.

Chris followed and looked from Dan to the dead zombie on the floor next to him.

"It's kind of late for introductions, but I'd like you to meet my brother, Dave. Dave, this is my friend, Chris."

Chris was not expecting that. He stood in shock for a moment. "Sorry, buddy," he finally whispered. "But we need to get out of here and head back to Joliet. They need us there. I'm sorry about your brother, but we have all lost loved ones in this mess."

Dan looked at Chris and then stood and walked to the kitchen. Rummaging through the kitchen cabinets, Dan found a stash of vodka and opened a bottle, taking a long drink. He grabbed two others and threw them in a plastic bag he found in a drawer.

He took another drink, turned and stalked out the door towards the truck. "Let's get the fuck out of here!" he yelled. "It smells like yesterday's sweaty ass in here!"

Dan climbed into the passenger seat, took another drink, and lit up a cigar. Chris jumped in, fired up the big Ford and headed back down the drive. When they reached the road, they traveled in silence for about thirty minutes before coming across a vacant looking house near the highway.

"Pull over," Dan ordered, now slightly intoxicated.

They both got out while Chris scanned the area for threats. Seeing nothing out of the ordinary, Dan kicked in the door and pulled a chair up to the empty kitchen table before finishing off the bottle of vodka. Chris took it upon himself to clear the house.

"I'm tired and don't give a fuck anymore," Dan announced. "We are staying here tonight."

The next few hours went by slowly for Chris as he picked through a couple of MREs and drank bottled water while cleaning his rifle and topping off magazines. Dan started on his second bottle of vodka and was soon incoherent.

"Thank God he's not an angry drunk," Chris said aloud after listening to Dan's conversation with the bottle he was holding, "or I would really be in trouble right now."

The sun was starting to go down, so Chris found a good place upstairs to sleep for the night and went through the routine of securing the house and checking the area with binoculars. They were time consuming chores but were quickly becoming second nature. Dan became quiet as it grew dark, and when they settled down and tried to get comfortable, little was said. They both knew where they stood.

"Hang in there, buddy."

Dan didn't reply, but nodded his head slightly.

*

Stephen carefully walked over to the conversion van and cleared the front before he opened the back door and found the woman that the gang was talking about. She was a middle-aged woman who they'd left naked, bound and gagged, and very much dead. Stephen couldn't tell if she had suffocated on her gag or maybe just gave up after being repeatedly raped by the now dead gang of filth. He quietly closed the van door and made his way back towards his quarry. He checked for usable weapons and located two Romanian AK-47 style rifles and a small backpack with ammunition. The group only had two magazines for each rifle and they were duct taped together. Stephen left behind the older sawed off shotgun and a bolt action rifle that had been damaged in the blast. He didn't bother checking the bodies for handguns or ammunition. He noticed the motorcycles parked near the van but found nothing of any real use in the saddlebags other than a couple of cans of stew. He had to sling a backpack along with three rifles, making for an awkward hike.

With it now fully dark, Stephen pulled out a flashlight as he made his way back towards the truck. He managed to trip twice on the railroad ties and re-aggravated his knee. A lone zombie walked up on him when he approached the railroad bridge, and he shot it with his pistol just as it got close enough to raise its arms and hiss.

"It's creepy as fuck out here after dark!"

Approaching the truck, he cried out for Amber and made sure she knew it was him coming from a long ways off. It was very dark now, and the last thing he needed was to be smoked by friendly fire this late in the game. When he arrived at the truck, he found her on edge due to the gunshots and explosion, clutching her pistol in her hands.

"Sorry that took so long," Stephen said, "but everything is okay."

He gave no explanation for the delay, threw the captured gear in back, climbed in and started the truck. Only after being incessantly bombarded with questions while they drove past the roadblock did Stephen finally admit to killing the bandits. Amber listened to the story in silence and then asked numerous times how he could be sure they were bad men. Stephen continuously assured her that they were and said little else. Sensing that Stephen wasn't telling her everything, Amber continued with her pestering interrogation

"But what if they—" she started to ask.

By now Stephen had tired of her insistent questioning of his decisions. "You really want to know how I knew they were pieces of shit?" he asked her angrily. "Maybe it was when they were talking about killing refugees and laughing about it. Maybe it was them talking about ass raping some poor woman. Maybe it was the naked dead woman I found duct taped in the back of their van, horribly beaten and brutally raped!"

Silence dominated the cab of the truck as he continued to drive.

After a bit, Amber quietly whispered, "Sorry."

"No, I'm sorry," he replied, calming himself a bit. "You had the right to know. I was hoping to spare you the details."

With the adrenaline wearing off, Stephen realized he was tired. When they reached a small railroad bridge over a very deep ravine, he parked in the middle of the bridge and announced it was as good a place as any to stop for the night. Any zombies in the area should find it nearly impossible to navigate out onto the tracks, and they should be safe there. Stephen rolled out sleeping bags in the back of the truck along with air mattresses and brushed his teeth before crawling in. Amber joined him and lay there quietly looking at the man who had just killed four people and didn't even seem fazed by it. She was a little scared that it didn't bother him but at the same time felt safe lying next to him. They were soon both fast asleep.

*

The cold wind reminded me that I forgot my damn jacket in my camper. It hadn't been that cold when I started my workout. Some intense sets of push-ups, sit-ups and chin-ups followed by a slow jog around the inner side of the wall had me working up a sweat. Now, walking a second lap to cool off, I was again reminded it was late October and the weather could fool you. It would be plenty warm during the day but quite cold at night, and nightfall was coming earlier and earlier now. It wouldn't be long until snow started to fall, and I hated the cold.

Yet, as I continued my walk I couldn't help but be impressed with the improvements to our home that had been completed in a relatively short period of time since moving in. The teams of refugees-turned-landscapers had transformed an old overgrown jungle of a prison yard into a nicely manicured courtyard that any homeowner would be proud to have. Buildings had been cleaned, repaired and painted. Steam could be seen venting from the prison's laundry room and power tools could be heard from the machine shop as parts to solve most any mechanical problem we could think off were being fabricated. The interior yard was safe and well lit. Laughter could be heard from inside the campers we had brought back to the prison.

What we needed to do when we get the time was find one of the large franchise fitness workout businesses and bring some weight equipment back. I'd been slacking in that department. Everyone could benefit from some weight training, and it would be nice to have it up and running before winter.

Sadly, we never had the time to collect the extra stuff we wanted. The list of urgent supplies kept getting longer as the days grew shorter. One thing we had learned was how the danger grows at an expediential rate if you were outside after dark. The undead were unhindered by the darkness.

Seeing a familiar big man up ahead standing outside the old prison firehouse, now refurbished as our new command center, I steered myself towards him. I looked around for his sidekick, Jeff Kleaner, but he was not to be found.

"Hey, Logan, where's Jeff, and how are the security upgrades you made panning out?" I asked.

Logan smiled and put out his smoke. "Jeff's making his rounds of the guard stations to ensure they are not sleeping," Logan said. "I know it's boring work, but we'd rather they be bored than a zombie chew toy during their nap. As far as the rest, come on up, brother, and I will show you."

I followed him upstairs, where he pointed to some recently installed LCD monitors. The images were black and white but surprisingly clear. Individual zombies could clearly be made out shuffling towards the prison.

"Looks like an old black and white horror movie."

"It's all going to be gravy from here on out, brother," he said with pride. "The infrared cameras we installed today pick up those zombie bastards a long ways off at night, don't they?"

"Stephen was right to pick you two to head up the prison security," I said. "We have a lot of people entrusting us with protecting them and their loved ones." I swore I saw him swell with pride. "Carry on, soldier." I walked out of the building and started making my way back to my RV for some shut eye.

On my way back, I was forced to stop and talk to a bunch of people from our growing group of survivors, most of whom wanted to know when Stephen, Dan and Chris were coming back. Their absence was noticed, and everyone was curious as to their whereabouts.

"They should be back in a day or two," I told everyone who asked. "They are checking on family out of town, and I'm sure they are fine."

Since Dan and Chris had left to check on Dan's brother down in the lower part of Illinois, a lot more responsibilities were dumped onto my shoulders as a result. Stephen got word from Eddie that the area in Wisconsin along the Mississippi River where he grew up was utterly destroyed. Not from zombies, but by refugees and gangs of humans looting and raping as they fled the masses of undead. This news had forced Stephen to take off, leaving me extra shorthanded.

What was I to do? Tell them no? What was done was done.

I entered my humble abode, showered, changed into a pair of shorts, and quickly hopped into the bed, cringing at the freezing cold sheets. Mattie was not back from her rounds checking on the new intakes, and although I wanted to wait up for her, I was thoroughly exhausted. Sleep quickly settled in, and my mind drifted towards a mission I had in the works. I was still working out the details, but the basic plan involved setting large zombie traps to kill them in bulk, sparing us all the brutal and up-close killing that was wearing us all down.

*

Stephen awoke to a strange sound. It was just after dawn, and Amber was lying on his shoulder fast asleep. He didn't mind the small puddle of drool on his shoulder and merely chuckled. She was good looking enough that it didn't bother him in the least. The noise again caught his ear. He eased Amber off his shoulder and sat up in his sleeping bag. Behind the truck, a lone zombie had attempted to walk out onto the bridge and had fallen, becoming wedged between two railroad ties. Somehow the creature had fallen all the way through the railroad ties and got hung up on its head. Stephen sighed, put on his boots, grabbed his pistol, and walked out to the zombie dressed in only his boxers. It was cold, but the rising sun felt good on his chest. Approaching the zombie, he made out that it used to be a young man who, from the looks of it, had survived up until recently. He was missing a large part of his belly where he had been bitten and turned. Although clearly stuck, he was nonetheless hissing and clawing away, trying in vain to reach Stephen. He raised his pistol and prepared to fire a round into the zombie's head, paused and decided instead to handle it by hand, or in this case by foot. Stephen raised his hard-soled boot and brought it down with all his weight right into the creature's face. With a few additional stomps and a loud bone crunching crack, the thing's jaw and skull were forcefully crushed through the railroad tie gap and it was sent howling to the waters far below. Amber shot up in the back of the truck, wide awake now from the howl and splash.

"Fucking zombies," Stephen muttered, walking back to the truck. "Have you seen my pants?"

"Umm yeah, they're right here," Amber replied, throwing them at him. "Why aren't you wearing them?"

They both got a laugh as Stephen sheepishly stepped into his BDUs.

The pair took the time to cook breakfast over a small propane stove and Stephen's stomach rumbled when the instant pancake mix turned from a watery mix into a delicious breakfast. Piling on the syrup, he wolfed down two stacks and polished it off with a glass of powdered milk.

"I'll handle the cleanup, Amber," Stephen offered with a smile. "Thanks for cooking, it was delicious. I'm starting to think you're the total package."

"Oh really," Amber laughed. "Well you haven't seen what a bitch I can be when I'm pissed off and not getting my way. And I'll take you up on that offer on the dishes. I hate them!"

After cleaning up and putting on fresh clothes, Stephen studied the map for the tenth time before they hit the tracks for the day. They had to drive around yet another stalled out train, this one just north of the Illinois/Wisconsin state line. The engines were deserted and their cargo had only been coal. Stephen stopped to take a few pot shots at passing zombies, but didn't risk getting punched for teasing Amber this time around.

"See, you're learning," Amber remarked and jokingly tousled Stephen's hair.

"Do you know how to cut hair?" Stephen asked, suddenly serious.

"Uh, I don't know, never tried cutting a man's hair before," Amber replied.

"I like my hair nice and short, but there seems to be a shortage of barbers these days," Stephen said. "Maybe you could give it a shot when we get back? I'm tired of trying those stupid hair clippers by myself."

"Your haircut does leave something to be desired," Amber laughed. "I tell ya what, you get me back alive, and I'll give it a shot. It can't come out any worse."

Shortly before noon, after stopping outside of town for a bathroom break, Stephen and Amber rolled in to Prairie-Du-Chien. True to Eddie's word the town was completely destroyed with nearly every structure in town burnt to the ground. The empty brick shells of all the retail stores were picked clean to the bone. It looked as if a massive army of locusts had moved through the area, destroying everything in its path. The main roads were nearly impassible with burnt cars littering the streets. A large traffic jam, probably originating near the bridge over the Mississippi, had left everyone with nowhere to run.

"Looks like the road coming out of Kuwait City during Desert Storm," Stephen remarked, looking at the destruction. "The Highway of Death I think they called it."

Amber rolled her eyes to yet another history reference, wanting to tell Stephen she was two years old when that happened. Instead she remarked that they had not seen a single survivor all day. Stephen shrugged and took a shot at a lone zombie shambling their way.

"There aren't many of those either," she mentioned as he

dropped the bulky zombie woman. "No zombies, no survivors, nobody at all."

"It *is* awfully quiet," Stephen commented, "and this doesn't look good. Some people had to have escaped and wandered off into the woods."

Finally stopping on Highway 27, outside of the city limits, Stephen pulled into a driveway that led to a roadside property where two houses once stood. Both were burnt to the ground, and trash from refugees was piled high in the adjoining yards. Stephen got out of the truck and walked around quietly for a while and then returned.

"That used to be my parents' and brother's places," he said quietly, pulling back out of the driveway.

He drove back west into town without saying anything. Amber rested her hand on his knee and gave it a comforting squeeze.

"The houses were burnt too badly to find anything worth saving," Stephen noted as they drove. "I'm just glad I didn't find any bodies."

Driving carefully around abandoned cars, Stephen reached the large bridge that stretched west across the mighty Mississippi. It was jammed solid with stalled cars, completely impassible by vehicle. Stephen stopped the truck in the parkway in front of the bridge and climbed out, leaving it running.

"This's where I grew up. If we could have gotten across the river, I was going to show you the view from the state park," Stephen sighed, pointing to a big bluff that overlooked the river from the Iowa side. "It's just outside of town. My grandma's property is over there too, but it's not practical to go see it. If we found a boat we could use it to cross maybe, but the marina looked deserted when we drove in. And to cross the bridge on foot would leave us trapped if any undead or looters showed up..." Stephen's voice drifted off and he was lost in thought for a moment.

"It sure is a pretty area," Amber said, seeing the hurt in his eyes.

She stood silently by his side while he stared across the river. After a few minutes movement on the bridge caught their attention. Grabbing his binoculars, Stephen focused on the bridge as the lead elements of a zombie horde came into view. Weaving through the abandoned vehicles, they advanced in a deep wave.

"You see that?" he asked. "Bet they heard our truck. That's where the entire fucking zombie horde went! The rotten bastards chased every living person to the west side of the river!"

Stephen grabbed his rifle from the truck, lined up a quick shot and squeezed of his first round. Amber jumped from the rifle's report and listened to him curse after missing. Firing again and again, Stephen quickly ran his magazine dry. Pulling a spare from his vest, Stephen turned to Amber.

"Get my ammo bag from the front seat!" he snapped.

"There must be a thousand of them coming, Stephen!" she replied in shock. "Are you crazy? Let's go!"

"Get me my fucking bag!" Stephen screamed and started firing again.

Amber ran to the front seat and retrieved the bag, tears welling up in her eyes. Dropping it at Stephen's feet, she again pleaded for them to leave, but Stephen ignored her and continued firing into the approaching mass. Scores fell, but the number facing them grew ever larger and ever closer. By the time the evil mass closed to within half a football field, Stephen had a pile of empty magazines at his feet, and the hand guards on the rifle were hot to the touch. While he was loading yet another magazine, Amber pleaded for him to take her away from this awful bridge.

"Please," she sobbed quietly, "can we leave? *Please*?"

Stephen turned and looked at Amber, who had tears streaming down her face, and snapped out it. Suddenly he looked stunned and very much afraid at how close the zombies had come.

Stephen practically tossed Amber through the open driver door. "Shit! Get in the truck, let's go!"

He frantically turned the ignition while the truck was still running, causing a terrible screeching sound, which made things even worse. The lead zombies slammed into his door right as he hit the gas. Far too many had to be run over as he spun the truck around. One flew up onto the windshield.

Amber screamed.

Stephen realized how badly he had fucked up. "We get stuck and we're screwed!"

Fortunately they didn't get stuck, and they left the horde in their wake.

After driving a few minutes in quiet, Stephen apologized.

"I'm sorry, Amber. I just lost it for a minute. I suddenly realized that my family was gone, and I would never see them again," Stephen said with genuine remorse.

"I understand I guess, but don't let it happen again! You really scared the shit out of me." Amber forced a smile while wiping away the last of her tears. "Or I'll be forced to slap you silly! You're not as big and tough as you think you are!"

"Maybe not," Stephen relented.

"Where are we going?" Amber then asked after looking out the window and seeing that they were now moving north, farther away from Joliet.

Stephen told her that he wanted to check on his property several miles northwest of town before heading home, as there might yet be some things there they could use. It was a quiet drive down an empty gravel road, and they soon reached the remote property and the shooting range Stephen had built. The very same place he had enjoyed with Mike and Chris that seemed like months ago but was really only hours before the virus went rampant. It looked like some fleeing refugees had found it and trashed the place, leaving garbage strewn about. All his firewood had been used up, and the shed Stephen kept his target stands and such in had been broken into pieces and burnt for fuel. Looking around, Stephen found a shovel near what looked disturbingly like shallow graves, and walked over to the outhouse which was set back in the woods. He promptly tipped it over.

"What are you doing?" Amber asked. "Have you lost it again?"

Her question went unanswered. Stephen dug a small hole next to the shit pit and retrieved two metal tins wrapped in heavy plastic.

"Each sealed tin contains 700 rounds of 7.62x39 ammo," Stephen said triumphantly. "They'll work in those rifles I got off those shit bags back in Galena."

"Why did you have them under the outhouse?" Amber asked with a look of disgust.

"For when the blue helmets come," Stephen replied as if it was obvious, "or zombies I guess. Don't you remember how scarce ammo got awhile back?"

"Uh no, not really."

Now it was Stephen's turn to look confused, how could anyone not remember the panic buying shortly after Obama got reelected? You couldn't even find a box of .22lr on the shelf for quite some time.

"Hey, how about some target practice before we leave?"

The confused look on her face only intensified. "Now?"

"Can't think of a better time or place to blow off some steam. That's why I built the place after all."

He went about setting up four target stands on the range. He located some ear protection and first showed her the proper stance for shooting her pistol and how to properly align the sights. Stephen always enjoyed teaching people how to shoot, and this was no exception. He had her put nearly a hundred rounds downrange with the 9mm, practicing headshots, and then moved on to his AR-15. After a good hour, Stephen wrapped up with some transition drills, using the opportunity to get in close to Amber. He had his arms wrapped around her from behind, showing her how to quicken the transition from the slung carbine to her holstered pistol. Finally Amber stopped, put her pistol in the holster, and kissed Stephen on the mouth.

"You're welcome," Stephen joked as he grabbed Amber around the waist and pulled her in close.

"I've wanted to do that for a while," she whispered softly.

His hands slid down, grabbing her ass as he kissed her again. After a moment he paused. "What perfume are you wearing?" he asked softly. "It's intoxicating."

"Pink Friday, and at some point you are going to have to find me some more."

Stephen's sudden good fortune was interrupted by movement off to his left. A lone zombie had arrived, drawn by all the gunfire. It looked vaguely familiar to Stephen as it stumbled in their direction.

"I don't fucking believe it!" Stephen brayed. "My gun hating, liberal, asshole neighbor is a fucking zombie. This is awesome!"

Amber looked at Stephen again with a curious gaze.

"It's a long story. Okay Amber, it's time to graduate from Stephen's basic firearms class," he said with an air of authority in his voice. "Go out and kill that zombie!"

Amber calmly walked towards her intended target. It was dressed in overalls and wearing a tool belt. She drew her pistol smoothly, turned back to Stephen and asked, "You used to know this guy?"

Stephen laughed and nodded his head. Amber turned and aimed the pistol at the zombie that was now mere feet away. She fired a single shot, and the zombie's head snapped back from the impact of the round. He dropped onto his back like a puppet with its stings cut and went motionless.

"A plus!" Stephen cheered, walking up and playfully smacking Amber on the ass. "Let's roll! I really wanna be home by tomorrow evening."

"Tomorrow is Halloween," Amber said. "I bet you didn't know that."

"I sure didn't," he admitted. "Where has all the time gone?"

Back on the tracks, and after a quiet drive, Stephen and Amber spent the night on the same railroad bridge as the night before. After a dinner of Mountain House dinners heated up using a camp stove, Amber prepared the bedding in the back of the truck while Stephen set up a camp shower and heated up some water. He and Amber finally had a chance to clean off the dirt and grime accumulated from their long journey. Stephen insisted on cleaning the guns, and after he finished he stripped down to his boxers and slid under the sleeping bags. He was happily surprised to find Amber, whom he thought was asleep, in her bra and panties.

"You smell like gun oil," she laughed.

"Wow... and you don't," Stephen replied, pulling her close.

"You have been amazing the last couple days," she said coyly. "Now let's see if you can finish undressing me yourself."

*

Chris awoke at dawn with Dan still passed out from his late night with the bottle. He wanted to get underway quickly, eager to get back to the prison, the only home they had left. The truck was all packed before Dan started moving again and Chris forced a couple of cups of coffee down his throat to wake him up. Finishing breakfast, Chris loaded up the truck, and to his surprise Dan was following along with the program. When they were getting ready to leave, Dan headed for the driver's door.

"I'm driving today, kid," Dan remarked bluntly. He headed down the driveway and turned left, back towards Peoria. Not the way Chris wanted to go.

"Where the hell are we going?" Chris asked. "Home is the other way."

"Back to the property," Dan replied. "We are going to kill every zombie we see and bury my brother. You are going to help, and then we will go home."

Chris realized he had no choice as they soon enough pulled back down the drive to the cabin. He checked his carbine and pistol to make sure they were both loaded.

Dan stopped the truck, jumped out, and yelled at the top of his lungs, "I'm here motherfuckers, come and get some!"

They could hear rustling in the brush, and soon the relentless ghouls appeared from the tree line, shambling towards Dan. Dan screamed a cry of pain and rage and charged the small horde, firing wildly. Thinking that Dan might get himself killed, Chris decided to stay near the truck, just in case. Jumping into the truck bed, he rested his arms onto the roof as a shooting platform and began picking targets that stumbled dangerously near to Dan. For his part, Dan had his rifle on full auto, killing fifteen zombies at close range, and burned through a full combat load of 270 rounds in minutes. Chris only needed to kill seven or eight from the truck's roof and expended less than one magazine.

After the targets dwindled, Dan and Chris began the difficult task of digging shallow graves for Dave and the other identifiable bodies in the group. The labor was intensive, and despite the cool afternoon, both were sweating profusely. By the time it was done, both were completely exhausted, and it was after dark.

"Thank you, Chris," Dan said. "I feel a little better now. I'm sorry that took so long. We will have to take off in the morning, get an early start and hurry back."

Exhausted, Chris nodded and prepared another hobo dinner on the road. Dan played with the HAM radio in the truck and located an operator twenty miles west of Peoria. The guy was on his way to the West Coast, hoping to make it to the government safe zone. He also relayed how the National Guard Air Lift Wing in Peoria had been overrun.

"Saw it happen myself, firsthand," the stranger said. "When zombies hit the runways it was all over. A few other civilians were camped out there with my family and there wasn't enough room on the remaining aircraft. They were down to a skeleton crew at that point. The last plane to try and take off crashed and burned on the runway."

Dan speculated how the noise of the planes had likely drawn in a massive number of zombies. He also questioned the man's decision to try for the West Coast and offered a spot at the prison, which the man politely refused. He had family out west. They continued talking until the man's signal started to fade out and they wished each other good luck. Dan was unable to reach anyone else on the air that night. The radio didn't seem to have the power to punch back out to Joliet and the radio in the cabin had been destroyed by errant gunfire.

While Dan wound down, Chris searched the cabin for anything useful that they might be able salvage. He found a couple of cases of Coca-Cola and chocolate bars under the sink, along with a few odds and ends. Returning to the truck after gathering everything he wanted to take from the cabin, Chris found Dan asleep behind the wheel. Not wanting to wake him, Chris loaded up the supplies quietly. When he was done, he crawled into the back of the truck and tried to stay awake to keep watch. It had been a long and laborious day, however, and Chris soon dozed off.

7

October 29
Day 65
Oklahoma, USA

Matvei kicked the steel casings of 5.45 x 39 around in the dust. He bent over and checked the head stamps on a few of them, which confirmed his suspicions. The rounds had belonged to his men.

"I missed them again," he muttered. "Will I ever catch up to them?"

Another firefight had played out here, the third he had come across today alone. They were most definitely one-sided firefights between his men and the infected hordes. It was obvious, however, from the camouflaged bodies strewn about that the undead were not the only ones taking losses. They made up for what they lacked in weapons and tactics with overwhelming numbers and unrelenting determination. Matvei was now well aware of the fact that he had severely underestimated his enemy when planning this ill-fated operation.

He was now outside of Allen, Oklahoma, some 170 miles north of Dallas and had been chasing his fragmented army north for several days. They were undoubtedly moving towards a rendezvous point in Missouri and as of yet he had been unable to catch up to them. The remote gas station had been his only promise of fuel for miles, and it looked like his men had beaten him to the punch. He had fallen behind while holed up, licking his wounds, awaiting a rescue party that never showed. Matvei initially began his chase on foot, with operational vehicles surprisingly scarce. Eventually he found transportation in the form of an older Dodge Caravan. Since then,

Matvei had been scrounging up fuel and avoiding traffic accidents while moving north. Shortly thereafter, he began coming across signs of his advancing men. Shell casings and dead bodies around cleaned out gas stations and looted stores. Any living person that Matvei saw in the distance was unwilling or unable to make contact with him. All the traffic headed north was drawing the infected with them, and Matvei did not have to shoot many himself, only passing the occasional straggler along the highway.

After looking around in the service station and not finding anything of value, Matvei carefully moved into the town of Allen on foot looking for more suitable transportation. His van had been run hard and wasn't sounding too good. Everything he had fit into his rucksack, and he made his way down the side streets. The silence was deafening, with only his own labored breathing to keep him company. House after house was gutted and vacant. Large crows stared down from dead power lines, almost as if they were casting judgment. More than once he glanced up, expecting to see a bunch of carrion birds above him, circling, waiting for him to give up. The birds in Chechnya haunted him at times, as he watched them peck out the eyes of the dead.

Block after block was completely burnt, with no fire department to contain the blaze. Finally, on a dead end street, Matvei found a newer black Dodge Ram truck in the driveway of a single family residence. It was approaching dark, and Matvei decided to check the ranch style house for anything useful and maybe get lucky and find the keys. Kicking in the front door, he used the weapon light on his rifle to clear the house. He found the house in disarray but the keys on the table in the blood-soaked kitchen. Catching movement in his peripheral vision, Matvei turned towards the hallway leading towards the bedrooms, and his light illuminated a white male, sickly and pale with a blood-stained mouth and torn clothing. The 160 lumen LED bulb would have blinded any normal attacker, but this creature didn't even flinch. Matvei whispered a Russian prayer, and quickly dispatched the infected homeowner with a quick three round burst from his assault rifle.

It was all quiet again, and Matvei waited for nearly half an hour for any other infected persons to show up, but thankfully none did. Securing the rest of the house, he found the homeowner's wife. Her corpse was mostly eaten, and Matvei simply sealed off the room because the smell was overpowering. The refrigerator stank of rotten food. Matvei decided he would set up camp in the attic. It was the only place free of putrid decay. He rummaged through the den and located boxes of ammunition that would work in his guns, but no actual firearms. The truck had a half full tank of gas and Matvei found five additional gallons in the lawn shed in the backyard. This was a much needed stroke of luck. He dragged the corpse of the homeowner outside into the yard and returned to the safety of the residence. Dragging furniture in front of all the doors and windows, he kept as quiet as possible, not wanting to have any more run-ins with the infected. He found various canned goods in the pantry and ate four cans of cold beef ravioli before loading the rest into a box. Finally he managed to drag a twin mattress up into the attic and place it near a small window which he would use to keep lookout. Matvei laid out his bedding and cleaned himself with wet wipes before promptly passing out, his last thought being how his quarry was probably growing increasingly distant by the minute.

8

October 30
Day 66

I was up again with the sun, awakened by a knock on the door. I lay motionless in bed, hoping that whoever was knocking would just go away and let me sleep a few more minutes. Unfortunately the knocking continued, and I was about to get out of bed and make them pay when I heard Mattie answer the door. She had unknowingly saved the unsuspecting soul a royal ass chewing. I decided to let Mattie handle it and hit the shower. I didn't take hot showers for granted; hot water was definitely a precious resource after the zombie apocalypse.

When I exited the shower, I was hit by the rich smell of coffee. I never drank it much before the world went to shit, but now even I had a greater appreciation of what a luxury a cup of coffee was. When I walked out of my room, Mattie handed me a hot, steaming mug.

"Black and bitter, just the way you like it."

"I could get used to this real quick," I answered, taking the mug. "I might have to keep you!"

"You'll have to catch me first," she laughed while pouring herself a cup, "but I gave away my camper to a new family and may need a place to stay."

"The way you run, that may be difficult," I said, "but you are always welcome here. By the way, who was at the door?"

"Just some guy asking where Stephen was," she replied. "He was having a problem with his pistol and knew that Stephen was a gun guy and hadn't seen him around. I told him that Stephen was out on a long range patrol and would be back soon."

"He had to wake us up for that?" I asked. "What an asshole!"

"I figured you would be pissed so I spared the guy an ass chewing," Mattie added then asked what my plans were for the day.

"More of the same," I replied. "We are going to hit the area of Columbia and Henderson hard today. The houses are packed in pretty tight over there, and I would like to get some of them torn down to create a fire line. Any number of things could start a fire that would quickly get out of hand."

"I've got a lot of loose ends to tie up around here today, but I would love to go out on a raid tomorrow," Mattie said. "I would like to see some action, helps keep me sharp."

"Ask and you shall receive," I replied then went back to my room to retrieve my gear.

*

Brother Jonas slipped away from Mike's RV window after listening to their conversation. He grimaced under the weight of the heavy propane canister in his grasp. Checking and swapping the tanks on various campers gave him the perfect alibi to eavesdrop at his leisure. He walked past the two security bosses who were standing at the entrance to the small circle of motor homes. They were arguing over if they should ask Mike or Mattie if they could wear badges of some sort to make them appear more official.

Amateurs, he thought, shaking his head in disgust. This could be the perfect time to take the woman that Father Kettle was so infatuated with. If Kettle said not to harm her he wouldn't.

Jonas replaced the propane tank to its rack and meandered off, planning his next move.

Those other clowns were a different story. Them he could kill. Since three out of five of the main players were gone, that only left the big bastard, Mike, to take care of for now.

Settling down on a bench at the campfire he built outside his camper, Jonas warmed himself in the cool morning, drew his blade, and began to whittle a piece of wood, sending the chips into the flames.

And I got something for that bald fucker, he thought with a wicked smile. But first thing's first, he was going to need to get another message out. He needed to let the others know that Stephen was gone as well, and tomorrow may be their best opportunity to strike since Mattie may be out of the prison on a raid. He needed to be on that raid, and figure out a way to get her alone.

*

Father Kettle looked up from writing his latest sermon when he heard a knock on his office door.

"Enter."

The door opened, and Kettle's brother entered with a toothy grin on his face.

"I have news from your man inside the prison compound," Lewis said, waving a piece of paper in his hand. "It was given to me by one of the men shadowing that stupid prison."

"Well don't keep me in the dark," Kettle snapped, waving his hands for Lewis to give him the parchment. "Let's see what he has to say."

He scanned the poor writing that his man had used to transcribe Jonas's message.

"It says here that three out of five of those assholes are no longer on the property. It looks like it's Mattie and the big aggressive one with the shaved head are left at the prison," Kettle read from the paper. "The other three left and are currently out of town."

"Didn't a couple of them shoot up some of your guys?" Lewis asked, but quickly dropped the matter after receiving an unsettling glare from his brother.

"It also mentions that Mattie will be outside of the prison walls tomorrow,," Lewis continued, nervously reclining in a chair across from Kettle. "We should act while those knuckleheads are still gone, and the woman is ripe for the picking. I don't like the idea of kidnapping anyone, but if it will result in the destruction of their imperfect idea of a safe zone, then I'm all for it."

"Yes, I was aware that two of them were gone," Kettle responded. "Indeed, they blew the head off of one of my men on their way out of town. I did not know about the third leaving. And if Mattie will be vulnerable tomorrow, we must act."

"Beware of the big guy, he hits like a truck!" Lewis chimed, rubbing his badly healed crooked nose. "Trust me, I found out the hard way."

This brought a chuckle from the men who were standing guard outside Kettle's open office door. Kettle lowered the paper and looked at his brother. He seemed obsessed with showing up those former police officers, although Kettle was almost positive that those men didn't even know Lewis was alive. Kettle figured they didn't give two shits about his brother, let alone want to outdo him. His brother Lewis felt otherwise. Hell, from what Kettle had been told by a few survivors that showed up, the safe zone Lewis had been in charge of fell as a direct consequence of Lewis's subpar leadership. Kettle was sure his brother blamed the cops for that as well.

"Our team shadowing them will capitalize on those three being absent. Get word to them as soon as possible to be ready to move on Jonas' signal, snatching Mattie the first chance they get," Kettle ordered, returning to the task at hand. "We need to question her to find out the group's strengths and weaknesses."

"I'm on it." Lewis grinned in satisfaction and got up to leave. "We'll put a plan together to grab her first thing."

His wooden door slammed shut, and Kettle took a second to sigh in growing anticipation. He dropped the dispatch on his desk and retrieved a key ring from a drawer. Pushing back the chair, he stood and walked to the door, opened it, and he stuck his head outside.

"I'm not to be disturbed until I tell you otherwise," Kettle told the guards. "I am going to be in deep prayer with almighty God."

"Yes Father!" both guards responded in unison.

Closing the door, Kettle locked it, walked to the rear of his office and pulled aside a decorative curtain, revealing a second wooden door which he unlocked and opened. He next grabbed a tray of leftover food off the nearby coffee table, mostly discarded table scraps and chunks of dried bread. Kettle paused a minute to light a few candles in a silver candelabra as the stairwell leading down was pitch black, having no windows to let in the sunlight. Passing through the doorway and walking down the creaking wooden stairway, he quickly moved down the stairs and unlocked another wooden door located at the end of a short hallway. Kettle pushed it open and looked with anticipation at the captured women tied to the old fashioned cast iron radiators on both sides of the basement room. Setting the tray of food down on the floor, he turned to face them. The faint whimpers soon turned into cries for help and begging to be set free.

"Free?" Kettle mocked. "Why would I set you whores free on my unsuspecting followers to tempt their hearts with your evil ways?"

Many of them shied away from his presence, trying in vain to go unnoticed, but one of them dared to stare with defiance into his eyes.

Stopping in front of her, he pushed the feeble candlelight over her. The faint glow showed a scantily clad woman in a ragged black dress. Untying her bonds that fastened her to the radiator but keeping her hands secured behind her back, Kettle pulled her upright.

"What is your name, woman?" he demanded.

"Does it really matter, you filthy pig?" she hissed and spat in his face.

Kettle's hand rocked across her face with a resounding slap. The defiant woman cried out at the sudden pain and fell to the floor.

"I see that the power of Satan runs deep in this one," Kettle said aloud to his harem, looking at the woman's shapely ass as she had landed chest first on the ground.

"Even subconsciously you tempt the virtues of men," he preached, his passion growing unchecked, "but what else would I expect to find among such filthy whores? You are good at what you do."

"Fuck you, you sick motherfucker!" his captive hissed, crawling to her knees in insolence. "Let me go, and we'll see how big a man you really are!"

Feeling the surge of holy righteousness flow through his blood at her audaciousness, Kettle jerked her to her feet and dragged her, screaming in protest, into an inner chamber which used to hold coal for the church's original furnace. A heavy curtain hung over the doorway, and Kettle brushed it aside, revealing a bed and small table along the back wall. Kettle set his candle holder on the table, dragged her over to the bed and sat down on it, pulling the screaming woman across his lap on her belly. Kettle then pulled up the woman's ragged dress and began to spank her like a child. At first, she kicked and screamed as he slapped her hind end viciously, but there was only so much resisting that she could do with her hands tied behind her back. Added to that, the woman had been sleep and food deprived for more than a few days, and the fight was quickly and literally beat out of her. Sadly, the screams of denial were switched to whimpers of pain and acceptance, and Kettle grew more and more aroused until he suddenly threw her face down onto the bed where she let out a faint grunt of pain.

Shaking with barely contained lust, he began ripping his garments off. Kettle climbed onto the bed and forced her legs apart. As he brutally entered her from behind, his twisted mind took her screams of pain as screams of pleasure as he thrust again and again inside of the helpless, restrained woman. Her whimpering pleas for him to stop were heard as pleas to continue, to give her more, to use her tainted flesh as he saw fit. Soon the poor woman was half unconscious from the trauma, her screams turning to animal-like grunts as he slammed his manhood into her. Kettle grabbed her bruised hips hard as his pleasure reached a crescendo. Sweating profusely, he slammed his member into her violently faster and faster yet until he finally felt himself spill his seed deep into her trembling body.

Shaking with pleasure, Kettle withdrew from the woman and used her torn ragged dress to clean himself off. He then donned his priestly garments.

"Soon, my dirty little girl, and only after you give your soul over to the power of God's unending mercy, you will see that you have brought all of this onto yourself," Kettle said. "Until that day comes, we must continue with our little sessions."

The woman couldn't muster the strength to respond, which brought Kettle further satisfaction. He dragged the woman back across the floor and secured her to the wall. The others cowered at his presence. Grabbing his candle off the small table, he left the basement rooms, locking the door behind him. Kettle was in a hypnotic daze now, already fantasizing of Mattie's tight young body being restrained by his hands. Smiling in anticipation of the soon to be had pleasure, he ascended to his office. Behind Kettle, unseen and now unheard, women sobbed in the darkness as they began fighting over the meager scraps of food.

*

As the darkness and its accompanying cold crept in after another long day of door-to-door raids with myself and the others, Casper, the former postal worker, struggled to carry boxes of canned goods into the old gymnasium. Finding clear floor space, Casper dropped the heavy cardboard box with a thud. Taking a breather, he looked at numerous stacks of unopened boxes containing military surplus MREs.

Looking around and spotting Mattie, Casper walked over and inquired where the group had located the Meals Ready to Eat.

"Those were not from a raid," Mattie said. "They came from Logan and Kleaner's place. We brought them when we picked them up after the RV run."

"No kidding?" Casper replied. "I happen to know of a huge stash of this stuff at a place I used to deliver mail to. I totally forgot about it till now when I saw those boxes."

Mattie looked at Casper to gauge if he was being serious. When she knew he wasn't joking, she nodded her head. "Come with me."

She led him over to where I was working nearby, just out of earshot.

"I think you need to hear what Casper has to say, Mike," she stated. "Go ahead and tell him what you just told me, Casper."

Casper cleared his throat as I turned my attention onto him. He looked a little nervous at first.

"Well, I was helping unload canned food into the gymnasium when I noticed the cases of military issued MREs," Casper said. "I think I know of a place that probably has hundreds of those cases. It was on my mail route, and I completely forgot about it until now. It is a very unassuming building. I think the guy intentionally kept it like that so as not to draw any attention. Not sure of how many times I delivered to the address over the past few months, but it was a shit ton. UPS and Fed Ex were always leaving boxes there too. I'm sure we will find something."

He suddenly had the attention of everyone in the room, and I was very excited about the possibility.

"Would you mind taking a team over and check the place out?" I asked.

"Not at all," Casper replied. "Like I said, it was on my route, and I know the place well."

"Then hit it. In the morning assemble some volunteers, take three trucks and see what you can find," I requested. "But be careful. If the guy was that prepared he might have his own team together and still be alive, and he may not want our help. If that's the case, respect his wishes."

"Yes sir!" Casper said.

After Casper left, I turned to Mattie, who was standing there with a sly grin on her face.

"This could be huge, Mattie," I remarked. "If he's right about this, we could get a leg up on food supplies and start to focus our efforts into other areas."

"I knew you'd like it," she replied as she sauntered away. "Looks like you owe me one."

Shaking my head to break the hold the hypnotic rolling motion her hips was having on me, I got down to fleshing out my idea of thinning the ranks of the zombies that seemed to be getting thicker around the prison. My plan, while good on paper, was probably only good until first contact. That's where Murphy's Law ripped up many a good plan and proceeded to wipe his ass with it.

My plan was simple enough to work. I wanted to rig up a large building in the downtown area with flammable items and accelerants. I had scouted out several and found the perfect candidate. We would lure a shitload of zombies inside of it with bait of some sort, most likely me, until it was filled to the brim. A team stationed outside would then barricade them in from behind, sealing the entrance. The "bait" would use a zip line to rappel down off the roof to the roof of a lower building located next door. Then we'd torch the place. I hoped to round up and kill thousands zombies without firing a shot. It sounded simple enough.

The details could be worked out in the morning, so I made my way back to my RV. I parked my tired ass on the sofa with much anticipation. I needed a break, and looked through a stack of movies Mattie had added to our growing collection. Settling on *Captain America*: *The Winter Soldier*, I popped it into the player just as Mattie came in for the night. She offered to make popcorn and then plopped down next to me on the couch. We passed the next two hours as regular people on a random Friday night. Sadly, after the movie ended I fell asleep without even making a pass at Mattie.

9

October 31
Day 67

After a rare good night's sleep and a hearty breakfast, I readied my gear and walked out to my newly completed ride. The formerly city owned dump truck I now called my own sported a newly installed heavy snowplow. I could personally attest to the plow's ability to push through layers of decaying, animated corpses. My pride and joy was now parked outside my front door. Tossing my gear inside, I turned around and walked smack dab into Mattie.

"Going somewhere?" she asked, hands on her hips.

"Um...yeah...I-I was going to start work on a trap I thought up," I stuttered.

"So you planned on leaving me here?" she replied testily. "I thought we had a deal. I need a break from these walls."

I chose my next words carefully. "Well if you really wanted to go, I would love to have you along."

Mattie walked back inside and came out holding her backpack and AR-15 rifle. "That's what I thought."

Tossing her gear into the huge truck, she hopped back down and put on a pink Chicago Bears cap. "So what is this grand idea that you came up with?"

I explained what we needed to do to set it up and the risky part of playing "dinner" for probably hundreds of hungry zombies before it was over. I was showing her all the tinder I had preloaded into the back of the dump truck when Mattie stared at me like I had grown a second head.

"So let me get this straight," she said, placing her hands on her hips. "Your plan is to play follow the leader with hundreds of zombies and lead them into a burning building?"

"That about sums it up, yes," I replied with cool confidence. I knew it would irritate her, so I added a shit eating grin.

"Are you serious?" she asked, not amused in the least.

Reaching up into the cab of the truck, I grabbed one of my favorite props. "But, I have a bat," I said, still grinning, and reached out to show it to her.

With a heavy sigh, she rolled her eyes and turned to walk to the command center.

"We need to get back before it gets too late tonight," Mattie called back. "I want to pass out some candy to the kids for Halloween before they are all asleep."

I followed Mattie up to the command center where we kept a log of all current and upcoming raids. Casper and several other men were already present, and I helped lay out the two missions that we would be doing simultaneously—my zombie trap, along with Casper's run to the mail order guy's place. Casper gathered three trucks, with one of them pulling a flatbed trailer, and was taking a total of fifteen people to help with security and loading responsibilities. I was taking the dump truck, a large SUV loaded with volunteers, and a Honda four-wheeler to use to gather up wandering groups of zombies. Loud and agile, they made the perfect bait car. At my request, Casper circled the area of town he was heading to on a map in case he needed help, and I gave him a radio to reach the prison with if he got into trouble.

"Looks like we got it nailed down," Casper grinned. "It's game time!"

*

A pothole in the road awoke Chris from his slumber when his body lifted from the bed of the truck before slamming back with a sharp whack. He checked his watch and discovered that it was just after seven in the morning and they were already on the road. He knocked on the window and talked Dan into stopping to let him in the cab, and wasn't surprised to find Dan in a foul mood. The trip went on without Dan speaking a word, and he started to swerve the truck on purpose, to hit mail boxes and sideswipe abandoned vehicles. They were clearly not taking the same way back, but Chris didn't dare ask if they were lost. According to the sun they were headed in the right direction.

After what seemed to Chris to be an eternity, they turned onto a gravel road that started to parallel a blacktop road about five hundred yards to the north. Chris noticed some cars clumped together on it ahead, and as they closed the distance, five or six cars and two semi-trucks came into view. Chris wondered what kind of goodies were in those semis and what had happened to the drivers of the other vehicles. Dan was looking at the cars now too, and noticed that one small imported car was disabled with two flat tires with people standing around it trying to get in. He stopped the truck, jumped out and looked through his binoculars. He stated out loud that the four people standing around the car were in fact zombies.

"Why do you think they are trying to get in that car?" Chris asked, glad that Dan was now talking again.

"Only one reason I can think of. Must be people in it," Dan replied. "Let's give them a hand."

"Roger!" Chris exclaimed. Now not only was Dan he talking, he was being proactive. "Maybe we can still save someone on this trip."

Dan grabbed "Betty" and placed her across the hood of the truck. The vehicle was about six hundred yards away, and Dan settled down his breathing as the first round found its mark and one of the zombies at the driver's door lost its head. Dan fired his second round and then two more, finishing off the zombies in only four shots.

"Nice shooting!" Chris bellowed. "It looks like that was all of them."

"Yeah, let's go over there and see who we saved," Dan grumbled. "Those .375 H&H shells aren't cheap. Hopefully they have something to offset the cost."

Driving over two barb wire fences and through a large soybean field, they reached the small traffic jam on the highway. Both men exited the truck cautiously, not wanting any sudden surprises. As they were poking around, Chris heard something coming from the car. It was a soft moan, or maybe a cry.

"Shit, what do we do about this?" Dan sighed after looking into the backseat.

In the back, still strapped into a car seat, was a baby boy. Chris and Dan both stood there, each waiting for the other to say something. Finally Dan mentioned how he probably shot the kid's parents who had gotten bitten while trying to open the trailer looking for supplies. They must have not been here long since the kid didn't even have a dirty diaper from the smell of it.

"Lucky little fucker," Dan concluded. "He would have died slowly and miserably if we hadn't shown up."

Chris carefully removed the car seat and placed it into the back seat of their big diesel and then went back for the diaper bag and formula. He took his time tightening the straps and making sure the car seat was put in properly.

"The police department sent me to a class to learn how to properly install baby car seats," he mentioned to Dan, who was giving him a weird look. "I wouldn't want you to give me a ticket."

Dan laughed and told Chris to step it up.

"Since you are the fucking expert, you're responsible for feeding and changing him too, smartass." Dan added with a scowl. "Babies don't seem to like the smell of my cigars."

*

Casper and his men raced ahead of us towards their destination in the southern part of town. My truck had been the lead vehicle on my convoy. If any zombies tried to walk in front of us, I had a nice steel snowplow that could easily swipe them aside. Now separated, I made my through the downtown area of Joliet, trying to stay clear of the area controlled by that preacher man, Kettle.

"We don't need any more drama with that wacko," I reminded the others.

After a short drive into the business district, I slammed on the truck brakes and screeched to a stop in front of our former local state Senator's office. A sinister smile cracked my face.

"You don't think we will be needing representation from our bleeding heart liberal Senator anytime soon, do you Mattie?" I put the truck in reverse, cut the wheel hard and backed up to the office. "It is time to put our tax dollars to work for once!"

Mattie rolled her eyes at me and shook her head.

I stopped the truck, engaged the hydraulics, and dumped the load of combustibles onto the sidewalk. Lowering the truck bed, I killed the engine and hopped out as a couple of others set up for perimeter duty. The rest walked over to carry the kindling inside while I booted the door. When I walked back to the truck for my coiled up rope for my escape part of the plan, I saw a familiar face. I recognized him easily, despite the dumb looking scarf he had wrapped around his neck.

"Hey, glad to see you finally make it on a raid," I commended, grabbing his arm. "We can always use a new set of hands to do some heavy lifting around here."

The wiry man looked down at his arm then back up at me. "I thought about what you said about not helping," he said with a fake smile, "and figured I might as well start now."

"Well, we've got plenty to do. Don't let me hold you up, buddy. Say, what was your name?"

The man hesitated for a split second then answered, "The name's Jonas."

Grabbing the length of rope, I turned to head back into the building then up to the roof to find a place to secure a zip line or to anchor a rappel line to. Mattie was entering with an armload of scrap lumber to drop off inside.

"What do you think you are doing?" I asked her.

"What does it look like? I'm helping with the wood," she replied. "Just because I'm a woman doesn't mean I can't do some manual labor."

I scowled. "But that's why I brought these guys. You can help me on the roof."

"I don't think it's a wise thing to be around you while tying a knot that will save your life in a bit," Mattie laughed. "Best I not distract you from your work."

Damn, she had a point. I would most likely end up tying my shoelaces together or something. I trudged through the late Senator's office to the stairwell leading up to the roof.

*

Casper's convoy pulled to a stop outside what appeared to be a long string of old abandoned warehouses patched together. Exiting his truck with his SKS rifle in hand, he motioned to the designated four man security team to set up guard. They had strict orders that if the zombie contact became too intense, they would give the signal to evacuate and try again at a later time. This was basically a scout mission, with gathering supplies a secondary concern. Piles of fallen leaves were pushed up against the building by the wind along with loose garbage. The place looked like it had been deserted for years. But looks could be deceiving.

Casper looked over the outer facade of the large building which took up the entire north side of the block searching for easy entry points, which didn't look promising. Since the building was located on the east side of town in a rough neighborhood, most entry points appeared to be fortified. The windows that he saw had bars bolted into the bricks. The heavy steel doors had two to three deadbolts on them. Finally deciding to see if anyone was inside, Casper banged on the entrance where he always made his deliveries.

"No answer," Casper concluded after waiting for what seemed like forever.

Suddenly gun shots rang out behind him. Spinning, Casper watched a zombie drop to the pavement.

"They didn't take long to find us," he remarked to the anxious man standing next to him.

Knowing where there was one zombie, there was bound to be more, he knew he had to get the show on the road. Casper had the biggest man in the group hit the door with the ram. The door rang like a church bell but gave slightly.

"Come on man! Put your back into it!" Casper urged.

More than a few swings with the ram and lots of cursing eventually succeeded in breaching the portal. Casper entered the building, and a few of his other men followed to clear the dark warehouse. An ominous low growling sound came from a dark corner of the building. Using hand signals, Casper had his men fan out as he and the others turned on their flashlights.

"Somebody's home," he whispered.

More gun shots rang out from outside. The blasts made Casper turn momentarily back to the open door.

Focus Casper, he reminded himself.

Whirling back around, he was almost tackled by a gravely chewed up zombie wearing mechanic's overalls. Reflexively firing his SKS into the assailant, he sent the creature sprawling back onto the concrete floor. The recoil of the rifle made Casper stumble backwards. Luckily, his teammates did not hesitate, and before the zombie could regain his feet, they pumped half a dozen shotgun slugs into it, pulverizing its skull.

Shaking from the intense adrenaline dump, Casper thanked the men who simply shook their heads and resumed clearing the warehouse floor.

Looking at the bullet-riddled corpse, Casper assumed it was the property owner he'd delivered all the stuff to, for he knew that man to be a mechanic. Letting his light fall on the surrounding area, he found that all his deliveries were indeed still on hand. Boxes upon boxes lay stacked on the floor, including the now familiar crescent moon symbol of the MREs.

A low whistle escaped out of Casper before he could silence it. "We're going to need more trucks," he said. 'This guy had a major operation. I wonder what the hell happened to him."

He descended deeper into the building, taking a mental inventory. He came to a locked room. He had no idea what lay on the other side. Only one way to find out.

He jiggled on the door handle and tried to ram the door with his shoulder, to no avail. Casper called a man over and requested he bring up the ram from outside. After the man left, Casper heard a female voice quivering with fear from the other side. It was faint but audible.

"Don't come in!" she warned. "I have a gun, and I'm not afraid to use it!"

10

October 31
Day 67

The fall day had started off cold, but now the scarf served not only as a symbol of his identity, but also a suffocating irritant, his sweat causing it to cling to his skin. Manual labor was not Jonas' idea of a good time. Going through the motions of carrying in armload after armload of scrap lumber, he kept an eye out for movement. Not the shambling of the undead but the covert movements of Father Kettle's men that he knew to be somewhere nearby.

If only they would send the signal, he could remove the wretched garment and get this over with.

The plan was simple but required some adlib. The men were to seek him out and then set up a trap for him to lure his prey into. A signal mirror would indicate they were in position. They were to then carry Mattie to Father Kettle, freeing him up to take out the remaining unbelievers.

He wondered why there was a delay? Jonas labored on.

After a considerable amount of time had passed, Jonas started losing hope that Father Kettle's men were out there at all. Exiting the building and grabbing at the annoying scarf, Jonas first saw movement in the window of a business across the street. A second later the mirror flashed across his eyes.

Finally!

He made himself look preoccupied near the truck until Mattie returned for more wood. The silence on the street was almost deafening. The small perimeter team had swept the area and then set up down the block in both directions. From what Jonas had gathered, the rest of the group had gone off on ATVs to round up a bunch of the undead to consume with fire in this building. Eventually Mattie reappeared. She too was starting to sweat from the exertion, and as she prepared to get more scrap wood, Jonas piped up.

"Hey, Mattie, you look beat, wanna take five?" he asked. "I was poking around across the street earlier, and I think there is some stuff we might be able to use. Want to have a look with me?"

Mattie paused, wiped sweat off her brow and gazed to where Jonas referred. Shrugging, she nodded her head.

"Sure, why not?" she replied. "I could use a quick break."

Mattie walked to the large dump truck and retrieved her rifle. Jonas raised an eyebrow at her weapon.

"You think you are going to need that?" he asked. "We have men on perimeter duty."

"Better safe than sorry," she replied. "And I can take care of myself. Come on, let's have a look."

Crossing the debris-filled street, they approached the front door of what looked to be an old cell phone store. The glass front door had been shattered along with the windows from some previous looters who thought stealing cell phones was a good idea while the country was being overrun by the undead. Seeing the display cases smashed and thoroughly looted, Mattie stopped.

"So what are we looking for again?" she asked Jonas.

"I know there were some two-way radios in here somewhere," Jonas replied. "We can always use more of those."

He went over and started sifting through some cabinets behind the counter, while Mattie turned her back to him and checked a small storage closet.

I should just kill this bitch now and be done with her, he thought, seething in anger.

It took all of the will power Jonas could muster to heed Father Kettle's warning of wanting Mattie unharmed.

"I'm not seeing any radios here," Mattie decided, turning to face Jonas.

"The back storage room," Jonas countered, snapping his fingers. "That's where I saw them."

Mattie rolled her eyes. "You didn't remember that till now?"

Jonas only smiled and waved his arm in gesture, "Ladies first!"

Walking across shards of broken glass that crunched underfoot, Mattie led the way to the rear of the building. When she passed through a doorway into the back room, she stopped in her tracks.

Standing before her were five dangerous, hard looking men. They all had weapons at the ready, but made no move. Mattie whipped her rifle up to a shooting position. They had not yet uttered a word, but Mattie didn't have to be a psychic to tell her that they meant to do her harm. One of them was clothed in what looked like an orange prison jumpsuit.

"Who the hell are you people," she demanded, "and what are you doing here?"

The tall lanky man in the middle stepped forward. "We're waiting for you, my sweetmeat," he replied with a smirk.

The other four laughed loudly at this.

"Jonas, go get the others," Mattie ordered. "I'll keep them at gunpoint until you bring help. If any of you so much as move a muscle I will—"

The tall man who first spoke interrupted her. "I'm afraid that is not going to happen, lady."

"Oh really? And why is that?" Mattie snapped back confidently.

With her attention focused on keeping all five men in her line of sight, Mattie was taken off guard when an arm snaked around her throat.

"Because all is not what it seems!" Jonas hissed into her ear.

Mattie struggled mightily, but Jonas' arm was like a steel rod across her throat. Just before her vision faded from lack of oxygen, she reflexively squeezed the trigger, her rifle round striking one of the five men in the neck. The man grabbed at his throat and stumbled back into the wall, gurgling blood through the gaping wound. It was a horrible way to die, choking on your own blood, but the other men didn't even give him a second thought. Jonas cursed loudly then brutally slammed Mattie's head into the nearby door jamb. Letting up on his chokehold as Mattie slumped in his arms, he looked up at Kettle's men.

"Someone kill that fucker already," he snarled. "Then I want you all to get the hell out of here now!"

Jonas tossed Mattie's rifle to the ground and slung her unconscious body over his shoulder.

The tall man walked up to his dying partner, who was clenching his throat as crimson blood oozed from the wound. A sickening gurgle filled the man's throat as he looked at his demise with panic-filled eyes.

"Sorry man, but dead men tell no tales."

The tall man pressed his boot down on the dying man's neck. By the time he stopped struggling, blood splatter covered the wall and floor.

"We can't cover up this mess," Jonas decided, nodding at the corpse. "You all have to beat feet now!"

Jonas shifted the weight of Mattie's unconscious form across his shoulder, stroking the inside of her leg and ass roughly. One of the others pulled the holstered pistol from her belt and stuck it in his waistband.

Yes, Father Kettle will be quite pleased, he thought. *God has finally granted his wish.*

After the men gathered their meager belongings, Jonas handed the tall man Mattie's limp body.

"Take this filthy slut to Father Kettle," he commanded, staring each of them in the eye. "And do not stop to take your turns with her! He will not be pleased if he finds her to be defiled. I know you guys fucked up your last two chances at hitting these cops, so let's not fuck *this* up."

Watching until the last man disappeared out the back door and down the alley, Jonas looked around until he found the proper prop for his plan. Locating a stout piece of wood that would work as a club, Jonas hurried over and smeared it into the fallen man's blood. Satisfied, he walked over to the door and violently slammed his forehead into the edge of the wooden door frame. Reeling back from the pain, Jonas fell to one knee. As his head was bent over he saw blood splatter onto the floor coming from the gash in his head. He tossed the club onto the floor and sprawled out next to it, not a moment too soon either apparently. He heard voices approach from the other room, drawn by the shot from Mattie's rifle. Soon shouting and excited voices rang out, calling for the first-aid kit and for someone to get Mike.

*

Fastening the rope to the air conditioner mounted to the roof was an easy thing to accomplish. After making sure the rope actually reached ground level and pulling hard several times to determine that it would hold my weight, I began working my way to the ground floor, helping the guys prep the building to become a zombie bakery. When I paused to take a drag on my water bottle, someone from the perimeter guard duty came running in yelling that someone had attacked a member from our group and that Mattie was missing!

"Fuck me!"

I sprinted across the road, following the man. When I entered the room and saw the wiry man, Jonas, being helped into a sitting position with a nasty head wound I stopped short. Glancing to my left, I saw another man I didn't recognize with most of his throat missing from a gunshot. My blood ran cold seeing Mattie's rifle sitting in the middle of the floor.

"Did that guy get bit?" I asked the others.

Not from the looks of it," one of them answered after inspecting the body. "Found him dead and this guy here knocked out cold, along with what looks like Mattie's rifle."

"What the fuck happened here?" I screamed at Jonas.

Jonas winced at my shout. "I don't know, man. I heard Mattie scream, followed by a gunshot. I ran back here to help, then got smacked in the head and knocked clean the fuck out. It looks like Mattie got one of them before they took her."

"They... who the fuck are *they*?" I screamed in rage.

I didn't realize I had snatched the man up off the floor and was shaking him like a leaf until I heard him stammering.

"L-l-let g-g-g-go of m-m-m-me pplleeaassse!!!"

I dropped him to the floor and turned to leave. Exiting the back door into the alley, I headed north, looking for any clues as to where she had been taken. It looked like one of the kidnappers had stepped in blood, and was leaving a faint trail. A short distance down the alley, a bit of bright pink on the ground near a hole in the fence caught my eye. When I got closer, I recognized it as Mattie's Bears cap. It must have fallen off when they carried her through the fence.

Not even stopping to retrieve the hat, I squeezed through the gap, drew my pistol, and rushed ahead recklessly to catch up.

Big mistake, because apparently I wasn't the only one tracking the gory footprints.

I rounded a blind corner at full speed and with pistol raised, I was inadvertently tripped by three zombies, who were bent over sniffing the bloody boot impression. They sent me sailing through the air straight into a metal dumpster. My Glock sailed off into oblivion. I saw a blast of stars and nearly succumbed to the darkness.

Struggling to stand, I searched in vain for my weapon. It was nowhere to be found. And my bat was in the truck. So was my rifle.

"And I'm an idiot!"

I now had the full attention of the three zombies, who rose and scurried my direction, their loathsome faces locked onto mine.

Realizing discretion is the better part of valor, I hobbled back the way I came, the zombies groaning and stumbling relentlessly in pursuit. I yelled for help like a girl as I squeezed through the broken fence and struggled back to the others. Stumbling to a stop in the alley, gasping for breath, I cried for the man inside holding Mattie's rifle to toss it to me.

"Huh?" he replied staring at me with his mouth hanging open.

"Toss me that fucking rifle now!"

The zombies were now only a few paces away and closing fast with their shambling gait. My teammate, not seeing what was approaching me, shrugged and nonchalantly tossed the rifle out to me. Snatching it from the air, I could sense that they were now too close to use it as the manufacturer had intended. I continued my spin and slammed the stock into the nearest zombie's head.

A large piece of the hardened plastic collapsible stock and chunks of zombie brain scattered across the alley as the decaying figure was blasted sideways. I lashed my boot out into a front kick and launched a second zombie onto his back with a squishy splat.

Something tugged at my boot.

"What the hell?"

Slimy ropes of intestines wrapped around my foot, and I couldn't shake them loose. The third zombie closed in, and I rammed the barrel into its gaping mouth hard enough to come out the back of its neck. Of course, that didn't kill it and its hands clawed at my face. Sweeping my left arm across my torso, I knocked its hands free and pushed it backwards to the ground with the rifle swaying upright from its bloody mouth. The sickening creature fell down onto the one whose guts were twisted around my foot. I struggled to maintain my balance, gazing in amazement as the creature pulled the rifle from its mouth while both of them stumbled to their feet. Looking over to the side, I noticed I finally had the attention of my crew. They were in the doorway, gawking at me in disbelief.

"A little help would be nice right about now!"

That broke the ice and they unleashed hell on the zombies. I was not quite sure how they missed me with their spray and pray gunfire. After the zombies were dispatched, I backtracked to Mattie's hat.

Where the hell were they taking her? And this direction? That preacher had his walls not but a few blocks to the north.

A couple of my guys wandered a little farther ahead, returning a short time later with my pistol, claiming they found it tucked up under the dumpster.

Standing there with Mattie's hat crumpled in my fist, I gazed up ahead at a landmark in the distance, rising high above all other buildings. It was a looming structure, and its presence made everything crystal clear.

"Son of a bitch," I cursed.

Saint Joseph's Catholic Church...those were Kettle's men! It all made sense now. The creepy way he had stared at Mattie when he first met her, the numerous invitations to join his congregation. After our refusal, the strange zombie attack when returning with the RVs, followed by the attack on Dan's truck while leaving the city.

We were at war with more than just zombies and didn't even know it!

11

October 31
Day 67

On the outskirts of Joliet, a ragged, beat up truck crested a hilltop. The vehicle was covered in dents, and most of its grill was missing. It made its way through clogged streets, weaving around wrecked, abandoned vehicles. Chris was riding silently next to Dan and looked over at him with his peripheral vision, quite worried about his mental state. After seeing his family's cabin in ruins and finding that his own brother was cursed with being a zombie, Chris knew without a doubt that Dan had become even more unstable, if that was possible.

He was positive that if he had not been there Dan would have kept killing the zombies wherever he found them until he himself was bitten and turned. Dan had randomly slammed into so many mailboxes and sideswiped so many abandoned vehicles on the way back, their truck now had a very bad shake to the steering whenever it got over thirty mph, and pulled badly to the right. His salty friend was never one for conversation before the depressing trip, but now he hadn't said ten words in the last five hours. Dan didn't even want the CD player on. The infant they'd picked up had thankfully remained quiet. Chris thought Dan would have thrown both of them out of the truck if the little guy started crying again.

But the nightmare road trip was almost over. Chris felt anticipation as Dan eased his truck over the Cass Street Bridge onto the east side of Joliet. *Just a few more minutes.*

Suddenly the truck made a hairpin turn to the left and skidded to a stop. Dan slammed the gear selector into park and got out.

"Dan, where the fuck you think you're going?" Chris yelled from the cab.

"My grandpappy's pistol from World War II is in that goddamn building!" Dan said over his shoulder, pointing ahead to a pawn shop. "It's the only heirloom I have left from my entire family, and I am not leaving until I have it back. Now you promised to help me retrieve it, so get your ass out of the truck!"

It wasn't the fact that Chris had promised to help that made him scramble for the truck door release handle. It was due more to the crazed, maniacal look in Dan's eyes.

Chris glanced into the back seat and saw that the baby boy was still asleep in his car seat. Chris then got out of the cab and was digging for tools in the truck bed when he heard the booming sound of Dan futilely kicking the pawn shop's front door.

"Hold your horses, you damned fool!" Chris barked. "I got some tools that will help."

Dropping an acetylene tank and torch onto the ground near the shop's entrance, Chris grabbed Dan's left arm to pull him back from the door.

"Hey asshole, you watch for the fucking zombies, and I will get us inside," Chris said, trying to get through Dan's thick skull.

Dan stared at Chris, breathing hard for a few moments, then stalked back to the truck without a word and grabbed his rifle. Shaking his head in frustration, Chris knelt down, put on the tinted safety goggles and picked up the acetylene torch and the striker. In a short time, Chris had a shower of sparks flying as he cut through the locking mechanism of the steel door. With a metallic clang the door almost literally flew open.

"I got it, Dan!" he bellowed, cutting off the torch's flame.

Chris was promptly trampled over by Dan, who literally walked up Chris' back from where he knelt in the doorway. Looking up at Dan's backside as he picked himself off the ground, Chris heard glass breaking inside. Dan was breaking open display cases, searching for the pistol.

"Say, Dan... the pistol is probably locked in the vault," Chris said looking at a huge steel door back near the office. "Why don't you look for the keys somewhere?"

While Dan proceeded to tear through the desk drawers and cabinets of the office, Chris walked over to some of the display cases. Looking around and finding a large duffle bag, he began to load it with handfuls of diamond rings and necklaces. The pawn shop had been secured very well and had been spared the looting that spread wildly throughout Joliet as everything fell apart. Moving over to another display of coins and bullion, Chris calmly dumped tray after tray into the duffel bag, a greedy twinkle to his eyes.

Eventually society would get back to some sort of barter or currency, and a man couldn't go wrong with gold and silver. Plus, with the huge diamonds on the rings, he should be able to barter a little something with the ladies at the prison.

He heard Dan cursing along with the crashing of desk drawers.

"I've had enough of this!" Dan yelled. "Let's rip that door apart with the torch!"

"I don't know, Dan, that may take a while," Chris warned. "Plus we have no idea who or what might be inside."

"I know all I need to know about what's inside there!" Dan roared. "My grandpappy's pistol is behind that door!"

"Fine, whatever," Chris sighed. "I need you to stand back and give me some space to work with here. Keep an eye on the truck too, would ya?"

Grudgingly, Dan stepped aside while Chris retrieved the torch, put on his tinted goggles and got the gas torch roaring with flame once again. Studying the door, he looked for the locking points to figure out what needed cutting without burning the place down in the process. The hot blue flame gradually bit into the steel door. There were three deadbolts on this bad boy, and he hoped that there was enough gas left in the torch tanks. After the first deadbolt was cut through, Dan's foot flashed over Chris' shoulder and slammed into the door, scaring the shit out of him.

"What the fuck! Do you mind?" Chris asked, while looking over his shoulder angrily. "I'm trying to work here. Go check on the kid in the truck, keep yourself busy."

Growling something unintelligible, Dan stalked away.

Getting to work on the next deadbolt, Chris saw that his progress was slower and figured the door must be made of some sort of case hardened steel.

It took a good ten minutes to make the cut, and as that lock was torched through, a large blade flashed past his left ear and wedged into the door frame, and Dan began feverishly trying to pry it open.

"What the hell, man!" Chris shouted. "You could have taken my ear off!"

"Just get on with it," Dan thundered, pointing at the door with the big knife, without the hint of an apology.

Sighing heavily again, Chris went to work on the last deadbolt. This one looked intricate, so he figured the best way to attack it was to cut the entire area out of the door. Kneeling down to get a better view of the lock, he couldn't wait for this to be over with. Sweating profusely from the heat of the torch and the hot molten metal, Chris started the slow process of getting the steel up to temperature to cut.

Jesus, he's really starting to piss me off now, Chris thought when Dan began pacing back and forth. He couldn't wait for this to be done and over with.

The door finally gave way and opened slightly. Chris sat back, took off his goggles and was about to let Dan know he was successful when Dan roughly shoved him aside and pushed the vault door open with his left hand.

"Goddamn!" Chris yelled. "Can you wait till I turn off the torch?"

Dan looked back at Chris while holding the door open with his left hand. "Outta the way, kid," Dan replied. "I have been waiting way too long to be reunited with... aarrgghhhh!!"

Dan jerked his arm out of the vault room. Along with a zombie attached to his left hand by its teeth.

Chris, while holding the burning acetylene torch, quickly drew his pistol and blasted the pawn shop t-shirt wearing zombie point blank in its head. Even as the zombie dropped to the ground and without any hesitation, Dan turned and laid his badly mangled hand onto the display case with the injured part hanging over the edge.

"Oh shit, oh fuck, shit, shit, shit!" Chris cried. He gaped in horror at his friend, thinking that he was soon going to have put him down.

With a roar of rage, Dan raised his blade high and swiftly brought it down upon the bitten appendage.

"Holy fuck!" Chris was dumbfounded. "You just cut your own hand off!"

Screaming with pain, Dan spun around, blood jetting from the amputated limb, and snatched the burning torch out of Chris' numb fingers. Jamming the heavily bleeding stump into the flame, Dan cauterized the wound with the torch. Howls of anguish and screams ripped from Dan's throat as he fell to his knees from the pain, all the while burning the wound shut. The smell of burning meat filled the pawn shop as Dan finally finished and shakily handed the torch back to Chris, who then shut off the flame.

"Did that just happen?" Chris whispered.

Struggling to his feet, Dan leaned heavily on Chris, and then pushed him away, stumbled into the storeroom, and disappeared from sight. A minute later, Dan reappeared with a dazed look of victory. Holding his grandfather's pistol in his remaining right hand, he shoved it into his waistband and then promptly passed out.

Chris looked down at Dan in shock and then set his face in determination and grabbed Dan under his arms. Grunting from the weight of the full grown man, he dragged Dan back to the truck and placed him inside with considerable effort. The baby had woken up from all the screaming and was now crying. Chris felt like crying himself, as the commotion had drawn the attention of a considerable zombie horde that was now headed his way. Not wasting any time, Chris got behind the wheel of the truck and hit the gas.

*

Stephen breathed a sigh of relief when the familiar sights of Joliet came into view. He was glad to be back. They had made good time on their return trip and would indeed be back at the prison well before dark. After keeping him company all morning, Amber had finally drifted off to sleep. She had dozed off on his shoulder and looked comfortable there.

He had assumed the worst regarding his family prior to the trip, and saw nothing that changed any of that.

"Everyone alive today has lost someone," Amber said before drifting off, and it was true. Why should his situation be any different?

After coming to grips with it, Stephen let his mind drift on ways to improve their new life behind the enormous prison walls. He even jotted down a few ideas along the way, that task made easier by the fact that the truck sort of steered itself while connected to the train tracks.

After crossing over the river into the east side of town on the railroad bridge, he noticed the stronghold held by Father Kettle in the downtown area was as big as ever with new and larger barricades.

He wondered how long they would hold out. Without permanent walls, he didn't think they would make it in the long run. Not if they got hit with what they saw at the high school. He'd definitely need to ask Mike if he knew anything about what that weirdo had been up to.

Stephen sensed a bad vibe from the preacher, and although it should be the living versus the dead, it seemed to Stephen that it would never be that simple. There would always be evil men as long as there were men alive. The bandits he was forced to kill in Galena only reinforced that.

Raising the lever, Stephen guided the truck off of the tracks and the sharp bumps woke Amber from her nap. Rubbing her eyes, she sat up and peered out the window.

"Home sweet home," Stephen said with satisfaction.

"Thanks for getting us back safely," Amber replied with a wink. "Sorry I slept most of the way, but your shoulder makes a pretty firm pillow!"

"I didn't mind at all," Stephen said. "You obviously needed the rest."

Amber stretched her arms over her head as the prison came into view. "I need to get cleaned up and see how my uncle is doing. What are you going to be up to?" Amber asked, pretending not to notice his gawking.

"I'm sure there will be a list of chores with my name on it to take care of," Stephen replied, "but I wouldn't mind running into you later."

"I'll see what I can do," she answered with a smile.

Stephen came to a stop in front of the gates so the guards could dispatch the few zombies who had gathered near the entrance. He was impressed when one particular guard managed to hit two zombies in the head with the same bullet. His task was made easier by the fact that the first zombie, formerly a tall man, was standing directly in front of a short older lady who took it right in the forehead.

"Looks like Logan or Kleaner showing off again," Stephen chuckled. "Those boys have been getting plenty of practice from the looks of it."

With the gates now open, Stephen pulled the truck in and continued until he stopped in front of Amber's uncle's camper. He exited the truck, grabbed Amber's bag and set it on the steps to the camper. Amber followed and leaned in for a hug as Buddy came bounding up baying like he was hot on a rabbit's trail.

"Somebody is happy you're home," Amber laughed. Stephen reached down and rubbed his dog's ears.

They were both distracted by a vehicle honking at the main gate, which was now reopening. It opened back up just enough for a vehicle to slip through the crack, and Stephen recognized Dan's truck when it tore into the compound and raced towards the medical trailer.

"From the looks of that truck, they must've run into some problems!" Stephen shouted, running towards the truck.

Stephen, Amber and Buddy reached the truck right as Chris came to a sudden stop.

"What the hell happened, Chris?" Stephen asked when Chris threw open the driver's side door and quickly ran to the passenger side. Stephen could see Dan slumped over against the dashboard.

"And why's there a baby in the back seat?" Amber asked, peering into the truck.

"It's a long story, but could you take the baby until we figure out what to do?" Chris asked Amber. "I need to talk to Stephen for a minute."

"Sure," Amber replied and grabbed the baby and the diaper bag from the truck. "I'll catch up with you later, Stephen."

Amber walked away with a concerned look on her face and a crying baby in her arms.

Chris took a deep breath and paused. Stephen could tell that he was worried sick.

"Dan got bit by a zombie while we were trying to get that pistol of his out of the pawn shop. It was really fucked up!" he whispered. "He cut his own hand off before passing out. I think he cut it off in time. It's been a good fifteen minutes, and he hasn't turned into one yet. What should we do?"

"Let's get him inside and maybe cuff his good hand to a bed just in case. I'm sure if he hasn't turned yet he is probably good to go, but let's not risk it. Tell the doc what happened, and let him take care of it. Losing a hand is bad enough by itself. He will need antibiotics and plenty of rest." He moved to help Chris carry Dan inside. "By the way, how was Dan's brother?"

Chris shook his head and frowned. "How was your trip?" Chris asked.

"The same," Stephen replied, and they left it at that.

*

Casper stared at the heavy steel door and wondered how someone could be on the other side of it after all this time.

"Miss, we are not here to hurt you," Casper said calmly. "If you need help, we have a safe zone of sorts set up, and you're more than welcome to join us."

"I don't believe you!" the woman sobbed from behind the door.

"It's a trick!"

"It's not a trick," Casper sighed. "We're here to help if you want it."

"Go away!" the woman screeched.

Casper resisted the urge to pound on the door with clenched fists as he looked at the other men standing around him.

"Start loading what supplies are out here," Casper urged. "This place will take a return trip, but we need to take as much back with us now as we can."

The others nodded and headed off to get started. All the while, increasing sounds of gunfire from outside echoed throughout the building.

"Look here, lady. We are not your enemy," Casper said to the woman behind the door. "We're on the same side here, both fighting these zombies for our very existence." Not getting a reply, he continued. "If you want to stay in there, that is your choice, but you have my word that no harm will come to you if you would like to join us."

Still getting no answer, Casper figured to give the woman some time and space to think about what he said and walked away. Besides, they had plenty of supplies to load up.

As the last of the vehicles were loaded, and after saying goodbye, Casper heard the faint sounds of the door lock disengaging. Pausing in his place, Casper looked over to see the door cracked open slightly. Seeing a wide and frightened eye peer through the crack and watch him and the other men silently, Casper shrugged and took his armload out to the trucks. Upon returning, Casper saw that the woman had opened the door and stood a couple of steps outside the room.

Oh dear Lord! he thought. *Surely you have sent one of your angels down to this wretched place for guidance, for I am beholding one of them now*!

"Did you really mean it?" she asked timidly. "I can come with you guys?"

Casper's teeth clacked shut and realized he had been staring hard at her with his mouth wide open.

"Yes, and again, my promise of safety stands," he replied gently.

As the woman slowly approached him, Casper saw that she had long, flowing, if a bit snarled, red hair. She was tall, and a bit thin from malnutrition. She also looked kind of like the girl he first saw from the rooftop of the Post Office.

Casper waved a man over.

"Take her to my truck and see that no harm comes to her," Casper ordered.

The redhead clutched onto Casper's arm. "No!" she said firmly. "You promised me, so I'll stay with you!"

Just her touch made Casper's blood sing. "Um, okay, let's lock up that room for the next trip back here. What's your name sweetheart?" Casper asked.

The redhead looked at him with emerald green eyes. "My name is Holly, and that room is filled with nothing to eat, just a bunch of guns and stuff."

Casper's eyebrows arched up. "Guns and stuff?"

Walking over to the open door, Casper saw rows of rifles and stacks of military type hardware that he didn't recognize. Stacked up on pallets were cases upon cases of what was most likely ammunition. It took a moment for him to realize what a score this was really turning out to be. He wondered how it all ended up here and for what purpose. Somebody had been planning some heavy shit. The type of shit that would have made his little postal shooting look like back page news.

"Wow!" he said dumbly, looking at the cache before him. "We'll definitely be making a return trip."

*

Seething with fury and wanting to give immediate chase to Mattie and her captors but realizing the futility of it at the moment, I relented.

"Mount up!" I growled. "We're going to the prison to get more men, and then we are gonna to open a giant can of whoop-ass."

The others started up their trucks, but my mind was such a raging wall of red that I only vaguely remembered the trip back and didn't snap out of my haze until I heard the steel prison doors slam shut. It took a few moments to pry my white knuckled grip off the steering wheel and then cut off the engine to the dump truck. I saw Stephen heading my way, apparently having made it back from Wisconsin in one piece.

Stephen looked worried about something as he walked up, but apparently the expression on my face was worse. I didn't know where to begin.

"You don't look happy to see me. Not even a 'glad to see you're still alive'," Stephen joked. "Well I had to put down some shitheads, dude, wait till ya hear the story! And I got other not so good news in regards to Da—"

"I'm not in the mood, man," I interrupted drily. "Mattie has been kidnapped. I think by Kettle's men."

Stephen's eyes bugged out. "What the fuck!"

After giving him the cliffs notes version of what little I did know, Stephen began firing questions at me one after another. Putting both hands up, I shook my head. "I don't know, bro," I responded, pointing at the man who was being helped into the field hospital trailer. "You'll need to ask those questions to the man that was with her at the time. His name is Jonas. He was there when it went down. I would love to stay and catch up on how your trip went, but I need to suit up for the hell I'm going to unleash on those fucking zealots."

I left Stephen behind while he went to question Jonas. He had stormed into the medical trailer and was already yelling as I walked away.

Maybe he could get some answers.

On my way to my RV, I noticed Dan's truck was back. It was beat to hell, and didn't seem to have a spot that wasn't covered in blood, gore and dents.

It must have been a wild ride, I thought. It was a good thing he had returned, though. We would need the crazy bastard's help on this one.

Entering my RV, I started pulling out my S.W.A.T gear for the coming assault. Night was falling, and the sky was darkening. I felt as it was an omen, as if time was running out. I picked up my shotgun, racked a shell into it. Feeling the anger surging like waves hitting the shoreline, blood pounding in my brain, I looked towards where I knew the church would be.

"Hold on, Mattie, help is coming."

I slammed my fist on the table at the thought of what they may be doing to her.

I reigned in my anger, not wanting to let it loose just yet, and started to formulate a rescue plan.

*

Mattie gradually clawed herself awake. For some reason she could neither see, nor could she move her hands. It took a minute or two before she realized that her hands were most likely tied to a chair, as she was in a sitting position, and that there was a bag over her head.

"Mmmppfff-hhufff..."

And there was a gag over her mouth.

"Ah, I see that Sleeping Beauty is awake," an oily voice said.

Turning her head towards the sound, Mattie struggled to loosen her bonds and was rewarded with laughter.

"Who knew that your men would actually pull it off?" a different man spoke up.

"That is enough out of you, brother. You may take your leave," the first voice responded.

"But she just woke up!" the man protested. "I want to see her holier than thou attitude get crushed like a grape."

"Brother, do not test me. I want you to leave. If she knows your identity, it could hurt her attitude towards future opportunities."

"Fine!" the man relented. "I hope the bitch gets all she deserves."

Mattie heard a door slam shut behind her.

The original voice began to speak to others she couldn't hear or see but could tell stood directly behind her.

"I want to commend you fine gentlemen on an outstanding job," the oily voice purred. "It took many days to pull off, but I must congratulate you men for persevering through the trials that were put forth to battle the will of my faithful servants. Others before you failed and were met by death."

Mattie could tell from the man's voice that he was moving around, most likely shaking their hands. And something about his voice sounded familiar.

"As a reward for doing as instructed and following those instructions to the letter, I have a surprise for you Soldiers of God."

Mattie heard what sounded like a desk drawer open and some keys jiggling.

"Here, take these," the man said, throwing the keys to a man who grasped them from the air, it sounded like.

"Follow the stairs down behind this door," the man said. "At the end of the hallway is a locked room. Inside the room is the reward for you four to use however you wish. Do not worry, my children, the taint has been removed from them, so enjoy! Just make sure they live."

Soon the sound of people filing out of the room stopped and was followed by an eerie silence. Mattie could hear him breathe, so she knew he was still there. Was this freak just staring at her?

She felt a hand graze her shoulder. Then a hand brushed her left breast. Mattie struggled and tried to scream around the filthy rag that was tied around her mouth. The bag over her head was ripped away, revealing the man she was beginning to suspect culprit all along.

"Kettle," Mattie said, recoiling in horror.

"Mattie, Mattie, Mattie...look at all of the pain and suffering you have caused," Kettle chided, shaking his head and sitting on the corner of his desk facing her. "Why, I bet you had no idea that a man died today trying his best to follow orders." Kettle shook his head with false sadness. "Now he is dead after you shot him in the throat for nothing."

Mattie tried to use some of the more interesting swear words she'd learned from Dan, but the mouth gag muffled the words too much to be effective.

Starting to walk behind her, Kettle kept talking. "So much hate, so much seductiveness, so tainted," he whispered, rubbing her long, lustrous black hair.

Mattie jerked her head loose to Kettle's laughter.

"Oh, you are a fighter?" he laughed. "That is the evil wickedness coming out that we must purge from your soul!"

Iron hard fingers locked into a fist in her hair and jerked her head painfully to the left causing tear to leak from her eyes. Kettle's other hand snaked down the front of her shirt and grabbed her left breast hard.

"Listen, you dirty harlot," he hissed. "I will no longer let you taint my church, my people, or my community with your very presence!"

Kettle paused to lick her neck from the base all the way to her right earlobe.

"Delicious...tastes like sin," he whispered into her ear. "What is going to happen next is this. We are going to someplace secluded, where I will be able to cleanse your soul of evil without interruption."

After an eternity, Kettle let go of her hair and breast and stepped back over to the desk, trembling with white hot need, breathing heavy and hard.

"I must be strong," Kettle ranted. "It has to be perfect in order for Satan to be vanquished. I must avoid the temptation of the seductive pleasure placed before me and perform the ritual correctly."

The guy was bat shit crazy, Mattie concluded, staring wide-eyed back at him. Did he actually believe what he was saying?

Visibly restraining himself against his desk, Kettle turned back to Mattie.

"Your heathen comrades will no doubt be on their way shortly. I will have my men take care of them. I have recruited the most vicious men, and they do my absolute bidding. I'm sure you're saddened that they will soon be dead, but unfortunately we will not be here to see them perish. If you must cry, do so now. In the eyes of God there is no room for weakness. Tonight you will learn the extent of your wicked, tempting ways and will pay for it accordingly."

Kettle bent over hands on knees in front of her, looking her in the eyes. "Tonight's going to be a very special night indeed."

Grabbing her face with both hands, he leaned forward and kissed her full on the mouth right over the gag, heedless of her attempts to scream. He grabbed the hood and placed it back over her head. Walking to the door, Kettle opened it and ordered the guards outside to carry her, chair and all, down to the truck waiting outside. Watching her get carried out to the truck, Kettle licked his lips again.

Oh yes, he thought. *There is a God after all.*

12

October 31
Day 67

Casper wearily exited his truck and took a pull from his almost empty water bottle. The convoy had finally made it back to the prison in one piece and the huge outer steel doors clanked shut behind them. Casper looked over at his passenger, who was looking around wide-eyed with wonder at her new home. The raid was more successful than he could have ever dreamed it to be. All three trucks as well as the large flatbed trailer were filled to capacity, and that was just foodstuffs. There was the entire armory to go through, but that would take another trip to recover. Looking for someone familiar to tell about all the toys that were left behind, he saw a big man he recognized yelling something his way, barely heard over the tower guards engaging the parade of zombies that had followed his trucks back.

“Hey, Casper, I see your raid was successful! That’s freaking fantastic!” James said enthusiastically. "Look at all this shit!"

Casper stumbled when the man’s mammoth hand pummeled his back in congratulatory pats.

“Yeah, it was well worth it," Casper said. "There was enough stuff to outfit a small army. Nobody was using it, and I'm glad I remembered delivering it!"

“Good job, brother. If you need to find Mike, he’s in the Command Center at the moment," Logan told Casper. "I’m sure he would like to hear your raid paid off. So, who’s the hot tasty morsel next to you?”

Casper looked to his left and saw that Holly had walked up to his side and was looking around nervously.

"This is Holly," Casper replied. "We found her at the place we just came from."

"She's a beauty," the big man said holding out his hand in greeting.

Holly shied away from Logan, clinging to Casper's arm.

"A little shy I see. Oh well, don't let me hold you up. Great job again locating the supplies," Logan said as he walked off, directing the other trucks to take the goods to the gymnasium to be unloaded and inventoried.

Casper turned his head towards Holly. "Come on, let's go introduce you to the guys in charge around here."

Grabbing his gear, Casper led Holly to the former firehouse that the group had converted into the command and communication center. Trudging up the creaking wooden stairs to the main office, Casper heard raised voices up ahead.

"Look, I don't care how many of these religious nut jobs there are. We cannot wait all night to go get her back!"

A voice of reason cut over others. "I want her back just as bad, guys, but if we don't do this right, it will be a bloodbath, and not only their blood will be spilled."

Casper entered the top floor, and when he walked into the room, he saw Stephen standing over a map spread out on top of a table. Over by the window stood the big shaved head man, Mike, hands gripping the window sill hard enough that Casper could hear wood creaking. Chris was calmly loading AR-15 magazines, watching them argue over some unknown raid they were about to attempt.

"Hey guys," Casper announced as they all stopped to look at them. "I found someone on my raid I wanted to introduce you all to, and also go over what supplies I mustered up today."

Casper moved to the side revealing the redhead girl for the others to see.

"Holly! Holy shit, you're alive!" Stephen cried, making it obvious to Casper that they already knew her.

"How do you guys know Holly?" he asked, sounding a bit amazed by the whole thing.

"Well, we originally found her outside of a grocery store a few days after the virus hit," Chris replied. "She ended up at the city's safe zone with us, but we assumed that she was killed in the battle when it was overrun."

"What happened to you, Holly?" Stephen then asked.

Holly, until now a bit shy and timid, began to relate what had befallen her since her escape from the safe zone. After fleeing the thousands of zombies that poured into the safe zone perimeter, and realizing that it was hopeless to try and reach the safety of the school building itself, she'd fled south out of the safe zone on foot.

Holly then told the group around her that moments after fleeing the safe zone it was destroyed by a monstrous explosion that knocked her off her feet and twisted her ankle pretty bad. After wandering for a few days, holing up in abandoned houses, she came across some people that said they wanted to help her. She had no idea that they had plans for her other than protection and housing. All too soon her joy of finding shelter and safety turned to horror as she was made into some demented rapist's sex slave.

Tears started to course down her face as she relived those dark days. Many days passed where she had prayed for death, even wishing she had been bitten earlier by a zombie as to no longer feel pain.

"I wasn't expecting to get hurt by living people," she sobbed. "I had only been worrying about the zombies."

At a time when she had given up all hope, she noticed that the man guarding her was no longer at his post. Taking the slim chance at freedom, she escaped, knowing that she would be beaten, raped and even worse her if they caught her.

"They always said that if I tried to escape they would kill me," Holly said as more tears came.

But her freedom was short lived, for she was then chased by groups of zombies to a large brick building. All the doors and windows were locked, and she thought she was trapped with zombies closing in on all sides. At the last second, she found a fire escape ladder which led up to the roof. On top she was able to gain entry into the building through a skylight. She had found a small apartment inside the warehouse, located on an upper floor loft. When investigating the actual warehouse floor, she was attacked by a zombie stuck inside the building. She then retreated into a secure room that was filled with weapons and luckily some military rations.

"Unfortunately I had no clue how to work the firearms in the room I was stuck in," she said sadly. "That zombie stood on the other side of the door banging on it for days."

The men fell silent at the sickening trials this poor woman had endured, their former arguments forgotten. The lone female in the room, the compound's current dispatcher sitting at the radio desk was crying in sympathy. Casper put his hands around Holly's shoulder, comforting the poor woman.

"But I was not alone!" she suddenly cried.

"What do you mean?" Stephen asked.

"Kettle had other women he was holding there. He raped them too," she replied, "and when the guard left during my escape, it was to rape one of the other women himself, against Kettle's wishes. I'm sure Kettle killed him as punishment. He's pure evil, that man."

"Did you say Kettle was the man's name?" Stephen asked, clenching his jaw.

*

Jonas fidgeted in his chair while the attractive female medic attempted to stitch his head wound shut. It wasn't the act of getting his head sewn closed; it was having this unclean harlot's large chest jiggling inches from his eyes that bothered him.

"Sir, if you do not sit still, my stitches will not be very good and you will have a substantial scar when your wound heals," Shelly said testily.

Jonas kept his eyes tightly closed, feverishly praying that it would be over soon before his resolve folded.

A growling voice sounded off from the darkened end of the trailer, "Relax, kid. Chicks dig scars."

Looking over, Jonas saw that the voice belonged to Dan, one of the men that had left for downstate Illinois earlier this week. He was unconscious when Jonas had returned and looked to have just woken up.

Dan was also pointing to the huge scar along the side of his face. Word had it that he got it from some crazed knife wielding heroin addict.

"I'm not out to get myself a girl," Jonas replied.

Dan raised an eyebrow at the remark. "I see," he murmured quietly, but not quite enough for Jonas and the medic not to hear. "Guess there's one in every bunch."

"Hey, what happened to your head?" Dan then asked much louder.

"Some guy used it for batting practice earlier on a raid," Jonas replied. "Why are you here?"

"Zombie bit my hand," Dan answered, as if he was talking about the weather, and showed Jonas his bandaged stump, "so I cut it off with my machete, and then cauterized the wound shut with a cutting torch."

Jonas stared at Dan as if he had seen a ghost. *Jesus Christ*! he thought. *Here I thought I had some big stones for slamming my head into the wall, and this man cuts his own hand off*!

"Lady, could you come over here a second?" Dan asked. "I need to try something."

Finishing Jonas' stitches, Shelly walked over to where Dan sat. He casually stuck out his bandaged stump towards her chest.

After a few seconds the woman said, "Well...what is it?"

"Wow that is really neat," Dan said staring at the woman's chest. "I can still feel my fingers, and guess what they are grabbing?"

"Y-you're a pig!" she stammered, and with a sniff.

As the woman turned to walk away, she was pinched on the butt. Turning quickly back to Dan, she saw him staring at his stump in surprise.

"Phantom fingers," he said with a shrug.

Ignoring Shelly's look of outrage, Dan leaned around her and asked Jonas who hit him in the head.

"What? Oh it was a group of big guys I have never seen before who knocked me out and then kidnapped Mattie," Jonas replied. "I guess they left me for dea—"

Dan shot up out of his chair.

"*WHAT*!?" he screamed. "When did this happen?"

"D-During M-Mike's zombie trap test run," Jonas stammered.

Dan grabbed his jacket, slid his 1911 .45 back into his waistband and stomped out of the trailer without another word.

"I would hate to be those kidnappers with those men after me," Shelly remarked while Jonas subconsciously nodded his head.

*

Kettle glanced over at his brother Lewis with annoyance at all the questions, one after another.

"I don't need to give you a reason for my needing to leave the safety of the church. Be assured, I do have my reasons, but you don't need to know what they are. You will be in charge while I am away, however," Kettle said. "I am entrusting you to keep things running smoothly and to be ready for any attempt of rescue of Mattie by her comrades."

Lewis puffed his chest out. "You can count on me, brother."

Not likely, Kettle thought. Aloud, he said, "Try not to turn my church into a smoking crater by the time I return, please? We don't need a repeat of your last performance."

Leaving the office, Kettle gave the two men guarding the door a priority order. "If my brother fucks up bad for any reason, I want one of you to come get me at my former church where we first went after our escape from the penitentiary."

"Yes, Father Kettle!" the two men said together.

Kettle stared at them for a few moments, then picked up a large duffel bag near the door and exited the church. Walking quickly to the truck where Mattie was kept, he hopped in the front passenger seat.

"Take me to my former place of worship, Brother," Kettle ordered.

"Yes, Father," the driver said and put the old Ford truck into gear.

Moments later, they pulled up in front of the old church a few blocks away. The structure was safely inside his compound's perimeter, and old memories arose in his mind.

It feels as if it has come full circle, Kettle thought.

"Let's get the woman inside," he told the driver. "Lucifer has his talons sunk deep into this one. It shall take quite an effort to break his grip free."

Muscling the chair with Mattie tied in it was not easy, and Mattie didn't help either. She kept shifting her weight as much as possible trying to get them to drop her, hoping it might break the chair, thus freeing her of her bonds. Finally, the driver and Kettle dragged the chair and Mattie into the church and secured the door. Lighting several candles around the altar area, Kettle prepared for the 'cleansing' of Mattie's wickedness. Opening the duffel bag, Kettle began laying out the items enclosed within on the altar. First was a large white sheet which he laid out onto the floor. Next was a bundle of assorted lengths of rope. Following the rope were rolls of duct tape and a bottle of prescription pills that increased physical sensations such as pleasure and more importantly, pain.

Looking over at Mattie, who was still wearing the hood, Kettle walked over and gently removed the cloth.

"I want you to see what I have in store for you," he said with a sinister smile. "Battling against the evils of fallen angels is never a good idea without weapons."

Reaching into the duffel bag, Kettle grabbed his old worn bible with a large crucifix and placed it on the altar. He reached into the bag again and removed a Catholic school girl outfit, complete with red plaid skirt, white shirt, matching tie and white stockings.

Holding it up for her to see, Kettle remarked, "I need you to change out of those man clothes and put on this proper feminine attire."

Mattie tried to say something but was unable to talk around the gag still in place.

Kettle reached over and removed it.

Mattie worked her mouth open and closed a few times and finally spoke. "Take these ropes off of me, and I will show you what a real woman looks like in a skirt," she said with a dazzling smile.

13

October 31
Day 67

"We need to cause a distraction at their wall and enter in a different spot undetected," Stephen said, staring at our drawing of Kettle's compound. "Slip in the back door while all the action is going on at the front."

Intrigued by the idea but unsure of the timing, I mentioned that if we did not secure Mattie and the other women before the assault then Kettle's men most likely would kill them before we reached their location.

"What we need is a covert entrance, breach their perimeter and dominate them before they can act," I countered. "Then we evacuate Mattie and the others before any of the others catch on. Once they are safely out of harm's way, we utterly destroy them so we don't have this same problem again later down the road."

"How do we manage to do that, Mike?" Chris asked. "We have no idea of their numbers or armaments."

A plan had been forming in my head, and I laid it out for the group.

"This is what I was thinking. Your input is appreciated if you see anything you would like to add, guys," I said, looking at each of them in turn. "First off, the three of us will enter from the northeast side of their encampment. It doesn't seem they have enough men to be everywhere at once, and we should be able to slip by. Going off of Holly's description of the church layout, we need to reach the priest's office to locate the basement stairwell that leads to the room where the women are being held. Once they are secured, we radio to the assault team, who then notifies two volunteers who will have been gathering as many zombies they can scrounge up with the quad runners. Once the signal is given, we use the front end loader to smash through their vehicle barrier from the south. A transport vehicle will follow through and be driven to the side entrance of the church, where we will load the women. From there, we follow the front end loader northeast where it will smash out their perimeter at the train viaduct and get the women to safety. The guys on the quad runners will follow the transport vehicle into the compound, leading the zombie pack into their breached south perimeter. They will then escape out through the breach to the northeast."

"Isn't that a bit cold? To use undead to kill all those people?" Chris said with a shocked look on his face. "Are they all involved in this?"

"From what Holly said," I answered, "the current residents there are not like our refugees. Most there are of the criminal elements that prefer to prey on the weak. The survivors that make it there either agree with how things work or are killed. Any attractive women are apparently taken for Kettle's sick pleasure. The ones not deemed worthy of him are given to his men to use as seen fit."

"Sounds like a decent plan, Mike," Stephen decided. "Leaves a lot to chance though. There are a lot of unknown factors to consider. We should send out a recon team. With more information we could leave less to chance and hopefully all make it back alive."

"Only information we need to know is that a deranged serial rapist has Mattie in his clutches," I said with annoyance. "If we don't act fast, it'll be too late to save her. He will, without a doubt, rape her— most likely several times— before he loses interest and has her killed. Or worse, hands her over to his men."

"Okay, let's do this," Stephen said. "I'll gather the rest of the team. I am going to want two guards on the front end loader and four in the short bus as shooters. I also want a couple of volunteers to slip into the woods west of here and make their way nice and quiet like down to the northern edge of their walls. With all those zombies pouring in from the south, I'm sure most of those bastards will try and make a break for it."

"Ambush their escape route," I nodded. "I like it."

Stephen wanted Logan and Kleaner to drive the quads, and Eddie would operate the front end loader. He walked down the stairs and ran right into Dan, who was storming in his direction, demanding to know what was being done to save Mattie.

Eyeing Dan's missing hand, but knowing how stubborn he could be, he seamlessly inserted Dan into the role of the short bus driver. Stephen quickly found six volunteers to ride shotgun for the trip and four more for the ambush. As vehicles were quickly loaded and made ready, I noticed a familiar figure get into the short bus and start it up. Veering over, I noticed Dan sitting behind the wheel, as salty and grim as ever but looking sweaty and feverish.

"Dan, you don't look good, bro, why don't you sit this one out?" I suggested.

"What are you, my mommy?" Dan snapped back. "Worry about not fucking up and getting Mattie and any of the others killed."

"Whatever jackass, listen up! If you're set on tagging along, I need you to get Logan and Kleaner on the horn."

I gave him a quick rundown of what we had planned.

"They are going to be our 'bait' on the quad runners," Dan said, nodding in understanding. "I like it."

Calling the two eccentric mall cops over, I explained why I needed them.

"Can I count on you two to do this for me, for Mattie?" I asked.

Logan and Kleaner turned their heads to each other, and then a huge grin grew on each of their faces. With a loud whoop of excitement they gave each other a chest bump.

"Hell yeah you can count on us! We won't let you down, bro," Logan said while knuckle bumping Kleaner.

"Outstanding. Now go get the quad runners gassed up and ready to go. We leave in ten."

Leaving the rest of the operational orders for Stephen to look over, I stomped over to my huge RV to finish loading my gear for the raid. I cranked up the stereo to get the juices flowing with a little Metallica and some Five Finger Death Punch. In the small closet in the kitchen area of the bus, I looked over my current weaponry to use tonight. Deciding to leave the rifle, I grabbed the 12 gauge shotgun instead. We'd be doing some CQB (close quarters battle) inside the church and I wanted some knockdown power. I grabbed the shoulder holster for my .45, put it on, and slid the stainless steel handgun into it, along with four spare magazines in the pouches. I looped my Ontario spec plus survival machete onto my belt.

I hadn't yet had any opportunities to see what this bad boy could do. Maybe tonight we would find out.

The last thing I grabbed was a medium size "go bag" that I loaded with extra .45 rounds and a few bottles of water, along with a few protein bars. As an extra precaution I packed some first aid supplies in it— bandages, antibiotics, stitching needles, etc.. Two small special items I had been saving for a rainy day complete my kit. Hopefully I didn't have to use them for they were quite noisy.

Trying to plan for Murphy's Law was a bitch, but it was better to have and not need than the other way around.

Finished with my outfitting, I went to throw on my old bulletproof police vest and realized I needed to take my shoulder holster off.

I wanted to take my trusty baseball bat, but hopefully we wouldn't be fighting zombies...much. I would take the ballistic shield, however. Having the added protection against handguns would be worth the extra weight when we got into the church. I slung the shield across my back with the long neck strap, and headed out the door ready to make some serious war.

*

Kettle stepped back and looked at Mattie with a mixture of suspicion and lust.

"I will let you loose of your bonds, however, be assured that if you try to escape or attack, my guard here will not hesitate to hurt you in a most unpleasant way," Kettle stated coldly. "Once the clothing has been swapped you will be restrained for further prepping."

Mattie looked behind her to where the large man stood guard. She looked for a way out of her current situation but did not see any. She'd have to play along with this sick fucker for a bit longer. Hopefully her friends would rescue her before this asshole had his way with her.

"I promise to do as told," Mattie said in the most reassuring voice she could muster. "Besides, I need to use the little girl's room. You wouldn't want me to piss all over you while you are ridding me of my dirty thoughts, now would you?"

Kettle almost clapped his hands in excitement at hearing this. "Remember what I said. If you try anything stupid, we will forego the purifying segment and get down to the intensive 'cleansing' segment," Kettle said with an evil grin, "with the help of my large assistant of course."

Mattie sat motionless as Kettle produced a long, wicked looking knife from the left sleeve of his priestly garments and cut her free.

Rubbing the blood and feeling back into her hands, she took her time getting to her feet. Kettle tossed the Catholic school girl outfit onto her lap.

"You may use the bathroom off to the right and then change into the clothes. There isn't any water to flush, but that is the least of your problems," Kettle said then looked at his guard. "Take her over and make sure she doesn't leave your sight, even while taking a piss."

The hungry look in the guard's eyes made Mattie shiver with dread. The burly man grabbed Mattie by the arm and dragged her to the restroom. The man then shoved her into a dark room and stood there with crossed arms and stared unblinking at her.

She guessed he really was going to watch her the entire time. However, she kinda did have to pee.

She walked over to the toilet that had not worked in several years and dropped her pants to do her business.

She was grateful that it was really dark inside without any lights. The only illumination was from the few candles out in the main area that Kettle had lit.

After she was done, she turned her back to the guard and took off her clothes. The man grunted in pleasure when Mattie slid off her pants and shirt, revealing her bra and panties. As she prepared to put the skirt on, Kettle leaned around the shoulder of the man watching her.

"You can lose the undergarments my dear," he said with a sinister smile, waving his knife, "or I'll cut them off. You decide."

Not seeing any alternative, Mattie slowly unhooked her bra and tossed it to the floor, quickly followed by her panties. Standing there fully naked in the weak candlelight, she could feel the two men's hungry gazes devouring the sight of her nude flesh. She knew the longer she distracted them, the longer she would postpone the inevitable rape, hopefully long enough to be rescued.

Lazily, she slid the skirt up her shapely legs, wriggled her hips into the material and zipped up the small zipper in the back. Next, she pulled on the shirt and unhurriedly buttoned it up, followed by the stockings and tie. She bent over and picked up her shoes. Straightening up, she faced the men and told them she was done. Kettle's man nodded, took her by the arm, and led her back to the chair where Kettle had retreated to await her return. The effect of the fantasy outfit she wore was plainly visible when she stepped into the candlelight. Kettle shook with obvious need while the guard pushed her back down into the chair and reapplied her restraints.

"Yes, much better," he whispered.

"What do you expect to gain from all this?" Mattie asked, looking down at her outfit.

Kettle looked at her for a few moments then answered, "It is simple, my wicked temptress. Lust for a woman is what drove Adam to listen to Eve and disobey God. It is also what drove many fallen angels down from heaven. Lucifer is the evil that is in all women which makes men weak, and I must cast him out. You will thank me when this is all over, for I do this for your own good." Kettle shrugged. "Who knows? You may even enjoy it."

Mattie shuddered. This was one deranged, sick motherfucker. *Hope the boys get here soon, or this wacko— and probably the guard too— are going to have their way with me.*

*

Our small assault team, consisting of three people, set out from the prison. Chris was on point, followed by Stephen, and I brought up the rear. Chris and Stephen were both dressed in all black, and both had night vision goggles mounted on Kevlar helmets. I had a night vision monocular, all three sets graciously donated to us for the raid by Logan and Kleaner. Stephen had borrowed Dan's suppressed rifle for the raid since we needed to infiltrate covertly as much as possible, and any sniping would be done by him. Stephen carried his Sig .45 for the inside work, knowing that the hard hitting .45 would be better against humans who were obviously vulnerable to body shots. Unlike zombies though, people shoot back, which was why Stephen and Chris each wore their police issue body armor.

In the distance, the roar of the quad runners faded, as did the voices of Logan and Kleaner yelling and shouting to draw in the hungry undead for their phase of the raid. The front end loader and the short bus followed far behind the quad runners in order to get to their pre-determined positions. The ambush team had left the same time as us, and should have plenty of time to set up. Since we were on foot, we took a little shortcut of sorts. Behind the prison to the west was a set of train tracks that ran north and south through town. These same tracks also passed near the border to Kettle's compound. In fact, Kettle's men used the elevated train tracks as a perimeter wall on the east side of their stronghold. In theory, all we needed to do was follow alongside the berm of the elevated tracks to the south, scale it, and hop down off them to breach their perimeter.

We followed the tracks to the south, the night vision goggles lighting up the landscape in emerald green for Chris and Stephen. I glanced behind us to the north now and then to make sure we didn't get undead company along the way. When we reached the area of the berm we needed to scale, Chris went first, carefully crawling up the steep grassy side. We watched with our own goggles, until we saw him signal for us to ascend to his location. We kept low, the tall dry grass crackling beneath our bodies, sounding like firecrackers going off to our amped up senses. We peeked over the top and saw the colossal church where Kettle had set up shop.

They had several bonfires around the perimeter with guards along each side. Farther in, there was a lot of activity at the front of the church from the number of people near it and the bonfires they used for light. Holly had explained that she escaped the church through a side service entrance located near Kettle's office in the rear of the church. Using the dark area as concealment, Stephen noticed a roving guard was walking down the tracks in our direction on patrol. Carefully taking aim, he downed the man with his suppressed rifle. We quickly crossed the tracks and lowered ourselves down the other side with a rope, which was a sheer drop of twenty feet. Chris motioned for us to stop as he watched a guard moving away from us through his goggles. Seeing no more guards in sight, he rose to a crouch and sprinted while bent over across a parking lot, then across Scott Street.

Once in place and as yet undetected, Chris signaled to us to move up to his location. By the time my old ass made it to Chris, I was puffing like a lifetime smoker.

"Calm your breathing, old man," Chris whispered. "I could hear you from across the street."

I coolly give him the finger and Chris chuckled.

Using the shadows, he maneuvered around the edge of the brick Catholic school building we were next to in order to get a good look at the rear entrance to the church.

Long, agonizing minutes ticked by before he finally returned to say there was a guard posted at the door.

"Hopefully it's unlocked or he has a key," I replied, signaling to Stephen to take the guard out with the suppressed rifle.

Stephen nodded back and moved into a decent shooting position without making himself into a silhouette. He did this so quietly and effectively that I heard the guard fall to the ground after what sounded like a loud cough. We quickly jogged over to the body to make sure he was dead. He was lying face down, a trickle of blood flowing from his chest. I leaned over and grabbed the man's weapon, a shotgun with the barrel sawed off. It was not going to be of any use to us, so I tossed it into the shadows. We moved quickly up the steps to the door, Chris turned the handle, and we were rewarded with it being unlocked. Stephen and Chris filed inside while I dragged the dead guard in behind us.

"So far, so good," Stephen whispered.

I crossed my fingers hoping the rest went this well.

*

Lewis paced his brother's office, becoming more annoyed as time went by. Most of the desk drawers were locked, and the ones that were not had boring supply inventory lists in them.

What was he supposed to do when his brother didn't tell him what needed doing? Lewis needed to have a talk with Kettle. This was bullshit, being treated like a kid Lewis used to be a city councilman!"

Lewis exited the office and asked the two guards posted there where his brother went.

The two guards looked at one another over the top of Lewis' head.

"He had some special work to do," one answered. "He did not want to be disturbed."

"Well, I am going to disturb him," Lewis said angrily. "He left me in charge in his absence, so I order you to tell me where he went!"

The guards stared at each other with a bored look, wishing they could pound this little man into the floor like a nail. To get the dork to shut up, one of the guards pointed to the front exit of the church.

"He went out those doors," he replied. "After that, we do not know where he went off to."

"Thank you, good man, I will have my brother go easy on you when I report your insubordination," Lewis said while walking away holding a clipboard. "Now where did those other two guys go that I just saw walk past?"

"They went that way," the guard pointed down the hall.

When Lewis got out of ear shot, the man turned to his fellow guard. "What does 'insubordination' mean?" he asked

"I don't know," his partner replied, "but that little worm is an asshole."

*

The three of us froze in our tracks when Lewis rounded the corner in front of us. He was glancing at a clipboard while ordering two smaller men following him to pay better attention. He paused and glanced over at where we stood.

"You men," he ordered, looking in our direction. "Get back to your posts. There will be no loafing on my watch."

"Yes sir!" Stephen said, disguising his voice.

Lewis seemed glad that he was rewarded with obedience and continued past, lackeys in tow, without another glance.

"I thought that motherfucker was dead!" Chris hissed.

"Whew, that was close," Stephen whispered.

"Damn right," I replied. "It was his lucky day he didn't look too close at us."

I refastened the strap holding in my machete, which I had drawn at Lewis' sudden arrival.

"Looks like a bunch of people we thought were dead are not," Stephen replied. "Come on, time's a' wasting."

*

Outside the perimeter, Dan sat behind the wheel of the bus wishing he was with the guys assaulting the church.

He looked at his stump with its missing hand. It could have been worse, he guessed. The rotting bastard could have bitten him in the crotch. A man had to be grateful for the little things.

Behind the bus about a block away, Dan heard the quad runners make another pass. Looking in the mirror, he could dimly make out a mammoth undead horde swarming after the quick vehicles.

"Hope those guys reach Mattie soon. Those undead fuckers sound hungry," he said with a whistle.

Ahead of his bus sat the front end loader waiting for the signal to start up and ram the vehicle barrier that was two blocks ahead. One of the shooters sitting on the large tractor was growing impatient and ran back to Dan's bus.

"What's the hold up?" the man asked.

"Sit tight, rookie," Dan ordered. "We'll be moving in shortly. Just pray those damn fools get those girls out in one piece."

Dan was more worried than he thought he ever would be after

seeing his family destroyed by this damned virus. So many people he cared for were now in danger and here he sat as a spectator.

"I'm going to need to fashion a fucking hook or something for this dang stump," he grumbled at the man. "Damn thing itches too."

"You know what?" the man replied. "I think I'm going to go wait back up at the tractor."

*

The stiff hairbrush was leisurely pulled through her thick black hair almost sensuously. If it wasn't for the fact that it was done by a sexual predator like Kettle, Mattie was afraid to admit that it felt fantastic.

The fact that he had her dressed up as a Catholic school girl didn't make her any more comfortable either.

What was it with men and their damn school girl fetishes? She wondered about it, trying to distract her mind from what was transpiring. Unfortunately, she had to go along with Kettle's sick fantasies until— hopefully— her friends located her. She just needed to play along and drag it out, keep him distracted long as possible to put off the inevitable rape that was without a doubt destined to follow.

Now the man was pulling her hair into ponytails. He wasn't kidding that he wanted this to be perfect.

Kettle was now looping her thick, long, black hair into braids. She could tell that he had not done it many times before and was having difficulty doing it properly. To try to appear compliant, she offered to do it for him.

"Need a hand with that, Father?" Mattie asked. "I can tell you haven't done this before."

Kettle paused at his weak attempt at hair braiding and looked at her hard with suspicion.

"Very well, you may do it, but I'll be watching," he decided. "Any tricks and you shall be disciplined and tied up once again."

Mattie agreed and Kettle untied her restraints. Free of her bonds Mattie again massaged the feeling back into her hands. She shook free the sloppy hair braid and brushed out the tangles with the hairbrush. Grasping a handful of hair, she separated the hank into three sections and began to expertly braid them into a thick ponytail. As she did so, she bounced her crossed leg up and down. It had the desired effect. Kettle's eyes narrowed as he stared at her stocking covered foot with hunger as it swayed.

She needed to keep him occupied, and hoped an opportunity would present itself..

Kettle paced unhurriedly around her, not saying a word, breathing heavily as he watched her, his eyes glazing over.

Oh dear God, she thought, trying to keep herself from shivering in fear. *Boys, if you're going to save me, you better hurry up.*

14

October 31
Day 67

We shoved the dead guard into a dark storage closet and set off for the office. Stephen took point with his suppressed rifle, Chris followed next, with me bringing up the rear. Entering the long dark hallway, we noticed an area up ahead that was lit up which, according to Holly, was our target. We had to assume that security had been upgraded since her escape, but we were counting on the fact that Kettle had not moved the girls. Up ahead, two guards stood outside the door keeping watch. As we neared the light, I heard two faint percussions when Stephen shot both guards without breaking stride. One hit was fatal, the other not so much. The second man grunted and then drew in a large breath to scream his pain or sound an alarm. I wasn't sure which it was, but I didn't want to find out, so I clubbed him unconscious with the butt of my shotgun.

"Check the door!" I whispered to Chris.

Chris tried the handle, and it twisted open. Ducking his head in, he saw it was the office and was unoccupied.

With Chris motioning for us to enter, both Stephen and I grabbed a guard and dragged them into the room. Unfortunately both guards left a trail of blood, but that couldn't be addressed right now.

"Lock the door, Stephen," Chris said while I tied up the wounded guard, "and let's find the basement door."

It wasn't hard to locate, as it was only concealed by a set of drapes. Chris opened the door, saw the stairwell was dark as coal, and signaled he was ready to move. He pulled his night vision goggles down. Chris had point again, the three of us slowly making our way down the steps. With the lack of depth perception of the night vision goggles, we did not want to go tumbling loudly down the steps and alert the entire church of our presence. Navigating to the bottom of the stairwell seemed to take forever. The hallway itself presented its own hazards for trying to be quiet. It was packed with decades of clutter. Boxes were stacked shoulder high and looked as if they were purposely placed wherever space was found.

We made our way to the end of the hall and located a closed door. We could hear the muffled screams of women and the grunting and laughter of more than one man. Seeing the bright light leaking out from under the door, we took off our night vision goggles as to not be totally blinded when we made our entry into the room. We allowed a few moments for our eyes to adjust, and we grimly prepared to kill ourselves some ass clown rapists.

I slung my shotgun and drew my pistol. Slinging buckshot all over the room ahead and hurting a friendly wasn't a good idea. Stephen and Chris did the same with their rifles and drew their handguns.

Stephen wanted to take point on entry, followed by Chris, and with me bringing up the rear. I gladly handed the ballistic shield to Stephen. Fucking thing got heavy fast, and I had been lugging it with me since leaving the prison. Stephen took the shield, and I exhaled silently in relief at the lessened weight, shaking my arm to get the blood flow and feeling back into it. Stephen readied himself with Chris close behind. I stepped forward to breach the door, and prepared one of my little surprises I brought with me. I retrieved one of my two CTS Model 7290 flash bangs from my bag. The stun grenade, as most people think of them, generated 175 decibels of sound and 6-8 million candelas light with a 1.5 second fuse. This, in layman's terms, was really fucking loud and blinding if one was not ready for it.

Judging by the sounds coming from behind the door, the men inside had other things on their minds at the moment. I pulled the pin on the flash bang; my grip kept the spoon from flying free. I nodded to Chris, who tapped Stephen that he was set. Stephen nodded at me that he was good to go. Rearing back, I lashed out my right foot, making contact with the old wooden door next to the door handle. The wood splintered from the force of the kick. By the time shouts of alarm sounded off the room, my surprise had already been deployed into the candle lit room. The thunderous blast of noise accompanied with the huge strobe of light was quickly followed by

Stephen entering, picking his targets and letting loose with his pistol. Chris followed closely behind Stephen with me right on his heels. I peeled to the right once I cleared the doorway, as Chris should have done, to engage targets that were not visible from the hallway. However, before I cleared the doorway into the room, a loud roar came from the unseen and still unsecured corner of the room.

I saw Chris crumple to the floor from the edge of my vision, but I could not stop to see what he'd tripped over. In front of me was a fat naked man with a shotgun, racking another round as he started to swing it in my direction preparing to fire. I fired my own pistol, double tapping him in the chest and the head, and continued my path into the room. Seeing another man grabbing at his eyes in pain from the flash bang, I kicked him hard in the teeth. As he collapsed unconscious, I turned and shot a third man in the back who, was scrambling for his pistol lying with his clothes on the floor. At the same time, Stephen shot him twice in the side of his torso from the other side of the room.

The sound of gunfire and screaming women was deafening. Luckily, I saw that none of the women appeared to have been wounded by gunfire as I quickly scanned for Mattie.

From behind me I heard Stephen say my name, "Oh my God, Mike!"

Not wanting to waste time to see what he wanted, I continue to search for Mattie, as many of the women were covering up their faces and I had to physically pry their arms away to look at them.

"Mike, it's Chris. He's dead."

The finality in his voice etched with pain made me pause and look.

There sprawled on the floor was Chris, missing a large chunk of his head.

The shotgun blast I heard upon entering must have hit him in the face.

Goddamn. Poor bastard probably had no idea what hit him.

To make matters worse, it looked like Mattie was not even here.

Stephen finally restored some semblance of order amongst the prisoners, and they figured out that we were here to save them, not to rape or kill. He quickly cut their restraints and set them free while I walked over to the unconscious man I had kicked in the face.

One of the women separated herself from the group, not even bothering to cover her nakedness, and walked over to the man's pistol that was lying next to him.

"He laughed and raped me after I told him I was pregnant. He can burn in Hell," she spat and shot the man in the head.

This, of course, got the women screaming again, and I gently took the firearm from the limp grip of the stunned woman. I calmly took her by the shoulders and turned her away from the gory scene. She burst into tears as other women gathered her into their arms.

Stephen calmly but firmly took charge by insisting they gather what clothing they had, get dressed, and prepare to quickly follow us to safety.

"Need to hurry, girls," Stephen urged. "We made a lot of noise and someone was bound to hear."

While they got dressed, I asked if they had seen a new girl that was brought here earlier today. No one had seen anyone new for some time now.

Kettle must have taken her to a different location...but where?

*

Lewis was mad as all get out. His brother had put him in charge, but from what he saw from everyone he met so far, that authority was apparently in name only. Everyone he dealt with held open contempt and disgust on their faces when he asked where his brother had gone off to. Being of a frail stature with little physical strength, Lewis could not back up any threats he wanted to make. It was so much easier before society crumbled when with nothing more than a signature, he could ruin a man's career or sue the living shit out of someone. The majority of the people he asked ignored his questions or just plain told him, "Go fuck yourself."

Swallowing his growing fury, Lewis was eventually able to glean the information as to his brother's whereabouts.

It seemed that the destination happened to be Kettle's former church where he'd preached before his unfortunate incarceration. Angrily, Lewis stalked towards the old abandoned church that was nearly two city blocks away, all the while his temper soaring.

"Why would he move her?" Lewis muttered to himself. "It doesn't seem worth the risk."

Lewis kept his head on a swivel on his walk toward the church.

He knew those asshole cops were going to come for her, and he had his doubts that his brother's men would be able to handle them.

*

Mattie put the finishing touches on her ponytails and secured them with some pieces of red ribbon. This freak had his fetish planned out to the smallest detail. Unfortunately, she had stalled as long as she could without making it seem too obvious.

Kettle walked around her, staring, but not saying a word. It was nerve-wracking and creepy as hell.

"I must say, you're the picture perfect symbol of temptation," Kettle purred from behind her. "Satan's little whore.

Turning her head over her right shoulder, Mattie tried to appear as innocent as possible, which was kind of hard to pull off dressed as someone's sexual fantasy come to life.

Continuing to walk around her, Kettle stopped in front of her, literally rubbing his hands together in anticipation of what was soon to follow.

"Now, my dear seductress," he said panting with lust. "Now we shall begin the process of breaking Lucifer's grasp of your soul."

*

The path back upstairs to the church office went as quickly as one can move carrying a two hundred pound corpse who used to be a very close friend while trying to usher several bawling, starving, sex slaves up a pitch black stairwell.

When we reached the office, we found the wounded guard I had knocked unconscious groggily trying to get to his feet. Setting my friend carefully to the floor, I stalked over to the woozy man and questioned him as to Kettle's whereabouts. Blood was flowing heavily from his shoulder wound, and I knew he would bleed out.

At first the man refused to answer, but shortly after the third broken finger, and when I pulled out my large Ontario survival machete and calmly lined up the blade to his other hand, the information literally flew from his lips. Apparently Kettle wanted complete privacy while he tended to the woman that had been captured. He had taken her to the old abandoned church where he used to preach, located at the intersection of Ohio and Scott Street.

I thanked him for his input, then slammed the hilt of the knife into his head a few times to knock his ass back out. After retying his hands and feet, Stephen and I threw him down the old creaking flight of stairs we'd just come up. Tumbling down the stairs like the sack of shit that he was, he crashed to a stop at the bottom in the darkness.

"Stephen, get on the horn and call in for pick up and start phase two," I said. "The clock is ticking!"

I heard Stephen relay the message to Dan that the hostages were secured and we were ready for extraction. As soon as he put the radio away, a commotion could be heard in the hallway outside the office.

"Mike, we got company!" Stephen whispered. "Ladies, hit the deck!"

From outside the room, we heard men talking as they approached the office. They weren't being very quiet and one of them said, "Holy shit!" at the sight of the blood on the floor in front of the office door. It was clear from all the bumping noises coming from the hallway that they had stacked up to the left of the door and were probably getting ready to storm the office.

"Sounds like at least four guys," Stephen whispered. "Shoot through the door when they try it, Mike, I'll take care of the rest."

The door handle rattled. "It's locked," I heard the man say just before I sent a 12 gauge slug through the door. One thing I learned when doing any type of tactical shooting was that a wooden door or wall plaster would not stop a bullet. It wasn't like Hollywood, where a simple wall barrier would make bullets magically ricochet. We knew this, but Kettle's men seemed painfully oblivious to that fact. Stephen emptied his suppressed AR-15 into the wall in a shallow arch from right to left. By the time I fired my second slug and lowered my shotgun, Stephen was finishing a reload, and everything was quiet in the hallway. Stephen haltingly opened the shattered door and checked the mangled, bloody corpses in the hallway.

"Good to go, Mike," Stephen stated from his position in the hall. "Let's move. And ladies, watch your step. It's pretty messy out there."

*

Logan looked over his shoulder at Kleaner on the other quad runner and then at the huge crowd of zombies behind him howling for their blood. If they didn't have to drive so damn slow in order to keep them motivated to chase them, it wouldn't be so bad. But they had to move just fast enough to gather them in and keep them following without getting themselves killed. There had to be several hundred by now, but it was hard to tell with it being so dark out. Logan had to constantly check with his LED flashlight to monitor how close or far back the hungry fuckers were.

After dozens of passes, he saw the signal from Dan's position. It was finally time to lead the horde into the church perimeter. Yelling over to Kleaner, Logan let him know that it was time to sow some destruction.

"Kick the tires and light the fires!" Logan cried.

Kleaner whooped eagerly and the quad runner engines roared in response.

Ahead of them the front end loader began to move, followed closely by the short school bus Dan drove. Further up the street, the vehicle barrier loomed out of the darkness, illuminated from within by the many bonfires inside Kettle's compound.

*

Lewis stormed into the old church where his brother formerly preached. He found the front door unlocked, and he stopped dead in his tracks when he entered. Kettle was standing in front of the captured woman, Mattie, who was dressed up like a school girl. It almost appeared they were doing some weird sexual roleplaying shit.

"What the fuck is going on here?" Lewis asked. "I thought you were questioning her for information regarding her friends at the prison."

Kettle spun towards his brother. "I thought I told you I was not to be disturbed!"

"I came to find you because your people refused to follow nearly every order I gave!" Lewis roared back.

"You will leave now and not return," Kettle roared. "I'll come find you when I finish my business here!"

Mattie took the opportunity to try and add to the argument.

"Why not let your brother stay, Father? I have never had two men at once," she purred lustfully. "Let alone two brothers."

Lewis was taken aback. "What in the hell is she talking about?"

Kettle spun back at Mattie and soundly slapped her face, making her ponytails swing from the blow.

"I see the evilness of your soul shining true," he sneered. "We shall see how long Lucifer can keep his hold when God's cleansing has begun."

Turning back to Lewis, Kettle said angrily, "For the last time, brother, if you wish to see morning, you will leave now!"

Backing up slowly, Lewis retreated towards the front door.

Never had he seen the fanatical, almost homicidal look in his brother's eye before. Reaching the door, Lewis did as told and fled the church, but once outside, ran to the north side of the building to try to find a window to look through. He found several that had been boarded up but a suitable one for his purpose, one from which he could peer between the boards in order to watch with a sickening fascination what was occurring inside. So deep was his attention focused as to what was taking place that he failed to notice the screams he started to hear were not coming from the restrained woman inside the old church.

*

Inside the perimeter wall it was business as usual, which was fucking bullshit boring according to Gus and his dumb but loyal young friend Kevin.

"I cannot believe we got stuck on night watch again!" Kevin bitched, holding a rifle and only halfheartedly peering out into the darkness. "And now one of Kettle's men tells us to keep an extra eye out for anyone approaching the wall. He said to shoot anyone living on sight. He didn't fucking think it important to give me a reason. Could it be that they are expecting trouble?"

"I heard a rumor that Kettle found himself one fine piece of ass," the older man replied. "Hopefully we can find ourselves a female survivor, and we can get a chance at her before we hand her over to Kettle's boys. I'm getting mighty tired of the old worn out pussy they hand down to us. I want a feisty bitch with some fight left in her."

Kevin laughed loudly. "I hear that. Something that squirms and screams instead of just lying like a corpse would be real nice right about now. Might as well try fucking one of them zombie critters! At least they move!"

Both men laughed long and hard at their pathetic attempt at humor.

In the distance, somewhere in the darkness, the rumble of a loud diesel engine grabbed their attention.

"What do you make of that, Gus?" Kevin asked, stepping up to the vehicle barrier wall, peering out into the night.

"Hmmm, I'm not sure," Gus stated. "Earlier we heard those crazy bastards on the quad runners, but they never showed themselves. I can't make out what the other noise is from. Those damn bonfires have ruined my night vision."

"Should I go get some help?" Kevin asked nervously.

The two stood and watched, pondering what to do, and it became all too clear what made the noise. Without a chance to even curse their shitty luck, a huge front end loader roared out of the darkness and slammed into the protective vehicle barrier in front of them. The screeching of metal and crashing of breaking glass preceded the pain as the vehicle in front of them spun away from the impact of the heavy equipment and right into them. Momentarily stunned, Gus gasped for breath and struggled to hold onto consciousness. The sound from the tractor was deafening, and as it passed, Gus thought that another vehicle had followed in its wake. Unable to stand, Gus at first couldn't figure out why. Shaking the cobwebs from his vision, he was finally able to weakly lift his head enough to see that a small compact car had fallen off the barrier wall onto his legs.

Gradually, the roar of the front end loader and following vehicle receded and was replaced with an all too familiar sound that made his asshole pucker in fear. He groped around on the ground in vain near where he lay, looking for the rifle he had been clutching.

"Come on, kid, we got to get out of here!" Gus gasped in pain, trying to wiggle out from underneath the frame of a smashed Pontiac.

It should have crushed his legs, but with a good tire still on the axle, it only trapped his prone body. It hurt like the devil, but he would live.

When he received no reply, Gus frantically looked to where he last saw his partner. His mood sank low when he noticed Kevin's limp form crushed by a vehicle which had fallen from the barrier wall. Now the dreaded sound he heard quickly turned into an ear piercing howl as zombies poured into the perimeter like a flood wall giving way.

Gus had to curse at the ironic events that happened to let the zombie that was to kill him be a female that definitely did have some fight left in her. She was all too willing to accept his punches as he fought in vain to keep her teeth from his flesh.

"You fucking bitch!" he cried. The zombie's teeth clacked shut, tearing a chunk from his face. "I don't wanna die!"

His cries were cut off quickly and he vanished under the hungry mob of undead that swirled around him.

*

Willie passed the bottle of moonshine to the guy on his left before rubbing his hands together and placing them over the fire to keep warm. The word had been passed that Father Kettle was expecting some sort of trouble tonight and Willie and his crew had been placed on some sort of alert status. Five others were out on a roving patrol, and when they returned he would lead the others out into the darkness.

"It's not even our night to work, and they got us out here freezing our asses off," Willie griped to the other four men who stood around the burn barrel.

"You didn't complain when that tall dude sent us out here," Willie's buddy Waldo snorted. "You kissed his ass like always."

Willie had to admit that he had done just that. If you crossed one of Father Kettle's commands, you found yourself dead.

"Yeah yeah," Willie scowled. "Well the rumor is those dudes grabbed a woman for the good Father tonight, so I'm sure they think they are king shit. Kettle put them in charge, so it's best not to cross 'em I guess."

"Whatever, pussy," Waldo laughed and adjusted the rifle he had slung over his shoulder. "Now hand me that bottle, whoever gots it."

A sudden loud crash could be heard to the south. Something had smashed into their wall, and the sound of a diesel engine was getting louder by the second.

"What the hell was that?" Willie asked.

Waldo had dropped the bottle of corn whisky, shattering the glass bottle on the pavement, and slipped his rifle off his shoulder.

"Let's go check it out," Willie ordered. "Follow me guys."

As the men moved cautiously forward, a large tractor loomed into view. Then men froze under the tractor's looming spotlight like deer in the headlights. It wove recklessly up the street, seeming to deliberately smash into buildings with its enormous steel bucket.

"Kill those fuckers!" Willie cried, raising his shotgun to fire.

Rounds clanked harmlessly off of the tractor as Willie and his men began to fire. Instantly, unseen shooters returned fire with lethal accuracy, spiting deadly projectiles which tore into the hapless bandits. To make matters worse for the crew a short bus, that came out from directly behind the tractor, sped on past, flanking the group of men who jumbled together when the shooting started. A torrent of bullets cut Willie and his men to pieces just as they glanced ahead to see a flood of undead descending into their encampment. Waldo managed to drag his mangled body away long enough to see the men in the bus pause momentarily to throw Molotov cocktails into a few of the inhabited buildings. Waldo then bled out, but not before watching the bus tearing off in the path of an undead avalanche.

*

Dan's school bus screeched to a stop on the north side of the massive limestone church. The impressive structure was hard to miss, and I let out a sigh of relief as he pulled up. The four guards that rode with him jumped out the rear emergency exit and fanned out around the bus. Already the undead were flooding the area, and gunfire and screams could be heard in the distance from Kettle's doomed men. The guards dropped the few animated corpses who had already wandered in too close.

While the doors were still sliding open, we had the women rushing ahead to board the vehicle. The women were crying their thanks at the valiant rescue, many pausing to hug and kiss the snarling face of Dan, who was hastily urging them to move their asses and get on board.

When the last one climbed on, Dan looked out at us with a raised eyebrow.

"Don't worry, bitches," he said, "I don't want hugs and kisses from you fuckers."

That was when he saw the limp form across my shoulders. I reverently laid our comrade onto the bus floor, and Dan's jaw stiffened in anger.

"Mattie wasn't with these girls. She was taken to a different location," Stephen said.

"What the fuck!" Dan brayed. Stephen rapidly explained where she was being held and that we were going to go get her right now.

"Well, I'm not leaving without her!" Dan said. "I suggest you two hurry the fuck up. The party crashers we invited sound hungry. We'll try to slow them up from here."

Sure as shit, the howling did have a ravenous sound to it. Hopefully, with the amount of screaming and gunshots behind us, Kettle's followers would keep them busy until we could evacuate out of here.

Hurrying north on foot, Stephen and I rounded the corner of Clay and Scott Street and observed a figure exit the old church that we were heading for.

"I hope that wasn't Kettle," I said. "I don't want to have to hunt that fucker down with all the undead that will be arriving here shortly."

"He didn't have on priest robes," Stephen replied, panting for breath. "I don't think it was him."

To the west, we first heard then saw the front end loader drive across Scott Street ahead of us, crashing through the vehicle barrier that secured the Ohio Street train viaduct portion of Kettle's stronghold. The two guards that were manning the position were pinned down by rifle fire from our men on the tractor and were unable to avoid the destroyed wall when it collapsed on top of them. Following closely to the tractor, Logan and Kleaner screamed past on the quad runners, heading back to the prison as planned. Glancing behind us, I caught a glimpse of two of Kettle's men being chased by an enormous throng of zombies, firing handguns wildly as they ran, not hitting anything before being cornered and eaten.

"This place is already becoming a dead zone," I pointed out. "We're running out of time."

I scrambled up to the front doors of the structure where Mattie was supposed to be, praying that we were not too late.

*

The scream of revulsion and violation that ripped from Mattie's throat seemed if anything to only further Kettle's arousal. Having her arms tied to the chair was bad enough. After her first kick caught Kettle in the scrotum, he also restrained her legs spread open. After the pain in his groin faded, Kettle began spouting some tainted form of bible verses at her while he fondled her breasts and licked at her throat. Mattie couldn't remember what the crazy sicko was saying and kept repeating a mantra mentally in her head so as to not react to his manipulations. It was going well enough until he rammed his fingers deep into her vagina and violently thrashed them about. Unable to hold it back, Mattie screamed out her horror and helplessness to the rafters and the altar before her, the altar with the Cross of Christ on it that appeared to be burning from the reflective candle flames.

*

When we approached the double doors of the church, we heard a woman scream like the souls of the damned. Stephen reached the church first, but when he ripped open the door, I raced past him. Immediately inside the vestibule of the church was a single guard, looking quite panicked. Not slowing my stride, I raised my shotgun and fired into his chest. The shotgun slug ripped through his torso and out his back, coating the wall behind him with chunks of meat and blood. The man had little chance to recognize that we were the enemy and died without uttering a word.

I had already stepped over the dead man before he finished falling to the floor. Ahead of me, before the altar, my blood froze at what I saw.

Kettle, that sick fucker, had one hand between Mattie's legs and his other hand was twisting her head back by her hair. He was also biting her shoulder hard enough to draw blood. So caught up with what he was doing, it took him a few seconds to realize what was going on. Kettle whipped his hands free and stooped to pick up something from the floor. He stood up, and a gunshot blast went off right next to my left ear. I flinched from the unexpected noise, and saw Kettle spin to the ground. Stephen stood to my left, and had deafened me once again with his muzzle blast.

"Really?" I asked him, gripping my left ear. "You couldn't move a little to the side?"

"No time, crybaby," Stephen said, and then started shooting again at Kettle, who had made it to his feet and darted away. Stephen's hurried shots appeared to hit wide of the mark and Kettle disappeared behind the altar.

"Fuck!" Stephen shouted, firing again to try and keep the wounded Kettle pinned down. "Careful, he is probably armed!"

I ran up to Mattie, who appeared to be unconscious, and made quick work of her restraints with my knife. Shaking her gently, I attempted to wake her up.

When I didn't get a response, I figured she had gone into shock, and I called Stephen over. I picked her up from the chair and handed her limp form over to him.

"She is alive, but I think she's in shock. Get her to the bus. I will finish this."

Stephen tried to say otherwise but registered the cold look in my eyes. He holstered his .45 and laid her over his shoulder.

"Fine, I will get her to Dan but then I will be back for you," he replied.

I watched him until I was sure they were out safely, and then turned to follow to where that snake Kettle had gone. That was when

I noticed numerous small fires had sprung up from the candles Kettle knocked over while dodging Stephen's gunfire. The fires were quickly getting larger, the flames hungrily tearing into the dry wood with a vengeance. I had better make this quick. Locating the trail of blood drops Kettle so kindly left for me, I stalked my injured prey while my anger grew as hot as the flames eating at my back.

*

Outside the church Lewis stood in shock. One second he was morbidly turned on by what his brother was doing to that woman, then the next second he was stunned by the arrival of those motherfuckers, Mike and Stephen. All the recent pain in his life he could directly relate to those assholes. Now to top it all, they shot his brother! Finally he had his brother back, and now those sons of bitches were trying to kill him.

Maybe I can take care of the meathead, Lewis thought. He'd already missed his chance at Stephen and the woman. But the big fucker was still inside chasing his injured brother. All while he was standing there like some dumb bystander.

Lewis crept to the front door, and while doing so, noticed Stephen was now running down Scott Street southbound, with the woman slung over his shoulder like a duffel bag.

Now was the time!

Opening the door, he darted inside and almost tripped on the corpse of the guard that was killed earlier. Lewis shrugged because it was no big loss. The guy treated him like shit anyways, but he did stoop to pick up the large revolver the idiot had dropped. Lewis only paused long enough to make sure it was loaded. Now armed and with greater courage, he quickly jumped over the increasing flames and followed where the big bastard had gone.

*

Stephen's progress was slowed down by carrying Mattie to safety, watching all the while for approaching zombies. With few of Kettle's men left alive, he had gained the attention of a shit ton of howling, hungry zombies.

Drawing his .45 with one hand, he shot the five closest to him, emptying his pistol in the process.

At the sound of an engine roaring, Stephen looked up and saw

Dan approaching rapidly with the bus. Skidding to a stop and almost hitting him, Dan ripped open the bus doors.

"Get the fuck inside! We've got to get out of here now!" he screamed as Stephen laid Mattie onto the bus floor.

"I can't!" Stephen screamed back. "I gotta go back for Mike! He stayed behind to take out Kettle!"

"Hey asshole, look behind us!" Dan growled. "Your only choices are to get in now, or I'll take off for the prison and try to draw them off with me while you find some cover."

Stephen leaned back and looked where Dan had just come from. Filling the street behind them and closing in fast were several dozen corpses stumbling along in relentless pursuit. Now to the north, gunfire could be heard as well. Some of Kettle's men had abandoned their savior, only to walk right into a well laid out shooting gallery manned by the good guys. He paused, soaking it all in.

"Fuck it!" he spat, listening to the gunfire all around. "I'm not leaving Mike! We already lost one of our friends tonight, and I refuse to let another die! Get back to the prison. We'll both meet you all there. When you're safely out, call in the ambush team. I think their work is about done."

Not waiting for a reply, Stephen grabbed a fresh magazine for his pistol from his belt and reloaded on the run, running back towards the church while Dan sped past him in the bus. Lungs burning from the long day's exertions, he noticed the smoke and flames that were already starting to work their way out from the boarded up windows of the abandoned church. He holstered his .45 and gripped his AR-15. He was oblivious to much of what was going on around him. Only being concerned with zombies in his immediate area, the fate of many of Kettle's nearby followers was decided without Stephen's knowledge.

A block over from where Stephen was standing, Kettle's few remaining loyal followers had barricaded themselves in an abandoned house waiting for Kettle to provide a miracle. The four men huddled in fear, armed with a pair of handguns and two pump shotguns with very little ammunition between them. One of the men was trying to hold the front door closed against the pressing horde while the others fired wildly out the open windows. Their miracle did not come. Rotting arms finally reached through the gap in the doorway and pried the heavy door open. Falling back, the man failed to warn the others that the house was compromised and simply stuck his gun in his mouth and pulled the trigger. The other men were not even afforded that luxury and were eaten alive after their guns ran dry. Kicking and screaming, they felt their flesh ripped from their bones in bloody chunks.

As each doomed scenario played out, it quickly turned into a chaotic mess, and without any discipline, each man and woman scattered and ultimately died alone. Down the block, two former outlaw biker gang members made it to their motorcycles, but a wave of putrefying undead knocked them down and engulfed them. A lone teenager who only yesterday had raped a helpless woman while she cried for mercy now sobbed and begged for the same as several rotting corpses grabbed his legs and pulled him down from a fire escape ladder to his death. Many more chose suicide when it became obvious that they were going to be eaten alive in mere moments. Some refused to do that, and after being bitten, soon rose as a howling undead creature, filling the air with their screams.

*

Inside the rear of the church, I tried my best not to cough from the billowing smoke and give away my location. Still following the thickening blood trail, I finally caught up to where Kettle had dragged himself and collapsed. Apparently, Stephen's entire second round of shots did not all miss their intended target, and a few had struck true. Kettle had a nasty left shoulder wound which had drenched his robe wet with blood and another in his right thigh. He was whimpering in pain and coughing from the thickening smoke, trying to apply a pressure bandage to his leg when I stalked into the room.

"What's the matter, little man? Where is your God now?" I taunted the despicable man before me.

"You!" he gasped. His face twisted up with rage and he shook a blood-covered fist at me. "You have brought ruin upon me because of some worthless whore who deserved nothing less than what I was to give her!"

Walking forward, I tossed my shotgun down to the church floor, wanting to do this by hand. I grabbed his right arm and the front of his robes, pulling him upright and leaned in close to his face. I didn't even notice that Kettle's blood was drenching the front of my shirt.

"Tell me something," I snarled as the flames behind me started to brighten the room. "Does your broken arm hurt?"

My odd question caught Kettle off guard.

"You fool! My arm isn't...arrgghhhh!" He screamed in pain when I slammed my forearm into his right elbow that I had locked into a straight position.

With a sickening crunch, his elbow folded the wrong way. Kettle went white with pain and he fell to the ground onto his back. Disbelief was etched in his face as he stared at his mangled arm for a few seconds before the pain reached his overloaded brain. His bloodcurdling screams made me smile.

Thinking of how I last saw Mattie being violated by this man, I dropped all 225 pounds of my pissed off frame onto his groin with my knee. Kettle's eyes bulged outward in unbelievable pain as all air rushed out of his body. He tried to draw a ragged breath back in to scream again. I gripped the front of his robes in my left fist and lifted his torso off the ground as I blasted him in the teeth with a thundering right fist. Reaching back down, I wrapped both of my hands around his head and lifted him off the dirty floor.

"Look at me, you sick fuck!" I growled into his bloody, petrified face. "I want be the last thing you see before you die."

Kettle, clearly about to go into shock from pain, hacked a glob of bloody spit into my face, chuckled weakly and mumbled, "Go to Hell."

"You first, bitch."

With a surge, I flexed my shoulders and twisted my arms. Kettle's neck bones snapped with the sound like a tree branch breaking. His eyes rolled back into his head as the air escaping his body made a "k-k-k" noise. Kettle's body jerked and then went limp.

I dropped his lifeless corpse to the floor.

"Fuck me."

*

Scrambling through the smoke and flames, Lewis made his way to the rear of the church. Finally he made it to the room where his brother and that asshole cop Mike were located. Lewis observed the big man break his brother's arm and then his neck without hesitating. Stunned with seeing his brother killed by the very man who'd broken his nose and brought about the demise of his safe zone, Lewis shook with the pain of loss and rage. He remembered the heavy weight in his right hand belonged to the large revolver he was holding. Lewis whipped it up and pulled the trigger while howling his anger. With the deafening first blast, he saw the accursed man stumble, and with the righteous feeling of vindication emptied the revolver at him.

*

From behind, it felt as if some jerkoff had just hit me with a sledgehammer in the back. Twisting to my right from the impact, I felt another impact slam into my sheathed blade tied to my leg. Pain ripped across my thigh as it spun me around to the left and down onto the knee of my injured leg. Looking up, I saw a figure backlit from the flames that were increasingly devouring the church. I could not make out the face due to the light and the billowing smoke. The armed assailant screamed in rage and emptied his weapon at me. Two more shots struck me in the chest, another crushed into my head and one missed. That was what I was hoping, as I fell back onto the floor. Faintly I heard the sound of the revolver clicking on spent rounds, followed by severe coughing and curses.

My assailant rushed to stand over me and stared at the blood covering my chest and face. He snarled a curse at me and kicked me hard in the ribs.

Luckily I was already passing out beyond the ability to react.

*

A burst of adrenaline rushed through Lewis' body. He did it.

He fucking really did it!

He had killed that asshole and avenged his brother's murder.

Giggling, he did a little victory dance until he was suddenly wracked with a prolonged coughing fit, bringing him back to reality. He realized the rear passage of the church was now totally engulfed in flames.

"Holy shit!" he shouted. He'd have to celebrate later.

Pausing to spit on Mike's body and then reach down and close his dead brother's staring eyes, he quickly ran to a rear exit that had been boarded over. It took a number of frantic kicks, but he was able to breach a ragged hole in the door and crawl free from the burning building. Once outside he saw the chaotic remnants of his brother's safe zone completely overrun with undead.

"Those other cops will also pay for what they have done," he howled. He fled the oncoming zombies and encroaching flames of his brother's pyre. He ran west, ran for his life, and he alone made it to safety just as his brother's fortress became consumed by fire and those howling demons. Also as when his safe zone fell, Lewis escaped death.

He was alone again. Alone but alive.

*

Stephen stood outside the church doors, amazed at how fast the fire was spreading.

"MIKE!"

Covering his face, he ventured as far as possible into the raging inferno.

"Mike, where are you?"

Chunks of falling, burning wood forced him to retreat back towards the entrance.

"Goddamn it!" he screamed, ducking from the falling debris. "Answer me you asshole!"

The only answer he received was with a loud crash when a large section of the outer wall collapsed outward in a roar of flames and sparks.

"Goddamn it!" Stephen shouted again, shielding his face.

The waves of heat started to make his hair smoke and his clothes singe. With portions of the roof now falling to the floor in flames, he finally admitted defeat and retreated from the burning structure with a heavy heart.

"Fuck!"

After all this, he'd lost two of his closest comrades in the span of one hour. And this wasn't a damn video game with a start over button, or with extra lives. This was the real shit.

Retreating outside and evading or killing the few zombies that braved the flames, Stephen observed from a safe distance as the fire finished consuming the structure.

*

The pain in my ribs from attempting to draw a breath dragged my ass out from the blackness. Heavy smoke billowed around me and was filling the room as I struggled to sit up. My throbbing head made the room spin. I tenderly felt my temple and could feel the wetness of blood running from my head injury.

No entry wound, just a long gash.

The shooter must have narrowly missed and dug a furrow along my skull. Or my head was so hard it ricocheted off.

Oh well, Dan says chicks like scars.

Struggling up onto my knees, I stayed low and felt the soreness from where the man had shot my torso, front and back.

I had finally outsmarted Murphy!

My attacker had luckily managed to hit my bulletproof vest. Fucking ribs hurt like hell, but I did not think any rounds had penetrated. A bout of severe coughing reminded me of more pressing issues.

My sense of direction was now all fucked up from the thick smoke, but the wall of heat on my left told me that was not the way to go. Trying not to panic as the old church was quickly turning into an inferno, I felt a brief wave of cooler air from my right. Choking on the thick smoke and coughing badly, I crawled blindly towards the coolness.

Sudden pain jerked me fully awake and I discovered the source was a burning piece of wood that landed on my arm, catching my sleeve on fire. I slapped out the flames, wondering how long I was passed out. The roaring of the conflagration behind me and the cracking sounds of the structure's roof caving in was motivation enough to get my old ass moving. Gasping for air, I painfully pulled my battered, bleeding and cooked slightly medium rare body along the floor. Groping ahead of me, I felt a blast of cool air and then was gripping the edges of a hole in the wall. I pulled myself ahead, falling through an opening and out into blessed fresh air.

I rolled out of the burning building and lay there in the weeds trying my best to catch my breath. I was just about to thank whatever Gods were watching over me when three zombies stumbled around the corner and came howling for blood. Damn things must have smelled the blood that covered quite a bit of my char-broiled ass.

I fumbled for my pistol in the shoulder holster, mentally judging that I had a very small window for taking them out or becoming an unwilling snack for these fuckers. My pistol refused to come free from the holster, and my frantic jerking only encouraged the creatures. They came at me hard. Murphy must have finally felt pity on my sorry ass, for as I was about to throw in the towel with drawing my weapon, the outer wall of the church collapsed in an avalanche of burning wood, dropping directly onto the shambling corpses. Sitting there in an upright position with my mouth hanging open in disbelief, I could barely believe my good fortune.

Waves of blistering heat beat at me as unholy screams erupted from within the blaze, and I watched the creatures attempt to reach me even as they were fully engulfed in flames.

"Fuck me!"

I unsteadily rose to my feet, struggling to hold onto consciousness, and forced my way through the pain just to place one foot in front of another. I stumbled off into the darkness leaving the inferno in the distance behind me until I found myself before an open doorway of a building. I dragged my exhausted body inside and fell to the floor. I managed to shut the door and sat up against it, hoping that my dead weight would hold it shut if any undead attempted to open it. Resting my head against the door, I was too tired to be alarmed that the blood streaming from my head was running down my face and blinding my right eye. With the trauma and blood loss, I was too out of sorts to make sense of what had happened or where I was. As blackness ate away at the edges of my vision, I unknowingly fell over unconscious onto my side, and a small pool of blood formed on the floor where it dripped from my head.

Outside in the dead of night, a gigantic fire raged unchecked. As the smoke and sparks from the structure fire spiraled upward, it was pushed to the south over the heads of hundreds of howling, hungry zombies that searched tirelessly for flesh to devour.

A fair number of the undead were drawn off by a lone person screaming curses at the abominations, firing again and again into the encroaching horde. This man had lost two close friends this night, and was taking his revenge in the only way he knew how, one 5.56mm projectile at a time. Predictably, the sheer number of remaining undead forced him to retreat. With a final look toward the remnants of the church, he fled into the darkness towards his fortified prison compound. With hundreds in pursuit of the man, Kettle's destroyed safe zone gradually fell silent. The only sounds remaining were of the burning building crackling as it was consumed by the flames and distant moaning of the damned.

15

November 1
Day 68

A chilly breeze flowed in from the north, soft and slow but with the patient force of nature that gradually pushed and pulled along with it a faint stench of something much more dreadful and feared than a late fall shower. A virus had spread throughout the land, a virus which turned ordinary people into flesh craving creatures that spread their sickness as they consumed the living. And with the death of civilization, the ability to adequately fight fires in urban areas had also died. All night long, the guard tower personnel had reported a dull glow emanating from a massive black cloud far to the north. It now appeared likely that a massive fire was burning unchecked in Chicago.

The rising sun brightened the quiet landscape. An occasional crack of rifle fire interrupted the tranquility, giving way to the rustling of living people getting prepared to tackle another day in the new "fight or die" reality that had gripped the nation and most likely the entire world. As the people emerged from their various campers and RVs, the overall mood was quite somber and subdued. Word had spread that two of the prison compound founders were killed in yesterday's rescue of Mattie and others. Stephen stood in one of the watchtowers, staring out at the landscape, thinking of the events that led him to this point in time, focusing on what happened last night in particular.

There was a battle last night with a nearby encampment of fellow survivors. However, that group's ranks were filled with rapists, murderers, and pretty much all that was evil in mankind.

They were led by a pathetic individual who claimed to be a man of God. Hiding behind the holy symbols of that office, the leader whose name was Kettle allowed himself and his followers to commit acts that just a few months ago would have earned them a lengthy prison sentence. The refugees that looked to them for help were sadly mistaken once they entered. Countless rapes of the surviving women and children were what they had to look forward to when captured. The lucky few were killed for resisting or trying to escape. Kettle himself had his own personal harem of kidnapped women that he kept shackled inside a room deep within an old church. He would use those poor women to fulfill his sick fantasies and abuse them sexually and physically.

Those malicious thugs were destroyed by the valiant men of the prison stronghold. Mattie and several women that had been captured were rescued. Kettle and his minions were killed. His base of operations was destroyed and put to the torch. The only stain on the joy and euphoria from the successful raid was the two brave souls that had perished so that others may live.

Stephen's friends, Chris and Mike, had helped found the prison community and did not return alive. Chris's body now lay in the prison chapel awaiting burial. Burial was a luxury no longer afforded to most that died during this pandemic.

Movement out in the area that had been cleared by the prison encampment personnel caught Stephen's attention. He peered at the stumbling figures, snorting in anger and disgust.

"Fucking zombies."

It was unbelievable to Stephen that these monstrosities actually existed. He had killed countless numbers of them with head shots, yet the fact that they existed at all was still hard to grasp. They were all too real, though, and one small bite from them would turn you into one yourself. That was the main reason he and the others were holed up inside this old abandoned prison. The stone walls protected them against the mindless, unrelenting hordes of rotting creatures that were even now pounding against the walls with their fists.

However, time marched on for the living. A funeral was prepared for Chris this very day. For the most part, the majority of the refugee population didn't know the two men personally. However, they respected the way they had treated everyone in the camp as equals and had selflessly risked their lives for others. They had personally formed tight bonds during all the supply raids and zombie fighting, and all had benefited from the tactics and knowledge that they always gladly shared with anyone who asked. Those closest to them, Stephen and Dan, were affected the most. They had personally known, worked with, and treated each other as family for years. Dan was given a large amount of room to grieve. He had taken to working out his grief with his favorite relative, Jack Daniels.

A ceremony would not be performed for Mike, for his body had not been recovered. It was most likely totally consumed in the blaze that sent smoke and sparks spiraling into the air, which had been visible from the prison. Dan refused to admit that Mike was really dead and rejected any symbolic funeral for him until he saw the charred bones for himself. Stephen was sure that Mike was deceased, but seeing the raw pain in Dan's eyes made him agree to go back as soon as it was possible to look for any sign of his fate. He gazed out at the faint plume of smoke that came from the scorched remnants of the church where Mike had fought Kettle and ultimately where both had died in the structure fire.

He had spent the entire night standing guard over Mattie after she was cleared by the compound's medic. She had been moved into the huge RV Mike called home and where Mattie often stayed, and placed into the large bed. No one was to bother her while she healed physically and mentally from her ordeal. Stephen's dog Buddy had jumped onto the bed and lay at Mattie's feet, waiting patiently for her to awaken. She had not yet regained consciousness and had no idea that Chris was dead and Mike was missing and presumed dead. He stayed at her side for hours until he needed to get some air, and came up here to this tower to clear his head. Now with the rising sun, he tiredly made his way back to Mike's RV.

Once inside the bus, he pulled the window shades down so the bright morning light wouldn't awaken Mattie before she was ready. Wrapped securely within the soft comforter, she slept the sleep of the exhausted. Stephen watched over her, attempting to keep awake by going over mentally what they could have done differently that might have kept those two fools alive. Many times he broke down and tears filled his eyes. He refused to allow himself to weep like a little girl who'd lost his dolly. He opened the cabinet where Mike kept his spare firearms and took inventory of the remaining arsenal if for no other reason than to keep his mind off the fact that his dear friends were not coming back.

However, the inevitable weariness of being awake for more than twenty-four hours straight— and battling for his life for most of them— weighed heavily on his eyes. Unable to last much longer either physically or mentally, Stephen locked the outer door of the RV, lay down upon the couch and within seconds was snoring soundly.

*

Lewis scrambled to his feet, looking around for what had snapped him out of a fitful sleep. Standing frozen in fear, he heard the moaning and groans of more zombies closing in on his position yet again. Shaking with exhaustion, he was too tired to curse his luck and merely sighed. After he had shot that asshole cop Mike and escaped the blazing inferno that had been his brother's church, Lewis fled into the darkness outside the vehicle barrier that surrounded his dead brother's former stronghold. Now several hours later and after attempting to hole up in many different buildings, he once again was required to evade the unnatural, rotten flesh smelling creatures that were relentless in their pursuit of him.

He was in near panic when the first of the zombies began clawing at the cheap front door of the abandoned home he was in. He ripped open the rear door, and ran down the back steps just as more of the vile creatures spilled around the backside of the home from both sides. He jumped the backyard fence of the residence, which he knew would slow them down only briefly, and ran down the alley. Lewis hoped by crossing countless city blocks that he would lose them, yet no matter how far he went or how many times he tried doubling back, they eventually found him.

He knew the first thing he needed was a solid, firm structure in which to barricade himself. Then he needed a weapon, food and water. Without any of those he was doomed, for the zombies tirelessly pursued him. All the while he was running on fumes, and he desperately needed rest. Bursting out of yet another front yard, he frantically scanned up and down the street looking for familiar landmarks. Finding a sound brick house with windows set high off the ground, Lewis wearily stumbled through the sturdy iron wrought fence gate and secured it behind him.

As luck would have it, the front door was unlocked and the house appeared undisturbed from the infected creatures that were everywhere. The repulsive individuals seemed to be able to track living people somehow, and the fact that none were around was a good sign. Lewis closed the door and secured a heavy deadbolt before turning and inspecting his new home. Whoever the former owners were, they had left in a hurry, as most of their personal belongings were still in place. Family pictures lay haphazardly on the floor showing happier times with the smiling faces of three proud generations. Lewis kicked at the pictures out of sheer frustration over his present circumstances and then paused, taking a second to catch his breath and regain his composure.

After calming himself down, he swiftly checked the home for any of the foul smelling undead. Finding it clear, he checked the windows for signs of pursuit from the previous group of zombies. Seeing that, for now at least, the coast was clear, Lewis raided the pantry and cupboards for any food that might have been left behind. After the third bare cupboard, Lewis hit the jackpot. The former owner must have overlooked this section, for it was packed with canned goods and bags of dried beans and rice. Locating a can of Spam, Lewis eagerly sat at the kitchen table and devoured the canned meat like it was a juicy steak from a five star Chicago steakhouse. With his hunger taken care of for the time being, Lewis began barricading the windows using a hammer and nails to pound broken shelves and boards over the openings. He left the front and rear doors to be secured with furniture to allow for entry and exit. Unaccustomed to manual labor, and with a full belly, Lewis was rapidly growing more and more tired. He plopped himself onto the large sofa he used to help secure the front door and was fast asleep within seconds.

*

A loud crash dragged Mattie from a dreamless slumber. Not knowing where she was, she frantically scanned the room. Slow to gather her wits, she backpedaled herself clear off the soft mattress onto the floor. Scrambling out from the claustrophobic grasp of the blankets, she put her back to the small wardrobe closet gasping for breath. Gradually recognition set in. No longer was she imprisoned by the deranged sexual predator Kettle. No longer was she tied to a chair with her legs spread to be used as his personal sex toy. She was safely ensconced within Mike's luxury RV.

It's not a dream. They did come for me!

A familiar whimper from the bed got Mattie's attention and she looked back to the bed to find Buddy awake and wagging his tail. She sat on the edge of the bed and was greeted by a lick to her face and a friendly bark.

Breathing a sigh of relief and getting her hammering pulse under control, she looked down at herself and noticed that she was still wearing the Catholic school girl outfit that Kettle had forced her to wear. She stood and quickly tore at the clothing as if they were on fire and was soon standing there naked and panting as she stared at the outfit that was thrown onto the bed with disgust.

She opened Mike's wardrobe and picked through his slim assortment of clothing. Shaking her head at the selection she had to choose from, she finally decided upon a Lamb of God concert t-shirt and a pair of blue basketball shorts with a set of workout pants to go over them. She then made her way to his bathroom and prepared for a shower.

Mattie shook her head, this time at the lack of bathing options, but she didn't really expect to find feminine shampoos or soaps. The usual Head and Shoulders and Zest were all she found. Frowning at his lack of civilized selections, she got the shower running and was pleasantly surprised when hot water came from the tap. She scrubbed her skin almost feverishly, trying to physically wash away the mental touch of Kettle from her person while occasionally tearing up and sobbing. Even with Mike's poor taste in shampoo, she soaped her long black tresses into suds-filled lather several times and then rinsed it clean. The water temperature went from hot to lukewarm to downright frigid. Unable to take the now cold water spraying her, she turned off the water and climbed out. Taking a towel, she dried herself off and stared at her now cleansed body in the bathroom mirror. The difference a shower made was wondrous; what before was a tired, worn looking woman now appeared vibrant and alert.

Well, she'd slept in his bed, stolen his clothes and used all his hot water. So Mattie brushed her teeth with Mike's toothbrush and shaved her legs with his razor.

"I'll make it up to him," she said aloud with a mischievous smile.

Now that she felt renewed, she realized she was famished. Throwing on her commandeered clothes, she exited the bathroom to see if Mike was about and to locate some food he might have secreted away somewhere. Outside the small bathroom, she heard the sound of someone snoring like a saw cutting wood. Mattie giggled to herself quietly as she tiptoed over to see who was sleeping on the couch in the dimly lit cabin of the RV. Upon closer inspection she saw that it was Stephen. On the hardwood floor next to the couch was a stainless steel 1911 pistol which Stephen must have been holding and dropped to the floor.

That must have been what woke me up, she thought. The man even slept with his guns.

Shaking her head slightly in wonder, she quietly picked up the handgun and placed it on the nearby end table.

She returned to the couch, leaned over, tucked in the blanket covering him, and smoothed his hair back, then kissed him gently on the forehead. Standing upright, she pondered her fate for a moment. She knew that Stephen had been involved with her rescue. She just did not know how it came to be that one minute she was being molested by Kettle, and the next she was waking up in Mike's RV.

What was stranger was that she couldn't even remember how the fuck she got caught by Kettle in the first place. She rubbed the sore lump where she must have hit her head on something.

She was positive there was a fascinating story to be told, but she'd wait until they were all together so as not to hear four different versions.

Mattie went in search of something to snack on until Stephen woke up. There was no popcorn left from the other night, and after checking a few cupboards and drawers, she finally found a box of peanut butter flavored protein bars. Ripping open the wrapper of one, she took a large bite, and quickly her mouth scrunched up in distaste. Mattie looked at the protein bar with disgust.

"Yuck!" she said aloud. "He eats this crap?"

However, seeing there was nothing else to munch on, she valiantly managed to finish the entire thing. When she went to throw away the wrapper, she closed the cabinet door hiding the trashcan a little too loudly. Mattie heard Stephen groan as he started to wake up. She saw that he was now sitting up, and rushed over to wrap him into a big hug.

"Thank you for rescuing me from that horrible man, Stephen!" Mattie cried.

Stephen said nothing.

"I can't wait to see the rest of the gang and give each of them a hug."

At the mention of the others, Stephen froze. Mattie felt him do so and leaned back to look into his face.

"What is it, Stephen? What's wrong?"

Stephen avoided looking into her concerned face. He cleared his throat and attempted to speak a few times, and eventually managed to blurt out the bad news.

"Chris and Mike..." he started.

The look on Stephen's face made Mattie's blood run cold.

"They didn't make it, Mattie," Stephen whispered. "Chris is dead. Mike is missing. I'm so sorry."

*

I didn't realize that taking a nap in a grassy meadow could be so refreshing. The warm sunlight shining down wasn't too hot, just right for sleeping. The tall grass waving in the gentle wind made for a soft bed to lie upon.

What a perfect summer day!

Poke.

Still somewhat half asleep, I ignored the irritating feeling and eased back into the welcomed darkness of sleep.

Poke.

What the fuck?

Poke.

Cracking open one eye as I laid there with my hands laced behind my head, I stared at the largest crow I have ever seen perched on top of my backpack.

Poke.

It leaned over and smacked its beak right into my forehead.

Poke.

"Go away, bird," I said sleepily and shooed it away with my right hand. "Can't you see I am napping?"

The crow squawked, flapped its wings, rising to avoid my hand. When I shut my eyes again, it settled right onto my chest.

Poke.

My head, as hard as it was, was starting to hurt from the repeated strikes.

Poke.

I tried to hit it, and it lashed its beak forward into my right hand.

"Ouch, why did you do that?"

I sat up onto my elbows and sucked on the injured hand.

The enormous bird settled back onto my backpack, tilted its head and looked at me with one eye.

"You need to wake up!"

My eyes widened in disbelief. I laid there dumbfounded. Did this bird just...*talk*?

Poke.

"Stop that!" I tried to sit up.

The bird flapped its wings furiously and hopped back onto my chest. It grew to enormous stature and its weight crushed me back down into the grass.

"You really need to wake up, asshole!" it roared, and as I struggled for breath, its dagger-sized beak streaked for my eyes.

I turned my face away from the blinding sunlight that was shining through the door. As I did so, something struck me in the face. I cracked an eye open and looked up to see a fucking zombie pawing at my face with its fingers. When I passed out I had fallen over against the door, and the zombie must have been able to jimmy the door open just enough to poke me in the head with its fucking hand. It dropped to the floor, lapping at the small puddle of blood that leaked from the gash on my head to under the door outside.

Weakly, I pawed at my shoulder holster and drew my Colt Commander. Knowing that noise brought more of these damn things, I needed a way to muffle the blast a bit.

Seeing the zombie lapping at the coagulating pool of my blood gave me an idea. I smeared the barrel of the handgun in the blood.

"Hey shithead," I croaked.

The rotten fucker looked up at me and howled. I eased the gun barrel out the door. The dumb bastard couldn't help but take the bait, and it immediately began licking at the blood. When the lips of the zombie wrapped around the barrel like a cheap whore, I rammed the barrel quickly and violently down its vile throat and pulled the trigger.

The percussion was greatly diminished as I blew the back of the zombie's skull off with great effect. Smug with my ingenuity and sighing with relief, I shut the door and forced myself into a sitting position. Groaning in pain from my leg, I noticed that somehow I had wrapped an Israeli bandage from my bag around my right thigh at some point during the night. Looking at the blood soaked bandage, I dreaded seeing what the wound looked like. I really needed to take care of my injuries before infection and the ensuing fever set in. I unsnapped my "go-bag", dragged it out and onto my lap and took a few seconds for the black spots from my spinning vision to fade. Gradually I regained my strength enough to open up the bag and set out my meager first-aid supplies. A stitching needle and thread, some bandages and dressings, antibiotic cream, Tylenol, and a few alcohol pads rounded out my med-kit. Not much, but better than nothing. Grimacing with pain, I untied the dirty blood-drenched rag around my right thigh. My machete strapped to my leg got in the way, however. I noticed that the machete's sheath had a large tear. When I pulled the blade out, I could tell that whoever shot at me must have hit the metal blade with one of the rounds. The thick blade had reflected the projectile, and the fragmented round tore across the meat of my thigh instead of through it.

"Looks like I cheated Murphy that time," I chuckled.

When I removed the bloodied rag, I saw the fragmented projectile had ripped up my thigh pretty good. Luckily only one of the jagged tears looked like it needed stitches. I sighed. I really hated needles. I grimly and shakily managed to get some thread onto the slim piece of metal. I cut off a section of my pant leg above the injured part and psyched myself up for the pain. Taking a fresh bottle of water from my kit, I tried to clean the wound and remove any shrapnel the best I could. I knew that this wasn't the best use of my drinking water, but it was all I had. After drying the wound, I wiped the needle and my injured area down with a few alcohol pads. Wincing, I grabbed the two edges of the ragged thigh injury and jammed the needle through the meat. That fucking hurt!

Time to man up, pussy, and Mommy isn't here to do it for you.

Pulling the thread through, I jabbed my leg again and again. I cinched up the stitches tight, knotted it, cut off the excess thread and then looked at my handiwork.

Christ! It looked like I had just laced up my fucking boot.

I finished up by slapping a bunch of antibiotic cream onto the wound and wrapped it all with a large bandage and dressing. I also threw back a handful of Tylenol with a mouthful of cool water. I stowed my med-kit, struggled to my feet, and went about locating a mirror in this place. Judging by the looks of it, it used to be a small home unused by regular tenants for quite some time.

Finding the bathroom wasn't hard. I just had to follow the stink. Homeless people would find these empty homes and squat in them until someone kicked them out. If the water happened to be turned off, they shit and piss into the toilet anyway. At least the homeless vagrants hadn't been here for a while, with the zombie apocalypse and all. Trying not to vomit from the stench of human waste, I wobbled over to the stink, ripped the medicine cabinet door off and limped into the kitchen area with the mirror to work on my head wound. I frowned at the bloody visage staring back at me, I set to the task of cleaning the chunky blood off the wound. It looked worse than it really was. The injury wasn't that bad, head wounds just bled a lot. The bullet had skimmed across a section of my skull instead of carving a tunnel through it. An inch to the left and I would not be here today. After cleaning the head wound I realized that it really didn't need stitches, so I washed it the best I could and slapped a bandage over it. Good thing too, my hands were shaking from blood loss and fatigue so badly that I would most likely have stitched my shirt sleeve to my face.

I hauled an abused looking chair over to the mirror and sat my worn ass into it. Gingerly, I lifted my shirt over my head and pulled off the Velcro straps to my bulletproof vest and removed it. It was just as I had thought. I had cheated Death more than once last night. Whoever it was that ambushed my dumbass must have used a revolver, for from what I recalled six shots had been fired. One hit me in the middle of my back and as the impact spun me around, another round hit my knife/leg, two more struck the trauma plate in the front of the vest, the skimming headshot, and the last must have missed high when the recoil raised the muzzle. I touched the sore spots that lined up with the bullet slugs, and it didn't feel like any ribs were broken, just very sore.

I leaned back, exhausted, closed my eyes, and contemplated my next move. I needed rest more than anything and could not even think of trying to get back to the prison today. I would end up a tasty, if somewhat hard to chew treat, for any nearby zombie.

No, better to rest up today and try for the prison tomorrow. Settling into the most comfortable position the lumpy, smelly chair could give me, I quickly fell into a deep dreamless slumber.

*

Stephen could only take so much crying and sobbing before it started to get on his nerves.

Boy, does she have a lot of grief to bawl like that, he thought. *I miss them too, but guys obviously handle sorrow differently than women.*

"I got some things I need to check on and there's still hope that I can track down Mike. I'll let you get some rest," he said to Mattie, "and check in on ya later. Buddy can keep you company."

Stephen bolted out of the RV as another wail came from the back bedroom. The normal noises of day to day living were soothing to Stephen while he made his way past the clanking sounds of the makeshift machine shop and other different jobs that they had found for people to do. It filled him with pride to see how well things were going since their arrival. However, the minute he started feeling good, he would see the things that Chris or Mike had a hand in doing and it would bring the sadness back in full force.

Deciding this was as good time as any to check the fire ravaged old church for Mike's remains, Stephen double timed to his own RV and prepared a light backpack for his trip. He didn't want to drag others along, as they would most likely slow him down, so he grabbed his assault rifle, pistol and a shit load of magazines. Last he saw of the area it was heavily infested with zombies that had chased him all the way back. He jogged to the main gate, where he ran into Amber, who had been walking in the direction of his camper.

"How is she taking it?" Amber asked. "And how are you holding up?"

"She is taking it pretty hard," Stephen responded, "but she's been through a lot. I'm not too bad at the moment. Just got to keep busy with other things."

"Where are you going now?" she asked. "You look like you are about to start a one man war."

"I'm on my way to check on the guys outside the wall. Like I said, keeping busy."

"Well when you get back, let me know," Amber responded. "I can fix you up some dinner or something, help keep you company."

"That would be fantastic," Stephen said with a hint of a smile. "I'll let you know first thing when I get back."

They parted and Stephen reached the main gate. He gave Kleaner the same little lie of wanting to check on the corpse burning detail to make sure they were doing their job. By the time Kleaner figured out that the corpse burning detail was off today, Stephen was long gone.

Long before Stephen saw the charred ruins of the old church, he saw the smoke and sparks that crashed upward whenever a piece of wood fell into the smoldering shell. With no fire department to put out the flames, it had also consumed two nearby buildings and would probably continue to smolder for days. The church butted up against the elevated train tracks at the intersection of Ohio and Scott Street. Standing on the elevated tracks, he could see down into the smoldering structure. The entire roof was gone, and one of the thick outer walls had tumbled down. After Stephen lowered himself off the train tracks, he made his way around the outside of the building towards the back where he last saw Mike run to. The rear door was missing, burned away most likely, and he carefully entered the very hot interior part of the building. Stephen moved around the ruins, moving pieces of wood with still glowing embers and large piles of ash, looking for remnants of his friend's body. It wasn't long before he found a corpse. He had no way of knowing who it was. All clothing and damn near all the flesh had been devoured by the intense heat of the fire. All that was left was charred bones complete with a skull. The only way to verify the body was by DNA testing that was far beyond anyone's means these days.

What Stephen found near the bones was what sealed it for him. Partially covered in ashes were the burnt remains of what was a Mossberg shotgun. The same configuration that he helped Mike assemble, complete with the loose heat shield that Mike always bitched about. Tears brimming in his eyes fell onto the soot covered steel barrel as he picked it up and inspected it.

"Damn," he whispered.

He didn't have long to mourn, however, as his presence was detected by a nearby group of undead.

"You fuckers picked the wrong time to show up!" Stephen said, bringing his rifle on target.

16

November 1
Day 68

"They are both gone," Mattie gasped softly as she lay upon the bed hugging a pillow. "Chris dead and only God knows what suffering Mike may have had to endure. And all while trying to save me!"

Mattie had been faced with a rude awakening. After the horrible ordeal with Kettle and passing out, she did not know that Chris and Mike had been killed in the attempt to save her and the others. She now blamed herself in a large part, for if Jonas and she had not foolishly searched that building, she would not have been knocked unconscious and taken captive by Kettle's minions who ambushed them. The little she had pieced together from Stephen's accounts was that Jonas had also been knocked out when she was taken. She was then transported to Kettle's church where she was sexually molested until her rescue hours later.

Mattie explained to Stephen that she did not remember exactly how she was attacked and had only a vague recollection of being assaulted then passing out.

"If only I'd stayed with Mike and helped him with his stupid zombie trap, then none of this would have happened!" Mattie screamed, and punched the pillow she was holding.

After a time, she fell into a fitful sleep, dreaming of being a captive again and of times spent with Chris and Mike. She awoke some time later and then went in search of Stephen and Dan. The former she couldn't find. Dan, she was told, was in a nearby guard tower. Making her way to the top, she heard several gunshots followed by cursing like she had never heard before. She exited the stairwell into the observation deck, where she saw that Dan had been shooting zombies, and judging by the amount of shell casings, quite a few of them.

And he was drunk, very drunk.

An empty Jack Daniel's bottle rattled on the floor and stopped against a pile of empty cans of beer when Dan dropped it and grabbed for another thirty round magazine. Slurring badly while swearing, Dan finally was able to lock and load his fresh magazine. Mattie noticed he seemed to be having a bit of trouble, more than from just being intoxicated.

"What are you doing, Dan?" she asked as he looked through the optic of his rifle.

"Leave me alone, girl. I'm not ready for talking yet," he snarled back. "I got me some dead fuckers that need killing again."

Dan turned his sight back out into the hungry horde that howled outside the walls and fired his rifle repeatedly. The noise was deafening in the small room. He was not using the suppressor today.

Mattie then noticed the large wrapping on his left arm where his hand would be.

"Dan," Mattie asked, "what happened to your hand?"

"The correct question would be 'where is my hand', and since you insist on flapping your jaws, I might as well answer to get you to leave me be."

Dan stood upright, a bit wobbly, and faced Mattie. He let the rifle hang from its one point sling and stuck out his stump.

"I cut my fucking hand off after it got bit by a zombie. Right now, one of them is probably using it for a Scooby snack or something."

When the only reply was a horrified look, Dan looked out the tower windows towards Collin Street where more zombies made their way to them at a snail's pace.

"Chris saved my ass that day too, saved it more times than I am worth since this nightmare started," Dan said with grim determination. "Excuse me a second," he said, looking at her with a side glance. "You might want to cover your ears."

Mattie's hands flew to her ears while Dan sighted on a small group of undead and let the lead fly. It took him a full thirty round magazine to down the seven or eight creatures in the group. Several rounds would tear through their torsos without effect before their heads would snap back and cause them to collapse to the ground. Shortly after, letting the rifle hang again, he calmly reached into the side pocket of his cargo pants, pulled out a Pabst Blue Ribbon beer, cracked it open and took a long pull from the can. Grabbing his lit cigar from where it rested on the window sill, he popped it in his mouth and faced Mattie again.

"Now, pretty lady, I know you have been through a lot yourself, but nobody has come through this untouched," Dan lectured. "And I usually refuse to be the rebound boyfriend, but for you I'll ignore my own rule."

A look of outrage and embarrassment filled Mattie's face. She fled down the stairs, but not before calling him an asshole.

As her footsteps faded, Dan took another pull from the beer can. He crushed the empty can and tossed it into the corner and fished out another. Cracking the new beverage open, Dan chuckled at his brilliant move to shut her up.

He sat down to continue sniping and loaded a fresh magazine as new zombies that had gathered during his little rant got into effective range.

"Keep right on coming, fuckers!" Dan encouraged. "I got something for ya!"

After the latest group had been put to ground, and looking at the dimming sky, Dan realized he had better hurry if he was going to make the funeral proceedings that were prepared for Chris. He also was supposed to check in on the HAM radio tonight, making his usual contact with other similarly holed up groups. The prison was faring much better than most of the other groups and strangely, more and more of them hadn't checked in the past few days. Dan didn't like it. As if they didn't have enough to worry about. Now something was happening to the north, near Chicago, something that may be coming this way.

"I'll have to worry about that later," Dan decided and stumbled down the stairs and over to his camper to get cleaned up. Dan, who could be called a functioning alcoholic by some standards, actually cleaned up pretty well and was seated in the front row before it started.

Most of those in attendance at Chris' funeral didn't personally know the man, but all respected him greatly. He was one of the original founders of the prison compound, and every refugee here owed him that much respect to show up. Many women held their recently adopted little ones and whispered to them that a young man had died and that they should hope to be like him when they grew up. Men and women that he ran the raids with had tears in their eyes for their fallen brother. Many more of the single women were sad that a potential husband was gone, and from the looks of it, he had more than one of them on the line. Almost all were in attendance with the exception of the perimeter guards. Stephen, who had returned, accompanied Amber, who had her hands full caring for the baby that Chris and Dan had brought back. Mattie and Dan were in the front row, with Mattie surprised to find Dan only slightly reeking of alcohol.

An older, stately looking man opened the ceremony by declaring that he had grown fond of Chris while they passed their spare time playing cards and checkers. He said Chris was the guy who had rescued his family while on a supply run, and he was the reason why his family was alive.

All of the people in attendance openly grieved at the loss, all but one man. That man stood in the back away from view of most, away from prying eyes that would see that his face was filled with hate, not grief. Standing in the deepening shadows, Jonas shook with anger. He recently heard that these men saved the group of dirty whores, including Mattie, from Father Kettle's church, and then they brutally killed the saintly man.

How could a few men destroy an entire flock of God's children? How could it be God's plan when a good man like Father Kettle was cut down by these heathens?

After all the effort it took to capture Mattie, these barbarians saved her and in the process of doing so, destroyed all that he held dear within hours!

At least two of them died, Jonas thought, *and if I have anything to say about it, I will see them all dead before this is over*!

If anyone did see Jonas, they would think he was quietly sobbing in sadness instead of shaking with righteous rage before he walked away.

Stephen gave a short version of the rescue to the gathered audience, allowed anyone who wanted to say a few words to do so, and the service was soon over. The volunteer pallbearers picked up the closed casket and gently lowered it into the pit that they had dug outside of the church near the west wall. Stephen pulled the American flag off the casket and handed it to Mattie, who started to cry again. After a few more spoke quietly to Stephen, Mattie, and Dan, who stood by the open grave, several men grabbed shovels and began filling the pit. Dan helped dig, not caring that his having only one hand hindered more than helped. He stayed there shoveling until it was done and long after it was finished. The others touched his shoulder in sympathy as they left.

Dan finally came out of his daze, his remaining hand hurting from gripping the shovel handle. He dropped the shovel and looked at the fresh dirt covering his friend.

"I will miss you, brother," he whispered, "and so will everyone else. We even took the time to bury you when bodies are littering the streets and being burnt by the hundreds around here."

He made his way back to his camper that he had shared with his fallen friend.

Each of them looked for solace in their own way. They were not mourning just Chris because Mike was missing too. Dan worked on a twelve pack of beer, while Stephen cleaned his rifle and reloaded empty magazines as he visited with Amber. Mattie cried into her pillow softly. One by one, they each fell into a troubled, dreamless sleep. The night passed, and when they awoke, they knew that they had to go on without their friends and continue to live their lives.

When Stephen made it into the command center, he was asked by Casper when they planned on returning to the warehouse for the supplies and weapons that they found on his raid the other day.

"I don't know, Casper," Stephen said, rubbing the sleep from his eyes. "We need to get a raid crew together along with the vehicles to pull this off right."

"I can get started on that," Casper volunteered.

"But before we do, I need to go talk with Dan," Stephen said. "I have some news for him. I'll hook back up with you later."

Carrying a long object wrapped in a cloth, Stephen walked over to Dan's camper. He knocked and entered without waiting. Inside the camper, his nose wrinkled at the wave of booze and vomit stink that enveloped him.

"Good god, open some windows in here!" Stephen said while gagging.

He yanked the t-shirt off one of the windows and opened it up, allowing fresh air to enter. He located Dan's unconscious form covered in old vomit and surrounded by empty beer cans and empty containers of Spam.

No wonder he'd puked. What a combo. Stephen kicked the empty cans out of his way, grabbed the front of Dan's shirt and heaved him into a sitting position. Kneeling next to him, Stephen slapped Dan in the face.

"Dan! Wake up you salty fucker!"

After the shaking, yelling and slaps, he managed to get Dan to crack an eye open. Stephen grabbed a water bottle and upended it over Dan's head. Dan shot to his feet, sputtering and slamming into the walls, thinking he was under attack or something.

"Good morning, sunshine!" Stephen said loudly. "Glad you decided to join the living!"

Dan's face scrunched up with obvious hangover pain.

"Could you not shout please?" Dan asked in an unusual cry for sympathy. "I happen to be feeling a mite tender this morning, if you can believe it. You better have a damn good reason for waking my ass up."

He ripped off his soiled shirt and threw it in the trashcan, and reached into his duffel bag for a fresh one, all of this made more difficult by his missing left hand.

"No, I'm not happy to see you. That's my pistol," Stephen said, reading the caption on Dan's t-shirt aloud.

Stephen shook his head but said nothing and tossed the cloth-covered object he'd brought over to Dan.

Dan removed the cloth and saw the scorched, heat warped item it covered.

"That's what is left of Mike's shotgun," Stephen explained. "I found it near the last place I saw him, the church. Close by was a set of badly burnt human remains. I can't be positive they belong to Mike, but we can't sit here and think he's alive at this point."

Dan sat down. "Who else knows this?" he asked.

"It's just the two of us at this point," Stephen replied. "Nobody knows I went back to look."

"We need to keep this between us," Dan said as he nodded in understanding of the situation. "Mattie still has hope Mike is alive, and if she hears of this, it might push her over the edge."

"Agreed. Get rid of that shotgun barrel, and we won't bring it up again," Stephen said. He turned and left the trailer while hearing the cracking sound of another beer can opening behind him.

*

I felt like clown midgets beat me with baseball bats all night while I was asleep. I fucking hurt everywhere.

Even my pride hurts.

The slightest movement either sent a wave of pain and nausea spiking through me or made my joints pop like bubble wrap.

I took a few moments of heavy breathing to gather the energy to get up, and managed to get myself somewhat upright on my feet. A brief wave of vertigo made the room spin, and after I tamped it down, I hopped over to the crappy chair I found yesterday and fell into the seat.

Damn, I felt weak as a kitten. I reached up and touched my forehead. Fucking great. Now I had a fever.

I grabbed a handful of Tylenol and downed it with the rest of my bottle of water, tossing the empty down with the rest of the garbage on the floor. I reminded myself that I only had one full bottle left. I was going to have to make it last.

Luckily, I wasn't too far from the prison camp, but my current list of injuries and the unknown zombie factor might make a short trip into a long journey.

I figured I might as well get my ass moving. I hadn't seen any rescue parties looking for me, but had been unconscious for the most part.

Still, nobody had looked all that hard for me. It wasn't like I had been moving from place to place.

I gathered up my meager supplies and strapped my bag to my waistline, taking a few minutes to regain my breath.

Shit, I was going to need a crutch of some sort to help me walk.

Stumbling around the dumpy house, I located a closet rod that would work for a walking stick. The piece of wood was about six feet long and an inch thick, and looked to be made of oak.

Ready as I would ever be, I paused to look outside and saw that it was currently clear of the flesh biting bastards. I cracked open the door and saw that the zombie I killed yesterday was still there, smelly as ever, and I cautiously stepped over it out onto the porch. Holding onto the porch support pillars, I got ready to step down off the porch when I heard the low droning of an engine coming from above. It had been awhile since I last saw an aircraft, and I didn't know if I would ever see another. I scanned the sky until a large engine prop military plane came into view, slowly flying over the city.

The plane headed north toward the prison and disappeared from view.

Oh well, I couldn't do shit about it.

Limping and cursing, I began to make my way back to the safety of the tall prison walls.

17

November 2
Day 69

The sun overhead was peeking through the scattered clouds, and there was a mild wind coming from the northwest that made the surrounding trees sway to and fro slightly. Casper again went over the checklist he made for himself. Much of the manpower going on this raid would be first timers. That wasn't really a good thing, but most were going to be moving items, not fighting. He would be leading the raid since he was familiar with the location, with Stephen as second in command. Dan was staying behind, stating he had some work that needed looking into on the HAM radio. Mattie was recovering from her ordeal and was making herself busy speaking with and caring for the other women rescued from Kettle.

He did enjoy the quiet that resulted from civilization grinding to a halt, but that quiet was all too often shattered by the crack of a high-powered rifle or the moans of undead. Checking his watch, Casper saw that it was noon and time to get the show on the road. He signaled that he was ready to the gate guards, climbed into his truck, and waited for the few trucks in front to begin moving. The caravan wound its way southbound on Collins Street and then turned westbound onto Cass Street. They were delayed for a short time with a small number of zombies around Joliet Central High School. Something had drawn them to the area and they turned their attention to the convoy with a snarl. The crack of rifle fire soon cleared the problem, and the group moved on before others could arrive.

Shortly thereafter, the convoy of vehicles stopped at the

warehouse type residence that Casper had raided a few days before. While he and the rest of the raid members disembarked from their trucks, many just stood around staring at the neighborhood. Being one of little military training, Casper did not grasp the problem this posed. He was so excited about showing his fantastic discovery of supplies, that something as elementary as setting up perimeter guard escaped his notice.

"Come on, folks. Let's get these trucks loaded!"

Seeing Stephen nearby, he pushed his way to the front and motioned for Stephen to follow him inside.

"All the loot I told you about is inside, boss," Casper continued. "I can't wait to see your face!"

"Lead on, brother!" Stephen replied with a smile, his first since before Mattie's rescue.

The loud rumble of an airplane overhead made most of them stop in their tracks. Overhead and to the west, a large gray aircraft flew northward across town.

"That's a C-130 Army transport," Stephen said excitedly. "I wonder what they're doing out here? Maybe a recon flight of some sort. Doubt they're putting down anywhere close."

The ponderous aircraft flew north, and when it was nearly obstructed from view by buildings, they saw it circle back around then head north until out of sight.

"What do you make of that, Stephen?" Casper asked.

"Maybe they are done getting their asses kicked," Stephen remarked. "I'm glad to see they are still flying."

Casper shrugged. "Well we can't worry about what we don't know, so why don't we go get us some goodies instead?"

Entering the dark building, Stephen looked around at the dozen or so pallets of supplies stacked here and there on the warehouse floor. They looked to contain camping and hiking gear from various manufacturers.

One small pallet contained a dozen water filters. Another held enough medical supplies to outfit a small hospital. Many other pallets held an assortment of camping and military gear.

Stephen whistled appreciatively at the sight. "Wow, you weren't kidding," he said looking around.

"I know. It's crazy, isn't it?" Casper replied. "You haven't even seen the good stuff yet."

Casper briskly led the way into the dark structure with his flashlight lighting up the path among the numerous crates and pallets. When he reached a sturdy steel door, Casper turned the handle and pushed the loud squeaking door open.

He entered and moved to the side as Stephen followed and stopped in his tracks. The beams of their flashlights illuminated the windowless room, and Stephen's jaw fell open. Posted on a large bulletin board next to the door was a detailed list of everything that was in here, along with the companies, and even in some cases the countries, where the items were purchased or mailed off from. Next to the list, he found a phone tree of contacts. It appeared that the warehouse had served as a forward depot for a group of some sort. He scanned the inventory list, and several things made a low whistle escape him as he read it.

"Holy shit," Stephen remarked. "Some of this stuff is high end, well out of my pay grade."

According to the list, every member of the mysterious group owned one of the Polish Tantal AK-74's that were on a long wall rack. There were at a minimum twenty-five rifles, along with stacks of wooden crates containing sealed tins of Russian ammunition. There were about three crates of ammunition per rifle. Boxes that Casper said he remembered delivering contained hundreds of East German Bakelite thirty round magazines. This room also contained dozens more cases of military MREs.

"These guys were ready for war," he muttered, "and they didn't seem too worried about getting robbed or caught. I bet most of this stuff never went through Customs. From dates on a few of the shipping labels, it seems that most of the heavy stuff showed up not too long before everything went south."

The other equipment stacked on pallets made it evident to Stephen that the group felt something was coming and had requisitioned extra supplies and weapons for themselves and refugees they might want to take in. Similar to what was going on at the prison right now. Stephen scanned through the remaining list and was very impressed by the amount of firearms and ammunition it contained.

"You did a good here job here, Casper," he said with a grin. "This place is a goldmine! Let's put this shit to work!"

*

I was beginning to think that maybe I hadn't cheated Murphy's Law after all by surviving the gunshots and church fire. I think that fate is a cruel fucker, and intended for me to be injured and hurt like hell on purpose. Even though the weather was currently clear skies and cool breeze, I was sweating like a whore in church right now. As if Murphy planned it personally for my enjoyment, my nice easy walk back home to the prison was derailed when a group of seven howling undead stumbled out of the nearby tree line and took up pursuit of my ass almost immediately when I left the house. Altering my course to the east, the only luck I had was my current limping speed was slightly faster than the shambling pace of the zombies just behind me. The bad part was that *they* didn't get tired. The tapping of my makeshift walking stick and the dragging of my right foot was not nearly as loud as my ragged breathing.

I had only left twenty minutes ago, and I was already winded...from walking! The growing mob of undead behind me was motivation enough for me to keep going.

Taking a quick glance over my left shoulder, I saw that the mob had increased to about twenty-five. Unfortunately for me, some of the newcomers were somewhat quicker than others, and I had to pause momentarily and shoot several of them when they got too close.

I grabbed the water bottle in my bag, hurriedly gulped down a few mouthfuls of water, and seeing I had a bit of a lead, I quickly pulled out my battered can of Copenhagen tobacco to take what was a good chance my last dip of chew. When I opened the can I almost gave up, a look of pure horror on my face. I was out of chew!

"Goddamn...what else could go wrong?"

I chucked the empty can off to the side. Knowing that I had cases of it waiting in my RV almost had me damn near jogging to get back.

Scores of undead craving and howling for my flesh and blood behind me only managed to move me at a slow limping pace, but having no Copenhagen had me almost running in fear. My priorities are fucked up. I frowned at what was in front of me. Obviously Murphy hadn't forgotten about ways to make my life interesting. Another mob of undead cut me off on the road I was on. Cursing my luck, I veered off onto a side road and continued hobbling east towards Collins Street. All the while, my makeshift crutch made a frantic tapping sound as I fled the hungry fuckers behind me that now numbered closer to fifty. Grimacing in considerable pain, I pushed on, each step one closer to home.

*

Lewis was almost happy. He had spent the last few days in this brick home and not one time was his sleep interrupted by those damn zombies. Lying on the lumpy couch that barricaded the front door, Lewis mentally went over the loss of his brother and the revenge he took on that bald bastard Mike. A cruel smile that would have made Kettle proud crept across his face.

If only he'd had the time to hurt him more before he died. But that damn fire almost did him in as well.

"Now all I need to do is take out the rest of the glory hungry assholes," Lewis reminded himself aloud, "and their crappy safe zone will crumble just like ours did!"

Lewis stood and began pacing back and forth in the living room, plotting how to best bring this about. He always did his best work when he paced and thought through the answer.

Suddenly he stopped in his tracks.

Jonas was inside the prison! If he could get word to Jonas that he had an ally in Lewis, then he could use him to further his plans.

"Oh, this is perfect," he told the family in the large portrait on the wall while rubbing his hands together. "I can use that deranged killer to do all my dirty work and then make sure he gets caught in the act while I watch from afar! Who ever said politics wouldn't last past the fall of government?"

While standing there smiling over the many ideas and plots unfolding in his head, an odd repetitive noise gradually made itself aware to him.

Pausing with his head cocked to the side, he listened hard.

There it is again, he thought, frowning.

Moving from window to window, Lewis scanned outside for the weird sound. It was the loudest from the front of the house, and when Lewis looked out the window there, he froze in unbelieving shock.

Tap, tap, tap, tap…

A large, blood covered man with a shaved head was limping past the front of the house he was in, using a stick as a crutch.

Tap, tap, tap…

"No fucking way," Lewis whispered.

Face white with rage, he screamed. "I fucking killed you!"

Losing all control, he began clawing at the front door, forgetting the couch that was barricading it.

"I fucking killed you!"

With a great adrenaline surge, he shoved the couch to the side.

"I fucking killed you!"

Screaming through the window and shaking a fist at the retreating figure, Lewis was so focused on the limping figure that he did not see the giant horde of zombies that followed in his wake.

"No!" Lewis screamed. "You will not escape me again! You are dead!"

Grasping the door handle, Lewis jerked it open, screaming at his seemingly invincible enemy.

"You're dead! I killed you!" he shrieked as he ran out onto the porch and down to the street.

When he reached the street, Lewis abruptly slid to a halt as scores of undead turned their malevolent gazes on Lewis' pale face and howled as one for his pulsing blood.

"I killed…oh shit."

Lewis turned quickly when a chunk of the mob split off and gave chase like crazy fans chasing a celebrity. Scrambling back into the house, he almost got the door shut…almost.

Falling back from the combined weight of several animated corpses, Lewis crawled from the quickly filling doorway and got to his feet, running for the back door. Lewis didn't know it, but the sheer weight of the number of undead all trying to get to Lewis created a bottle neck traffic jam in the doorway. By the time the clawing and biting mass freed itself, Lewis had made his escape outside and into the neighborhood beyond. Inside the home, zombies shuffled from room to room, endlessly searching for the meal that was right in their grasp. A number of backyards away, Lewis seethed with rage and frustration.

He fucking did it again! Lewis thought angrily. The asshole just walked past and destroyed everything in his wake! This was the third time he had done this, and every time Lewis tried to kill him he failed.

"But how does he do it?" he wondered aloud as he climbed over another fence, putting as many obstacles between him and the zombies that doubtlessly were in pursuit.

"What could I possibly have done to be cursed like this?" he mumbled to himself as he ran madly through the neighborhood. He would need to expedite the plan to get Jonas on board and make these bastards paid, once and for all.

Knowing that he needed to get near the prison to make contact, Lewis took a parallel route to his adversary's stronghold, and since he was not wounded, quickly passed Mike's location. Lewis had never been much into physical fitness and was gasping for breath after the third block. He stopped to check on the zombies that had given chase. In the distance, Lewis could see the large group that was following him had turned and now were now flowing away from him, most likely heading back towards the big bald fucker.

"Good, hope they bite a chunk out of his ass," he said to himself.

Lewis turned back to the north and made his approach to the prison. When the mammoth stone structure appeared in the distance, Lewis found a spot to hide, wait, and decide his next move.

He needed to make contact with Jonas and stay out of sight. And stay clear of these damn infected bastards. No easy task.

Seeing a stand of trees near the prison and a large pile of burning objects with a truck near it, Lewis decided to get a closer look. After several minutes, Lewis finally made his approach without being spotted from the prison. The burning pile came into view, and Lewis observed that it was dozens of zombie corpses that someone had stacked up high and lit on fire.

If he could get word to Jonas and have him get on the burning detail, then they could talk face to face about what they needed to do to bring down the compound.

From what he could remember, the men who captured Mattie kept in contact with Jonas using handheld radios. They also had a camp nearby, probably in these trees, to run surveillance and keep in working range of the small two-way radios. Finding the camp didn't take long, and Lewis was rewarded with a case of bottled water and cans of ravioli. Greedily devouring the nourishment, Lewis watched the corpse burning detail work when the answer to his problem presented itself. One of the workers was talking on a two-way radio, and when he was finished talking, he opened the door to the cab of the truck and set the radio on the seat.

Using the billowing clouds of smoke coming off the corpse pyre as concealment, Lewis took a dirty shirt from the small camp and fashioned a mask similar to what the other workers wore, scrambled over to the parked truck, and hid behind it to catch his breath. Panting from the brief sprint, he stood to stare through the cab windows over to the men to see if he had been spotted. Seeing that he had not, Lewis breathed a sigh of relief and looked into the cab of the truck, spotting the radio on the seat. Quickly, while he still had the courage, Lewis opened the cab door and grabbed the radio from the seat. Again using the vast fire as a screen, Lewis made his way back into the wood line.

He tossed his mask to the ground and looked at the radio. Luckily for him, he was often involved in the communications between Jonas, the other men, and his brother. Lewis knew the channels that they used, and after turning on the radio and setting the frequency, it took only a few minutes for a reply.

"Who is this?" Jonas demanded.

"This is Councilman Lewis. My brother was Father Kettle," Lewis answered. "I need your help."

A few seconds ticked by.

"I was hoping that some of my Master's people had survived," Jonas finally said. "What can I do for you, Lewis? What has happened? The prison has been awash in rumors over the last few days."

Lewis told Jonas what went down in Kettle's stronghold, describing his brother's coldblooded murder as well as whom the killer was and his current predicament.

"I see," Jonas said with an air of confidence that lifted Lewis' spirits. "Now here's what we are going to do. Listen closely."

As Lewis listened, his current smile turned into a look of puzzlement and then into a frown as he heard Jonas' instructions.

"I want radio silence from here on out," Jonas finished by saying. "We will only contact each other on this channel every night around midnight."

At that, the radio went silent. Now that he knew he was not alone in his battle against those fucking cops, he felt much relieved.

*

Through the continuous stream of blood stained sweat running off my head, I could see the prison gradually getting closer. By the sounds of undead pursuit behind me, they were too.

Minutes dragged by with me thinking of nothing more than placing one foot in front of the other. The pain and exhaustion was starting make me hallucinate. I swore I heard someone screaming at me that I was dead a while back. I almost was, too, because I stumbled and damn near fell when I turned my head to look.

"Got to focus, take the pain," I grunted. "...need to get the anger burning."

Stumbling to the right to make my way around a stalled vehicle, I was brought out of my mental mantra by the shattering of glass next to me. Not slowing my pace, I turned my head slightly and looked to my left. In the middle of the spider webbed windshield was a nice big bullet hole.

"What the hell?"

The answer came a second later in the form of a rifle report echoing off nearby buildings.

*

Logan looked up from his high powered scope and glanced at Kleaner.

"Shit, I think I missed," he said.

"What?" Kleaner responded. "You make me sick. A kid could make that shot."

Logan stood up and set the rifle down.

"Are you nuts?" Logan argued. "That fucking ugly zombie that's in the front of the pack is damn near seven hundred yards away!"

"Move over, kid. Let me show you how it is done," Kleaner ordered.

After Logan moved aside, Kleaner bent over and picked up the .308 bolt gun and lined up the target after making a few adjustments with the scope.

"You might want to get a pencil and some paper and take some notes, rookie!" Kleaner stated as he steadied his aim.

His body jerked from the rifle's recoil as he sent his round downrange.

*

Step with left foot, place staff, drag right foot.

Step with left foot, place staff, drag right foot.

That was my entire world of focus right now. Plus the long list of injuries, the pain, the burning thirst and gnawing hunger.

And the now damn near one hundred hungry zombies that were gaining ground on me.

A loud buzzing insect flew right past my head, and before I could swat at the thing, I heard a meaty splat.

I glanced behind me quickly enough to see the zombie that nearly caught me from behind was on its way to the ground, missing its head from the bottom jaw up.

Again, a second later, the sound of a gunshot echoed from the prison.

"Wow, nice shot."

*

"Wow, nice shot," Logan said, watching with a set of binoculars, "but you missed the zombie with the stick."

"I wasn't aiming for that one," Kleaner lied.

"Bullshit, you were too," Logan argued. "You knew what one I was aiming for. Why would you pick a different one?"

"Are you calling me a liar?"

"Hell yes, you are a liar!" Logan roared, "And a terrible shot to boot!"

"Do I hear a challenge?" Kleaner asked.

"Absolutely! First to take out the zombie with the stick doesn't pull midnight guard duty for a week," Logan said, pulling a cigarette from his coat pocket.

"Deal," Kleaner said, shaking hands on it.

Logan grabbed the rifle back and steadied himself.

"Now don't you move, you ugly bloody fucker," Logan said while looking through the scope that lined up on the zombie's blood soaked head.

*

Great, my head wound had opened up again, and blood was running down my face and onto the front of my shirt. Gasping for air like a fish out of water, I took a breather for a second by leaning on a speed limit sign along the roadway. It was reassuring to know that the guys in the guard tower were taking out some of the zombies behind me. Any second I should be seeing a rescue party coming to save my injured ass.

Just when I began to move, I heard something slam into the metal sign above my head. Risking a quick glance up, I noticed a nice round hole in it, followed by the all too familiar retort of gunfire.

Suddenly my asshole puckered real tight.

Some jerkoff was shooting at me! I started waving my arms frantically, trying to let those assholes know I was not dead.

*

"You bitch!" Logan roared, turning to yell at his buddy. "You messed with the damn settings on the scope!"

Laughing at his buddy, Kleaner pushed Logan out of the way.

"Too bad, pussy, now it's time for my reward," he said as he looked through the optic. "Say... where did it go?"

Kleaner could not see the object of their wager anywhere. Scanning left and right he saw plenty of other targets milling around with a large chunk pouring onto a side street. Maybe they'd found a meal nearby. Kleaner held his shot. A night free of observation tower duty was huge, and he wanted to get a good night's rest. Settling in and getting serious now, he continued to look for the zombie with the stick that was covered in blood. A few minutes ticked by when the target came out of a different area, much closer than before.

"There you are, you disgusting flesh eating bastard," Kleaner said to himself as he squeezed the trigger.

*

Getting off the wide open road that led to the prison, I limped down a side alley with my group of undead friends behind me screaming and howling for a little taste of Nordic meat. I was running on fumes and even those were running out fast. I needed to get something between me and the horde dogging my steps. I cut through a yard and swung a little chain link fence gate behind me closed. It would only slow them down a bit, but I would take it. To further hinder their pursuit, I drew my pistol and killed the closest seven, causing a little more of a barrier for them to navigate. Doing a quick magazine change, I realized I was down to my last full one. If I wanted more I would need to reload them as I walked. Unfortunately I needed both hands to do this, but I could not walk unaided. I needed to use the staff and place most of my weight onto it while I dragged my injured right leg. It was either waste time loading magazines or put some distance between me and the mob behind me.

I chose to do the latter.

Now as I hobbled around the front of a home again in view of the prison, I attempted to hurry along, aware now that some asshole was taking potshots at me. Keeping an eye on the prison and not on what was in front of me was both bad and good as it turned out.

Bad, because as a police officer, you should always be aware of your surroundings, for shit always went wrong when least expected.

Good, because sometimes stupid shit would save your ass.

I did not see the beat up looking skateboard that was in plain sight on the ground in my path. As I set my staff on the ground and dragged my bad leg up, I stepped off and planted my good leg right onto the fucking toy. Naturally, my entire body flipped straight up into the air like a cartoon character stepping onto a banana peel, and I crashed down onto my back while the skateboard skimmed along the ground away from me. Assailed by waves of pain, I dimly heard the echoing and much louder bark of the rifle.

*

"I got him!" Kleaner whooped, pumping his fist in the air, thrusting his hips and chanting, "Eat it bitch."

Logan, refusing to admit defeat, ignored Kleaner and kept monitoring with the binoculars the hedge row where he last saw the target of their wager fall.

Right as he was about to throw in the towel and call it, he watched the wretched ugly zombie clamber back to its feet, still clutching that stick, and begin its stumbling limp towards the prison.

"YES! You missed him!"

"No fucking way I missed," Kleaner complained. "You saw him go down!"

"Look for yourself if you don't believe me," Logan said and handed his binoculars to the unbelieving friend while he scooped up the rifle.

"Don't worry, I might swing by with a few of those fine ladies that Stephen and Dan brought back the other night to keep you company while you pull my watch," Logan bragged, taunting his friend.

"I got something for you to pull, asshole," Kleaner growled back and scanned again with the field glasses.

Logan calmly let out a long slow breath and steadied his aim. "Shit, looks like it ran back into the surrounding buildings because I don't see him," Logan remarked. "He is a crafty fucker. Oh well. It will come back, and when it does, I will finish this wager once and for all."

*

Leroy had never been the most overachieving type person, and he would be the first to tell you. Before the current epidemic of flesh eating undead, he mostly sat around collecting a bullshit disability check from the government that came once a month. That, along with his dead mother's Social Security check, went towards supporting his alcohol and gambling addictions. He had lived in his deceased mother's home at the ripe old age of forty-two. With her house paid off, those government checks went a long ways. Sponging off of the generous taxpayers was his version of the American Dream.

Now all of that was shot to hell, and he had to actually do something productive or the current leadership here would throw his ass out.

"This damn supply run is bullshit," Leroy said to his buddy. "I'm disabled, ya know!"

His equally worthless buddy agreed. "Fuck yeah, definitely bullshit."

"What complete bullshit!" Leroy lamented. "These assholes have no compassion for the disabled."

Of course, his disability was a fake, but that was beside the point. Those assholes didn't know that.

Before the world turned to shit, he had found a "slip and fall" lawyer who had won a lawsuit for him involving a supposedly injured back and he was declared unable to work from that point on. He burned through the workman's comp check that he got within two weeks at the riverboat casinos located in Joliet.

What else was I going to use the money for? he once thought, justifying his behavior. He already had his parents' place to stay at for free. The hookers and drugs he had burned the money on were well worth it.

Now he was reduced to carrying some dumb shit's MRE cases and stacking them onto a truck.

"Where is the justice?" his friend snarled in contempt.

A couple of the others doing the manual labor were also of the same frame of mind as him and had been equally as useless in society before it all broke down. They agreed wholeheartedly that it was all so unfair how things had turned out. They managed to stay unnoticed since their recent arrival at the prison, but had been rounded up by the overeager Casper. Now, standing by the truck after another trip outside, Leroy waited until the others came out with an armload of goods.

"Hey guys," Leroy whispered looking around. "Let's go into a few of these nearby houses and look for some booze or drugs. I want to party, and a lot of these were drug houses. We just got to find the right ones."

"Hell yes," one of them replied. "I haven't got high since this zombie shit started. I sure could use a fix."

"Haven't seen any dead fuckers around either," another commented.

Keeping an eye on the others while pretending to be busy, they waited until nobody was paying attention and ran across the street to the rear of a large two-story home. Puffing from the quick sprint, Leroy waited to be sure nobody saw them leave and then forced open the rear door to the home.

"This's going to be fucking awesome!" he heard one say from behind.

They all ran into the home. None of them bothered to clear any rooms before searching. Most dangerous of all, none had brought a single weapon with them.

"Jackpot!" one of the men shouted, holding up a gallon-sized Ziploc plastic bag full of weed he'd found in a cupboard in the kitchen. The chorus of shouts of happiness was soon replaced with screams of pain.

Out of the rear of the residence, black men wearing assorted gang colors spilled into the room where they all stood. Normally gang members made people feel uneasy to be around, but when those same gang members were also blood craving, mindless flesh eaters, each sporting a large array of mortal wounds, it was enough to paralyze them with fear. The ensuing battle was extremely one sided. The only one to make it out was the short-lived ringleader Leroy, who used one of the men that came with as a "meat shield" to distract the zombie attacking him. However, Leroy also had three fingers bitten off, along with his right ear. Bleeding heavily, he ran screaming right back to where the bullshit raid was still in progress.

*

Stephen walked back out to his truck and looked over the inventory checklist on his clipboard he had brought with.

"I can't believe what a goldmine this place was!" he said to Casper, who was soaked in sweat from hauling the weapons and ammunition out, and was drinking heavily from his water bottle.

Casper was about to answer when a scream of pain and fear erupted from across the street. All heads swung to look at the source, a man who was supposed to be loading supplies, running at them from across the street. Close on his heels were several obvious zombies in full pursuit of their meal.

"What the fuck was he doing over there?" Stephen asked as he and the others opened fire on the encroaching undead. In the momentary confusion, nobody stopped Leroy until he was behind the other members of the raid.

After the zombies were quickly destroyed, they still didn't know a member of the raid had been injured. When a few noticed Leroy huddled near them, they approached to see what was wrong with him. They quickly found out. When they touched his back, Leroy abruptly stood and latched his teeth onto the face of one of them, ripping most of the man's nose and left cheek off. The others recoiled in fear, which only allowed Leroy to attack and injure three more souls until Casper walked up and shot Leroy in the head. Silence hung heavy over the area, only broken by the screams of the newly injured.

Casper calmly opened the cylinder of his revolver and replaced the spent shells with fresh ones. Snapping it closed with a flick of his wrist, Casper turned, and without remorse blasted each of the newly infected raid team members in the head with his side arm.

Casper was so fast dispatching the infected people that nobody near him could even react to stop him if they wanted to.

"This is why we have what we call a perimeter, people!" Casper screamed with rage. "When each of us refuses to do their job in times like this, people die! These men died because someone let this cocksucker out of our operating area without stopping him. Now others paid with their lives from his stupidity and our laziness!"

"Everyone back to their vehicles and load up!" Stephen ordered while loading a fresh magazine. "We leave now! All this noise is bound to get us a lot of attention."

The heavily laden convoy returned to their stronghold, the mood subdued and mournful. A few of the newly deceased had families back at the prison and would need to be notified of their loved ones' deaths.

The convoy turned onto Collins Street, which now was a straight shot back to home. Getting closer to the prison, the lead vehicle came across corpses in the roadway that they knew were not there on the way out. These were fresh kills, and it wasn't long before they saw the massive mob of grotesque undead clogging the road in front of him. Stephen stopped the truck, got out, and had the others behind him pull along both sides of his truck, forming a makeshift vehicle barrier. When the rearmost zombies in the mob discovered that more meals had appeared behind them, they howled for blood and scrambled to be the first to sink their rotten teeth into succulent flesh.

*

For the life of me I didn't know how I got myself into a clusterfuck like this. My leg was injured to the point I couldn't walk unaided, I had been shot repeatedly, almost died in a church fire, chased by hundreds of zombies, bleeding badly judging from the blood-soaked bandage on my leg and the stream dripping into my right eye, and now some jackass was trying to snipe me from the very place I desperately need to get to for safety and medical attention. Somewhere there was a divine entity having a gut busting laugh at my expense. At this point I could hardly remain conscious. The fall from the skateboard episode nearly made me black out. Falling onto my back reminded me how tender my ribs were from the .45 slugs that tore into my vest.

Each breath felt like someone was slipping a red hot knife between by ribs.

I dragged in a shallow breath and then coughed a blood-drenched glob onto the pavement. I didn't recall getting to my feet. I must have crawled a distance, for the prison was now much closer and loomed large, filling my vision as black spots danced in my eyes.

Sounds from around me now seemed faint, as if coming through a wall, like I had earplugs on. The silence was replaced by a roaring sound, kind of like a seashell held up to your ear. My pistol was empty, and I didn't have the focus or energy to reload, so I dragged out my machete and transferred it to my left hand, walking staff in the right.

With every remaining ounce of energy, I made my final push towards the prison, not caring if I got shot. I couldn't evade them anyways now.

I made it all of three steps when all of a sudden I found myself on the ground staring up at the sky, lying on my back.

Overhead on an electrical line sat a large crow staring at me with its beady eyes. I was in bad shape, and the prize for second place in this race wasn't something you get a trophy for.

*

By now, the yelling and shooting inside the guard tower had drawn a dozen spectators, all taking bets on who would kill the "stick zombie", as it had now come to be known.

Logan was heavily favored, judging by the odds being given.

"What the hell is it doing now?" Logan asked. "It just fell down without me even shooting the ugly bastard."

Several others threw out their opinions, none of them making sense.

For example, it couldn't be asleep because zombies don't need sleep. Another wondered if it was playing possum.

Either way it wasn't sporting to shoot a target that wasn't even trying to move.

"It wouldn't be fair," he said. Besides, there were plenty of other opportunities behind the ugly fucker that had sufficient sport left in them.

A loud barrage of gunfire in the distance tore through the afternoon air. Swinging the scope farther south, Logan discovered that it was Stephen and Casper's raid returning from their mission, and it was currently under attack from the mob that was led here by the target they had been trying to snipe from the tower.

"Hey guys, listen up!" Logan shouted. "For now, let's leave stick zombie alone and thin out the herd behind him. Stephen's convoy is on the other side and under attack from the remaining mob of rotten bastards."

No more needed saying as a dozen rifles were quickly stuck out of the windows, and the resulting sounds thereafter were deafening. Shell casings were now flying and bouncing all over the cramped observation tower room. Several people abruptly stopped shooting and started dancing jigs as hot brass went down the collars of their shirts or stuck to the bare skin of arms and faces, followed by cursing and shoving.

Down at ground level, the resulting combination was devastating. Chunks of rotten zombie flesh were shredded and ripped away by the hot lead that tore into them. Entrails from exploding chest cavities spilled onto the pavement causing other undead to trip or slip onto the ground. Limbs were severed and left twitching for a time, soon to be followed by the owners when they sustained head injuries.

The cross fire did the job, and all that was left was the mop up duty of walking among the corpses to find the ones that were not fully dispatched. Stephen picked out a group of five seasoned men to do the work, and as they made their way through the piles of dead meat, he got in his truck and drove over the squishy corpses directly towards the prison. It was a bumpy ride, and he quickly broke through to the other side. He slowed to a stop when he saw the most unusual zombie to date. This one was crawling on hands and knees towards the prison. It had a long wooden stick in one hand and was dragging a machete attached to the wrist by the safety loop of its other hand. Its head was wrapped in a blood soaked rag and it was dragging its right leg behind it as it crawled weakly away.

Putting the truck into park, Stephen got out, wanting to get a better look at this ugly looking bastard of a zombie before he killed it.

He had seen many undead wearing tool belts and items of their former professions before becoming undead, but never had they actually been *carrying* the items.

He grabbed his two-way radio, slid it onto his belt and drew his pistol. Stopping in front of the great blood-covered creature, Stephen watched in confusion as it gradually become aware that he was standing in front of it. Instead of gnashing its teeth and trying to bite at him, Stephen was surprised when it fumbled for and finally gripped the heavy blade.

Stephen's face went blank with shock, his mouth hanging open.

The zombie stared without seeing, swaying from side to side.

"Bout fucking time," the bloody figure said roughly.

Recognition flooded Stephen. His friend, who he thought was dead, was actually alive!

He was numb with shock as Mike's eyes rolled up into his head and he fell over onto his side unconscious. Stephen snapped out of it and lunged forward, pulled Mike into his arms and dragged him back to the truck. He frantically opened the tailgate and with adrenaline induced strength, tossed Mike's limp form into the truck bed. He ran to the cab, got in and slammed it into gear, racing for the prison.

"I have a wounded man down here!" he yelled into the radio. "I want every available medic ready to work on him, and get those fucking gates open now!"

The speeding vehicle screamed through the gates while they were still in the process of opening and lost a mirror on the passenger side in the process.

When Stephen slid to a halt in front of the medical trailer, a team of people with varying medical knowledge had already formed up outside the trailer. Within seconds they had transferred the wounded man from the truck to inside where they could better treat and assess his various injuries. Outside the trailer, Stephen frantically paced as he heard shouts of instructions and orders given inside. He couldn't stand to lose his friend after he got him back. And just when he had finally came to grips that he was most likely dead.

From behind him, he heard heavy footsteps crunching in the gravel.

"Hey brother, we heard you on the radio," Logan said as he and Kleaner walked quickly towards him. "Who was the injured person you brought in?"

"You will not fucking believe this!" Stephen said excitedly. "It was Mike! He's fucked up pretty bad, though. I found him outside the prison walls crawling on his hands and knees with a damn stick in his hands!"

Logan reached into the truck bed. "Y-You mean he was using this stick right here?" Logan asked, grabbing the staff.

"Yes, that is it," Stephen said nodding his head. "Oh shit. I need to tell Dan and Mattie that Mike is alive!"

Stephen grabbed Logan's arm and pointed at the trailer. "You two stand guard. I have to go tell them the good news!"

Stephen hurriedly ran off to tell the others, and Logan looked knowingly at Kleaner, whose face was white with dread.

Holding the stick in his hands like it was a live snake, Logan looked over at Kleaner. "We tell no one what we were trying to do from the tower," he whispered. "No one."

"Deal," Kleaner croaked.

*

Jonas stumbled slightly and dropped his radio. He could not believe what he just saw. The unbeliever, Mike, had been found badly wounded but alive. That asshole Lewis had failed to mention that little nugget of information. Jonas now stood there clenching and unclenching his fists. *What the fuck does it take to kill these assholes*?

The sound of his stumbling and the radio clattering on the pavement garnered the attention of the big man, Logan, who tossed a long piece of wood back into Stephen's truck and started walking over to him.

"Are you alright there, mister?"

Jonas shook like a dog to calm himself, then bent and retrieved his radio he had dropped.

"Yeah, I'm fine. I was just shocked is all," Jonas answered. "The only ones I have seen come back from the dead have been bitten. Are you sure he isn't infected? He sure looked like one of them."

Logan cast a sidelong glance at Kleaner. "Yeah, we kind of thought that too," Logan replied, "but we were wrong. He isn't infected, just beat up pretty bad."

Jonas stood there trying to figure out a way he could use the distraction of the man's miraculous survival, but he was interrupted by a woman's scream. Jonas whipped out his razor sharp knife in a blur as Logan and Kleaner whipped their assault rifles up to the ready position. From the inner circle of RV trailers and campers, a woman was running towards them. Kleaner moved to intercept the woman and was knocked down from a solid right hook to the jaw by Mattie, who was not to be denied. She stepped over Kleaner's groaning form and disappeared inside the medical trailer. Logan chuckled at his friend's misfortune, let his rifle hang from the one point sling and looked over at Jonas standing there with naked steel in his hand.

"Nice knife. Looks sharp," he complimented.

"You have no idea," Jonas said, sheathed the blade, spun around and stalked off in the opposite direction, needing solitude to think about the day's revelations.

First he'd been contacted by the brother of his dead mentor requesting a meeting. Then the big bastard Mike showed up very much alive after Lewis assured him that he was a dead man.

It appeared his appointed quest was not derailed after all with the murder of the Father Kettle. An evil grin appeared on his face.

No, it isn't over... it's just beginning to get interesting.

18

November 2
Day 69

Dan stood like a statue, staring at the large map they had erected showing each group of survivors that they made contact with using the HAM radios. His ugly facial scar twisted like an angry snake as he scowled with unease at what was beginning to unfold. The map had pins stuck in each area representing the location of survivors. The problem now was many of the groups no longer made contact with him at their designated time and channels. It first started early on, with the retired naval veteran Phillip in Chicago. He and his people were overrun and killed by waves of undead inside the city.

Did that mean the others were destroyed in the same manner?

Where there should be a pin, the spots that no longer were in contact had a large 'X' with a date of last contact next to it.

Each successive 'X' on the map crept south and spread out according to the listed dates. Many of the groups had reported a spike in the number of zombies prior to losing contact. Others had been facing radio or power source issues.

Dan was now staring at a newly added 'X' that he had not seen before. It was listed as today's date.

"Hey, cupcake," Dan said to the Latino woman currently manning the radio desk, "is this date correct?"

The woman scanned her log entry chart and replied, "Yes sir, they did not respond at 1600 hours yesterday or today as previously planned."

Turning back to the map, Dan told her not to call him sir and began stroking his chin until he realized he actually *wasn't* because that hand had been amputated, and quickly switched arms.

This latest contact lost was south of Oakbrook, a fortified position with over a hundred survivors. His eyes followed the marked highways and realized the need to get some eyes up there and see what was going on firsthand.

"Whatever it is, it's coming this way," Dan told the woman as he made radio contact with the much closer Bolingbrook and Romeoville safe zones.

These safe zones, just as the prison was, were not the FEMA camps, but small groups of resourceful individuals who had banded together for survival. They had both seen the C-130 that had flown over the area and told Dan that it seemed to acknowledge their presence. Dan wanted to know if they had seen or heard anything from the north or east. They had not but did confirm the reports from graveyard shift guards that a large fire was burning in the direction of Chicago. It appeared that the whole city was engulfed in an uncontrolled fire, burning to the ground. Dan told them to be extra careful and report any changes in the area around their perimeters, relaying his growing concern.

When Dan finished his conversations over the radio, he exited the command center for a smoke and some fresh air. Everyone's spirits had been lifted by the unexpected safe return of Mike, and Dan lit his third celebratory cigar. From inside the safety of the prison walls, many observed and heard the wailing of hungry undead filling the darkening landscape like a marching army of ants. The earlier gunfire and slaughter had gathered new shambling bodies in varying states of decay, each one sporting different repulsive wounds. Some suffered from simple little bites that made it hard to tell it was a zombie, only identifiable by its weird gait when walking. Others had horrible injuries such as missing arms or legs. Others had ripped open chest cavities with entrails dragging in the dirt and asphalt behind them as they walked endlessly around the prison, stopping to repeatedly beat their fists on the thick stone block walls.

The guards were ordered not to waste ammo on groups this size. When these situations arose, the men fired up the front end loader and the huge dump truck with the V-plow attached to the front. Those machines were used to crush the monsters into the dirt. Those same machines were then used to scrape what was left into the corpse burning area for disposal. It was quite sickening to watch, however it was a necessary chore.

*

Miles to the north and east of Joliet, a massive army of undead was being driven from Chicago by flames and hunger, and was pouring out into the surrounding suburbs. They flowed like a cloud of locusts that spread out in all directions, consuming everything living in its path. This was no small horde, but a mass exodus several hundred thousand strong and growing. The moans coming from the dead could be heard from a mile away. Already, numerous small holdouts of humanity had been swallowed with little advanced warning. A group of survivors near Oakbrook, Illinois, were overrun before being able to make radio contact with the Joliet group.

The Oakbrook group had up until this time mostly relied on stealth to avoid the undead and had only a defensive perimeter consisting of a chain link fence. Their sentries were woefully unprepared for the ravenous wave of undead. Before most of the survivors could even get to the fence to assist with repelling the undead invaders, the inadequate barrier was crushed by the weight of thousands of undead. When the person in charge of the radio left her assigned post and ran towards her husband for safety, she neglected to get on the air first to warn other groups of survivors to the south. Sadly, her husband was being devoured alive on the perimeter. She was too late to save him or herself, and they both joined the ever expanding horde of the undead on its relentless march.

*

Outside the safety of the prison walls, all was not going very well for Lewis. He was currently stuck in the limbs of a small tree. The tree was not very thick and bent dangerously close to the grasping hands of the creatures that surrounded him below.

Again he cursed that piece of shit former cop Mike; that man nearly got him killed. He added that as yet another reason to kill him and all he held dear. He still could not understand how that asshole had survived. He raised his fist at the formidable prison walls and screamed his rage, and was nearly dislodged from the thin branches for his foolishness.

The deafening chorus of the moaning wretches below him rose in level as the fingers of the zombies below him, for a moment, brushed

Lewis' feet.

He screamed at them in fury and kicked at the hands of the taller ones, knowing in the back of his head that the more he shouted and struggled that it would only bring more of the wretched creatures.

He had a most spectacular view earlier when he saw Mike struggling to reach the walls of the prison. Each time the bald fucker fell to the ground he cheered with glee, but then would curse when the big jerk struggled back to his feet. The last time he fell and remained down, Lewis could barely contain his excitement as the big mob of undead closed in. He stared in disbelief when the men and women from a returning raid party arrived just in time to slaughter the infected fuckers.

After several minutes turned into an hour of ranting, Lewis realized with alarm that scores of undead were now showing up and converging on his location. So thick was the press of bodies that he had no choice but to climb the tree in which he now was stuck. The little tree swayed back and forth as the horde pushed against it, but the mob surrounded it. As the mob pushed from one side, others opposite them pushed back against it, somewhat neutralizing each other. The result was the swaying of the entire tree. Lewis clung tightly to the trunk as the night wore on and prayed fervently that it held out until morning when he could try and escape.

The final bits of light faded, and Lewis looked down into the howling sea of rotten flesh grabbing at him and countless sets of gnashing, yellowed, cracked teeth.

He scrambled as high as the little tree allowed, tucking his feet up under him and gripped the branches tightly.

It was going to be a long night.

19

November 5
Day 72
Cotter, Arkansas

Matvei glanced warily into his driver's side mirror, not liking what he saw. The warning on the mirror advising that objects are closer than they appear didn't make him feel any better. In his wake was an ever growing mob of infected. Matvei was trying to cross the White River in northern Arkansas, and had been forced to backtrack, all the while picking up his ghoulish horde. He estimated their current strength at a hundred, minimum. The modern highway bridge on 62 was out, an entire span removed by what looked like an explosion, and after checking the map, he discovered his only alternative was an older bridge to the south that ran right through the small town of Cotter.

Now, with the distinct and nearly one hundred year old bridge looming ahead, his path was littered with destroyed cars. His pace was slowed to a crawl, allowing the slow but never tiring infected to keep pace. The bridge itself looked intact, with only a few disabled cars sitting on its deck. The last thing Matvei wanted was to have to leave his truck on the west side of the river and continue on foot. On the other hand, up on the bridge would be a bad place to get cornered, and he didn't know what dangers might be lying in wait on the other side. Weighing his options as he approached, Matvei caught movement up ahead. It looked as if survivors were up on the bridge, and a man was trying to push a stalled truck up out of the traffic lane. Matvei had cheated death many times in combat by making the correct decisions quickly, and once again he went with his instinct.

Deciding not to try and double back, he eased his truck up onto the bridge and wove his way around the first set of obstacles. The bridge then opened up for a short distance, allowing him to put some precious distance between him and his pursuers.

Once they caught up and started out across the bridge, he would be sealed in. There was no way out but forward.

Matvei slowed his truck as he approached the man, who was struggling to move the stalled truck. It was wedged between the railing and a school bus that was rolled onto its side, blocking both lanes. Matvei instantly realized that the truck had to be moved. A third vehicle was sitting directly behind the wedged truck, and Matvei deduced that it must belong to the man. It was a station wagon loaded to the hilt with gear, along with two hysterical women in the front seat.

Matvei pulled to a stop, sizing up the man on the road. He looked middle-aged, balding and slightly overweight. He wore an older set of woodland camouflage Army fatigues that looked like they might have fit him twenty years and forty pounds ago. The man looked spent.

"We don't have much time," Matvei said as he exited his truck, motioning back towards his pursuers. "Where we at here?"

The name Allen was stitched on the man's breast pocket, and his eyes widened with fear when he looked back to the west. The screams coming from his station wagon grew even louder.

"That's my wife and mother-in-law in the car, along with my newborn baby girl in the back seat. We're trying to reach family up in Kentucky, and this is the only way over the river. I broke the steering column in the truck and managed to get it into neutral, but I can't get the wheel turned and push at the same time." The man seemed to be growing more desperate as he spoke. "My wife is having a full blown panic attack and is no help whatsoever. Her mom is even more worthless."

Matvei hadn't noticed the baby in back, but now heard her start to cry through the open driver's window.

"Get behind the wheel," Matvei ordered, ignoring all the commotion. "I'll push, now hurry."

The man did as he was told. Matvei looked back again and was dismayed to find that the infected had already significantly closed the gap. There wouldn't be enough time to move the station wagon and try to push the truck with his vehicle. Matvei also didn't have the ammunition to knock them down, so this *had* to work. He dug in his legs and pushed with everything he had.

"Cut it harder to the right!" he cried, his arms straining under the weight.

The front bumper of the truck scraped against the guard rail as it moved ahead. The incline was about level by this point and Matvei gave the truck a final heave, which cleared enough room in front of the bus for him to pass. Unfortunately for the man behind the wheel, the truck came to a stop with its driver door wedged against the railing, preventing it from opening. The passenger door had been damaged in the wreck, and wouldn't open. Matvei watched him struggling to free it.

Matvei realized he was out of time, and turned to his truck.

He estimated he had just enough time to reach it, and his estimations proved correct as he slammed his door seconds before the first infected began to tear at it. Matvei found himself face to face with a grotesque figure, its teeth snapping against the glass, dead eyes filled with hate. Throwing his truck in reverse, he slammed into the undead crowd, smashing several of them into the ground. The women in the car in front of him were now screaming so loud they could be heard above the roar of the zombies. Matvei coldly steeled his heart to what must be done. He lowered the shifter into drive and punched the gas. The station wagon blocked his only avenue of escape. He braced for impact when the brush guard on his truck slammed into the car, sending it through the guard rail. For a few seconds it stayed up, perfectly balanced. Then the infected were again clawing at his window and he pushed forward without mercy. The station wagon careened off the bridge, screaming grandmother, mother, baby and all, eighty feet down to the rushing water below.

Matvei quickly navigated the breach and unexpectedly slammed directly into the man on the other side, just as he was crawling out of the window of the truck. He bounced violently off the hood of Matvei's truck and flew over the roof, landing motionless in his wake. Matvei only glanced briefly in his mirror before speeding to the safety of the shore ahead.

It was them or him, and he didn't want to die today.

20

November 5
Day 72

Muffled voices made me twitch slightly as my subconscious tried to kick start my brain into full awareness. The dark void I was submersed in felt like a sensory deprivation chamber, cozy, warm, and dark. The faint sound of those voices sent ripples out into the darkness like tossing a stone into water. With those ripples came twisted versions of remembrance. Horrible visions of loved ones, long since dead, haunted my dreams. Gouts of blood rained down upon the images in a spray of sticky crimson. The visions laughed, and I watched them die time and again. Mercifully, the darkness began to drag me down again, and I eagerly looked forward to the oblivion descending upon me. Just as the blackness tried to pull me in, the horrible visions thankfully beginning to fade, I heard the voices again. The more I tried to listen to what was being said, the more I tried to recognize and understand the voices, the closer it brought me to consciousness.

Not one of my better ideas.

I gasped in sharp agony when consciousness slammed into me like a car hitting a telephone pole. I hurt so bad that I longed for the blessed darkness to return, which of course it didn't.

Well I can't be dead. I hurt too damn much.

Groaning in pain, I cracked open an eyelid slightly and looked around. I was in a large bed that took up the majority of a small room. I wanted to get a better look around, put faces behind the voices. I turned my head a tad, also not a smart move. The tight muscles in my neck caused the bones to crack loudly and a jolt of pain rushed up into my skull. My exhale of pain caused the noisy bastards near me to stop their conversation and look over at me.

"Look, he's awake!" a woman exclaimed loudly.

Suddenly the small room was filled with shouts of happiness and relief. Someone roughly pulled me into a hug, and before I could croak out a cuss word in protest, I felt some wetness on my shoulder. Whoever it was smelled good. Damn good.

Recognition slowly dawned on me that it was Mattie and that she was crying, sobbing out her relief and stress onto my sore shoulder, but damned if it didn't feel fantastic. I looked up at the other two, Stephen and Dan. They stood at the foot of the bed with huge grins on their faces. I started to ask where Chris was when I suddenly remembered the tragic sacrifice he made during Mattie's rescue.

Stephen walked around the other side of the bed and gripped my other shoulder.

"You look like shit, brother, but considering what you went through, it's a miracle you're alive," he remarked. "Besides, you always did look like shit, so it isn't a big drop in the beauty department."

I chuckled a bit and felt a sharp pain in my side. Wincing from the agony, I gripped my ribs and groaned.

Stephen now had a serious look on his face. "Take it slow, Mike, you have two badly bruised ribs, most likely from the gunshots your vest stopped."

Mattie let go of me, eased me back into my pillows, and looked at me sternly.

"You've been in and out of consciousness for three days," she said with a frown. "You also had a fever which finally broke today. We've all been worried sick."

"I even cut back on my drinking," Dan volunteered.

This made me chuckle again while Mattie scolded Dan for his remark. Sitting there on the bed, I began to take stock of my injuries. Feeling my head, I could tell that I still had a bandage above my eye. My left arm was wrapped in one as well. I dimly remembered that my shirt sleeve had caught on fire from the church blaze. The tight wrap around my torso protected my injured ribs. Continuing my body scan, I saw the large bandage wrapped around my right leg. My knuckles on both hands, while not bandaged, were scraped up good enough to have half-healed scabs on most of them.

Stephen, seeing me look at my wounds, started filling me in on the extent of the damage.

"You were half dead when we found you, bro. Like I said, you're lucky to be alive. You already heard about the ribs. You're also sporting a nasty leg wound that you apparently tried to stitch up yourself."

"Real shitty job of stitching it too, you dumb bastard," Dan chimed in with a smirk. "It looked more like you were knitting a sock than closing a wound."

Too tired to argue, I gave him the finger.

"Anyways, the medics said you damn near bled out," Stephen continued. "If our friend Dan here had not had the same blood type as you to give you a transfusion, you might not have made it."

I looked back towards Dan, now noticing the small bandage on his arm.

Thinking of all the trashy women Dan had been known to associate with, I tried to be calm, but the horror in my eyes had to be clear as day.

"You mean I have his blood swirling in my veins?" I asked weakly. *Maybe dying would've been better*, I thought after not getting the answer I wanted.

Stephen chuckled at my discomfort. "You also have a nice concussion from the head injury along with the assorted bumps, bruises and burns," he concluded with little sympathy. "In short, you look like shit."

Dan, who looked like he was getting ready to leave, gave me some caring, inspirational words to help me recover.

"Pussy," he snorted and stomped out of the cramped bedroom of my RV, but not before I saw the telltale signs of a smile on his face. Ah, what good friends I have.

"You feel good enough to fill us in on what went down at the church, Mike?" Stephen asked hesitantly.

My eyes drifted closed as I tried to picture what happened. It was kind of cloudy, but my memory was clearing by the minute.

"First, I would like to know how Mattie got caught. What happened when Kettle's men grabbed you, Mattie?" I asked.

Mattie frowned, dredging up the bad memories of what happened. "I have been having a hard time putting it together myself, Mike. From what I remember, I walked into the back room of that store with Jonas and was jumped from behind. Someone was waiting behind the door and grabbed me." She stared down at her tightly clench hands. "There were other men in the room, and I think, yes, they must have also attacked Jonas. I did manage to get a shot off at one of them before they knocked me out. When I woke up, I was tied to a chair at Kettle's church. I really cannot remember much from them hitting me in the head."

I saw that she had a nasty purple and yellow bruise on the side of her head and that talking about the ordeal was getting her upset. Stephen must have sensed it and quickly steered the story back to me. Taking a second to clear my head, I fought off the drowsiness.

"After I handed Mattie off to you, I went after Kettle," I said wearily. "I found him in the back of the church bleeding from one of the rounds you sent his way."

Mattie had picked up my left hand as I explained the events that transpired.

"What happened after that Mike?" I heard her ask.

Without even realizing it, I had started drifting off to sleep again. I opened my eyes slightly and looked into her deep brown eyes that always seemed to hypnotize me.

Smiling weakly, I whispered, "You don't need to fear him anymore. I broke that sick fucker's neck with my bare hands." I shifted and grimaced from the pain. "But like a damn rookie, I was so focused on him that I didn't check my surroundings and someone, I don't know who, ended up using me for target practice."

Now the heaviness of my eyelids was dragging me into sleep, and I heard her whisper, "Thank you".

Before I went under, I smirked slightly and whispered sleepily, "You owe me."

*

Jonas sat near the window of his camper and watched Stephen exit that asshole Mike's RV with a smile on his face. Dan had done the same thing minutes earlier.

Those damn bastards just refused to die! He lowered the binoculars. Every damn plan came up short. Jonas felt like that coyote always chasing the roadrunner.

He paused in his train of thought...

Well not really, for the youngest of the five, Chris, was currently worm food thanks to the assistance of a shotgun blast to the face.

Thinking on it hard, Jonas realized that actually most of the small group had been severely traumatized at some point.

Chris was dead, Dan lost a hand, Mattie was kidnapped and supposedly sexually assaulted, and Mike was literally almost beat to death. So all of them except Stephen and his fat beagle.

Stephen must have had a guardian angel watching over him. The worst he had to deal with was a bum knee weeks ago that seemed to have healed up well.

"But all of that will soon change," Jonas muttered. "I have a little idea that might change their mind on what pain truly is."

Pulling out a small scrap of paper, Jonas began to list certain items he needed his newfound ally Lewis to acquire. How the spineless bitch acquired them was not his problem, Lewis had better come through with what was needed. Finishing the list, Jonas pocketed it for his next conversation with Lewis.

He stood and stretched, full of restless energy, drew and fingered the edge of his ever present blade. Grabbing a large piece of wood covered with pockmarks, he placed it upright on the counter against one end of the trailer and then walked to the other end. Spinning in place, Jonas' hand was a blur. A split second later he was rewarded with a "thunk" sound which revealed his dagger quivering in the wood. Pacing back to the wood, he wiggled the blade back and forth to remove it. Returning back to the opposite end, Jonas spun and launched his blade into the scarred chunk of wood.

Grinning now as he pried the weapon loose, Jonas pulled up his shirt sleeves and tested the edge by drawing it across his left wrist. The extremely sharp blade parted the old scars that crisscrossed his wrists like paper. Jonas stood there with blood welling from the cut, cleaning the blood off the blade with a swipe on his pant leg. The pain of the flesh wound made his mind focus.

His uncertainty was banished.

His anger and hatred stoked white hot with clarity.

Now who shall be the next of the little group of heretics to die? he thought, staring out the trailer window. With Father Kettle murdered by that bald fucker and his friends, who deserved to die the most?

He went through his mental list of foes, tapping the blade thoughtfully against his lips. Mike was the easiest to dispatch right now but at the moment the most closely watched. Dan was a powder keg waiting to explode any moment and even with one hand was still no slouch in the ass kicking department. The unexplainably lucky bastard Stephen was not a welcoming target either. It was common knowledge that Stephen slept with his damn guns.

That left Mattie. He thumbed the razor sharp blade in his hands.

"I should have killed that bitch when I had the chance and risked

Father Kettle's wrath," he muttered. "Now he's dead, and that harlot yet fouls the air with her breath!"

Looking out the window as Mattie emerged from Mike's RV, Jonas' right arm lashed out to the side. Not even looking, he heard the dagger slam into the wood again when it found its mark.

"I won't make the mistake of trying to purge the bitch of evil as Father Kettle attempted," he barked. "Oh no...the only thing I will purge will be the blood from her veins."

*

Lewis stood shaking his head in disbelief, staring at the list he wrote down as relayed by Jonas over the radio during their last communication. The list looked like a weird chemist's grocery list of things that he was going to have to locate for Jonas. Some of the stuff he had never heard of except in the movies.

And Lewis was supposed to find all this shit in three days. Didn't the idiot know there were fucking *zombies* out here? Lewis had barely escaped with his life the other night in that tree, and now he had to go on a fucking Easter egg hunt for that deranged fuck.

Scanning the area carefully, he knew he had to get out of there quickly to avoid being spotted by the guard towers and more importantly, the ever present undead. He retreated down the block to where he had stashed his new wheels, a working truck that he had located earlier that day. He climbed in, locked the doors, pulled out the list from Jonas, and looked it over.

What the hell did he need this stuff for anyway?

No explanation had been given, no orders for after the stuff was gathered, just the simple message, "I need everything on this list in three days. Don't fuck it up."

Lewis tossed the paper onto the seat next to him and rested his head on the steering wheel in exhaustion, lamenting that he was so tired. That was mainly because he hadn't had a good night's sleep in quite some time. Not since he had been stuck in that flimsy tree all night surrounded by hundreds of zombies, all clambering for his flesh and blood that was just inches out of their reach. Lewis had been tempted many times on that mentally and physically exhausting night to throw himself headfirst into the pulsating mass and get it over with. But his intense hatred of those cops, especially the big one, Mike, kept him from killing himself. The true reason why he didn't though, was that he was deathly afraid of dying.

It was a good thing he was a coward at heart. Not too long afterwards, dawn arrived and with the morning rays falling onto the stone walls, the massive steel doors of the prison clanked open. The noise drew quite a few zombies away from his small tree. Then from inside the prison, a front wheel loader and a city dump truck with a V-shaped snowplow on the front came roaring out and slammed into the encroaching mass of undead scum. The truck and loader continued running the zombies over again and again until they were decimated. The loader then scooped up the flattened corpses and dumped them into the burning pit area for cremation later in the day. It was horrific to watch and worse to hear. The smells and the squishy popping sounds some of the corpses made caused Lewis to vomit until he could barely hold onto the tree as he dry heaved. His stomach and ribs still hurt, and that was three days ago.

A sudden impact slammed into the driver's door, shook the truck and jerked him awake and upright. Outside his window was a badly mauled creature missing a majority of its face and throat. It pawed at the window and clacked its teeth together, trying to bite at him through the glass. The ruined windpipe caused the zombie to make a hissing sound like air escaping a balloon.

He really needed to find himself a weapon when he got a chance. He needed to kill these smelly bastards— running all the time was bullshit.

So focused he was on the zombie outside his door of the truck, Lewis did not see the others that approached his vehicle from the front until they began to bang on the hood and fenders relentlessly.

"Leave me alone for Christ's sake!" he screamed. "I can't get a moment's rest without you moaning assholes finding me!"

He angrily started the truck, slammed it into gear and stomped on the accelerator. The truck jerked and bounced as it lurched forward, running over a handful of the attackers. In his mirror, Lewis saw that he had crushed a few and, stealing an idea from the prison compound folks, decided to take his anger out on them. Backing up, he struck more of the undead as they turned to pursue him.

He continued back and forth until the zombies were a gooey pile of meat on the roadway. Feeling much better with the satisfactory release of pent up anger, Lewis started his task of acquiring the items on the list.

It would help if the arrogant prick would let him know what all this crap was for. He steered his truck away from the nearby prison to start his scavenger hunt.

"I should be the guy calling the shots, not that lunatic."

21

November 6
Day 73

My alarm clock woke me from my slumber. The nap I just took felt great, if you can call sleeping for five hours straight after breakfast a nap. I had knocked out a few pages of that damn *Dark Tower* book, thankfully finding it right on the nightstand where I left it, but soon after fell back asleep. I woke up today feeling much better, nonetheless. Since pulling out of my semi-coma yesterday, a lot of my pain had diminished. It now felt more like muscle soreness from an intense workout. Carefully easing my bad leg over the edge of the bed, I gingerly stood and shuffled my way to answer Mother Nature's call. Using everything around me to hold onto to keep from falling, I carefully made my way to the facilities. Judging from the contractions in my lower intestine I'm guessing that's what woke me up from a dead sleep.

Barely made it there in time too, and after a lot of grunting and groaning from the stench, I finished my tour of duty. Since I was up, I figured I might as well hit the shower. It took several painful minutes to remove the bandages and hop into the small stall. Reaching up blindly, I grabbed for the bar of Zest soap on the soap tray, and I came back with a pink bar of something that smelled like flowers. Confused, I looked up where I got the soap and saw some kind of frilly looking bathing sponge and more than a few bottles of girly body wash.

"Where did my soap go? And what the heck am I supposed do with a sponge? I'm not washing a car."

It looked like my part-time roommate Mattie was becoming

more and more permanent these days.

Guess I'll have to smell like a girl, I thought. I shrugged and got down to working up lather.

The hot water worked wonders to undo the mass of knotted muscles in my back and shoulders. It took a while to wash around my list of injuries, and by the time I finished, I felt great but still as weak as a kitten. I checked my reflection in the mirror, quickly losing track of the purple bruises that crisscrossed my body. Grimacing, I grabbed the toothpaste, scrubbed my teeth and then prepared to shave.

Finished with my beauty treatments, I again limped back to my room and replaced my bandages, then struggled to dress myself. I had to take a few breaks as I got lightheaded a few times and broke out into a cold sweat. Judging by the angle of the sunlight peeking through the shades, it was getting late in the afternoon, approaching dark. I figured if I was going to get some fresh air I had better do it now.

I shuffled to the RV's door, passed the couch, and saw that Mattie had apparently taken up refuge on it. It was usually me sleeping there while I let her use my bed since she was frequently between trailers. Every time she got a new trailer, another group of refugees arrived to take possession of it at her insisting.

It looked like my man cave was no more, but the first decorative candle I saw was going in the garbage!

I hobbled down the stairs out of the RV and stood outside breathing in the crisp cool air. Leaning against the RV door was the thick wooden pole I had used as a crutch during my quest home. Good, I would need something to help my lame ass limp around.

My attention was suddenly diverted by raised voices.

To the north I heard a bunch of yelling, and I decided I had better see what the problem was. Limping that way, I saw Stephen standing around with a whole group of guys from the prison. I recognized some, but there were many new ones. Stephen saw me walk up and turned my direction.

"What the hell you doing out of bed?"

"Cabin fever," I replied and nodded my head towards the commotion. "What is going on over here?"

Stephen looked over at the large group that was now breaking up into smaller formations while getting screamed at by someone who reminded me of my old drill sergeant from basic training.

"I thought I'd run our people through a little boot camp to give them an idea of what we expect on raids and guard duty," Stephen said with a chuckle. "The angry man screaming at them is Rodney. He keeps everyone on their toes. We have just over two hundred people in our compound now and out of those about one hundred and forty are combat ready. Or will be after we are done with them. The rest take care of most of the group chores around here."

"Good idea," I replied. "Is this because of the raid to Casper's place? I heard it went bad. What happened?"

Stephen's face went grim with anger. "Saying it went bad is an understatement. We had a lapse in security, and paid for it with the lives of far too many guys. I'm thinking it will take maybe three or four days of training to get everyone somewhat up to speed. After that it's on the job training."

He explained what went down on the raid, and I had to agree it sounded like quite the clusterfuck. It sounded like this training would be beneficial to the men. Instead of throwing raw recruits into the fire, this would give them some idea of what to do.

"Hey, I got a surprise for you," Stephen said, changing topics.

He picked up a Motorola walkie-talkie and got in touch with Logan. After a brief conversation, he told me to hang on a minute, and walked back to where Rodney was demonstrating a proper knife thrust.

After a good fifteen minutes of watching the recruits go through scenarios, my attention was broken up by an electronic whine as Logan pulled up in a little electric shopping cart. Seeing the Wal-Mart sticker on the side told me where they got it. They were usually driven by very obese people who acted handicapped but most likely were just too lazy to walk and push a cart. Logan had a huge smile on his face.

"Here ya go, broke dick," he chimed as he climbed off the cart. "Figure to give your bum leg a break, you could scoot around in style."

While Stephen, Logan and several of the others chuckled, I swallowed my pride and gratefully sat down on the contraption.

"Very funny, assholes," I replied. "You could have mounted some belt fed machine guns or something on it."

"We never thought of that," Stephen said. He handed me a shoebox. "But we did get you this."

I opened it up and found a little horn, the kind that small kids had on their bikes.

"Wouldn't want someone to walk out in front of you, bro," Logan joked. "Those carts are quiet. Now we can hear you coming from a long ways off."

Trying not to laugh myself, I scrunched up my face to look pissed and drove off at top speed...all of five mph, after giving a courtesy honk and the finger.

That got a shit ton of laughs.

Maybe I should have stayed in bed.

*

Dan sat uncomfortably in his chair in the command center. He was used to being the one dishing out the verbal abuse and didn't like being on the receiving end.

"How many times am I going to have to chase you down?" the stern old nurse continued her harangue. "And all of this drinking... I told you not to drink alcohol with the medication you are on."

"Yes, ma'am," Dan replied. "Where's the nurse with the big tits that usually sees me? Nurse Shelly."

All his comment got him was a slap to his face.

"I'm all you get today you dirty old man," she scolded. "Do you want to die from infection? Amputation is a serious matter. You don't look that good right now as a matter of fact. Let me take your temperature. I bet you are on fire!"

It was true, Dan had not been feeling all that well the last couple of days, and his stump was sore to the touch. However, losing his hand was far better than becoming a zombie. Now with Mike alive and recovering, maybe it was time he took a step back from the edge.

But he did have his well-crafted reputation as a heartless asshole on the line.

The old nurse abrasively shoved the thermometer in his mouth. If only this was Nurse Shelly paying him a visit.

At least she put the thermometer in my mouth, he thought. *Not the other....*

"Under no circumstances are you to consume alcoholic beverages," she continued with her harsh lecturing. "On top of everything else, you're still weak after donating blood to Mike."

On a shelf in the corner of the room sat two small digital AM/FM radios that Dan had set up after finding them on a raid. There had not been any broadcast on the radio for quite some time, but Dan left the units plugged in and turned on. One was constantly scanning through the AM band and the other the FM band, searching for any signal from the outside world. There had been nothing for months. Until now.

The thermometer dropped from Dan's mouth as the radio scanning the AM band stopped at 1000AM and picked up a strong signal. Dan rushed to up the volume before sitting back down, feeling faint from the sudden movement. He and the nurse sat quietly together listening to the broadcast without saying a word. As soon as the message was over, it began to repeat itself from the beginning. It continued this looping pattern over and over. It was short but offered a message of hope. There were other survivors and maybe all was not lost. The broadcast, they were told, originated from the USS Normandy, a Ticonderoga class guided missile cruiser now located in Lake Michigan. Dan quickly found Stephen, Amber, Mike and Mattie, who returned to the command center and listened to the broadcast. After a lot of trial and error and cursing, Dan was able to rig a signal through a stereo receiver and broadcast the message through a number of loudspeakers used to pass information and assignments in the prison compound. When it started again, Dan turned up the volume for all those gathered to hear.

"My fellow Americans, this is President Greer. Before the current crisis I was the Secretary of Veterans' Affairs, and now as the senior surviving government leader and in line with our Constitution, I am acting President of the United States. I am currently recording this message from the USS Abraham Lincoln off the West Coast of the United States. This great flagship is now the acting capitol of the United States.

I send this message with a heavy heart. We are all aware of the terrible epidemic that has been brought upon not only us, but the entire globe. We have all lost loved ones and family members. I myself am included in this. This terrible virus spread swiftly and quickly consumed most of the population. Much of our armed forces were annihilated in a vain attempt to quarantine the larger cities and defend civilian safe zones. The entire National Guard was mobilized, but it was too little and too late to help. Most of our soldiers fought bravely, and deserve our gratitude as they allowed many of our citizens to survive. As would be expected, we also had a portion of our soldiers at home go AWOL in an attempt to try and save their families and loved ones. This epidemic has taken a devastating toll on our country. Many safe zones were established by FEMA but often proved inadequate to the disaster which unfolded. I will not deny that what transpired nearly brought about the end of our entire government, but I am here to tell you that we are not finished as a country or as a civilization.

Now I'm sure all of you have questions that you want to ask, like when is help arriving? Many also want to know where the disease came from. Well... as for the latter, our scientists tell me that it is an advanced biological weapon most likely developed by a rogue state and deployed by a terrorist group such as Al Qaeda. This is not, I repeat not, a result of some military experiment of our own government gone wrong. It is, however, a highly advanced virus crafted with considerable skill. It is speculated that the weapon was first deployed from Mexico with humans used as the delivery devices. At this time, where the virus came from does not really matter anymore. Unfortunately, there is currently no vaccine available despite the best efforts of our top scientists, but our research is ongoing. We have the best surviving minds from our top hospitals and universities working on a vaccine. The consensus is that the infected are beyond saving, but a vaccine could be produced to immunize the survivors. Now I'm also sure that you are aware firsthand that the only way to stop the spread of the virus at this time is to neutralize the host. This can only be efficiently done by destroying the brain of the carrier. The virus does not live long outside of the human body. The only known way you can be infected is by being bitten by a host patient. If you are bitten by an infected, the virus will quickly take over your body, and you will develop the same symptoms. It is also unknown at this time how long before an infected subject dies off on its own, but studies are being done to find out.

As for help, don't lose hope, all is not lost. Around the globe there are islands and pockets of humanity not affected. Our own nation had many ships at sea during the outbreak, and some stateside ground units remained intact. To this end, all available elements of our armed forces have been ordered to the nearest National Federal Safe Zone. On the East Coast this was located at the Cherry Point Marine Corps Air Station near Havelock, North Carolina. Perhaps you had heard that and were headed that way. Regrettably, we were forced to abandon it due to severe pressure from the infected. A new, more secure installation has been set up at the recently closed Ft. Monroe in Virginia along the Chesapeake Bay. On the West Coast the safe zone is Whidbey Island Naval Air Station near Seattle, Washington. Both of these safe zones are completely secure and well-fortified. As additional ships have arrived and resources made available, these safe zones have been expanded to include neighborhoods and farm land. Survivors are already being settled in these new areas, and the secured areas are growing daily. We are now patrolling the skies, searching for pockets of survivors. Perhaps you have seen our aircraft, which are reporting back with news of survivors. In the western states, many small communities have fortified themselves without federal assistance. We encourage them to continue this, and to seek out and assist their neighbors. Eventually we will all become united again and restore hope to our stricken nation, and encourage everyone to work with agents of our government in the future.

To this end we are setting up a lifeline across the country. Soon, soldiers will begin to clear a route across the country. Using Interstate 90 out of Seattle, they will head east to Interstate 25, then 70 to 64 to 57 to 24 to 40 into the eastern safe zone. Units from there will be heading west out of Fort Monroe at the same time. As circumstances permit, we intend to set up outposts every hundred or so miles along the route. Hard work is also going into restoring our railroads along this same route. Folks, we have eleven aircraft carriers at our disposal, amphibious assault ships, and many hard working soldiers, marines, sailors and airmen. Our nation's infrastructure is largely intact and valuable materials are strewn across our vast nation, waiting to be picked up. Combine this with the spirit of the American people and we will overcome this and rebuild. We encourage anyone who is able to move to the safe zones for their own safety and help us rebuild together. We have the resources but need your help in this fight. For the sake of this nation you must fight, you must survive! If you cannot reach the coast, you can try to reach a point along our route and make contact with our patrols, which can lead you to safety. We look forward to your safe arrival. I hope to broadcast again soon with good news and further instructions. Geographically specific instructions will now be given out on different stations, detailing evacuation points along the coast or in your area. Locally secured areas will also be identified in your regions and instructions on how to proceed to them if possible. These small communities, once safely secured, will one day rise up to form the backbone of a new America. God bless you, and God bless America."

A new voice took over.

"This is Captain Brokaw of the U.S.S Normandy. We are currently operating in Lake Michigan. Unlike coastal areas, we are not performing water evacuations at this time. Our ship is not equipped to take on refugees, and we are merely tasked with recon duties. We soon

hope to be bringing a larger ship into the area and may attempt shore rescue in the future. This will most likely taken place in the remote areas of Wisconsin and Michigan, but again, no timetable has been set. Several depots of survivors have been observed from the air in this listening area, with the most prolific being Munising, Michigan, located in the Hiawatha National Forest on the Upper Peninsula. A secure area has been established there, and the remote location is being considered for the home of a future civilian, provisional regional government. At this time security is very tight at that location, and supplies are severely limited. Martial Law is being strictly enforced. I do not recommend you try for that location at this time. As resources permit, rescue missions will be sent out to bring you there.

I do not wish to paint a rosy picture here, folks. Our big cities are destroyed, and the countryside is filled with roaming bands of these infected, as well as the criminal element. Horror stories of atrocities committed by the living are pouring into our safe zones. Travel can be very dangerous. I hope to bring you better news in the future, but for now, I need you to stay strong. Keep your head down and your powder dry. Help is on the way. Captain Brokaw out."

Finally hearing that we were not the only freaking people alive in the country was a big relief for everyone. After a good hour discussing the ramifications of the broadcast, it was decided that although encouraging, nothing much could be done about it as of now anyways.

"Fuck the Feds!" Stephen shouted. "I don't trust 'em and I don't need 'em bossing me around again. How long before they're going to start wanting tax money again?"

That gave us all a chuckle, and everyone returned to their tasks, the air abuzz with conversation. Limping down to my new scooter, I hopped onto it and prepared to take off. When I raised my eyes, I saw some asshole was having a bit of fun at my expense. Right in front of the scooter someone had planted a handicap sign, and they had given me a handicap parking ticket. They'd also put an improvised "boot" on the little scooter tires. A faint laughter drifted out from inside.

I shook my head with anger and humor. "No respect, assholes."

From behind me Logan approached and saw my immobility dilemma. "Hey, Chief, need a hand?" he asked all too nicely.

I looked down at the boot then backed up slowly to Logan. "Looks like my unpaid parking tickets have caught up to me at last," I chimed, making light of the situation. "Can you help me out?"

Logan dropped an armload of colored sticks he was carrying and removed the tire block. "It appears someone has a poor sense of humor, boss," he replied, grinning ear to ear.

"Oh yeah, I'd be rolling on the ground if it weren't for the bruised ribs," I said. "What's with the sticks?"

"Kleaner and I are making range markers and putting them out into the killing fields for those that are not as good of a shot as they think. To help cut down on some of the wasted ammo."

"Great idea. What else you two got cooked up?" I asked. "You guys always have something going."

The look of eagerness entered his eyes. Logan always got that look when explaining a new project. "Well, we're working on putting together a documented experiment on whether or not .22lr ammunition is powerful enough to put down a zombie. We have a metric ton of .22lr and would love to put it to good use. That is another reason for the markers. To see what the effective kill range is, if there is one. It will be a couple days before we get going on that, though. It's getting dark now anyways, and Stephen had us busy all day teaching a bunch of new recruits how to shoot straight."

Logan picked up his colored range markers and walked swiftly away. I turned the scooter around to head back to my RV. Mattie told me earlier she had a surprise waiting for me when I was well enough to be up and around. Judging from the look she gave me, the possibilities were interesting. After a short fifteen feet, the cart abruptly died. Someone had drained the batteries. As more laughter rang from out of the command center, I muttered angrily and fished my walking stick out from where I had it stuck it in the cart's basket, and limped away cursing those I had thought my friends.

22

November 6
Day 73

What should have been a short walk back to the RV took quite some time. I was looking forward to seeing Mattie, but I really enjoyed the walk. I made a lap around the prison compound making small talk and admiring all of our progress. Buddy was no longer the only dog in the prison, as he was leading a small pack of dogs in a game of fetch along with some small boys. I did my part and threw the stick myself a couple times. By the time my RV came into sight, I was feeling much better and even worked up a bit of a sweat in the process.

I limped up to the door and reached for the handle, just when it burst open without warning.

I recoiled in surprise, stumbling back a few steps.

"I'm sorry," Mattie said standing in a halo of light coming from inside the camper. She reached out for me and gently took me by the arm. "Come inside, Mike. Sit down, you look tired."

"So, what's the big surprise?" I asked, looking around. "What did I do wrong this time?"

"What? Oh, you didn't do anything, silly!" she looked shocked. "Why would you assume something is wrong?"

"Because," I said, "I messed up and got you kidnaped. I feel terrible and am so sorry. I should have kept you by my side."

"Don't apologize," she responded. "I wandered off without you knowing. I can only blame myself. I wanted to talk to you because I've realized something. I'm so thankful for you, and wanted to thank you for everything you've done for me. I'm alive because of you, by the way."

She paused and looked at me with her head cocked to the side. "I knew you guys would come for me, but what the hell took you so long?"

"See, I told you I was in trouble!" I said putting my hands up in defeat.

"I'm joking, silly," she laughed. "I really mean it, though. I don't know how to convey to you how much I appreciate you. Mike, when we all thought you were dead, I was a wreck. It was the first time I realized how much you matter to me. I couldn't stop crying. If I lost you..." She choked up, crying and unable to speak anymore.

I gently held her close. "Please don't cry, Mattie. I will never let anything happen to you. You knew I would come for you. I always will. And I'm here now. No one is getting rid of my old ass."

She pushed back enough to look at my face and let out a soft laugh. "You're ridiculous, you know that?" she said with a grin. "I'm sorry I'm such a crybaby sometimes. I can't help it when I feel strongly about something. And, I just can't stand the thought of losing you."

"Now you're making me blush," I joked.

"So," Mattie continued, "I asked you here so I could give a thank you, and I figured I could best do that by finally giving you that back rub you're always asking for."

"Sweet," I said, trying not to look too excited. "My shoulders are killing me!"

"Well, I do owe you big time, so I think I can manage that," Mattie said with a wink. "C'mon, get undressed and lay down."

If only it were that easy.

My stunned look might have given me away.

"Oh, goodness, you don't have to strip down to everything, but take off your shirt and your pants. Besides, it's nothing I haven't seen before, remember?" she teased.

"Just wanna give you fair warning, I don't mind stripping down to nothing."

"I will try to control my fear," Mattie chuckled. "Down to your underwear is fine."

I painfully shed my clothes as quickly as my injuries allowed. I disrobed down to my boxers and lay on my stomach. Mattie playfully slapped me on the ass and then straddled my back to begin the massage. As Mattie's soft hands started a very gentle rub-down, she seemed to keep in mind that I was still very sore and recovering from my injuries. Her fingers traced the dark bruises from me getting shot. It wasn't long before the RV fell silent with only soft groans and my heavy breathing piercing the silence.

"Are you okay? Am I being too rough?" she softly asked.

"No, don't stop. Please don't stop," I grunted as her hands worked at the knots in my shoulders which made audible popping sounds.

She giggled and moved down to my lower back, her fingers gliding across my skin. Her hands deeply kneaded my lower back muscles, and I exhaled, moving my right hand back to her right leg as I groaned.

"This is my dream come true."

After about ten minutes, I dared to ask, "Mattie, please don't smack me for asking, but, could you please massage my chest for a few minutes? It's tight across the chest and neck."

It was pretty pathetic sounding, but it was worth a shot.

"Hmm," she mused, clearly undecided.

"Promise I'll behave," I promised, "I won't do anything you don't want me to."

"Okay, but only for a few minutes."

I turned over, and adjusted myself comfortably on my back. She too repositioned and placed her hands upon my chest.

She inhaled deeply. "I'm finding myself distracted by your body."

"I know the feeling," I said as her hands worked their magic on the front of my shoulders.

"Focus, Mattie!" I heard her mutter under her breath. "Dammit, focus!"

Then she spoke louder. "Um, is this okay, Mike?"

I didn't answer.

"Hey, Mike?"

I had been gazing at her as if in a trance. My hands suddenly had a mind of their own. I felt my fingers creep underneath the bottom of her shirt and gently start to caress her waist. Her eyelids sank shut, and she tilted her head back slightly, grinding her pelvis into my groin. It felt so nice to be touching someone softly for once, instead of violently fighting for my life.

Before I knew it, I felt myself hardening underneath her. She started to move along with my hands, guiding her hips in a slow rolling motion. Her breathing quickened, and there was no way she couldn't feel my painfully aroused lower abdominal area pressing against her.

Indecision clearly written on her face almost made her stop.

After a few moments passed, she peeled off her t-shirt and took my hands, placing them on her breasts. I hesitated slightly before massaging them gently, soaking up the entire sensation. Finally, she leaned in close enough to kiss but not quite doing so, breathing me in.

"You told me you wouldn't do anything I don't want you to...Mike, I want you to."

I never imagined our kiss would feel like that. I felt as if someone hit me with a stun gun. I didn't remember how I got the rest of her clothes off, hoping I didn't ruin anything. I quickly found myself on top of her now. My hands explored her breasts, my mouth salivating at the idea of following in their place. My tongue wetly glanced across her nipples, with a subtle sucking. Her hands drifted down to my boxers, slid them off and grabbed my manhood. After a few delicious moments of her manual stimulations, she reached for my face and gently pushed my head down her exquisite body. I moved across her midsection, kissing her softly around the navel, moving down and settled between her legs as she moaned loudly with pleasure. I got down to work, and I could finally relate to those damn zombies always munching on their victims.

After a few blissful minutes, she pulled me up to look me in the eyes, wrapping her legs around my waist. She reached down and grabbed me, guiding me in. I could feel our hearts pounding and slowly pushed. She inhaled deeply and reveled in the experience. When I settled in on a rhythm, I saw Mattie's eyes roll back into her head.

"Don't stop, you feel amazing!" she panted. "I've waited so long for this!"

Faster and faster my hips pounded into her, and I didn't think it could get any better.

"Take me from behind," she gasped.

I stand corrected.

With one swift movement, I was on my knees and flipping her over, driving her face into the pillow. I grabbed her hips tightly, working myself in and out of her. Before long we rolled again and found myself underneath her. Mattie pulled my head into her chest as she worked me over. She began to spasm and arched her body, her sudden orgasm spilling forth. She tensed up, driving her fingernails deep into my chest before biting my neck in a scream. Her molten hotness then slowly started to send me over. I swore I felt it building from the tips of my toes.

"Cum with me, now," she begged.

And I did just that as she collapsed onto my body.

We lay together for some time, trying to catch our breaths. She climbed off and settled in next to me.

Mattie finally spoke, breaking the silence. "Well I didn't expect a simple back rub to turn into that."

I smiled. "Let's find out what happens when I ask you to make me a sandwich."

We both laughed and she sighed in contentment. After a short time I leaned over her shoulder and gazed down at her face. She was dead asleep.

I flopped over onto my back with my arms behind my head, a grin on my face.

"Hot sex and no pillow talk. Life is good."

23

November 8
Day 75

The next couple of days saw Stephen complete his training with the survivors in the prison that now made up the security forces. They completed courses in firearms, hand-to-hand combat, and small unit tactics. Physical fitness was stressed, and a few candidates got a crash course from Eddie in driving an 18-wheeler, Stephen included.

"They're great for hauling a lot of shit," he explained. "Plus, I always wanted to drive one."

Passing scores were required in marksmanship with Logan and Kleaner providing the test. I conducted the physical fitness training, along with hand-to-hand combat drills, for killing zombies up close and personal without getting bitten. It was a little comical to have me teaching hand-to-hand combat while leaning heavily on my walking staff. I also took the time to stress what types of clothing we preferred on raids. No loose clothing was allowed. Loose clothing let zombies easily grab hold of their victims and it was hard to make it let go. We recommended leather, canvas or anything dense that could slow down a zombie bite. Stephen conducted endless drills on movement and tactics, with the progress being evident almost immediately. He also picked out the natural leaders amongst the group, and upon completion sorted the men into a company level unit with four separate platoons. They were not to be the only line of defense; this is where our safe zone differed from other refugee camps. We expected everyone to be armed, so everyone could be called on in short notice if necessary.

The first three platoons, Alpha, Bravo and Charlie, were each complemented with three nine-man squads, for a total of twenty-seven. They were responsible for the always dangerous supply raids and would work on a rotating basis. The day after a raid, you were off and free to work on side projects or take care of personal matters. The third day you trained, pulled guard for the burn/burial crew, and kept on standby in the event of an emergency. Stephen made sure that each platoon was outfitted with as similar weapons as possible, rifles and pistols. Every rifle was to be magazine fed, with enough magazines for a full combat load. Stephen preferred seven to ten per man. Every pistol was to be issued with five magazines, mag pouches and holsters. The platoons were also equipped with medical and communication personnel.

Dan, Mattie, Stephen, Amber and I were in Alpha platoon, as we were in fact the self-described “A” team. The platoon was completely equipped with AR-15 rifles of various manufacturers. Bravo platoon was equipped with the AK-74’s. They also had the benefit of the camouflage uniforms that were located along with the rifles. Charlie platoon was armed with a variety of AK-47 rifles and a few SKS carbines. Side arms were mandatory, but left to personal preference. The forth group, Delta platoon would not participate in the raids and was permanently assigned perimeter duty and internal security. It was the largest by far, led by Logan, Kleaner and Casper. They were outfitted with the best remaining firearms, with upgrades constantly ongoing. They were broken up into three shifts daily, allowing for an occasional off day.

The one firearm that was in large supply was 12 gauge pump shotguns. So many Remington 870’s, Mossberg 500’s and Winchester 1300’s had been recovered in various configurations that one was issued to every adult in the compound along with whatever personal weapons they may have brought with. Every able-bodied adult was also issued a handgun of some sort for personal defense. All were taught how to safely handle and shoot the guns. The students had plenty of shooting targets in the form of howling undead to practice on. All in all I was feeling better about our situation every day.

*

Stephen was sitting alone in the command center and had just finished going over some updated numbers. Mike, who for the last couple days had this shit eating grin on his face, made some excuses earlier about being tired and scampered off to his RV.

That guy takes more naps than my dog, he thought, frowning while he looked out a window at Mike's RV.

Speaking of which, he looked down at his beagle, who was napping by his chair, and gave him a scratch behind the ears.

"What ya up to?" a feminine voice asked, catching him off-guard.

Glancing up, he saw Amber standing in the doorway, dressed in a Colt's sweatshirt and jeans, with rosy cheeks from walking in the cold.

"Finally finished up some paperwork. Hey, someone built a nice sized campfire outside and cooked some chili over it. Let's grab a bite and warm up."

"You read my mind," Amber replied. "Just took a walk around the inside of the walls, and I'm cold and hungry!"

"Love the look!" Stephen teased, while tapping the pistol that Amber was clearly wearing under the sweatshirt.

"You like that?" she teased back, giving him a playful shove. "Well, hands off my piece, Mister."

"Your uncle has the baby?" Stephen asked, referring to the small child Chris found outside of Peoria, as they headed to the campfire.

"Actually, no," Amber replied. "Dan found a Latino couple who adopted the baby as their own. He said they named him Chris, in honor of the man that found him."

"Don't let him fool ya," Stephen said knowingly. "He comes off as an asshole, but he has a soft spot somewhere in there."

They ate hearty bowls of chili and cornbread by the fire, and Stephen brought up the idea of the radio station, something she'd mentioned on their trip to Wisconsin.

"Made some inquiries over the HAM, found a guy at the Bolingbrook safe zone who used to work at a radio station," Stephen told her. "There is the old WJOL 1320AM station on the other side of town, and he seems to think that we could get the equipment needed from there and mount the antenna on the top of that old smoke stack in the center of the prison yard. Thinks we could have a broadcasting AM station with very little trouble at all. And with no FCC to interfere, we should be able to really crank up the power and punch a signal way out there. He's coming down here in the morning and is gonna go over there with us."

"Us?" Amber asked.

"Training is all done, babe," he said, and then reassured her with an arm around her shoulder. "We're in Alpha platoon and are up tomorrow. Broke dick Mike is gonna sit this one out. I'm gonna be in charge."

"Well, that's tomorrow." Amber replied. "I have other intentions for you tonight!"

Seeing the gleam in her eyes, he replied, "Now you read my mind!" and led Amber back to his RV.

When they entered the camper, he popped open a bottle of wine and turned on some music.

"Do you think you could try giving me a quick haircut?" he asked. "I hate it when it touches my ears!"

"Now?" Amber asked, rolling her eyes.

"What?" Stephen responded. "You said you would give it a try. I picked up the proper tools from a barber shop. Let's knock this out."

"Fine," Amber relented. "Grab me the clippers and sit down.

Amber had to admit that he had put together a nice barber kit and was also impressed that he had managed to locate some of the high end hair care products she had asked about. He had them gift wrapped in a large box.

Stephen sat frozen in the chair as she worked the clippers. It seemed at first she knew what she was doing.

"Don't forget," he reminded her, "a three on top blended into a one on the sides."

After a while it became evident that the whole thing was taking way too long. Amber had stopped talking and had a worried look on her face as she moved the clippers from one side of his head to the other.

"Everything ok?" he asked.

When he didn't get an answer, he turned and looked at his reflection on the glass window on the oven door. He was greeted by a half bald reflection with a cowlick in a place where there shouldn't be one.

The look on his face said it all, which sent Amber into tears. It all happened so fast and Stephen found himself having to backtrack.

"Hey, it's nothing we can't fix," he pleaded, trying to sound convincing. "Cut it all down to one length, just not bald like that ugly bastard, Mike."

"Oh, there will be no next time," she said and roughly pushed Stephen back into the chair and hit him with the clippers with a bit more force than last time around. "And this is your fault anyways."

After a few minutes of awkward silence, he said, "You know I like it rough."

He then spotted the handcuffs in Amber's hand and a wicked grin on her face.

*

The following morning he did not want to leave the warm bed but Buddy's constant whining to be let out, combined with Dan's increasingly vulgar remarks over the loudspeakers, finally drove him out. Arriving in the command center, Stephen was introduced to Derrick Booth from the Bolingbrook Safe Zone.

"This's the radio guy I was telling you about," Dan said after a brief introduction. "He seems to think we can make this little idea of yours a reality."

"Nice to finally meet you in person," Derrick said, offering an extended hand. "Love what you've done with the place. From what Dan's shown me you've got the infrastructure in place you should need. Everything else can be grabbed at radio station facility.

"About that," Dan interrupted, "Mike and Mattie won't be joining us today. They're going to be giving the head guy from Bolingbrook a little tour of our personal paradise while we're out. I think his name is Kirk. I got two fill-ins from Bravo team who volunteered for some trigger time."

"Let's roll," Stephen replied. "The sooner we get this done, the faster we can get on the air. Be in the conference room in ten."

Dan smiled. "Way ahead of ya, the coffee's already on."

Alpha platoon was already gathered when Stephen arrived. There was a sense of eagerness and confidence in the team now. Training will do that, and the one good side effect of the last botched raid was that the herd was culled of its deadbeats. Unfortunately, those same losers increased the ranks of undead that continuously hammered at the prison walls. He watched Amber walk up and gave her a smile as he began the briefing. A hand drawn map on a large table showed the layout of the target building and surrounding area. Scouts had gotten the layout down the previous day, and they reported only a moderate infected population in the general area. Props were used to show the battle plan. Toy plastic soldiers and plastic cars showed the exact layout for every assignment so nothing was left to chance.

Alpha platoon was broken down into three squads and security assignments were given out. Several large trucks were going to be used in the convoy, with twelve additional volunteers to help provide the leg work of moving all the necessary equipment. These pickers, mostly from Bravo and Charlie, had been at it awhile now and were good at their jobs. Derrick from Bolingbrook was going to be riding with Dan out front, and Amber volunteered for rear guard, a spot sure to see plenty of action since a convoy always drew a crowd of zombies in its wake.

With all the plans explained and questions answered, Stephen gave the order to lock and load, and the convoy personnel loaded up. Squad leaders met with their teams while he laid out the convoy's order of travel. After a radio check, they were let out of the prison by Logan and Kleaner, once again amongst a hail of gunfire. Forty-one souls moved out on a mission that if successful, would allow them to broadcast over a vast area and perhaps save even more lives. Dan rode shotgun in the lead plow truck and called out zombie contacts along the way. Other than that, the radios were quiet as everyone anticipated the coming action. Some of the roads had been used frequently, but as the convoy went north out of Joliet city limits, they entered an area where they had not yet done any salvaging.

When they pulled up to the small radio station, two squads set up the perimeter while Stephen led the third squad inside to clear the building. He heard the rear guard call out contact before engaging as they folded into the perimeter. So far, it appeared the training was already paying off. Those same well-practiced tactics quickly dispatched the two zombies milling about inside the radio station's front lobby. He assisted by putting them both down with head shots from his newly suppressed AR-15, courtesy of Casper's raid. From their grotesque, withered condition, it was obvious that they had been stuck inside the building since they had turned and were unable to feed. A third corpse was found in the broadcast room. The disc jockey looked as if he'd died from thirst or hunger, unwilling to try to escape. Stephen shuddered at the painful, yet cowardly way he died.

With the building cleared, Derrick was able to show the movers what needed to be taken. The remaining men dragged the decaying bodies outside and joined the outside perimeter. The line was going to need to be held for quite some time due to the disassembly work that needed to be done. Thankfully, Derrick had explained that the antenna itself did not have to be removed, and a sufficient replacement could be built on site at the prison.

Stephen walked up to Amber and checked her position. At least thirty zombies were in this area alone, and he was glad that they brought as much ammunition as they did. She picked the two closest targets, zombies that had managed to get in close by walking out from behind a blind spot near a stalled conversion van. One was a white male, his suit tattered from the elements. The other was an older black female in a jogger's outfit. Without hesitating, she fired at the female and the round penetrated her forehead. A second shot glanced off the side of the man's head, a wound that would have been fatal to any mortal human. The zombie lost its balance and fell to the pavement before slowly trying to scramble back to his feet. She finished him with a third round, splitting its head wide open.

"Nice shooting, sweet thing."

"Now's not the time for flirting!" she shouted over the increasing gunfire.

He was going to mention how hot she looked shooting a gun, but a radio transmission for assistance told them that some extra guns were needed on the north side of the perimeter. Amber gave him a reassuring look and told him that they had this end locked down and to go have a look. Silently nodding over the gunfire, he peeled away while she loaded a fresh magazine into her rifle from her pouch. Pausing long enough to grab three extra trigger fingers, he jogged to the north perimeter where he was greeted by a large cluster of undead that had pressed in way too close. There must not have been much else for the zombies to chase, as in the distance they now all seemed to be headed their way.

In the center of the crowd was a most unusual sight. Around twenty former high school football players were pressing to the front. They were still in their football uniforms and must have been at practice at the beginning of the outbreak. Their uniforms were caked with mud, blood and gore. After becoming zombies, they must have been unable to remove their helmets. The facemasks on their helmets were encrusted in filth.

"Those would make it hard to feed," he told the guy next to him, "and probably make them really fucking pissed off!"

Only able to soak in the sight for a moment, he was quickly forced to engage the group before they risked having their position overrun. The perimeter was small enough to not allow for any fallback position. As he put rounds into the plastic helmets, the zombies closed the gap to the point where he could smell the stench of the rotting flesh. The remaining football players in the center were now in pistol range as their flanks were cut down by lethal crossfire. When his rifle ran dry, he transitioned to his Beretta and fired with two hands. The charge reached its high-water mark as the closest zombie shambled to within a mere ten feet before being cut down. The line held.

The gunshots tapered off for the moment, and they all took a few precious seconds to regroup, staring at the mound of rotting bodies. It would have been too much for many of them to handle a few weeks ago before the training, but everyone had become quite desensitized by now. An occasional shot rang out while they reloaded their weapons and took a quick drink of water.

“We need to get some improvised barriers up to our front,” he ordered. “When they hit us again in we might need something to slow these fuckers down. Let’s see what he can scrounge up.”

Time permitted a quick barricade building detail, and he was able to share a bottle of water and candy bar with Amber.

“Got anything stronger?” she asked, “This is rough.”

"Sure thing, after we’re back," he replied. “I’m buying the first round.”

“How’s it coming inside?” she asked, “I was ready to go ten minutes ago.”

“Will advise,” Stephen replied and headed off to check.

Just as he was checking the progress of the pickers, the gunfire on the perimeter intensified. Satisfied that the station was being dismantled as quickly as possible, Stephen went back outside and was informed that the zombie traffic was again picking up. He found their words were true enough and was greeted on the perimeter by a new, heavier wave of undead.

He made several passes around the perimeter and checked on their remaining ammunition supply, not wanting to run dry at the worst possible time. On his third pass, a squad leader asked for an update.

"It's been a couple of hours, they should be getting close," Stephen replied, looking back at the radio station where boxes were being hauled out at a feverish pace. Nearly on queue he received word over his radio that everything was loaded, and the convoy could pull out. All perimeter units verified the order, and Stephen coordinated a timely withdraw. He returned to his truck to find Dan firing his AR-15 with the barrel stuck out the open window of the driver’s seat.

"Let’s go, fuckers!" Dan yelled over the noise. “I’ve gotta hot date tonight and can’t be late!”

Pausing to make sure that everyone was indeed loaded, Stephen boarded the truck and ordered the convoy back to the prison. The plow truck in the lead crushed a path of carnage through the thickening zombie mass, and it became clear that it was a good thing that they left when they did.

"They just keep coming," Amber sighed with a tired look on her face. "No matter how many we kill."

From the trucks, the guards fired at the zombies as they passed, which usually resulted in a miss. By the time they reached the prison, everyone was clearly exhausted, and others were waiting to unload the radio gear and begin setting it up. Stephen found Mike and Mattie in the command center working on some figures involving the prison's food supply and a revised wish list. He informed them of the raid's success and the lack of any casualties.

"Good job, Stephen," Mattie said. "All the training certainly paid off. Nobody got hurt and soon we'll have one of the few working radio stations in the world from the sound of it."

"Thanks! You two are definitely going on the next one!" he jokingly said, then headed back to his camper to shower. "I'm tired of pulling all the weight around here, gonna go grab a beer!"

When he returned to his camper, he saw that Derrick was already ordering the equipment unloaded and reassembled in the building designated as the new radio station. The work went way into the night. The perimeter team reported heavy contact in the wake of the convoy returning.

"They really stirred up a hornet's nest out there today," Kleaner remarked as he shot a rather fast zombie in the head at a cool two hundred yards. "We gotta thin these fuckers out or they'll have us sealed in by morning."

*

The following day saw the rest of the work on the radio station antenna completed. Derrick set up the finishing touches on the equipment and showed all interested people how to operate it. That stuff was way over my head, and I left it for the "Geek Squad" and those that were into that kind of thing.

"We'll be ready to go online tonight, Mike," Derrick said, "and being that this is an AM signal, we ought to be able to reach out even farther after dark."

After much debate, it was determined that we would send out a message that would give directions to our location for any survivors that could hear us. We would also give assurance that we were honest and responsible and able to provide shelter, company and protection for anyone willing to help. This message was recorded by Mattie and would play over a loop in between single songs.

"I always wanted to be a DJ!" Dan said enthusiastically.

"What kind of music are you going to play?" I asked.

"Both kinds," Dan replied. "Country *and* Western!"

Dan picked through a stack of music, then announced that his first song was going to be, "A Country Boy Can Survive" by Hank Williams, Jr.

When I walked back into the command center, I was greeted by Stephen and Eddie, who had just concluded a small HAM radio meeting with the few remaining safe zones. Another one located in Grayslake had initially reported heavy zombie contact and was now off the air as well. This left a feeling of uneasiness in everyone's stomach, and it was agreed that all remaining safe zones would send scouts up towards Chicago to look for trouble. There were six remaining contacts on the air in the area, with the two closest in Bolingbrook and Romeoville, both whom had fared pretty well due to the large number of warehouse industrial parks in their areas. We would be sending out a pair of scouts on the quads tomorrow and needed volunteers. Stephen also advised the safe zones that beginning shortly we would be broadcasting continually on AM 1320.

Stephen signed off, and I told him of my plan to go up and see the Bolingbrook safe zone for myself in a day or two at the invite of their leader Kirk Simms, and that maybe our scouts would have solid intelligence by then.

"Sounds like a plan," Stephen remarked. "Now let's go watch Dan put his radio station online. I want him to play some Jamey Johnson!"

Amber walked in at that moment and rolled her eyes. "Not more Jamey Johnson," she sighed. "I'm going to need to assist in the music selection, or we risk you guys driving everyone off with your selections. We need more than just hillbillies around this place, ya know."

I had to agree with her, and we got a good laugh out of it at Stephen's expense.

24

November 10
Day 77
Wisconsin, USA

Chad Evanston looked up at the two remaining men that had survived the trip with him up to Wisconsin after they listened to the radio broadcast repeated between songs.

"What do ya make of that, Terry?" he asked. "First message was from the Feds and now this one from back home in Joliet. I'll be damned if it didn't sound like Mattie!"

Terry Coleman, a high ranking former supervisor at the Joliet Police Department and Chad's former S.W.A.T Commander, scowled as his mind processed what he had just heard.

"Not sure, Chad. We need to find better shelter for sure. We've been taking a beating on a regular basis lately and are low on about everything."

"I agree," Chad replied. "I don't think any of us realized the extent of the devastation or how bad it was gonna get. This is not something we can just ride out at a summer cabin."

Their current location was in southern Wisconsin, near the small town of Lagrange, at a summer cabin Terry owned outside a large state park. It was a simple cottage, neither designed for nor intended to withstand any type of siege. While the first few days after arriving went by relatively pain free, they were damn near destroyed by a huge influx of undead one foggy morning. After a long one-sided gun battle, they finally destroyed the large group of zombies. That was just the beginning, because the numbers were increasing day by day. The cabin itself was in a remote park only thirty or so miles from

Milwaukee. Their food stocks were adequate at first, but the wild game scattered quickly and the fish weren't biting like they used to. Terry did take some of the men to a nearby cornfield where they managed to harvest some field corn for cornbread, but they lost two guys in the process. They shot a big beef cow a few days ago, and that was what they were living currently. Now even the once abundant ammunition supply was running low.

Most of the coworkers that made the trip up here with them had died as a result of either getting bitten or murdered by desperate humans fleeing the undead dangers. A couple of others lit out to go find their parents out west. They had grown tired of seeing their buddies die, and the strain was weighing heavily on them all. Now it was down to just Terry, Bruce, and Chad. The trio was all that was left of the group of over ten able-bodied men that originally made the trip. They needed to get the hell out, and the sooner the better. Transportation was another concern. Only one of the three S.W.A.T vehicles they originally had was operational. The armored Bearcat had lost its transmission and had to be abandoned on the drive up. The equipment truck that held all of the police department's swat team hardware was destroyed by a large group of fleeing refugees. Angered that they couldn't take it, the mob vandalized the truck by smashing out the windows, slashing the tires and setting the damn thing on fire. The small riot only dissipated after several of them were shot and killed.

That left only the Ford Excursion. The big SUV more than likely would have been damaged in the flash mob; thankfully it was on a scouting trip at the time. After hearing Mattie's voice come across the radio, Chad recognized that there was an opportunity to join up with his old workout partners and their crew.

"I've wondered what became of those knuckleheads," he said to Terry. "If they have that old prison outfitted like they claim, then you can't get a more secure location than that."

"Those guys were always the worst case scenario types," Terry admitted. "I'm not surprised they made it and are actually ahead of the curve."

"I think we need to make our way back then," Chad decided. "We can't hold this cabin any longer, plus there's strength in numbers. Mattie said that they had almost two hundred people in their group. We need them, and they could use our skills, I'm sure."

"Well that settles it," Terry said, "and I'm sure Bruce will agree."

"Where did he run off to?" Chad asked. "I didn't see him leave."

Bruce broke into the conversation by shouting through the open front porch window.

"I'd hate to bother you two, but we've got a problem, a really big problem!" he cried. "You better get out here!"

Chad and Terry walked onto the front porch, and Bruce pointed down the driveway of the property and out onto the road. Across the road was a large grassy meadow, three hundred yards of open ground leading up to the edge of the nearby forest. The three of them observed five deer running towards them across the field from the tree line.

"I saw a big buck earlier and shot it for some dinner. Then three more ran past me so close I could've hit them with my hand. Something has the wildlife spooked," Bruce said.

"Can only be one thing," Chad mumbled under his breath.

After the deer bounded past the cabin, they soon saw a steady flood of smaller animals such as rabbits and coyotes exit the timber.

"I got a bad feeling about this, men," Terry ordered. "Get your gear together, we're leaving now."

The three of them didn't have much to pack. They threw the last of their duffel bags and weaponry into the back of the Excursion, and the reason for the frightened animals became all too clear. From out of the trees came a sporadic number of zombies that soon grew in number. Bruce fired rapidly into the growing mob with his AR-15, pausing to reload when his rifle ran dry. He noticed that even with the dozen that he had taken out, there were more exiting the forest into the open field than when he first engaged them.

"Mount up, Bruce! Let's get the fuck out of here!" Chad yelled out the driver's window of the truck.

"Looks like downtown Milwaukee just joined the party," Terry added.

Bruce scrambled around the rear of the truck to get in the rear passenger seat as the wall of zombies steadily approached their position. Chad slammed the Excursion into gear before Bruce shut the door. Slinging gravel from the rear tires, Chad sped down the driveway towards the road.

They made it to the roadway when the first edge of the mob reached them. Chad was grateful the vehicle they were in was a huge SUV and not some little car, for while the diesel engine roared in response, it also shook from the dozens of rotting undead bodies slamming into it as he plowed his way through them. Finally breaking free of the press of bodies, he took a moment to light up a smoke.

"Gave these things up a year ago," he said blowing a plume of smoke out the window. "If I live long enough to die from them now, it means I survived this bullshit."

The three men traveled in silence for a few moments, then Chad felt a tapping on his shoulder.

"Hey, bro, pass me one of those," Bruce asked. "I don't smoke but could use one myself right about now."

Chad handed his pack of smokes back to Bruce, who lit one and immediately started coughing.

"Fuck it, give me one too," Terry said holding his hand out.

Heading south down the small two lane road, they discussed the route they would need to take to make it back to their hometown.

25

November 11
Day 78

After an early start the next morning, Bravo platoon completed a successful raid of a full residential block and had returned ahead of schedule with plenty of supplies and no casualties. It was now midday, and Stephen was quickly walking towards the two men packing gear onto their machines for the scouting trip. When he was close enough to make out who it was, he was surprised to see that one of the riders was Casper.

“Casper, what do you think you’re doing?” Stephen asked.

“This is an important mission, boss,” he replied. “I think that I owe it to you guys to go up north to see what the problem is with the other safe zones that went dark on us.”

“I agree," Stephen responded, "but you don’t have to go. You’ve done great things for us here lately. You, along with Logan and Kleaner, have the guards running like a well-oiled machine."

“I know I don’t have to go, but I need to do this for you guys," Casper went on. "Mike can’t go because he is still a little banged up. Dan is missing a hand and, well...it’s hard to drive a quad with one hand. You have your hands full with day to day operational stuff and running these raids. And you remember Frank, right? He’s coming with me."

"Ah yes, the bridge tender," Stephen nodded in recognition. "And yes, I’m taking Charlie team out for the first time as a group in the morning."

Stephen reached out and offered his hand, which Casper and Frank both shook firmly.

"Make sure you take enough fuel and ammo to make it there and back," Stephen ordered.

"Way ahead of you, boss," Casper replied. "Each of us has enough gas to make it about a hundred miles each way, and we have a couple hundred rounds of ammo a piece. Fuel won't be hard to find out there, and we both have our Glock 17's. I have my SKS and Frank has his."

Casper and his partner climbed their machines and fired them up.

Stephen handed Casper a handheld radio. "Make sure you keep us updated."

"Roger that," Casper said and turned to Frank. "Let's move out."

"Hold up a minute," Stephen said. "I have something for you."

Stephen jogged over to the command center and quickly returned with a couple of items. He reached up and pulled a rifle and a bag from his shoulder. "This belonged to Chris. I want you to have it."

Stephen handed Casper the AR-15 that once belonged to Chris. "This should help. Take good care of it for him. The bag has ten loaded thirty round magazines."

"I don't know what to say other than thank you for entrusting me with it," Casper said. "I'll bring it back in one piece."

Casper gave the Honda four wheeler some throttle, and they headed out of the safety of the prison walls towards an unknown threat.

The trip north to the interstate was, for the most part, uneventful. The quickness and agility of the small machines easily evaded any random groups of zombies that approached them. They took Route 53 and passed through the town of Romeoville. It was devastated and desolate just like Joliet. Although Casper knew there to be a group of survivors somewhere in this town that had made contact with Stephen and Dan, he had no idea where they were located. Several times in the empty looking town they had to use the quickness of the Honda quads to evade groups of roaming zombies.

They reached I-55 and took the northbound ramp towards Chicago. The interstate was a parking lot, as expected. Here and there were traffic jams that even the small Honda four-wheelers could not get through. They had to find vehicles that still worked and either move or ram them out of the way to continue on their journey. They were heading northeast, but most of the stranded vehicles had been heading south. The resulting mess had caused numerous accidents and tied up the traffic even more in the early stages of the outbreak. Every time they stopped to move cars and trucks, they had to keep one on security. The highway was infested with zombies, and some were still trapped inside the vehicles. It was hard and very time consuming work.

On their approach to Kingery Road, the sun was beginning to set, so Casper looked for a secure place to spend the night. The roads were way too clogged with vehicles and debris, not to mention zombies, to continue north. They would have to wait till morning.

"End of the line for today," Casper called to Frank. "We're going to need a place to sleep."

After some time searching, Casper located a large semi-truck with a sleeper cabin and an attached trailer. One of them could sleep inside while the other pulled watch duties on the roof, out of reach of any zombies that might wander by. Taking the time to properly clear the truck and surrounding vehicles and not seeing anything out of ordinary, they deemed the area for the time clear of danger. Frank opened the truck trailer to see what cargo was inside, and was greeted by the sight of bed mattresses stacked to the ceiling. Frank made Casper help him throw one on the roof of the semi.

"Not bad at all!" Frank said with a whistle and a hint of satisfaction in his voice.

"Get some shut eye, buddy," Casper replied, "and don't forget to relieve me in a few hours!"

*

On the prison walls, it was business as usual for Logan and Kleaner, who sat in the guard tower in the southeast corner of the prison.

"Man do you ever suck, dude," Logan chided.

Kleaner stood up and looked over at his large friend. "It isn't my fault these little .22lr bullets lack stopping power at this distance," Kleaner responded. "I hit that last one eight times in the skull before it died."

Logan snorted, "Yeah I saw, but you're averaging 8.14 rounds per zombie kill, whereas it only takes me 4.76 rounds per kill."

"Are you kidding me? It took you nine rounds on that last one!" Kleaner snapped.

"Nope, that's where you're mistaken, my long range deficient sharpshooting friend," Logan laughed. "It took only four shots. I don't know where you counted nine."

"Oh really?" Kleaner answered. "And how do you figure this?"

"Simple," Logan said, pulling out a clipboard. "I have been keeping track of your sloppy shooting on this here chart I made."

"Let me see that," Kleaner said, snatching the clipboard from Logan.

"It really is quite painful to watch your inadequate sniper skills, but I try to stay unbiased for the sole purpose of this experiment," Logan taunted.

Glancing at the chart, Kleaner's eyebrow arched up. "Say, this is a very impressive chart."

"Thank you, I try to be very thorough."

Kleaner saw the marked score he was racking up and tossed the chart back to Logan.

"This's bullshit. You're fudging the numbers, asshole. I'm out of here. You can experiment on the remaining zombies by yourself," Kleaner replied angrily and stomped out of the guard tower and down the steps. "It's getting too dark anyways to shoot with any accuracy. We need to try this again, inside one hundred yards and with me keeping score!"

Logan couldn't pass up the chance to berate his best friend. Even if he was fudging the numbers to where he did win, that was beside the point. Logan kept on rubbing it in with Kleaner until he exited the guard tower and out into the prison yard before he let it go.

He stood there chuckling at Kleaner's expense, long after Kleaner had left the room. Logan noticed a bit of movement near one of the off limits areas that was abandoned and restricted from use because a large section of the roofing had collapsed and the floor and inner support walls were unstable. Curious as to who or what it might be, Logan crept towards where he last saw movement.

For being a big man, Logan could move surprisingly silently when he needed to. Creeping into the dark and empty structure, Logan heard someone muttering to himself up ahead. He came to a fancy Victorian style staircase and could tell that the noise was coming from above. On this top level the ceiling had collapsed years past and most of the windows were no longer intact. Silently climbing two flights of stairs, Logan heard a voice in the adjacent room.

"What the fuck does he mean he can't find the fertilizer?" the male voice said in anger. "The man's an idiot!"

Logan walked out from around the corner to confront the

unknown speaker.

"What are you doing up here? This area is off limits," Logan said, turning on his flashlight. "Who is an idiot, and what do you need fertilizer for?"

Jonas looked up quickly, startled that someone had not only found him but heard him talking to himself.

"Umm... a buddy of mine...I wanted to plant a garden. Need some fertilizer for it," Jonas said.

"Plant a garden?" Logan said, with a look of confusion on his face. "It's fucking November! Nothing will grow in this cold."

"It's for the spring planting," Jonas said easily. "One can't be too prepared nowadays."

Logan glanced down at Jonas' right hand. "What you got in your hand there?"

Jonas kept eye contact with Logan and slowly put the small paper scrap into his pocket. "Just notes from my deceased wife. God rest her soul," Jonas lied.

"I see," Logan answered. "Okay, listen, you can't be in here. It's not safe. You need to leave now."

Jonas put up his hands in surrender, walking towards the stairwell. "I apologize, sir. I didn't know that."

Logan stood there shaking his head. *He wanted to plant a garden when it's almost the middle of November*! *Who's the idiot here*?

"Hey!" Logan called, stopping Jonas in his tracks. "What are you doing up here anyway?"

"I come up here to get away, think about my family and such," Jonas replied. "The view is great. Hey, come over and take a look. I found a telescope and have it set up here in the other room. You can see for miles."

Against his better judgment, Logan's curiosity got the better of him. Jonas led Logan into the adjacent room and showed him a telescope set up near an open window. Logan glanced at it but then noticed that there were other items in the room. Stacked against a wall were six blue plastic 55 gallon drums that obviously had not been there long. He also saw several boxes stacked in a corner and began to turn back towards where Jonas was standing when he felt a sharp pain pierce his back near his kidneys.

The pain was so intense that he was unable to draw in a breath to scream.

Standing up straight, Logan tried to reach back to the source of his unbelievable agony when an arm snaked around his throat.

"I told you once this knife was sharp. What do ya think now, asshole?" Jonas snarled in Logan's ear.

Logan gathered his breath to scream.

"Now, now," Jonas purred, "we can't have you spoiling my fun."

Jonas wickedly twisted the knife in the wound then ripped the blade from Logan's back.

As blood pulsed from the knife wound, Logan couldn't believe how bad it hurt. He couldn't even breathe!

When Logan staggered, Jonas grabbed his shoulders and spun him around to face him.

"You just couldn't mind your own fucking business, could you?" Jonas said with satisfaction, cocking his head to the side slightly.

Logan leaned heavily on Jonas and tried to reach for his firearm.

Jonas glanced down, saw what Logan was doing and whipped his right elbow into Logan's face, crushing his nose. Logan stumbled back, and Jonas grabbed Logan's pistol from his holster and closed in on the big man again.

Logan feebly tried to push Jonas away but failed and fell back against the window ledge. Jonas stuck the pistol in his belt.

"You're not one of my intended victims," Jonas growled, stepping towards Logan, "but you will do in a pinch."

Rearing back, Jonas gave Logan a front kick to the chest, launching him through the open window. The large man fell down amongst the drooling, hungry jaws of the teeming undead that had gathered below. Jonas leaned out the window, pulse hammering with the sensual pleasure that a victorious kill always gave him. Smiling a big-toothed, grin he listened to the munching sounds down below.

Well, if the fall hadn't snapped his neck, then they could use him for target practice as a zombie tomorrow.

Jonas disappeared down the stairwell and made his way unobserved back to his trailer to ponder his next move.

*

Darkness fell and the moon began to rise. Casper had a great view from the rooftop of the tractor trailer. The bright moonlight lit up the surrounding area for several hundred yards easily. The advantage of moonlight quickly disappeared as a dense fog rolled in from the north. Casper watched as car after car was completely enveloped by the heavy mist. The road ahead of him dipped down into a slight valley which was slowly filled by the fog. The mist did stop and thin out at about one hundred yards or so in front of him.

This was not good, but at least they were out of reach of any undead clawing hands.

The night dragged past and Casper began to get sleepy. A quick check of his watch told him that he had another forty five minutes left of guard duty to go before Frank was to take over. Boredom and exhaustion crashed down, and his mind started to wander. He thought back to his decision to kill his coworkers at the Post Office and everything that had happened since, including Holly. She was in tears when he left.

Casper was relieved by Frank, and he was able get some shuteye. His dreams carried on where he had left off, however, and he found himself in Holly's bed. She was crying, trying to warn him of some impending danger which was coming for him. At first she was pleading for him to run, but then she turned into a zombie and lunged for his throat. Casper ripped himself awake with a scream, a cold sweat pouring from his body.

Unable to go back to sleep, he went outside and relieved a tired Frank early. The pre-dawn light was starting to brighten up the horizon, and it was quite chilly. Pacing along the length of the trailer to keep warm, it was when he was up near the tractor end of the trailer that he first heard something. Cocking his head to hear better, Casper watched the thick fog up ahead.

There it was again. It faintly sounded like coyotes howling, or maybe a herd of cattle.

"Sounds more like a fucking big pack of dogs," he muttered.

Packs of dogs were not unusual to see these days. Many family pets had been left behind, and the dogs quickly turned feral and now ran in large packs.

Casper stood as still as a statue as the howling got closer, and the closer it got, the more cold sweat began to bead his forehead.

Now he could clearly hear screams mixed in with the howling.

Cursing, Casper leaned over and slammed the stock of his assault rifle on top of the truck sleeper cab.

"Wake the fuck up, Frank!"

Switching his rifle off safe, he clutched it for dear life, ready to send some rotten zombie fucker a lead appetizer. The rising sun started to light up the landscape, and the fog to the north began to churn and roll. The screams got louder and louder. The sleeper cab jerked from side to side as Casper's friend gathered his equipment and exited the truck. The noise was rising and falling just like the fog was ebbing and flowing, almost as if the thick mist was alive. Casper saw shambling figures move out of the mist then. Their jerky, stumbling gait made it clear that they were zombies. Casper's rifle swung up, and he fired as the creatures cleared the white wall churning before him. When Frank entered the fight, his rifle echoed deep into the distance, drawing more and more figures towards the sound of battle.

Casper's rifle ran dry in seconds, and as he reloaded a fresh magazine, he saw more and more of the infectious bastards shamble out of the thinning fog.

"Get the ATVs started now!"

While Frank hustled off, Casper scrambled down from the roof of the truck. Reaching the ground, he began firing at the now much closer zombies.

During yet another reload, Casper froze in the act of sending home the rifle bolt.

Ahead of him, the rising sun was burning away the last of the fog.

In the quickly dissipating fog remnants, Casper gasped at what unfolded before his disbelieving eyes.

Clawing and howling for his blood every step of its way was a zombie horde so massive, so ungodly colossal, that Casper could not see its end.

Filling both sides of the interstate, packing over six lanes of traffic were thousands upon thousands of undead.

"I think we're going to need more guns."

He turned back to his ATV, seeing Frank's pale face staring at the monstrous undead army flowing towards them. Casper punched him on the shoulder.

"Snap out of it, pal. We can't do anything here," Casper said firmly. "Let's fall back and radio in what we saw."

After retreating back about a half mile, Casper pulled up to a stop and got out his portable radio.

"Dispatch from Casper, do you copy..."

No answer.

Now with more urgency, "Dispatch from Casper, do you copy, over..."

Frank was visibly sweating in the crisp morning air, and was nervously glancing to the east.

"Casper, maybe we don't have the range, let's fall back."

He ignored Frank and was about to try again when a faint voice broke through.

"Casper, this is dispatch, do you copy? Your transmissions are faint but continue, slowly and clearly."

With a sigh of relief at making contact, Casper filled the dispatcher in on what they discovered. Making sure that she relayed the information back to him correctly, he then told her that they would check some side roads for activity before making their way back to the prison with haste. Behind them, the screaming, howling mass of undead crept closer towards them with every dragging footstep.

26

November 11
Day 78
Alton, Missouri

Matvei sat on the hillside and scanned the small town below him with his binoculars. It was evident that his men had been there. In fact, the town looked similar to some he had passed through in Chechnya during the war. The evidence was spelled out in the burnt out buildings and the bodies of his former mercenaries lying in the street mixed in with the rotting corpses that had been the undead attackers. Matvei calmly observed the birds feeding on the corpses. He noticed how they seemed to avoid the infected that had been turned months before and only fed on the flesh of those who did not appeared to have reanimated. He had been forced to become very patient as of late after a few close calls, and spent a good half hour looking for movement. He found none save for the birds. Satisfied that it was safe to proceed, he got back into the black Dodge Ram he had been driving and made his way into town.

Matvei's mercenary army had long since split up in the last week from the looks of it. The signs all pointed that way. In fact, Matvei was beginning to think pulling his units back together was a pipe dream. He had been chasing them north in a vain attempt to regain his command. Twice, he had followed different groups that split off, and both times he had met a dead-end as they had either been annihilated by the hordes of infected or had simply disintegrated into small groups to fend for themselves. Now, he was convinced that he was on the trail of the last intact group and had been gaining on them the last couple of days. From what he could tell, they were about fifty to a hundred strong. That was all that was left of his entire Dallas command. Only the strongest or luckiest still lived it seemed. The others were long gone or dead. This group was sticking to the plan, however, and he had followed them all the way into Missouri.

Matvei got into town and exited his truck. He could tell that this battle had not been over long. Small fires still burned, and the smell of cordite was in the air. The others had left and headed north out of town. Judging from the tire tracks, it appeared that they were operating the command vehicle, which was a good thing. It would allow him to make radio contact with his ranch in Arizona to check on their status and let them know he was still alive. The fact that there were no infected around and that the fallen mercenaries had their weapons on them led Matvei to believe that the survivors were driven out of town by the ever present infected, who then pursued on foot. He walked among the littered bodies and empty shell casings, scavenging spare ammunition from his dead soldiers. He decided not to look through the rest of the town and concentrate on catching up to the others. He was not entirely sure why he hadn't given up on the chase and tried to reach Arizona on his own. After all the careful planning that he had put together and since had watched all turn to shit, he just wanted to try and salvage something from the operation.

"Call it foolish pride," he muttered, looking among the dead soldiers for supplies.

After stopping long enough to refill his gas tank from gas cans he found in the back of an abandoned vehicle, Matvei headed north out of town and shortly came to an intersection that split off into three different directions. He'd had this problem before and stopped to pull a worn map from his bag. On the map, Matvei had marked various spots, locations of supposed safety. Supply depots of the cartel. It appeared that the group was headed to the cartel compound that had been set up near Oates, Missouri, in the Mark Twain National Forest. The sign on the outside of town told him that he was just leaving Alton on Highway 19 and was probably the best route to stay on for now, at least until he reached Winona. Checking his map, he noted the other forward supply depots that were marked. These locations had been set up by the cartel as forward supply points located near various cities chosen as targets for the outbreak. This was to allow the Americans that were on the cartel payroll a place to fall back and reorganize during the initial outbreak. The hope was to have a nationwide network in place to facilitate a full takeover. Matvei now admitted to himself that this plan had been overly ambitious. The compound in Oates was by far his best option. It served as the fallback area for the greater St. Louis area. He glanced at his tattered map to see what the next closest location was in case more supplies were needed for the journey to Arizona.

"Joliet, Illinois," Matvei pondered. "Well, it's a little out of the way, but if I need to go, I need to go." He decided to see what Oates looked like first.

27

November 12
Day 79

Slowly weaving between stalled and wrecked vehicles, the enormous undead plague crept westward out of the now dead city of Chicago. Food was to be had to the west.

Hunger.

The ravenous hunger forced the gruesome beings to fight one another to get to the front.

Rage.

Blinding all-consuming rage from the constant hunger drove them on.

The monstrous army shuffled onward, following the other stumbling creatures in front of them. The food was out in front. They could smell the pulsing sweet blood.

Chicago was now emptied of living people. The fires that had originated during the panic-filled outbreak spread uncontrolled from building to building. Towering structures, with their support weakened from the blazes, collapsed onto neighboring ones, spreading the destruction and flames even further. Skyscrapers were turned into towering infernos, which sent vast plumes of smoke skyward to be seen from miles away. As the fuel for the fires was spent they left behind the scorched shells of formerly impressive structures. At night, the city of Chicago used to light up the night sky from its thousands of streetlights; now it lit up the sky with its countless flames.

In the streets below, the zombies had long ago lost their food source and began migrating out of the city into the suburbs in search of more living meat. Now, the intense heat of the fires drove them all out of the city. They entered the surrounding suburbs, their forces growing larger and larger, expanding outward from Chicago like a bubble growing in size. Roads and interstates became the arteries and veins for the undead army's march. Every major interstate leading out of Chicago was filled with what looked like a massive, ancient army on the move. Many would pour off the highways at every exit, relentless in their search of living flesh, flooding into the smaller towns' residential side streets.

Town by town, the sheer size and endless numbers of the horde annihilated every meager opposition it came across. Screams of pain and fear, along with the frantic gunshots of the living, were washed away by the hundreds of thousands of howling, forever hungry, accursed beings that fought and clawed at the creatures in front of them just to get a mouthful of fresh bloody meat.

Just a taste.

Just a little blood.

Just a bite of fresh screaming living meat.

Stopping the ever present hunger that pounded at them was impossible, so they kept searching and were always moving. There wasn't any need to rest, for they never grew tired, just as their hunger never stopped.

So they howled.

And screamed.

And moaned as the search for flesh continued.

Death and destruction followed in their wake.

As each location of living bodies were overrun, the thousands that showed up late to feed on succulent flesh screamed their hunger and rage to the skies when there was no more to be had. Eventually forgetting the near missed meals, their soulless eyes turned to the south and started their advance forward again to search for more delicious, screaming meat.

*

The new dawn light climbed its way above the horizon and spilled its golden light onto the frost-covered stone walls of the old prison. The sounds of activity inside gradually picked up in intensity as more and more living humans began another day protected by the very walls that used to protect them in the past by keeping the dredges of humanity locked inside them. Here and there, a rooster greeted the morning light with its call. The small herd of cattle and pigs made it sound more like a farmstead than a compound filled with survivors of a zombie epidemic.

In a corner of the old exercise yard, the sound of an axe biting into wood was currently mixed in with curses and grunts of pain. I was trying to split firewood in an attempt to work myself back into fighting shape. My injuries had made me weak as a kitten, but I couldn't take sitting on my ass any longer. The book I was currently reading could only hold my attention for so long. It now rested on my nightstand waiting for me to finish it. And besides, the laughing I got from riding in that damn Wal-Mart electric shopping cart was getting old and that needed to change. So there I found myself, sweating like I just fought ten rounds. Looking over at the tiny pile of split logs, I couldn't help but scowl in disgust at my weak attempt at wood splitting. Steam spiraled skyward off my sweat-soaked head and shoulders in the cool air.

When I got a chance, I needed to get that gym I wanted up and running. All that high end equipment out there and here I was, cutting wood to build my stamina back up.

I wiped the sweat off my face and took a pull from my water bottle.

"The fucking zombies won't give a shit if I'm tired. They will eat me just the same," I said aloud, trying to work up some motivation.

Picking up the axe again, I placed another log upright for splitting and got to work. Soon I got my second wind, and the pile of firewood grew as I sweated out my weakness. The ribs hurt like a bitch, but there wasn't much I could do about that. The leg wound hurt too, but I favored it as much as I could. For the next hour, I worked until my hands ached as badly as the rest of me. Sinking the axe blade into the large tree stump I used as a base, I plopped my sore carcass onto a chunk of wood and took another break. Like it or not, I was way off my prime at the moment and needed the rest.

I sat there breathing hard and feeling a bit sorry for myself. A cloud of smoke drifted past me. Looking to my left, I noticed Dan with his ever present cigar, perched on a chunk of wood waiting to be split.

"How long you been sitting there?"

"Long enough to make me tired just from watching," he said, blowing a fat, lazy smoke ring in the air which, of course, drifted right into my face.

"You could've given me a hand, you know," I griped.

Dan arched his eyebrows at me.

I realized what I said as soon as I said it. “Sorry. Bad choice of words,” I said, looking at the stump where his left hand used to be. “What did ya need? I know you didn’t come out here to stare at my tight ass.”

Dan stood up and looked around the prison exercise yard.

“Have you seen Stephen around?” he asked. “I have some questions about the Bolingbrook compound to ask him. We don't have a raid out right now, and I can't find him.”

Mopping the sweat from my forehead, I took a long pull from my water bottle and then put in a large, refreshing dip of Copenhagen.

“Nope, haven’t seen him nor anyone else for that matter since I’ve been out here," I remarked. "If he isn’t in his trailer, go check Amber’s. He hangs out over there too. I know I need to get up to Bolingbrook myself to check things out. I’m waiting to hear back from Casper first.”

“I hear you on that, and already looked over at Amber’s place. She said to look for you, said you might know,” Dan responded.

“No clue brother. Have you checked with Logan and Kleaner?” I asked. “I know he wanted to see the results of their zombie killing test.”

“Good thinking. I had a few drinks with Kleaner last night too,” Dan replied. “And hey… have fun with the wood splitting.”

“Are you alright, bro?" I questioned, giving Dan a closer look. "You’re pale as a ghost and sweating more than me!”

“Yeah, I’m fine,” he answered. “The antibiotic they gave me for the hand amputation doesn’t work mixed with alcohol very well.”

“Maybe you should try not drinking then, you goof,” I replied with a chuckle.

Dan nodded and began walking with some effort toward Kleaner and Logan’s trailer.

Watching Dan walk away, I was a bit shocked. Not once did he call me a derogatory name or swear at me. Something had him spooked, or he really felt like shit, or both.

Fuck it. I’m not a psychiatrist or one to ask people how they felt. Everyone could work out their own problems. I had enough of my own to worry about.

I glared at the large pile of logs in front of me.

“Like this damn stack of wood that refuses to split itself for me,” I said to the axe perched next to me.

I picked up the axe and set myself to get some more work in

before breakfast was served.

*

Kleaner woke up with effort with a pounding hangover. Groaning from the spear that was stabbed in his right eye, it took him a few minutes of slapping his own face before he realized that the spear was actually a ray of morning sunlight that, of course, perfectly lined up with his eyeball. Quickly twisting his head out of the way was also a very bad idea. Now it felt like some demented bastard with a nail gun was driving a nail into his skull in time with his rapid pulse.

"Logan," Kleaner croaked. "Will you close that fucking shade?"

Silence.

Fed up with the piercing sunlight and the pounding headache, Kleaner sat up and knocked over the empty bottle of Jack Daniels that he and Dan killed off last night. Cursing loudly, he reached over and pulled down the shade.

He glanced over at Logan's bunk and saw that his large friend had not returned.

"He might have hooked up with one of the girls we saved the other night," Kleaner said aloud to the black Labrador puppy they had adopted last week. It had wandered up to the prison and was practically begging to be let in when Kleaner risked his own neck to grab it. The zombies had been pretty thick that morning.

Kleaner stood up, and with the help of the walls and furniture, made his way over to the cooler that held some cold water bottles. He chugged down an entire bottle, and while he waited for his stomach to quit rebelling over the influx of liquid, he wearily sat on his bed and looked around for his boots. His new dog was always running off and chewing on them. He found his left boot and pulled it on. The trailer door opened, and Dan climbed inside. Kleaner squinted up at his drinking buddy.

"I know I feel like shit, but I sure hope I don't look as bad as you do," he said with a groan.

Dan plopped down on top of the cooler and rubbed his face with his hand. "I do feel like shit, I'm not going to lie," Dan grunted. "Think my stump is infected. I'm burning up with fever."

Kleaner only shrugged his shoulders.

"But that's not why I'm here," Dan said. "Have you seen Stephen around?"

Kleaner shook his head. "Hell no, I just woke up a minute ago.

Have you seen Logan? He never made it to his bunk last night."

"Negative. When was the last you saw him?" Dan asked. "Was it after the test you two were running?"

Kleaner nodded while looking for his right boot. "Yeah, that's when I ran into you, and we killed off Mr. Jack Daniels." Seeing his right boot sticking out from under a dirty shirt, Kleaner slipped it on. "I'm going to go look up in the watchtower. Try looking for Stephen at the Command Center. He might be playing with the new radio equipment."

"I already looked there, but maybe we're just missing one another," Dan sighed. "Guess I will look there again."

Dan headed towards the command center, his path taking him right past the medic trailer. The door flew open as he neared it.

Dan's favorite nurse, the one with the oversized chest, exited the trailer and stopped in front of him. Watching her healthy lungs shake in front of him would probably make even one of the zombies feel better.

"Dan, you look like day old dog shit!" Shelly scolded. "Have you been taking the meds I gave you?"

"Yes ma'am," Dan replied. "But instead of painkillers, I prefer the liquid 80 proof type."

"My goodness!" she exclaimed. "You know you cannot mix those meds with alcohol! Now it looks like you have a fever, and I'm guessing your amputation is infected."

Dan didn't need to answer. His guilty look said it all.

"Didn't you listen to anything I told you?" she asked, shaking her head in frustration. You need to quit asking me out, and start paying attention."

"But, Nurse Shelly, you're an Italian goddess."

"Get your ass into the trailer right now," she ordered, "before we have to amputate your whole arm."

Dan walked into the trailer with more fear than facing a room full of zombies with only a spoon for a weapon.

*

Stephen was currently heading back to the command center after a wild goose chase of his own in an attempt to locate Logan. He wanted the final results of the .22lr experiment. When he reached the guard tower Logan and Kleaner were using, he spoke with the current guards, who reported that they had not seen Logan all night.

They had, however, shown him the notes and rifle that Logan left out.

It was very uncharacteristic of the big man. He hadn't cleaned and stowed away his weapon for the night.

A search of the prison grounds also failed to bring Logan's whereabouts.

Entering the command center, Stephen walked upstairs to the communication room. He was hoping to try out his new radio equipment again today and check in on the other safe zones in the area when the dispatcher noticed him.

"Glad to see you, sir. This came in a few minutes ago from Casper, it doesn't look good," she said holding out a note for him.

"How many times have I said not to call me sir?" Stephen complained absently. He scanned the message from his scout.

"Holy shit!" he said when he read it. "You're certain this is exactly what he said?"

The dispatcher nodded her head. Stephen read the note again and then just stared, first at the paper, then at the dispatcher, then back at the paper. Not saying another word, he turned and ran out of the building at a sprint.

*

I was finished with the wood splitting chores and was stacking the final pieces into a pile when Stephen rushed up to me.

"What the hell are you doing chopping wood?" Stephen exclaimed, short of breath. "I don't need you to be out of commission again or sick like Dan, not when we have a problem like we have never seen before!"

"Whoa, slow down there, hero," I replied, holding my hands out. "What are you babbling about?"

Stephen was pacing back and forth like an expectant father. He stopped long enough to push a note into my hands and then continued with his pacing.

The more I read, the more my balls shriveled up into my belly as if I'd taken a cold shower.

"The scouts report about a hundred thousand zombies heading this way? Interstate's flooded as far as the eye can see with them? Are you sure this is correct?" I asked.

"Casper is out on the scout mission. He has no reason to make shit up," Stephen said, pacing. "If this is what he says he is seeing, I believe him."

"This's not good," I replied grimly. "No wonder we've lost contact with the other settlements. They probably didn't stand a chance. If an army of undead that size were to hit the other safe areas, they would be utterly destroyed. I think we would be safe in the prison, at least for a while. But once surrounded we would most likely be stuck in here with no way out."

"What are we going to do, Mike?" Stephen asked with a worried look. "These creatures are destroying everything in their path while looking for food, just like a pack of welfare recipients with their benefits cut off!"

I had to chuckle. It was good that he had not lost his sense of humor.

"We'll need to get a hold of Romeoville and Bolingbrook on the radio and give them a heads up," Stephen voiced with a tone of dread. "Judging from the location Casper gave and the pace that he said the zombies are advancing at, they do not have much time. A couple days tops."

"We need to meet these creatures out on the interstate where they're confined to a smaller area. In the open they'd spread out and surround this entire area."

"Meet me at the command center in thirty minutes. I'll pass the information onto the other safe zones in the meantime," Stephen said and took off at a jog, stopping only to yell back, "When you show up, we'll go over ideas on how to stop these rotten fuckers!"

I packed up my gear, put away the axe and returned to my RV. I climbed aboard, shivering from the cold outside. Inside the bus, I peeled out of my sweaty clothes. Sadly, it took me a bit longer than I planned. Lifting my arms over my head to put on a clean shirt, I grunted like a bull during mating season. Sharp, stabbing pains ripped through my ribs that were already sore from my exercise earlier. I sat on the edge of the bed and gasped for air with my new shirt stuck on top my head. I was about to make the attempt to put my arms up into the sleeves when a small, soft pair of feminine hands traced their way up my back to my shoulders. I groaned with pleasure as the hands began to rub the large knots from my shoulder region.

"Wow, does that feel awesome," I grunted when something popped behind my right shoulder blade.

"I love your shoulders and back," Mattie whispered into my ear.

Knowing that I didn't have time for the wondrous things her

hands were doing for my beat up body, I tried to exert my Alpha male dominance. I babbled something dumb and realized trying to come up with a coherent sentence while her hands caressed my back was damn near impossible.

I wasn't quite sure how I ended up face down on the mattress, but there I was with Mattie straddling my back, working out the stiffness and soreness in my shoulders.

Again, unsure how it happened, but during the pleasure filled massage, she had somehow managed to take my shorts off and from what I could feel she wasn't wearing clothes either. I reached back and grabbed a handful of a wonderfully smooth and tight butt.

Yup, she's naked, I thought happily as she playfully sank her teeth into my right trapezius muscle.

However, she had only managed to swap the stiffness in my shoulders for stiffness in another area. Mattie lifted herself just enough for me to rotate onto my back and then straddled me once again.

"Mattie, I am supposed to meet Stephen in twenty minutes. We got a big situation going down," I groaned as her long hair tickled my face and her hypnotic eyes captured me in their spell.

She ground her hips into me and grinned. "Feels like I got a big situation right here to take care of first."

My last coherent thought had something to do with images of silky bare skin and hot wetness.

*

By the time I limped into the command center, it was way past the thirty minutes that Stephen had allotted me. From the looks of things he had gotten started without me. A number of guys hovered with him over a map and batted around ideas.

Oh well. Too bad, I could just blame it on my injuries.

"You're late," Stephen said, glancing up from a map.

"What have we got so far, bro?"

"I made contact with Casper on the radio and received an update," Stephen replied. "He's on his way back here now. I also spoke with Kirk Simms up in Bolingbrook. They will get hit first, probably followed by Romeoville soon after. The zombies on the highway are definitely traveling somewhat faster and a hell of a lot more in numbers than any that are wandering through the neighborhoods and side streets. I also directed that our AM broadcast be changed to update the current situation."

Stephen pointed down at the map on the table and explained that while the zombie horde was now southwest of Kingery Rd on I-55, the slow but steady pace they were moving would allow for two or three days before they reached Highway 53 and poured off the interstate ramps right onto the Bolingbrook safe zone and its inhabitants. That path would lead them straight through Romeoville and then right to our very doorstep.

"I'm already coming up with a defensive perimeter and a plan to hold a line in the sand so to speak," Stephen said with some newfound confidence. "So we have three days to come up with and implement a plan to kill a lot of fucking zombies."

"I've been thinking about that, and do believe I have a couple of suggestions," I said. I leaned over the map and looked at the lines Stephen had drawn. "This is what we are going to do."

*

Lewis sat in his truck scowling at the list of items Jonas requested he find. It had taken him much longer than the three days Jonas gave him to find the right stuff and once he finally acquired it all, Jonas informed him that he wasn't ready and told him to wait.

He wasn't the least bit happy about it.

Didn't that bastard realize Lewis didn't have thirty foot stone walls protecting his ass like Jonas did?

Every night he had to move to different locations since the zombies always sniffed him out, forcing him to flee. He gave up days ago looking for a secure building every night, preferring to sleep in the truck and move as soon as the smelly fuckers showed up. Besides, it had taken him several days to acquire the listed items, and he didn't want to lose the stuff by getting separated from it.

Lewis sort of had an idea what the stuff was for, but being a lifetime politician did not give him much time to study anything other than how best to take advantage of his constituent's problems and fears. He dimly remembered something about a few of the items he gathered as being components for some form of weapon that the Homeland Security WMD classes focused on. However, he had slept through the majority of the meetings.

Knowing that he had hours before the next message was transmitted by Jonas, Lewis planned on getting some shut eye since he didn't see any of those damned zombies around.

"Of course that won't last very long," he said sourly.

He closed his eyes anyway and was fast asleep in seconds.

28

November 12
Day 79

"To really kill these fuckers by the thousands we need to get a lot of them together at the same time," I said to Stephen. "They're packed in so close on the interstate, the hard work is done for us by the design of the highway itself, with the fencing on each side and no ditch separating north and southbound lanes."

Stephen nodded in agreement and looked up from his notepad.

"Now here's what I was thinking," I said. I walked over to the dry erase board set up on the wall. Drawing a rough diagram of the highway, I explained the steps we needed to take in preparation of the coming fight.

"First thing I wanna try is to lay out a welcome mat for them. Take two fuel trucks, drive them up I-55 to meet the horde head on. We'll need to clear a path for the trucks on the highway and need to get on it right away. We'll turn those fuel trucks around, open the valves, and drive back southbound slowly with the zombies following as all the fuel leaks out. I want the zombies chasing the trucks and sloshing around in that gasoline real good. When the trucks are empty, the drivers bail, and we light it up. That should slow them down a bit."

Stephen had a grim smile as I explained this. "We may be able to implement that tomorrow," he said. "Maybe get two passes in if we have the time."

"Now this spot here, just to the northeast of Rt. 53, is where we want to make our stand," I explained, drawing out my ideas onto the marker board. "At that designated spot, we need to rip up some of the concrete barriers that separate north and southbound lanes. We need to park either several buses or semi-trailers set at an angle to funnel the zombies coming down the north bound lanes into the southbound lanes, which will create a bottleneck of sorts. We can also use bait to draw them into the southbound lanes."

"By 'bait'," Stephen asked, "you mean *us*?"

"Yeah us. Then we can set platforms along the bottleneck near the concrete dividers for our people to fire down into the zombies as they pass by. By doing this we can form a vast kill zone with a buffer from which we can throw Molotov cocktails and—"

"What about explosives?" Stephen interrupted. "Dan brought back a shitload from that rock quarry from his trip down south."

"I'm glad you brought that up, Stephen," I replied. "We'll need to improvise dozens of vehicles or fuel tankers to explode along the route these creatures will take, make them pay for every shuffling staggering step they." I grinned evilly at him. "And here's the best part. We need to send someone to the landfill and get one of those trash compactors with the big steel wheels. With that, we can drive up and down both sides of the highway, turning these zombie fucks into hundreds of tons of twitching hamburger. Between that, blowing them up, and burning them like candles, I think it's our best chance. Stop them on the interstate, or we get rolled over out in the open."

Stephen was also grinning. "I like your style, Mike," he said with a chuckle. "You always had a flair for destruction."

"We need to act fast, though. Remember these bastards might not move very fast, but they do not sleep or rest. They can cover a lot of ground in two days."

"I know," Stephen replied, "and I've factored that into the rest of my defensive plans. The Romeoville safe zone is in an industrial park, and they are relying more on stealth than anything. We don't have the time to properly defend it, and with that in mind I'm going to concentrate on Bolingbrook. The Romeoville guys seem a little skittish, but are promising to help out. I want Dan to lay out a line of explosives several hundred yards in front of their safe zone. Create a large kill zone and spread this over as wide a front as possible, to keep us from getting flanked by the zombies who are not coming from the highway. I don't know how many that is for now. In that regard, we need to try to prevent the zombies on the interstate that make it past your kill zone from getting off at the exits."

"We can seal the exits off," I suggested. "Hopefully keep them flowing right on past us. I don't know if a few parked vehicles would work, though, if they know we're back there."

"Anyway," Stephen continued, "the rest of my plan involves a little bit of running, gunning and scorched earth policy. I want to basically set Bolingbrook south of I-55, along with all of Romeoville and Lockport, on fire when the time comes. Burn everything, just like the Russians when they retreated from the Nazi's in WWII. We can have rovers in trucks lighting the fires and shoot any zombies that manage to make it through the flames. Again using ourselves as bait, maybe we can force or draw the zombies around Joliet, further south and west."

"That's going to take a lot of work and even more luck," I said, "but it's worth a shot."

Most of the others present nodded their heads in agreement. From the idle chatter, it seemed this was our only good option. The men quieted when Stephen spoke again.

"On that note, I'd like you to head up to Bolingbrook to meet with Kirk and set up your plan, Mike. I'll take Alpha platoon on a raid to the Exxon/Mobile fuel refinery near Wilmington and get as many full fuel tankers as possible to take up to your position. The fuel that we will get doesn't need to burn in engines, it just needs to burn. We'll also swing past the landfill along the way back to get the heavy equipment you want."

"Sounds good," I replied. "I'll be taking Mattie with me, and Casper once he gets back. I want Casper since he was an eyewitness to the size of this gathering. I also want to take both Bravo and Charlie platoons with me today, along with anyone else who can work. We'll have to leave a skeleton crew here of course, but we have a shitload of work to do out there."

"I'll get a message out over the loudspeakers to have all squad leaders assemble for a briefing within the hour," Stephen said, rubbing his face. "This is going to be a logistical nightmare."

"I'll see you before I leave then. For now I need to start getting myself ready." I hobbled outside and back towards my RV.

Grunting in moderate pain, I climb into the RV and noticed that Mattie was no longer there. A post-it note stated that she had gone over to visit the women we rescued the night of the assault on Kettle's church. It was good that the girls all seemed to be adjusting to no longer being some freak's sex toy. Surprisingly, a couple of the guards had started courting a few as their girlfriends. Some were still having a rough go of it, however. Flashbacks and such sent them into fits of uncontrollable sobbing and one girl had no recollection of what happened at all. Mattie herself had spotty memories of how she was captured and what she went through.

I pulled out my rucksack, preparing the stuff I thought I would need to pull off my plan. Other than a few necessities such as a few days' clothing and toiletries, the rest would be ammo and firearms and, of course, my bat and shield. Hopefully we wouldn't use too much ammo. My idea hinged mainly on burning and squishing more than shooting them. Stephen was the one who liked all the shooting. I just wanted them dead.

I also threw in my pack plenty of first aid supplies that we might need and also for my current injuries. Seeing that I had a little time I decided to grab a nap, for I had no idea when the next good sleep would be available to me. Plopping my tired ass on the bed, I quickly fell asleep with Mattie's faint perfume smell still on my pillows.

*

Jonas held the two-way radio in his hand. He was not looking forward to talking to that whining bitch Lewis. Jonas only turned on his radio at designated times, though, for he knew from the long rants that he had to sit through, they usually contained information of little worth.

He had long ago discovered that Lewis just plain loved to hear himself bitch.

The time to bring that insufferable prick inside the prison walls was drawing near. He had just heard that many of the occupants would be leaving shortly due to some zombie horde that was approaching from Chicago. From what he had overheard, they would be attempting to battle the creatures up north somewhere.

With the lack of people present to ask questions or investigate like that idiot Logan had done, it was a prime opportunity to bring Lewis, along with the requested supplies inside the walls.

Jonas walked to the main gate, met the other corpse burning detail workers, and prepared to go about his duty in order to continue the facade of pulling his weight. On the way, he had observed Mattie with several other women sitting at the area set aside for a campfire. They appeared to be having a little morning picnic and talking amongst themselves. Jonas recognized some of the others as being the women that were brought back from Father Kettle's church. They had never seen him while he performed his duties inside Father Kettle's church, and he was glad for it.

It was a blessing that the whore Mattie didn't remember it was him choking and knocking her unconscious when Father Kettle's men captured her. Otherwise his cover would have been blown the minute they brought the slut back alive.

Jonas stared hard at the ladies as he marched past them, his fingers itching to grab his razor sharp blade he had secreted under his jacket. With effort that made him tremble, he resisted the impulse and continued past them to meet the other burning detail folks at the gate. He quickly pushed sinful thoughts of the women out of his head. He had an important task to see to as soon as he could get outside. When they exited the prison, Jonas waited until the guards destroyed all the undead that had gathered at the gate and made his way to check on something before someone else from the detail beat him to it. He made his way towards the old administrative side of the prison walls, and there he saw what he was hoping to find. The mangled beyond recognition bloody corpse of the former security guard Logan.

"Looks like the fall killed you after all, eh big guy?" Jonas said quietly.

Fortunately the undead had snacked on his body quite a bit, as his weight had fallen substantially to the point where Jonas was able to drag the corpse unaided to the burning pit.

Once he made it there, he had another detail worker unknowingly help him toss Logan's corpse into the hot flames of the pyre. The worker had no idea. To him it was just another of today's dozens of loathsome, stinking corpses to burn. Dusting his hands off, Jonas dutifully helped the others collect and toss dead corpses onto the growing mound within the large bonfire. Things couldn't be going better. With so many leaving, it would be too late for anyone to suspect that Logan was dead. He could always spread a rumor that Logan left to go fight the zombies up north as an excuse for him being gone.

Besides, he reasoned, if any did begin to think otherwise, they could just be made to disappear like Logan.

Nobody noticed Jonas' grin. If they had, they would have wondered why he was smiling as he tossed armload after armload of wood and bodies into the flames to be turned to ashes.

29

November 12
Day 79

Over twenty men stood in front of a large marker board in front of the conference room located on the ground level of the prisons' command center.

"So that's basically it, gentlemen," Stephen told the group of gathered men who served as squad and fire team leaders in the three security platoons and that were going to go into action today.

He had just gone over the overall plan and today's assignments, and everyone was on edge after learning of the zombie horde headed their way.

"We're going to set up a bottleneck on I-55 to kill as many of these bastards as we can." Stephen said. "I want to turn the battlefield in front of the Bolingbrook safe zone into a kill zone. We'll try to create a wedge of fire and drive any surviving zombies out around and past Joliet. Get them on I-55 south and I-80 west, if possible. All exits off the expressways need to be sealed off, and a wall of fire needs to be put up several miles long, extending from Bolingbrook, through Romeoville and into Lockport, with our guns plugging the holes."

Stephen paused, letting the visual of what his plan entailed sink into the men's brains. They shook their heads, some with understanding, others with a bewildered look on their faces.

"I really don't need to say 'be careful', so I won't insult everyone's intelligence by doing so," he added. "There's a gigantic wave of zombies headed our way and with a little planning, and a lot of luck, we'll see this through to the end. And finally, keep in mind that we'll not only be protecting ourselves out there today but also all the extra workers we're bringing with us. We will be traveling farther and staying out longer than ever before. Everyone keep your heads on a swivel and stay alert out there. We do that, and just maybe we can all make it back here safely."

I was standing off to the side of the room leaning against the wall. The other men in the room nodded in agreement as they broke off into smaller groups discussing the plan's merits and making final preparations. Eventually they would need to gather their squads for the mission. Those men, in turn, would need to be briefed. Following them from the command center, I made my way to my truck with the large V-plow attached to the front. I was going to lead a twenty truck convoy of well over a hundred people up to Route 53 and I-55 to get started on the zombie traps and fortifications. Along with that, I personally needed to meet up with Kirk Simms, the man in charge at the Bolingbrook safe zone.

I climbed up into the big truck. The huge diesel engine fired up and sent a plume of exhaust skyward. Outside, Mattie and Casper said their goodbyes to the others who were staying behind. Mattie gave Stephen and Dan a big hug and wished them luck on their portion of the assault and raids. Casper stood off to the side and talked quietly with Holly, who was hugging him with tears in her eyes. She had taken quite the liking to Casper and he appeared to be similarly infatuated with her.

The only goodbye I received was "the finger" from Dan, who even though he was suffering from fever, was going to take a couple of guys and start preparing the explosives he had recovered from the mine. The explosive charges were going to have to start being deployed today due to time constraints, with the majority of the work completed by tomorrow.

He flipped me off and unsuccessfully tried to lock lips with Mattie, which showed me that Dan had begun to break out of his almost suicidal funk and was now back to his salty, obnoxious self again.

"Saddle up, you two. We got work to do!" I shouted out the window and blasted the air horn a few times for good measure.

Mattie and Casper hurriedly finished their farewells and climbed aboard the truck. The gates were already opening from the corpse burning detail returning, and we were able to squeeze through with little delay.

The big truck rumbled through the city streets with little

problem as we made our way to Route 53, the others falling in behind us. It was about a ten mile drive to our destination, which was farther than one might think when you add the living dead into the mix. Heading north now, I weaved the truck through abandoned vehicles and carefully shoved a few smaller ones aside with the V-plow. Knowing it was going to take some time, I tried to get comfortable and put my arm around Mattie like we were cruising through town on a date. It was a little hard to be romantic, though, when I was turning the random wandering zombie that got in front of the steel snowplow into road kill. Apparently the sickening sound of bodies slamming into the plow does not turn women on. Go figure.

It took nearly an hour and a half, but we made the trip without problems. I had taken the time to clear a path so future runs would be much shorter. Now that we were here, Bravo platoon was going to be pulling security while Charlie platoon started preparing the kill zone along with the others. It was now well past noon, and this was shaping up to be a long, cold day. Leaving them to their work on the interstate, I pulled up to the fenced-in Bolingbrook safe zone nearby. If I remembered correctly, the facility used to be a car and truck wholesale auction house for used cars prior to the outbreak. The place was monstrous, and the majority of it was parking lot. Looking around, I could see why they would be worried about the size of the army heading their way. They had little in the way of a protective perimeter other than a tall chain link fence with barbed wire on top and vehicles pushed up against it from the inside. Unfortunately, due to the size of the parking lot, they did not have nearly enough vehicles to line the fence with. Some areas only had a single car where I would prefer three high and two deep. I recalled how at our FEMA safe zone a single row of stacked cars got overturned by thousands of zombies constantly pushing into it. That was something we would need to address. Just their sheer weight would punch through this fence with ease if we didn't successfully stop them all out on the interstate.

There were several people waiting when I pulled up to the front gate. I shut off the truck and hobbled up to the gate where I was met by their top guy.

"How's it going, Mike?" he asked and stuck his hand out. "Good to see you again."

"I've been better," I said, pointing at my bad leg, "and you?"

Kirk was about my height but very slim. He looked to be about thirty years old, give or take a few, and had rugged good looks.

"I'm a few months behind on my mortgage, but I think the banks will understand with our current situation," he answered with a chuckle. "Come inside, and we can get down to business with what you think we can do about the mess heading our way."

I had Casper pull our truck inside a large sheet metal building as Kirk then went about explaining that he used to be an accountant here at the auction house and how he had helped his coworkers and family members survive the initial outbreak. The rest of the survivors showed up at random times thereafter, often ill equipped. He summed up his story and current situation by saying that while they did not have a lot of firepower, but that they were stacked deep with food supplies from all the shipping warehouses nearby.

"We've made significant progress, implementing some of the suggestions and ideas I learned from your compound at the prison while I was down there a few days ago," Kirk mentioned, "and we've put those extra guns you gave us to good use. We even found some more of our own, but we in no way match your firepower."

"That may be true, but you can't bank on guns as an answer," I said, "because someday bullets are going to be scarce and you better have an alternative."

Once Casper joined us, I had him relate to Kirk exactly what he had witnessed during his scout mission. Kirk's face became more attentive and then had a slightly frightened look.

"That definitely isn't encouraging to hear," he said when Casper briefed him. "What do you have in mind? None of us here have any police or military training."

Well that wasn't encouraging either. I went into detail about what our plan on the interstate entailed and what was required of him to help bring it about.

"We do have access to some heavy machinery and tools," Kirk said eagerly, "and I think we have some people who can operate it."

"Great, get them assembled immediately. I want to get started now, and even then we might not have enough time to finish. And Stephen wants a trench dug about two hundred yards off your fence line and filled with oil, cardboard, wood, anything that can burn. I stopped my tirade and looked at him gravely. "You might want to write this down. I know I am throwing a lot at you all at once."

After he grabbed a pen and some paper, I continued. "We need to prep all the buildings to the north and east of here ready to burn. Also, get a team together and have them start packing the kill zone to the east with abandoned vehicles to use as I.E.Ds. We have some explosives here now, but we are going to use those for the interstate. The rest should be here tomorrow. You folks also have a hospital nearby that we may want to check for medical supplies and equipment if you haven't already. I remember there being a U-Haul store across the interstate that we may want to hit up for personnel transport vehicles in case we have to hightail it out of here in a hurry."

"That's a lot to handle," Kirk said as he scribbled down my suggestions. "But nobody said this was going to be easy."

Kirk stood up and began yelling orders for bodies and the equipment needed. I saw people start to move in all directions. This was an expansive complex that could easily hold thousands of refugees during a normal crisis, perhaps maybe a natural disaster. But with the limited fencing and shelter, it was ill suited for a zombie siege.

"I'll have some guys up on the highway shortly to help out," Kirk told me before running off.

I waved Mattie and Casper over. "Come on let's get back to the truck. We need to get out to the highway and make sure they don't fuck this up. We're only going to get one chance, and I want it to be our best shot."

"Everyone is trying, Mike. Cut them some slack," Mattie said, along with a reassuring pat on the back.

"Fuck that, I'll cut them some slack if we live," I replied.

Gunshots from the outer perimeter team rang out as they dropped incoming zombies, but luckily the amount of incoming was sporadic at this time. This particular area was not near any major residential area. The interstate where we were setting up was clogged with abandoned vehicles, and the men were moving the cars either out of the way or into position, by pushing or towing them. It wasn't long before help in the form of manpower and heavy equipment began to show up from the Bolingbrook safe zone. The rumble of a large front end loader was music to my ears. Kirk was riding in it along with the driver. When it stopped near me, I climbed up and shouted over the roar of the engine where I wanted the first stack of cars set up as a barricade. Several truckloads of workers also began to pour in from Romeoville, adding to the frantic fray.

I directed a skinny man driving a forklift over to the concrete barriers and instructed him and a small team to begin removal of a large section of barriers, opening up a gap between all north and southbound lanes.

Now having a free moment, I glanced around for a dependable man, turned to see Casper nearby, and grabbed him by the shoulder.

"Casper, go get one of these trucks started that has fuel. I want you to assemble a small three man team to set up a forward observation post and take them up the road to get a visual on the location of the incoming zombies. Give them the portable radio and make sure they keep us updated."

Casper took off at a sprint as Mattie walked up next to me.

"What do you want me to do, Mike?" she asked.

"I need you to stand there and look hot."

She looked like she didn't appreciate the joke.

"Just joking," I said, and then quickly added, "I need you to get someone to locate a bus or semi-truck to park at an angle to help funnel the zombies into the bottleneck we are setting up. The zombies will be coming at us from the northbound lanes and into the southbound lanes where we ripped up the concrete dividers."

As she walked away, I took a minute to ogle her shapely ass. After a few delicious moments, I turned to check on the progress with the dividers and noticed that quite a few other men were watching her ass as well.

Well, I couldn't really blame them.

The forklift crew now had several concrete dividers removed and repositioned them at an angle in front of where the vehicle barrier and bus would be parked. While not the perfect solution, the barriers should slow the zombies down some and help greatly with funneling them to where we wanted them to go. The whole southbound lane needed to be cleared out so the zombies had room to move as they shuffled past. Both lanes were now in the process of being cleared out in front of us to make room for the heavy equipment to operate as well as to set up a kill zone.

There was so much work to do. I sighed. And so little time.

I walked up to the nearby forklift operator and asked him to remove as many of the barriers as needed and set them in a row down into the ditch all the way out to the fence that ran parallel to the highway. This was to be done on both the north and south side of the interstate. We didn't want any zombies getting around our defensive position on our flanks. They all needed to be funneled over into the southbound lanes. I added my muscle into helping set the barricades into position and lining up a layer of vehicles behind them. Abandoned vehicles were an asset and luxury that we had plenty of, but it sure was a shame to see a fifty thousand dollar BMW get a five hundred dollar clunker parked on top of it.

Casper returned not too long after that and stood by while I took a break. He reported roughly where the zombies were and mentioned that at their current pace they would probably arrive the day after tomorrow. Sitting there thinking of what we needed to do in the meantime, I grabbed my ever present can of Copenhagen and put in a big dip of chew.

"What we need to do now is set up some of these cars on the road to be used as I.E.D's. We will want them ready to blow when the zombies pass by."

"You leave that to me, boss," Casper replied. "I know enough about explosives to make pipe bombs. I'm sure I can fabricate what you're after by using some of the explosives that Dan brought up from that rock quarry."

"Pipe bombs? How the hell do you know how to make pipe bombs?"

"Don't ask, don't tell, boss," Casper said with a grin while wagging a finger at me, and walked over to the truck that had just arrived with some explosives.

That man has some serious issues, I thought as I spat some tobacco juice onto the pavement. I was damn glad he was on our side!

Rifle fire cracking in the distance in all directions reminded me that, although the old problems we all faced were behind us, a real and deadly problem in the form of the living dead was all around us and closing in faster than I liked.

A loud engine caught my attention, coming up behind me. I turned to see that it was Mattie, who had found a large Greyhound bus, and a few others behind her who were driving bread trucks and a semi-tractor. Mattie pulled up alongside of me and flashed me a brilliant smile.

"Will these work, Mike?"

"Those are exactly what we need. Good job," I remarked. "Park them alongside the barriers and stack of cars across the road up ahead. Those others vehicles will make excellent shooting platforms. Set them up parallel to the southbound lane, extending back towards our position."

As they did this, I went up to check on Casper. He had recruited and instructed quite a few people to move abandoned cars out ahead of the bottleneck along the path that the zombies would be using for their approach to our positions. He then got down to business rigging each vehicle to blow and had his helpers pack each car with any loose metal debris that could be found. The detonators Casper was attaching to the explosives were the same as used by the rock quarry that worked via a radio signal transmitted from a panel. Other fuel bombs were rigged to blow by firing a tracer round into a milk jug of gasoline sitting on the intended target. A few had old-fashioned fuses that needed a flame to light.

The crews removing the concrete barriers were then instructed to remove another section of highway dividers a quarter mile further up the road and bring those barriers back here to help with the funneling. Although they didn't understand why I needed this, they got to it, and I just advised them to trust me.

Walking back to our main position, I took the time to check in on the scouts who were monitoring the progress and location of the advancing zombies. A very scared and stuttering voice answered me and stated that the main force was a good mile north of the I-355 toll road, and there did not seem to be an end in sight.

The man quickly asked to return back to the compound.

"Negative!" I shot back. "I need eyes up front so we can gauge where we need to be when they get here."

I was answered in silence.

Whoever it was had better not sneak back here, or I would personally feed them my knuckles and send them back to the front.

It was approaching dark when I saw nearly a dozen sets of headlights approaching from the south. It appeared that Stephen's mission was a success, as he had several semi-tanker trucks filled with hopefully flammable liquid and an enormous Caterpillar 836H heavy equipment tractor with knobby steel wheels. It was on the back of a flatbed trailer that was borrowed from Joliet's smelly landfill.

"Glad to see you got what we needed!" I shouted to Stephen as he exited his truck.

"We were slowed up a bit from some infected bastards near the oil refinery, but our guys handled themselves flawlessly." Stephen shut his truck door. "It seems that our little boot camp training we put our troops through was very effective."

"Outstanding, things are going along as well as can be here," I responded. "Now that we have the tanker trucks, we need to set them out past the main kill zone. I would say just before the I-355 ramps. We will want the burn area pretty clear of obstructions so as to pack them in pretty tight. I also got some scouts up there keeping a tally of the zombies' progress."

"I'll let the drivers know where to go and radio the scouts to let them know who is coming their way," Stephen answered and left to go tell the drivers what we had planned for them.

While Stephen was working on that, I limped over to the truck with the trash compactor on the trailer.

"Hey guys, I need you to position this monster in the southbound lanes about fifty yards south of the bottleneck area," I instructed them, also pointing where I needed the enormous machine.

Watching them position my "ace in the hole", I noticed that Casper had returned from prepping the explosives.

"How did it go, Casper?"

"It was cake once I figured out how to rig the charges properly," Casper replied, "but it's getting too dark, and I am not that sure of myself to be messing with high explosives by flashlight."

"Good point," I agreed. "We'll be back at it at first light, and I want you to finish what you have left to do if you're able. The rest of the explosives should be ready by morning, but make sure you leave enough for Stephen. I think he was going to set some charges near Kirk's compound in case any get through."

"You got it, boss," Casper replied. "I'll check with Stephen and see if he is going to need help setting his charges in the morning."

I sighed, surprised by the cloud of visible breath in the process, made me realize how cold it had gotten when the sun set. On my way back to the dump truck for my thick flannel coat, I saw that Mattie had climbed aboard to keep warm.

"You got the right idea, girl!" I said as I climbed inside and rubbed my hands together. "Got cold as hell out there after the sun went down."

Mattie looked over at me with a concerned look.

Uh oh. I didn't like that look.

"What's bothering you, Mattie?"

"I'm worried, Mike. If there's as many of these zombies coming this way as Casper says, do you think we have a chance?"

I put my arm around her and pulled her close, trying to comfort her. "I won't lie to ya, Mattie. I have no idea," I said in the most reassuring tone I could muster. "but this is the best we can do on such short notice. We have to try or a lot of people are going to die. If not us, then some other poor group of survivors. The more we destroy now, the fewer we will have to worry about in the future."

She burrowed herself into my chest, wrapping her arms around my tender ribs. "I know, but it seems like we never get a break," she said softly. "It's always one emergency after another."

I didn't want to tell her that every major populated area in the country probably looked like what was coming our way. She was freaked out enough as it was.

"I hear you," I said. "This'll be a good way to test tactics in case we ever need to do it again.

She looked up at me questioningly.

"Never mind," I said shaking my head. "Look, we can't worry about the hand we are dealt. It's how we deal with it that counts."

Sitting there holding on to each other as if it was all that kept us sane, I swear I could faintly hear the tortured howling and screams far to the north. It was like the legions of Hell were coming for our very souls. Finally, I peeled myself from her warm grasp, grabbed my coat and left to check on the men and help out where needed. The next few hours flew by in what seemed like seconds.

When I eventually decided to call it a night, Stephen notified me that he had called the scouts in for the night and was taking some of the men back to the relative safety of the prison for the night. There was also another set of tankers at the refinery that he wanted to grab tomorrow.

"I didn't know you were afraid of the dark and a little cold weather," I joked.

Stephen jerked a bit at me basically calling him a coward.

"What do you mean by that?"

"I'm staying here tonight," I stated. "I'm not leaving. We have way too much to do here, and I want to get a jump on it at first light. Besides, I know you too well. You won't wake up till noon."

"Fine, you stay here and freeze all night," Stephen shot back. "I am going to keep warm with Amber's tight ass pressed into me. Maybe I will keep Mattie warm too, she's heading back with us."

"Just don't keep her up all night, she gets bitchy when she is tired," I replied nonchalantly. "I'm just busting your balls. Kirk said that any of us are welcome to stay at their place. They have plenty of room. Make sure you all don't forget and oversleep tomorrow. There's a party heading this way and we're on the menu."

"Some of the guys will probably elect to stay up here with you," Stephen answered with a grin. "But it's home sweet home for me! Amber is waiting with hot food and sexy lingerie. I told you about my side trip to Victoria's Secret the other day, didn't I?"

"You always had a thing for dirty girls!" I chuckled.

Both of us laughed as we went our separate ways.

I understood Stephen's reason for stopping the work at night. It got dark early this time of year, and we had worked late into the evening. It was just not safe to be out working in force after dark with all of the zombies milling about. Although they constantly moaned and howled, they had the uncanny ability to sneak up on you unnoticed. It was kind of like the people who live next to a railroad. After a while they didn't seem to notice the loud trains going by. We lost one guard today who didn't realize that the moaning sound of a zombie that he had heard nonstop for weeks was actually one very close by. The poor soul had been helping others prepare to move a car to set up as an I.E.D. and failed to see that trapped inside the vehicle was a zombie. After opening the car door, the ravenous creature latched on to one of the man's arms, ripping a large chuck of flesh free. The disgusting monster was quickly disposed of with a head shot, and before his buddies could do anything, the doomed man pulled his pistol and held it in a white knuckled grip. Without saying a word, he sprinted off into the darkness. We heard the faint retort of a gunshot a short time later.

30

November 12
Day 79

Jonas stood silently in the dark. He was back in the old off limits area of the prison where he'd stored some of the equipment needed to bring these cocky assholes to their knees. Outside the walls, he clearly heard the pitiful wailing of the hungry undead battering the thick prison walls with their mangled hands. Inside the walls, he heard the last vestiges of humanity in this area go about their useless lives.

Jonas held his arms out and savored the pitch black environment in which he stood. He truly loved the night. The darkness hid the ugliness that he saw in each and every meat sack that these pathetic survivors represented.

How was it that a pure soul such as Father Kettle was murdered while these wretched sinners thrived without retribution?

Jonas angrily clenched his hands into fists until his knuckles cracked. Yes, it was only in darkness where everything was pure and equal, no shades of gray to make the weak run astray from the true path that Father Kettle had shown him.

Thinking back, Jonas realized that most of his childhood and all of his adult life he had struggled to conform to what society deemed normal. When he was unable to conform to those ideals, it usually landed his ass in jail. And he was in jail many, many times. Many of his school counselors and juvenile probation officers had told his mother that he was only acting out from the lack of a father figure at home, but that was pure bullshit. The fact of the matter was that his mother was a whore, and he had many "father figures" going in and out of his mother's trailer park bedroom several times a day. Once, a school counselor decided to pay Jonas and his mother a visit at home. A short time later, that counselor decided to be a temporary "father figure". The noises he heard coming from his mother's bedroom made Jonas both disgusted and enraged. When that same counselor was found in a ditch near Jonas' trailer park home the next day with multiple stab wounds, the other social workers agreed he wasn't just acting out anymore.

When the justice system was unable to prove in court that Jonas had been the killer, he had gotten away—literally— with murder. It wasn't long before his mother turned up missing. Jonas subsequently was sent to a foster home. When the family's pets turned up missing, Jonas was suspected but again couldn't be proven as the culprit. Soon he was sent to yet another foster home. Within the week, the social worker handling Jonas's case got the frantic call from the kind foster family telling her to come get Jonas. The strange kid had scared the shit out of them by apparently standing over their bed watching them sleep. Not long after that incident, Jonas had been arrested for stabbing another foster child and was sent to juvenile prison and the case worker washed her hands of him. The years passed, Jonas became of an adult age, and was caught committing other serious crimes and had subsequently been sent to prison for twenty years. What the different law enforcement jurisdictions that had him incarcerated did not know about Jonas was the dozens of cold case homicides or missing persons for which he was directly responsible. And now they never would. It was in the adult prison system where he discovered that he didn't even fit in among the so-called scum of society. He was, as Father Kettle labeled him, a "special individual".

It was in general population where Jonas first met Father Kettle, and it was Father Kettle who had shown him that the "ends justify the means." Jonas had finally found his father figure and had learned from him that it did not matter what he did or who he hurt as long as his missions were fulfilled. His last mission, handed down by Father Kettle before his murder, was simple: make these bastards pay.

Standing there clenching and unclenching his fists, he longed for the pale throat of a lusting whore to throttle or the worn handle of his knife to plunge again and again into the putrid shell of a disgusting, screaming sinner. Just as he was beginning to shake with righteous anger, his two-way radio crackled to life.

"Jonas...can you hear me? Are you there? This is Lewis...answer me, damn you!"

Jonas unhooked the radio from his belt and raised it to his lips.

"Lewis, for the last and final time, if you try to contact me at a time other than the one I requested, I will gut you like a fish and feed you to the fucking demons outside," he said without a trace of emotion. "You need to be patient. A few more days at most, and I will be able to bring you inside the walls. Just be sure you have all items on the list."

A few seconds of silence went by, and then the radio erupted in an unintelligible shout of anger. Jonas calmly shut off the radio and blessed silence returned.

*

Lewis was currently inside the cramped cab of his truck.

"Be patient? What the fuck do you mean, be patient?" he screamed at the radio. "I've been chased and attacked and tormented every damn second of every day by these goddamn zombies! All the while, you sit all safe and secure behind thirty foot stone walls and you tell me to be *patient*!"

No answer.

Lewis stared at the radio.

"Jonas, are you hearing what I'm saying?" he screamed into the radio.

No answer.

With a strangled gurgle of rage, Lewis threw the radio onto the seat and beat the steering wheel in frustration.

Minutes crawled by, and Lewis' anger turned into despair.

"How long must I put up with that arrogant jackass?" he moaned.

He lifted his head to stare at his reflection in the rearview mirror, shocked by what looked back at him. The lack of sleep, proper nutrition, and personal hygiene had turned his middle-aged good looks into a poster child for someone who abused meth or other hard drugs. Deep, dark rings surrounded his sunken eyes, and his thin face was covered in days' growth of scraggly facial hair. Lewis' mismatched and ill-fitting clothing had been scavenged from random homes, as were his shoes that rubbed his feet raw and bloody on a daily basis.

"How have you fallen so far?" he cried to his reflection. "Look at yourself! You were almost mayor of this town, and now you're taking orders from some psychotic killer!"

Lewis' frame shook with sobs of anguish and misery.

Misery...misery and despair at how events had unfolded, from his failed attempt at a prestigious political career, and his botched safe zone leadership.

Anger and frustration at losing his brother after just getting him back, and how he utterly failed time and time again at ending the wretched life of that asshole cop Mike and his worthless comrades who he blamed for most of his recent hardships. Now unfortunately, his only hope for vengeance and retribution rested with Jonas.

Lewis knew he had no choice but to do as told, no matter how badly he wanted to tell the little man to shove his head up his ass. Otherwise, without Jonas, he would have to try and bring about the destruction of the prison by himself. Lewis knew enough about himself to recognize he knew absolutely jackshit about combat and survival, and he seriously needed Jonas' help. Lewis' mood was somewhat lifted at hearing that most of the inhabitants were heading north somewhere to battle a group of zombies and that he was finally going to be able to enjoy safety once he was smuggled inside the walls, at least long enough for Jonas and him to destroy those bastards and their compound. Shivering in the cold cab of the truck, Lewis was irritated that he couldn't run the vehicle's heater because the sound of the engine would bring the inevitable group of infected.

Once these imbeciles were taken out, he was heading for warmer climates. He rubbed his hands together, attempting to keep warm as the temperature dropped.

*

Kleaner wearily made his way back to his camper. He had checked all over the prison compound for Logan and came up with negative results at every turn. He didn't like not knowing where his friend was and was now worried for his safety. He asked almost everyone that was still at the prison if they had seen him. The answers he got did not sit well with him. He had last seen Logan yesterday evening while they were arguing over the .22lr experiment they were working on. Kleaner had gotten roaring drunk that night with the assistance of Dan and Mr. Jack Daniels, and most of the evening was a blank after that. The closest thing to a lead he had gotten today was from a short, wiry fellow who said he thought he saw Logan leaving in a truck with others to head up to

Bolingbrook to fight the zombies.

After that, he had the dispatcher at the Command Center radio up to Stephen to check for Logan. They were told he wasn't up there either. This was confirmed after Stephen and the others arrived back that night. The more Kleaner wracked his brain, the more it didn't add up. A man as large as Logan just didn't up and disappear with no trace. He had never done anything like this before.

There wasn't much more he could do tonight, so he decided he would get an early start in the morning with a formal investigation into Logan's absence.

He settled in for the night, but sleep was hard to come by. Kleaner was worried for Logan's safety, along with all of the other new friends he'd recently made here at the prison, many of whom were going to be carrying the fight to the zombies well outside the safety of the prison walls. Too wired to sleep and yet too tired to do anything useful, Kleaner stared at Logan's empty bed while the night wore on.

31

November 12
Day 79

Matvei drove down State Highway J towards Oates, Missouri. He was only about five miles outside of town and he was double checking his map and log as he drove. From his notes, Matvei read that the compound had been hastily built only weeks before the outbreak. Unlike in other areas of the country, the cartel did not have a foothold in the area prior to the start of this final operation. Meth was the drug of choice in this area, not cocaine. A number of steel buildings had been erected to provide shelter, and shipping containers full of supplies had been dropped only days before the country went dark. The location was going to be used as a fallback site for cartel members, but in the double cross and subsequent coup, Matvei did not know if anyone even made it there alive. Matvei was worried that, unlike other, more secure and developed safe houses, so many of his men also knew of the location due to the fact that he had mentioned the area and its remote location.

They had probably arrived piecemeal and leaderless. God only knew what they did with the place. He hoped they didn't clean everything out and then take off again.

This was just another of a long list of concerns for Matvei. Due to all of the bad luck that he had experienced lately, he prepared himself for the worst.

Guess I'll find out soon enough, Matvei thought as the small town came into view.

He passed the city limits sign and its billboard with a likeness of the former mayor offering a warm welcome. He saw evidence of a mass exodus that had probably taken place soon after the outbreak. The small town had been sacked from survivors, and fires had spread to nearby structures. The buildings that were not charred shells were damaged so badly from looters and the undead they were worthless from a fortification standpoint. Garbage was strewn everywhere. Items that were once prized possessions now littered the ditches. The fleeing masses had realized they had to cut weight and part with once treasured heirlooms. Matvei saw no signs of life as he prepared to make the right turn onto County Road 838. The town was set in a valley surrounded by tree covered hills. In the spring they would be in full green but now they were bare and cold. In a small town like this, Matvei was certain that the former inhabitants had felt safe from the outside world. But the undead and refugees had found them.

Matvei swore in his native Russian as he looked ahead. "What the fuck is this?"

He had come into Oates from the west, and once he reached the intersection, he saw a slow yet steady stream of infected trickling in from the east. Matvei stopped the truck to process the visual. The three closest infected became more aggressive due to his presence and stumbled up to the truck. They looked ravenous and gaunt.

"You are hungry bastards, aren't you?" Matvei said, taunting the pathetic beings through the glass of his driver's window.

Matvei was now aware of the sound of gunfire coming from the south in the direction of the compound.

"I'd love to stay and play," Matvei told the howling trio, "but I have somewhere to be."

He ran over the two closest infected and left the other in his wake as he drove off in silence. In the short distance he must have passed seventy additional infected persons shuffling down the road towards the sounds of battle. Matvei figured they must be on the move from the cities in a desperate search for food. He had the feeling that the undead could sense where there was live human flesh. The virus was not acting at all like Matvei had hoped, and he wondered what other surprises "Variant Z" had in store for him.

After the long journey of six hundred miles and nearly three weeks' time, Matvei came to the gated driveway to the 120 acre property. The buildings had been set far enough off the road so as not to be seen by occasional passing vehicles. The gate was torn from the hinges, and the steady sound of gunfire was much closer now, and much louder. Matvei had wondered during his long trip how to arrive at the compound and not get shot out of mistaken identity upon his arrival. He tried to resolve this by installing a makeshift flagpole and fixing a small Russian flag from his bag to it. Matvei quickly exited his truck and set the pole into a slot in the truck bed designed for side rails.

He hoped it worked.

Hardening his will and ready to press forward, Matvei pushed the accelerator to the floor and began honking the horn as the structures came into view. He was immediately greeted by the sight of abandoned vehicles that must have been the transportation for his remaining mercenaries. They were parked haphazardly in his path, causing him to have to swerve left and right to avoid them. The three steel buildings that came into view looked tall enough to have lofts and were about eighty feet long. The courtyard area of the structures was walled off by using orange shipping containers. There appeared to be no way in, and Matvei saw several men on the roof firing at a massive group of infected that were massed along the makeshift wall.

Ducking slightly in his seat, Matvei hoped that he would not be shot at as he drove up to the stronghold. To be on the safe side, he drew his pistol and rolled down his window, shooting at the infected as he approached. He was not sure if he made any kill shots, but it gave the impression that he was on their side. Matvei was now drawing the attention of the larger undead group and needed to act fast. It was a pipe dream to find a spot near the shipping containers that was not completely surrounded with infected, so he picked the nearest side and rammed his truck into the crowd, getting as close as possible. He jerked to a stop with his passenger door up against the outside wall, then grabbed his backpack and G36 rifle. He quickly jumped into the truck bed and up onto the roof of the truck. There were not as many infected in front of this particular container due to the fact that there was no one on the roof of it and most were crushed by his truck. Without hesitating, Matvei threw his pack and rifle onto the shipping container's roof and then jumped and scrambled up.

Breathing hard from the mad scramble onto the roof, Matvei stood up, holding his hands up in a non-aggressive stance, and immediately recognized one of the men who stood nearby on the roof. The man did not return the recognition until Matvei spoke.

"Raul... it is me, Matvei."

Raul stared for a second in disbelief.

“Boss, is it really you?” he asked. "I thought you were long dead!"

"Yes it is me," Matvei answered back, "and I’m very much alive. Now lower that rifle. I’m hungry, thirsty and tired. I want to know our situation and exactly what the fuck is going on here."

32

November 13
Day 80

The next morning everyone at the prison was up before dawn and greeted by yet another cold day of work. As always, it took Stephen awhile to pry himself out of bed.

Reaching He reached over and gave Amber a little shove. "Time to get up, girl," he said when she tried to crawl back under the covers. "You are coming with me today."

Amber briefly protested but soon was up and throwing on some clothes while Stephen geared up. He was already wound up over the coming fight. He noticed that even Buddy was on edge, as if he knew something bad was going to happen. He reached down and gave the loyal dog a pat on the head.

"You stay here and help Kleaner protect the prison," Stephen said as Buddy whined softly. "I'll be back shortly."

Stephen told Amber he would be back for her in a bit, and exited his RV just as the sun was coming up. He checked in at the command center and learned that Dan had already left, making the trip north along with the rest of the explosives to supervise their deployment. This was the first time he had worked with industrial mining explosives and wanted to make sure everything was deployed properly.

While he was grabbing a quick breakfast in the cafeteria, Stephen was approached by Kleaner, who told him that Logan was still missing, and he had no idea where he might be. Kleaner was beginning to worry that he might have fallen off the wall at some point during the night.

"I want to help check it out, as it definitely is rather strange, but my plate is full. So is yours, for that matter," Stephen said. "Our AM broadcast is working and has brought nearly thirty refugees to the prison in the last two days."

"I know," Kleaner said, staring at the tall prison walls. "You might find this hard to believe, but I've never had too many close friends. It is tearing me up not knowing what happened to Logan."

"Just try not to dwell on it, bro," Stephen said, laying his hand on Kleaner's shoulder. "We'll figure out where the big guy ran off to. In the meantime, please help the new influx of people settle in."

Kleaner nodded without saying a word and walked off towards the most recent group of refugees who were scheduled to be cleared from the observation cells.

Many of the new batch of survivors from the north reported being pushed out of their hiding spots they had held for weeks by an extremely large group of zombies. They heard the prison's broadcasts on the radio and knew of nowhere else to turn. A new vehicle showed up every hour, and Kleaner soon had his hands full trying to process the new refugees safely and keep the perimeter clear of the undead. There was now an overflow parking area outside the prison to the west for arriving vehicles.

Stephen left shortly after his talk with Kleaner to pick up more tanker trucks from the refinery with plans to take them up to the Bolingbrook safe zone. Each man had plenty to do and little time to get it done. Problems, such as where to place newcomers and surviving the next few days, quickly overshadowed investigating Logan's fate.

*

I woke early and grimaced. My body sounded like someone walking on potato chips as it cracked when I stretched. After taking a much needed morning piss next to my truck, I grabbed a quick bite to eat and made my way over to speak with Kirk Simms, who was standing near a construction tractor working on enlarging the moat we wanted dug around their perimeter. He reported making some decent progress on the list of chores I gave him yesterday. The ditch was dug in front of and to the east of their encampment. He hoped to have three more trenching machines digging today and wanted it a full eight hundred yards long by day's end. They were lining them with plastic sheeting and had emptied a couple of oil change stores of their flammables into the trench. They needed a lot more, however, and were counting on Stephen to bring the tankers.

Out in the distance, I saw that Dan had arrived early and was directing others on how to properly set up the explosive charges. They had fifteen set already, with plans for many more. Dan looked like he was feeling better today, and the only thing missing besides his left hand was his cigar. He had been forced to put it out after several complaints of him smoking near high explosives. I checked in on defensive positions up on the highway and aided in clearing a few stalled vehicles from our staging area. Our perimeter team was also reporting increased zombie contact, but nothing they couldn't handle. All of our activity was beginning to draw a crowd.

Towards midday, Stephen pulled up with a roar and six additional tankers in his convoy. Eddie had been driving the lead truck and he, along with the next truck in line, continued up towards the highway.

Stephen climbed down from the driver's seat. "Three or four of these are for your trench, Kirk. This one here I would like to have dumped into some kiddie pools or something and used to fill up any container we can find with a lid. We're going to need them to help start some major fires around town when the time comes."

"I'll see what I can do," Kirk said, and wandered off to find the scarce manpower for yet another project.

"What do you have for me, Mike?" Stephen asked.

"Well," I replied, "the highway is too jammed up with vehicles to get tanker trucks all the way up to the zombies' current location, so we are going to have to settle with one burn off closer to our front. There is just not enough time or manpower to clear the roads that far out. Your trench is only going to end up being half as long and not as deep as you wanted, so I'm not sure how much good it is going to do. But it is better than nothing. Kirk also said that they did not have time to get over to the hospital to look for medical supplies."

"That's not what I wanted to hear," Stephen remarked. "I hope this trench will be enough to keep them bottled up around the highway."

"Maybe they'll get bored and leave?" I joked.

"So what's the good news?"

"The good news I guess would be with the Bolingbrook and Romeoville people all up here, we have over four hundred people working their asses off trying to get this trap set up as best we can."

"Good enough then," Stephen responded. "I'm going to have

Eddie and the guys position their trucks and head back for more tankers. I would like to maybe have a couple more up here for the trench and a couple of reserves to cover a possible retreat. Whatever is left we can set up on the highway."

"Speaking of retreat," Mattie cut in, "I think it might be a good idea to get all of the elderly people and children from Bolingbrook and Romeoville back to the prison today. I don't think it's going to be safe up here in the morning, and we should evacuate them now."

"That's a good idea, Mattie, and glad you made it back today," I said. "Why don't you get started on that now? I see that they managed to get some of those U-Haul trucks I mentioned yesterday. See what supplies you can get down there. We're going to need them."

"And Mattie," Stephen added, "when you get back to the prison I need you to tell Kleaner that tomorrow I want a skeleton crew on the walls and everyone else out on raids to gather as many supplies as possible. And I mean everyone. Have him take all of the new people we just took in and any that might come tonight or in the morning, for that matter. They're going to need to hit all the high priority targets on our books."

Mattie arched an eyebrow at him. "Are you sure that is a good idea?"

"No, it isn't an ideal situation at all."

"And you still want him to take a bunch of untrained refugees out on their first large scale raid ever?"

Stephen nodded his head vigorously. "We are going to need the supplies if we're going to be taking in all these new people, and I don't know how long we are going to have to safely retrieve them. Plus, as if we didn't have enough to worry about, Logan has turned up missing. That distraction alone has left Kleaner without his full head in the game."

"I'll let him know," Mattie assured him, "and that is strange about Logan."

"Yes it is," Stephen agreed, then announced that he was going to go up to the highway and check on the progress.

"We're going to work way past dark again today, Mattie," I said as she went to start helping with the evacuation. " I'm going to spend the night up here again to be ready to meet them in the morning."

"I'll be back up here later today to be with you, Mike. I wouldn't have it any other way."

I watched her hurry away, shaking my head to get my mind back into focus.

There was much work to be done.

33

November 13
Day 80
Illinois, USA

Chad Evanston sat wearily behind the steering wheel of the large white Ford Excursion. Everyone had taken turns driving and it was his turn again already. He was supposed to get some sleep while riding in the backseat, but the trip was turning into one close call after another. The area between Milwaukee and Chicago was densely populated, and it seemed to Chad that every zombie there must have been migrating outwards from the cities in search of living flesh. The sheer amount of mindless, walking, rotting corpses was unbelievable and the trio had to be on constant watch so as not to drive into a dead end and get trapped in their truck with limited supplies. Twice in the last four hours alone they had run into a roadblock created by burnt and destroyed vehicles on the roadway and had nearly been overwhelmed, barely able to shoot their way out and around it. If not for the three AR-15s they possessed, and working as a team, they would surely have died at the last one. Now ammo was running dangerously low, and they needed to stop and scrounge for fuel and supplies soon.

"When we hit the I-88 toll road, I'm sure we are going to find the same situation as we did back on I-90," Terry said from the front passenger seat. "We're going to need to find fuel before then. That would be a bad time to run out."

"I second that," Bruce chimed from the back seat.

Chad threw the map back to Bruce. "Find us some alternate routes so we have them lined up in case we have to head west again to skirt this wave of zombies.

"Roger that," Bruce answered.

"I know a place outside of Elburn where we can maybe find fuel," Terry said. "I used to stop there and pick up beer on my way up to the cabin. It was a small service station, and the guy who owned it used to be a cop. We always traded old war stories when I stopped in, and I believe he had a gravity tank behind the building for filling up his snowmobiles."

"Just point the way," Chad said while chugging his last Monster energy drink. They drove on in silence, the sunlight fading into darkness, and they needed to be even more careful.

A short while later, Terry again checked the truck's radio for an update on the situation at the prison. The station's signal had grown considerably stronger as they approached Joliet. They listened intently while the announcer for the small station gave a live broadcast detailing the massive zombie horde believed to be approaching the area on I-55 and the steps being taken to combat it. They learned that the battle was expected to commence in the morning in the area of I-55 and Rt. 53, and anyone who could hear this broadcast and respond to help, would be greatly appreciated. The prison would be able to provide safety after the battle if necessary, and it offered supplies and shelter to all who could participate.

"Morning... that's probably about the time we will arrive," Terry said. "Looks like we are going to have a forced march and then get thrown right into the fight."

"I don't think those guys realize the full scope and size of this zombie push," Chad remarked. "We're going to have to give them a heads-up."

"It's like they say...out of the frying pan and into the fire," Bruce said. "Let's get some!"

34

November 13
Day 80
Oates, Missouri

It was dark outside, and Matvei and a few others sat around the small propane heater in one of the steel buildings. A grim but tasty dinner of canned soups and Coca-Cola filled his aching belly, but it had been consumed cold without heating it first. The bumps, cries and wails of the undead on the other side of the thin metal sheeting made for an uncomfortable setting for the small group. It was difficult to even carry on a conversation. Matvei learned that of his entire command only thirteen men had stayed with the plan and managed to survive the trip north. The small group had plenty of horror stories to share of losing comrades along the way, some to the infected, and others to desertion and fighting within the ranks. This further dismayed Matvei, who had begun this mission with such high hopes.

They confirmed that Matvei's second in command, Lt. Calderon, never made it out of Dallas. He learned that Raul's small group had only reached the compound the day before yesterday and found it mostly looted upon their arrival. There was no security team at the compound like there was supposed to be when they showed up. If there was anyone securing the compound prior to that they had been overrun or had abandoned it long ago. It appeared that an enormous number of refugees flooded the area at some point and picked it clean.

“Whoever found this place must have thought they had struck it rich,” Raul remarked. “Those shipping containers were full. It looks like a large portion of St. Louis did just that and came right through here."

"And they brought those demons with them," his friend Hector said.

Raul again relayed the dark tale of how they lost three men clearing the compound of the infected. A small child they thought was dead ripped the throat out of an unsuspecting mercenary. Another died after being shot by a man who had claimed the place as his own, and died defending his teenage daughter. The daughter, for her part, knifed the third mercenary in the gut during the subsequent attempted rape. He managed to kill the girl, but lingered to a slow painful death.

Matvei was going over his dwindling options in his head. His dreams of conquest were now long gone. Every contingency he planned for had ended up with him holding the shitty end of the stick. Survival now was a top priority. He and the others heard a radio broadcast from the U.S. government, bringing news of their safe zones on the coasts along with the plans for eventually linking up. The message was purportedly broadcast from a Coast Guard barge on the Mississippi River. It, along with two smaller cutters, was moving up the river from the Gulf on a scouting mission. They claimed to have plucked survivors from the shore and were establishing an encampment near Snow Lake, Arkansas. The mercenaries were not convinced that these reports were true, and figured them as propaganda. They were also not sure that the remaining military units could pull off a coast to coast mission after seeing firsthand the extent of the plague. However, they were in agreement that they needed to stay clear of the military in any case. They didn't need a repeat of their last encounter. Supplies here were almost nonexistent, and more and more infected were showing up by the hour. Matvei finally concluded that he only had three things left working in his favor.

The first was that the compound did have a working radio that had allowed him to make contact with his ranch in Arizona. Tamera had been worried sick about him, but Matvei was more concerned about his ranch and was relieved to find that his comrades from Russia had not deserted. They, along with his best men held the ranch and had had little zombie contact up to this point. Matvei knew that eventually, even with the remote location, they would be hit with zombies coming out of Phoenix some ninety miles away, but he figured they had enough firepower to manage. Matvei needed to get to his ranch, which led him to his other two aces.

The remaining men that he was left with were dedicated and skilled, and would be able to help him make the trip west. In order to do it, they were going to need supplies, and that was the last ace. Although it was three hundred and fifty miles in the wrong direction, a safe house in Joliet, Illinois had been set up in a discreet manner over a long period of time. Gear, food, weapons and ammunition were stored in abundance, and the group was short in all of the above. Those supplies, once recovered, would make the trip west much easier.

"It sounds like a no-brainer then," Raul stated after Matvei laid out his plan.

“When do we leave?" Hector asked.

"First thing in the morning," Matvei responded. "Let’s load up tonight and shoot our way out of here at dawn."

The small group gathered what few possessions they had remaining, their spirits lifted. Matvei was once again in command. If anyone could get them safely to the ranch in Arizona, they knew, it was him.

35

November 13
Day 80

With darkness upon us and another day of work under our belt, we settled in for a long night of waiting. It was well past midnight. All that I could think of doing was now done. Our plans were set, and we had drawn a line in the sand here on this abandoned interstate. We set as many I.E.Ds as possible and makeshift roadblocks had been set up at every exit off I-55 from Route 53 to I-80. Stephen made photocopies of our battle plan for the morning and assignments for everyone involved. He passed them out to everyone after work had stopped and made a joke that it didn't matter if the plans fell into enemy hands as he doubted zombies could read. That lame joke earned him a few chuckles.

Stephen also informed me that an old ambulance was retrofitted as a field command vehicle, and he'd selected a crew to help manage the radio traffic. Many were going to be sleeping in their vehicles tonight with the engines running due to the cold and ever present zombie threat. Mattie sat with me in the cab of the dump truck trying to stay warm and keeping me company.

"I'll trade you my chili and macaroni for your chicken fajita," Mattie said playfully.

"You really want to be in an enclosed space after me eating chili?" I said and handed over the meal. "It's your funeral."

We both had a good laugh and finished our meal talking of better times when the world wasn't filled with ravenous undead cannibals. When the stress of what was heading for us made for an uncomfortable silence, I decided to excuse myself to check on the perimeter guards before calling it a night.

I stepped out into the chilly night and made my way towards the front line barricade to a familiar shape nearby.

"Can't sleep either?" I asked Stephen as he came to a stop and stared out into the darkness.

"Hell no," he said and blew out a puff of held breath. "I don't know whether to scream, fuck, or go take a dump from all this waiting!"

"Why not do all three?"

Stephen looked at me out of the corner of his eye for a few moments until we both started chuckling.

"Just not all at the same time," he said, laughing. "That tends to turn off the women."

"I'm going to head back to my truck. I think I'll watch a movie with Amber and try not to shit on myself," Stephen said with a grin. "I might work on the screaming and fucking parts though."

He walked off a few paces, pulled up, and turned to say over his shoulder, "Casper is not happy about it, but I'm sending him on a scout mission to keep an eye on our southern flank in the morning. I trust him and need his eyes down there."

Shortly after walking the perimeter and making small talk with the guards that were on duty, I returned to my truck to find Mattie dead asleep. I quietly climbed in and settled in as comfortably as I could.

A few minutes later, Dan dropped by offering shots of Jack Daniels to take the edge off. He pretty much strong armed me into a shot and then wandered off to find someone to help him finish the bottle. It grew late enough for most to bed down for the night, and I thought that maybe I would finally get a little sleep. There had been little zombie traffic today and we had sentries posted well to the front to advise when the main host of undead approached. I was about to nod off when Mattie began snoring like a chainsaw tearing into a chunk of wood. Sighing, I reached into my coat pocket to retrieve my headphones and turned my old iPod on, falling asleep to the soothing music of Metallica.

*

All night long wails of pain and hunger arose from the odious creatures as they marched, sending the uncountable multitudes behind them into a frenzy of howls and screams. The slower ones were mercilessly shoved to the ground and trampled into the unforgiving pavement. The crippled creatures were stepped on by countless others, who were now agitated greatly by the smell of fresh meat and blood ahead. Even then, the wretched creatures that had fallen were cursed with a mockery of life; their mangled limbs barely twitching, rotten teeth clacking together with all their might to rend and tear at the fresh flesh that was out of their reach.

Food was near.

Ear splitting cacophony erupted from countless throats into the cold night air as they shrieked their unholy agony and hunger.

As if it was one enormous beast, mindless, but of one goal, it surged forward.

To eat.

To feed.

Slowly, so painfully slowly, it neared the source of their rage.

They could sense the sweet blood that grew stronger with every staggering step.

And so they howled. Screamed their fury. Surged forward with their thousands upon thousands until the very earth trembled and shook in their wake.

Until at last, in the distance the accursed multitude came into view of the very food they had sensed for the last few miles.

Finally they could rend flesh and gorge on sweet meat and pulsing blood.

Finally there was food to be had.

*

The sun began climbing over the horizon, its cleansing rays breaking across the horde that, incalculable in size had just now begun to reach the very outer edge of the perimeter established by the survivors perched behind barricades that already looked to be overmatched. Advance sentries first reported the contact as they fell back. With labored breaths and rapid pulses, every man and woman who was awake gripped their weapons a little tighter upon hearing the news. Here and there, they checked and rechecked their firearms to make sure they were loaded and started waking up their friends.

Inside the city street department dump truck I sensed them coming. I thought I could hear them. I leaned forward in the driver's seat, wiped the fogged up windshield clear and stared out at what approached our position with grim acceptance on my face.

Only one response came to mind that properly summed up what I now saw.

"Fuck me."

36

November 14
Day 81

I climbed down from the cab of the dump truck, taking care not to wake Mattie, who was fast asleep. There was no sense in scaring her yet.

How do I manage to continuously get myself into clusterfucks like this?

Every time one crisis was over, the shit hit the fan from an entirely different direction. The last couple of months had been like standing behind a manure spreader.

Although getting closer with every second that ticked by, the undead mob was still quite a distance down the highway. As it slowly came into view, it was obvious that it was a much larger group than we had ever seen. Grabbing my Motorola two-way radio, I tried to reach Stephen who was likely still sleeping.

"Stephen, this is Mike!" I shouted into the radio. "Wake the fuck up man! Our guests have finally arrived!"

No answer.

"Stephen!"

No answer.

I cursed long and loud. "What good are all these radios we passed out if nobody answers them?"

Continuing with a string of expletives that would wake the dead, I limped over to a rusty, dent covered Chevrolet S-10 that we had been using to run messages and equipment around. I climbed in and headed off to where Stephen's truck was located.

A few minutes later I found his Tahoe parked in the grass and pulled up to a stop. The windows were fogged up with muffled screams coming from inside, and the truck was rocking from side to side.

"Christ. Those two are like a couple of teenagers," I mumbled under my breath as I heard someone scream, "Oh God, yes!"

Kicking the truck door, I yelled out Stephen's name.

The truck stopped its movement and an irritated male voice shouted back.

"What the fuck you want?" I heard him reply. "I'm a little busy here!"

An irritated female voice demanded, "Don't you dare stop, mister!"

"The zombies are here. I'm heading back up to the highway!" I replied, now just as irritated.

A moment of silence followed.

"Oh...okay...umm... thanks...," Stephen called back.

Before I could even turn to walk back to the truck I saw that the rocking motion had started back up at about double the previous speed.

I returned to our defenses and met briefly with the truck drivers who were a vital part of our operation, again going over our plans on what they needed to do. I had each of them repeat back to me their task. Satisfied with what I heard, I sent them off with a firm handshake and headed back to my dump truck. I opened the door and crawled back inside. Mattie was still asleep and whimpered slightly when a blast of cold air snaked across the bare skin of her back where her blanket had fallen away. Closing the door gently and cranking up the heat, I waited until she fell back into deep sleep. I reached over and gently pushed back a few errant hairs from her face and enjoyed staring at her.

She was truly a beautiful woman. Too bad I had to wake her. She appeared to finally be sleeping through the night without the nightmares that had been plaguing her after the Kettle debacle. Outside the truck, dozens of our people were scrambling here and there to get to their positions.

I let out a weary sigh. This morning found me in a foul mood indeed. Why couldn't we just have a few weeks of peace and quiet for once?

I guess I had to look at the positive things. Like for instance, I was currently not a flesh eating zombie...at least not yet. And sleeping to my right was yet another positive. Reaching over, I gently shook her by the shoulder.

"Hey, Mattie, wake up, we got company."

She opened her deep brown eyes and looked at me sleepily. She sat up and looked out the windshield, gasping at what she saw. I had to remain calm. If she or others saw how badly I wanted to just say "Fuck it" and leave, then all chance of holding here would be lost.

"Relax, they are still a ways off yet," I said. "You have plenty of time to tell me what a great guy I am before they get here."

Mattie punched me lightly on the arm. "Don't you ever get scared?"

"I think the closest I came to being scared was when I found out you were taken by Kettle's men," I confided. "But even then I was so angry and busy with getting you back that I really didn't have time to be scared. I had to be strong. Just like I need to be strong now, and I need you to be strong too. If we don't hold these bastards here, then they will run through this area unchecked, and a lot of people will die."

Mattie nodded and took a deep breath. Letting it out noisily, she shook her entire body. "I will try to make you proud of me and be strong."

"Thatta girl!" I replied. "Stay close to me today. If we need to bail out of here fast, I want you near so we can get to the truck without trying to find each other in the confusion."

She nodded again, and we both paused, soaking in the gravity of the situation.

"Get dressed and meet me on the roof of the bus out front," I said. "That will be our observation post for the battle."

I opened the truck door, hopped down, and went about retrieving my weapons. Once they were all located I transferred them to the bus rooftop. My aluminum bat and ballistic shield I left in my truck since they would be useless up top. Standing up at this height, I clearly saw in the distance the extent of the zombie force that was descending upon us. As far as I could see, it was a solid, twitching mass of rotting bodies inching its way closer and closer. Seeing the fear and terror on many of the faces around me, I decided to give them something to keep busy with, to keep their minds off the horror that was heading our way. I grabbed the handheld Motorola and raised Casper. At least he answered when I called.

"What do ya need, boss?" he asked with only a hint of fatigue.

"I need you to go out to the tanker trucks and make sure the drivers don't fuck up their assignments. Take a small team with you for security and be careful."

Hearing a noise behind me, I turned and found that Mattie had arrived. I walked up next to her and slipped my arm around her waist. She wrapped her arms around my ribs, and we both stood there watching our enemy inch their way toward us.

"Think we have a chance, Mike?" Mattie whispered, looking up at me with those warm brown eyes.

"Damned if I know, but I do know I am going to make them pay for every fucking inch they take! If you are the religious type, you might want to say a few prayers now. I will take all the help we can get, but I will not hold my breath. The only thing I have faith in is what I can hold in my hands."

Mattie looked up at me again. "Your hand is on my ass...I don't think my butt will win this fight," she said with a smile.

"I wouldn't bet against it," I laughed. "Have you ever seen your ass in tight pants?"

So there we both were, giggling like kids as uncountable numbers of undead stumbled and shuffled towards us, howling their undying hunger all the way.

*

Lewis drove around the neighborhood slowly in the bread truck he was told by Jonas to acquire. In the back of the truck were all the items and materials he had located.

Jonas had better get him inside those walls soon. There were more infected showing up every time he stopped for more than a few minutes.

Behind him was a group of undead several dozen strong, with more joining their slow pursuit of his truck. Lewis squinted as he made another turn onto a side street, and the bright morning sun shined right into his eyes. The sudden blindness made him jerk the wheel, and his truck slammed alongside an abandoned vehicle, causing the truck to weave back and forth until he regained control. The rocking of the truck caused many of the items he collected for Jonas to roll around inside the cargo area. Some of the liquids sloshed noisily.

Lewis would be glad to offload all of this crap. Some of the stuff reeked pretty badly. He made yet another loop around the neighborhood.

Any minute now he expected his radio to come alive and hear

Jonas telling him it was clear to enter the prison, a place that offered relative safety and a chance at redemption. And every minute that passed made him sweat a little more.

*

Back at the prison, Kleaner was finishing up his appointed rounds of the compound and watchtowers. Even though many of the occupants had gone north to battle the zombies and the prison should have been empty, it wasn't, due to the fact that they sent back truckloads of new refugees. Finding shelter for them was an added chore that he really didn't need right now, and there were not nearly enough campers to go around. Thankfully, the stone building on the north end of the prison had finally been cleaned up and was now being used as a dormitory for these new arrivals. On top of this, even mealtime was turning into a mess as many of the new folks wanted to eat whenever they felt like it and expected the mess hall cooks to whip them up a meal at a moment's notice. Kleaner thanked God that the old prison cafeteria was up and running and allowed the food to be sufficiently secured.

These new people were going to have to start pulling their weight or he would boot them out himself.

Kleaner had to reach deep for self-control as he played moderator with all the petty disputes that arose when the new people bumped heads with his remaining security team.

Maybe this was what police work usually entailed, in which case he wasn't missing much. He pretended to listen to the current disturbance involving two ladies in front of him.

They'd gotten into an argument over some missing clothes in the laundry area, with both blaming the other. Eventually he had enough of the arguing.

"Enough!" he roared. "If you two can't come to an agreement, then you both will be pulling kitchen duties for the rest of the week!"

The women gazed at him in disgust, but by the time he walked away he was now the bad guy and the two women were chatting like best friends.

He guessed sometimes people liked to be told what to do. He made his way to his trailer, satisfied with his leadership skills.

"And on top of all this, I need to get out on a large supply run today!" Kleaner told his dog upon entering his camper.

His dog showed him some of the pity he was looking for and

walked over to rub himself against Kleaner's leg. Kleaner pet the dog for a moment and then threw his tired self into the chair, taking a deep breath of relief. Looking over at his missing friend's empty bunk brought Kleaner back to reality.

What the hell had happened to Logan?

It didn't make sense. Now, after three days, he feared that his friend was most likely dead, and nobody knew of his whereabouts.

Kleaner stared at Logan's empty bunk, deciding that when he got the time, he was going to tear this fucking prison apart until he found something that indicated what had happened to him.

Outside his camper Kleaner heard the enormous prison gates clanking open yet again as more people were escorted inside from Bolingbrook, and now even Romeoville. Kleaner sighed and stood, wincing slightly. All of this walking was killing his feet, and a nasty headache was brewing from all of the petty complaints. Squaring his shoulders, he exited his camper and went off to welcome the new folks and direct them where to set up. They, unlike the stray people showing up, were not required to be held in the observation cells. They were, however, going to be put right to work.

*

Jonas stood next to the prison gates and watched the latest group of refugees enter the prison with concealed disgust. Mastering the burning rage within him, he stalked to his trailer and closed the door.

Retrieving the radio from a duffel bag, Jonas turned it on and tried to reach Lewis.

"Jonas, it is about goddamn time you answered me!" Lewis' frantic voice screeched back at him. "You have to get me inside today. I have a dozen zombies trailing me all over this damn city!"

"Relax, Lewis. Do you still have all the items I asked you to acquire?" Jonas said calmly.

"Yes! I have your precious items. Now for God's sake get me inside those walls!" Lewis screamed back. "If you don't, I will leave your stuff for these disgusting creatures to play with!"

Jonas took a deep calming breath. "Your chance will arise soon," Jonas said into the radio. "There's a major operation underway up in Bolingbrook, and I'm sure it will fail. You have to wait until there's a bunch of 'em returning with their tail between their legs to enter, so yours gets lost in the confusion."

Before the whining worm Lewis could start to bitch again, Jonas said, "Now you'll just need to keep near but out of sight until the opportunity presents itself. Until then, radio silence is paramount. They use these same radios all around the prison, but usually not channel 13."

Jonas turned off the radio before Lewis could respond, knowing that the worthless man would most likely just be bitching. Standing at the window of his trailer, Jonas watched the prison doors clank shut and nearly shivered in pleasure at the thought of what his plan was going to do to this cesspool of unbelievers. With everything coming together and the end so close, he could now picture the final moments of the unbelievers' miserable lives. He pulled out his razor sharp knife and thumbed the blade, smiling at the thought.

37

November 14
Day 81

Mindless howls and screams echoed off the nearby buildings and surrounding structures as thousands upon thousands of zombies could now almost taste the living flesh and blood just up ahead. The sheer size of the undead horde was so massive that the ones far to the rear could not yet smell the nearby food but sensed it within the calls from the ones up front. The shambling, combined weight of bodies that were shoved up against the hundreds of abandoned vehicles pushed them aside with squeals of tires and crashes of breaking glass. The mindless creatures neither knew nor cared that dozens of its brethren were mangled and crushed after they were smashed up against the vehicles from the intense pressure of the others pushing and clawing their way past the obstacles.

All that mattered was the food ahead. Nothing would stop them from feeding.

A zombie in the front ranks, who wore an electrician's tool belt, howled in hunger. Behind him, a female zombie clawed back at the others, wanting to be the first to feed. Next to her, a hideously mangled creature that once was a stockbroker in Chicago pushed another zombie to the pavement, one wearing a McDonald's uniform complete with the visor. This was all the humanity the zombies had left, their old clothing. The souls of their previous lives were long gone. Thousands of jaws dripping with discolored fluid unlike saliva clacked together as they closed in on the tantalizingly close fresh meat.

The howls of hunger turned to shrieks of rage when the meat

moved away from them yet again. Mindlessly, the horde followed. The creatures had no choice but to follow, even if they had the power of choice, for behind them unimaginable numbers of others pushed their way forward relentlessly. The creatures stumbled after the living flesh in front of them, and another annoying smell filled the air. This new scent nearly overwhelmed the smell of meat, which just enraged the mob even more. Step by step they moved after the frustratingly close meals, not having the intelligence to wonder at the sudden splashing liquid that they now were marching through.

*

Far ahead of my position I saw the puff of diesel exhaust billow from the two fuel tankers as they inched forward. The trucks moved slowly toward us, southbound, one on each side of the interstate. Each truck also had a scout standing on the rear of the trailer. This person needed to have a seriously large pair of stones, for he had to remain within yards of the front ranks of the undead screaming for his blood. Each of these volunteers had a very important job to do. While the fuel tankers crawled back towards where the rest of us waited at the bottleneck we made, the men on foot held the large hose that led back to the fuel tanks. They marched back to us, holding steady the hoses that spilled the contents of the fuel tankers all over the roadway in front of the horde which unknowingly splashed its way through it. Moving it back and forth, the men coated the pavement with fuel.

Step by stumbling, shuffling step the mob moved deeper and deeper into the liquid covering the roadway. Through my binoculars I saw the fluid gradually coating the legs and the torsos of the creatures. Some were covered head to toe when they fell on the suddenly slick surface and got back to their feet to continue their march forward. The mindless mob had no idea that the powerful scent that mixed in with the meat smell and the liquid that they stumbled in was thousands of gallons of gasoline.

Back several hundred yards on top of the makeshift observation post, a rooftop of a Greyhound bus, I watched the first part of my plan go into effect as the fuel trucks continued their way back to us, leading thousands and thousands of undead deeper into my nasty trap. It was nerve-wracking to sit there watching the ungodly gigantic mob of creatures get closer.

I keyed up the radio to give Stephen an update.

"Yeah, what is it, Mike? We're working on finishing up the trenches and traps for the base over here," Stephen responded. "I got another surprise load of fuel this morning from one of the new guys at the prison. Kleaner made him drive a tanker up here."

"Well, you'd better speed it up. Our visitors are here and they look pissed."

Choice swear words came across the little radio speaker. He must have taken notes from Dan.

"Listen up, jackass. We got a whole lot of pain heading our way. Just be ready to send reinforcements if we need it."

"Sounds good, and fuck you very much," Stephen said.

Yep, he had definitely been hanging around Dan too much lately, I decided.

I managed to raise Casper over the radio and asked him to personally check on the progress with the fuel trucks. There were a few moments of delay before Casper informed me that the trucks were nearly done emptying their load. I turned to watch the mammoth mob closing in.

"Good enough. Tell them to wait for both trucks to be empty and then set it off."

Eddie, who was driving one of the Mack trucks, was signaled by the man at the rear of the truck to speed up since the tanker trailer was finally empty. Seeing that they put a safe distance from the front of the horde behind him, he parked the truck and got out.

"You ready for this, friend?" the man asked, holding a flare gun.

"Hold up a second, let's make sure the other team is ready."

A quick look over to the other northbound lanes told him that they were also done and waiting for the signal to begin.

"They're all set, let's do this!" Eddie said.

The man carefully took aim with the flare gun and fired it at the large pool of gasoline.

*

Just when I began to worry that something was wrong, that maybe Murphy had made an early visit, in the distance the interstate exploded in flames. Fire and smoke screamed skyward as the flammable liquid was ignited.

All around me the waiting men and women gave the same reaction as me.

"Ooooo...."

"Well what do you know?" I said aloud.

"That worked nicely," Mattie responded.

The results were unbelievable.

On both sides of the interstate, a fireball roared skyward and screamed away at an incredible speed along the trail of fuel that they had left. Thousands of zombies that had soaked themselves from trampling through the accelerant instantly became screaming, burning torches. The flames hungrily consumed the flammable liquid as it raced from subject to subject.

Thick, greasy black smoke billowed into the air. The blast of heat pulsed out like ocean waves to beat on our faces even at this distance. You could feel the hellish roar in your gut. Even as those initial creatures were incinerated, hundreds and thousands more zombies were pushed into the flames. Up ahead I saw Casper, Eddie and the others making a quick retreat back to our location. Waves of heat from the inferno were shimmering and the flames caused a slight breeze. Lifting the radio, I chirped Stephen.

"Hey, Stephen," I called. "Phase one has been put into motion, we'll be setting up phase two shortly. How's it looking at your end?"

"No contact as of yet besides the occasional random roamer," Stephen replied. "But that fireball looks damn spectacular from here!"

"Glad that part of the plan worked," I responded. "Keep your eyes open. I know they are not all on the highways."

"Hey, Mike, one other thing," Stephen requested. "Send Mattie down here. I've rounded up some more people that are not going to be able to help out much up here for various reasons. I would like her to take 'em down to the prison now, so they are out of the way. They can help with some of the chores at the prison. She also needs to make sure Kleaner gets out on that raid today."

"Roger that."

Clipping the radio on my belt, I looked around for Casper. He was standing near the front of the bottleneck with Eddie and the truck crew men, so I climbed down off the roof of the bus.

"Well done men!" I said, offering handshakes all around. "With how well the fuel trap worked I wish we had a lot more to dump out. While I'm at it I might as well wish for a small tactical nuke too."

I asked Casper to begin phase two, which was to begin with the spent tanker trucks that Casper had wired to blow. Watching Casper rocket down the highway on an ATV, I couldn't help but be proud of how well this unassuming former postal worker had become a dependable warrior in the short time I had known him. When I turned to walk back to the bus, I noticed Mattie had climbed off, and I walked over to her.

"Enjoying the show?"

"It's spectacular!" she crowed.

"I'm glad ya liked it," I said, then drew a more serious tone. "I need you to do me a favor. Go see Stephen down by the Bolingbrook safe zone. He needs you to run some folks down to the prison for him."

"I hate to leave now!" Mattie said with a smirk.

"It won't take long, and hurry back!" I urged. "We could probably use some extra ammunition anyways. The guards chewed up more than I figured holding the perimeter while we set up the trap."

"Okay, see you soon then," Mattie said, hurrying off. "I don't want you to start the main event without me!"

*

Lewis anxiously paced back and forth alongside the bread truck. He'd managed to lose his zombie pursuers momentarily, but he was sure they would locate him again shortly.

They always did.

Lighting up a cigarette nervously, he took a long hard drag on it and then coughed raggedly. After years of kicking the habit, Lewis had fallen off the wagon due to the stress of the past few weeks. The truck's former driver had a fresh new pack inside the truck so Lewis had "borrowed" it and lit one up the moment he found them. Shortly after that, he ransacked a mall store and had come across cartons of them. Now he had plenty to support his two packs a day habit.

Checking again to make sure the radio was on for the fifth time today, he snarled when he realized it was and that Jonas had not bothered to make any contact to check on his status. From where he was now parked, Lewis had a decent view of the prison and could see a lot of activity. Several convoys had arrived from other places and many vehicles had also left.

Hopefully he would be able to tag along with a group arriving and sneak in the way Jonas had suggested. With the confusion of so many new people arriving, he should be able to blend in amongst them easily.

Lewis tossed his cigarette down onto the ground, fished the crumpled packet out of his jacket and shook a fresh one free.

Lighting it, he took a long drag and exhaled the breath with a string of curses aimed at Jonas for taking his sweet fucking time making contact with him.

*

Mattie exited the school bus she rode in that was ferrying the last noncombatants from the Bolingbrook and Romeoville compounds back to the prison. After taking a few moments to say hello to some friends, she went off to locate Kleaner, and found him outside the Command Center looking like he needed a long vacation.

"Kleaner, glad I found you. Did Logan turn up?"

Kleaner looked up angrily at hearing his name, then seeing it was Mattie, softened his expression.

"Mattie, you're a sight for sore eyes," he said. "As far as where Logan is, I have no idea. He has been missing for days now. Nobody's seen him."

"That's disturbing, but right now we can't worry about him, even though he's missing. We have bigger problems," Mattie said ruefully. "Don't forget, Stephen wants you to take a team and go raid the warehouses south of town to get as many supplies as possible. With the huge influx of mouths to feed, we'll run short of food within a month or two if we don't find more."

Kleaner sighed. "And who am I supposed to take with me on a raid again? You folks took all of the trained fighters with you and left a bunch of sheep here with me."

Mattie ran her fingers through her hair. She was stressed as well and didn't have time to argue.

"I don't know, Kleaner," she replied sternly. "Maybe take just enough of your guard platoon for security and make the new arrivals go with you to load the supplies. I know it isn't what you would like to or want to do, but you must do it. The option of starvation is worse than the fear of failure at this point. It's the new people that will need the food so they are going to have to chip in."

Kleaner accepted what he had to do. "Fine, but I can't make promises it'll be pretty," he stated. "Half of the ones you left me here with hardly know which end of a firearm to point at the enemy, and they are the better half!"

Mattie took Kleaner's hand and looked at him seriously. Just her touch gave Kleaner a renewed sense of bravado.

"We need you to do this," she pleaded. "We know that you're not staffed how you'd like, but we need you to roll with the punches and go with what ya got. Now I have to get back to the battle up north. Please be careful but get it done."

Kleaner squared his shoulders and shook off his feeling sorry for himself attitude.

"Consider it done," he promised. "I won't let you down!"

Mattie grabbed the man and drew him into a hug. "I've got to go. Take care of yourself. I promise to help look into Logan's whereabouts as soon as this is over."

Mattie saw to it that several cases of ammunition got loaded onto the bus. She then boarded the school bus, along with a few new volunteers that had just arrived and wanted to fight. As the enormous steel doors opened and the vehicle moved forward, she could not help but worry that no matter what they did it would not be enough. She had run the numbers in her head before. They all had. Out of the 150,000 plus residents in Joliet, maybe seven hundred had survived. And there were roughly three hundred thirty million people in the United States. Using that ratio nationwide meant maybe only 1,800,000 survivors were left, spread across the entire country. And if half of those killed nationwide were intact enough to reanimate, there were about 150,000,000 zombies.

Mattie shuddered at the thought.

*

Screams and moans erupted from thousands of throats as the flames eagerly devoured the flesh and clothing of the zombies. They fell by the thousands, burnt and defeated. However, behind them, moving like an unstoppable juggernaut, many thousands more pressed on undeterred. That was the sight that greeted Casper when he braked hard and skidded to a halt next to his partner, preparing for the next part of the operation. The now empty tanker trucks were a mere two hundred yards in front of them. As the flames shrank and the smoke lessened, Casper could see in the distance the full extent of what was first blocked from his vision by the smoke and fire. Grabbing his radio, he informed Mike of the large group that was reforming in the burn zone.

Mike's reply was curse laden to say the least, but gave him one order: "Make them pay."

"Well alright then!" Casper said, reaching back for the large duffel bag. "That's one thing I can do."

Grabbing two detonators that had taped numbers on the sides marked 1 and 2, he handed one to his partner.

"On three," Casper stated as the zombies swirled around the two empty tankers. But even empty tankers still had fuel in them, and on the count of three, they were turned into giant balls of fire and chunks of twisted metal, which again consumed large parts of the lead elements of the zombie host. The resulting concussion shook the highway and was later reported to be heard from the prison a good ten miles away. Casper turned the ATV around and retreated a safe distance, waiting for the flames to diminish.

He didn't have to wait long before the damned creatures spilled past the scorched bodies and moved directly at him, howling every step of the way.

Casper sat patiently on the machine and waited for the roadway to be jammed full again.

When the time was right, Casper retrieved from the duffel bag a detonator clearly marked by him with a number three for the explosive that he had previously set.

"Hmm, this one's a gas bomb if I remember correctly," he muttered and tripped the switch.

A massive fireball exploded in front of him, as well as on the opposite northbound lanes. Stalled vehicles had been filled with fuel and rigged across the highway. It wasn't nearly as impressive as the gas truck bombs but managed to kill and set afire a large number of undead. Using the distraction as cover, Casper and his partner pulled back a bit more and readied the next detonator.

Staring at it, Casper thought for a minute. *I think this one's a shrapnel I.E.D.*

After waiting for the flames to die and the road to become a target rich environment, Casper ducked behind the cover of an engine block of a nearby abandoned car and triggered the remote. Another loud explosion rocked both sides of the interstate. Even from his vantage point the concussion wave knocked his breath away and made his ears hurt. The results were quite impressive. Scores upon scores of undead that had just been howling for his blood were now chunks of meat on the road's surface. Many more were missing limbs and were quickly trampled by the next ranks of undead who pressed on. When Casper was rigging the explosives, he'd sent out scavengers for metal scrap parts. One team discovered a machine shop filled with bins and tubs of all assortments of nuts and bolts and pieces of rebar set for scrap. Packing such items in tight around the explosives made for excellent shrapnel. Looking back to the bottleneck area, Casper tried to calculate how many undead each explosion had killed and how many I.E.Ds remained. He looked at the incalculable number of zombies left standing. Not liking the answer he came up with, he set himself to do his job of making them pay. Retreating back to the next point down the road, Casper waited for the next wave of zombies to arrive.

*

Chad had to steer his vehicle around yet another group of the stinking creatures on the roadway.

"Goddamn things are everywhere!" he swore out loud. "This's fucking out of control. Where the hell are they all coming from?"

Terry was currently hanging on to the "oh shit" handle as Chad ran evasive maneuvers on the road to avoid collisions.

"Our turn's coming up, Chad," he replied. "We take a left onto 119th street up ahead, and that should take us across Rt. 59 and onto Weber Road. That's near to where the guys have set up for the battle on I-55, according to what's being said on the radio."

Chad gunned the engine, cranked the wheel hard and sped off eastbound.

"They're saying the action's already started," Bruce reminded the group. "I hope they left some for us to kill."

"Careful what you wish for," Terry said with a grin. "I'm sure there will be plenty left to take a bite out of your lily white ass."

Bruce laughed a flipped Terry the bird.

Barring any major detours, Chad figured they would be there within the half hour. Glancing out the side windows, they saw random groups of zombies, all heading southeast.

"It looks like we aren't the only ones heading to the party," Chad said, nodding his head to show the others what he was talking about.

Bruce leaned forward to point out something. "That's probably where they're going," he said, "and I'm sure that's our destination too."

Far in the distance they saw pillars of thick black smoke billowing skyward. Chad gave the SUV a little more boost of the accelerator. The truck responded, and he gripped the steering wheel even tighter.

"looks like the dance has started without us," he joked. "We better hurry, before all the hot girls are taken."

Terry laughed while he checked over his Colt M4. "Like I said, I'm sure there'll still be plenty of action waiting for us when we arrive. Let's just get there in one piece!"

*

Mattie made it back to the Bolingbrook safe zone, where it was clearly evident that the battle had already begun in earnest due to the large amount of smoke and occasional loud explosions. Gunfire from several sharpshooters also filled the air. After notifying Stephen of her return, she assisted others with unloading the supplies and ammunition she had brought back. She saw Mike up on the bus roof. Making her way over to the makeshift observation platform, she climbed up top and got her first good look at the opposition they faced on the road before her. Spread out as far as the eye could see was complete carnage and destruction. Shredded vehicles that had been detonated, smoked as they were swarmed over by the zombies. Fires burned in the distance, and she noticed that many of the smaller blazes were moving. The mindless creatures were coming at them even while engulfed in flames.

They were filled with such hatred and anger, wanting to kill them for no reason. Mankind had been doing such things to itself all through history. This was really no different when you broke it down. It was just heartbreaking, all the loss.

*

Silently, Mattie slid up to me and hugged me from behind. My attention was so captured by what was going on down field from me that when I felt a pair of arms wrap around my torso, I almost instinctively prepared to break them. The tenseness in my rigid frame relaxed when I realized that it was her after a few seconds. Luckily before that happened, I realized a zombie smelled a lot worse than the fine woman behind me. Taking a deep breath, I let out a big sigh knowing that she had safely returned, and I no longer needed to worry of her whereabouts.

"Welcome back, Mattie. You missed the opening credits, but the main event is about to begin shortly."

"I missed you, you big meathead," she teased.

"As soon as Casper is done playing with our friends out there, it will get messy real fast," I warned, "so if you have a weak stomach I suggest you wait elsewhere, but close by please."

"I'm staying at your side, Mike," Mattie scowled. "I can contribute to the fight; remember I used to be a police officer, not some fragile China doll."

I chuckled and looked down at her. Yes, she was wearing her Glock 9mm, just as she did on patrol every day. And my AR-15 was slung over her shoulder.

"You know which end to point at the bad men?" I joked, tapping her rifle.

Mattie laughed and punched me in the arm after she pulled the assault rifle from me.

She checked the magazine, chambered a round, and made sure the weapon was on safe.

"Good girl!" I said proudly, and turned to watch Casper wreak havoc on the zombies pouring down the road towards us.

*

Casper retreated ever closer to the bottleneck and retrieved yet another remote detonator. Glancing at it, he made sure that he had the proper remote and waited for the right time to initiate it. Looking at the detonator, he had numbered and marked it with the letters "G" and "S", meaning "gas bomb", and "shrapnel bomb".

"This should be impressive," he said excitedly.

At the right moment, Casper flicked the trigger switch. He was correct in his assumption. It *was* a very impressive combination. The resulting hail of metal parts shredded all of the undead within a twenty yard radius, turning them into ground undead hamburger. Moving out farther, more were disabled from missing limbs and severe injuries. With the accompanying fireball added to the mix, scores more were killed or set ablaze with the makeshift Napalm of gas and soap mix. Much to his dismay, however, Casper saw that the I.E.D he had prepared on the other side of the interstate failed to ignite like it was supposed to.

"Shit!"

He toggled the switch back and forth repeatedly but got no response.

"Well, I did set most of these when it was getting dark. Must have forgotten to arm it somehow," he muttered to himself as he spun the ATV around and retreated with his partner.

Before he knew it, Casper had reached into his bag of detonators and retrieved his last one. As if that wasn't a problem, he now had several hundred zombies in the northbound lanes, on the other side of the concrete median divider, snarling and howling for his blood. Because of the malfunctioning I.E.D, he now had a shitload of zombies in the northbound lanes far ahead of the ones approaching him from the southbound lanes.

"I need to stall these bastards for a little bit."

Whipping up his rifle, Casper fired into the crowd of creatures clawing at him over the chest high barriers. His partner joined in, and the AR-15s they were carrying made quick work of the snarling mass. It was obvious that they were also getting help from the sharpshooters in the rear.

Chunks of brain matter and bone shards with clumps of greasy, mangy hair were blasted away from the previous owners, who then fell like puppets with their strings cut. Casper had to swing the rifle barrel back and forth to engage targets, as some of the infected were jostled over the barrier due to the amount of pushing and shoving from the other side. He was so focused on halting the advance of the creatures in the northbound lanes that he almost missed the other half in the southbound lanes. If his rifle had not run dry and he wouldn't have had to reload, he might have become a statistic. Swinging the rifle behind him on its sling, Casper gunned the ATV and pulled back for the final car bomb.

Moments later, he was able to deliver several pounds of high explosive goodness mixed with a large amount of carpenter nails into the very teeth of the unnatural enemy before him. Not waiting to gloat over his kill tally, he headed back to the bottleneck. His part here was done for now. He had to use the two ATVs that he and his partner were driving and scout out positions well to the south for Stephen, who was worried what he might find. He was met by cheers from the men as he rode past, and gave a victory wave in response. Casper stopped for a minute, loading up on food, water and ammunition before tearing off yet again.

Gunning up side roads, Casper looked out at the overpass of the I-355 toll road, where a mass of zombies had been funneled and were moving southbound. The mindless things were following the path of least resistance and were shoved onto the road by the group in front of him and could not get off. Even now he watched hundreds of them climb off the sides of the bridge and plummet down onto the heads of other on the roadway below them, still trying to reach him. Stretching away as far south as he could see down I-355 were untold quantities of the enemy.

"Doesn't look good," his partner said with a whistle.

"That's an understatement," Casper replied, turning south and gunning his ATV. "Let's see where they're heading!"

38

November 14
Day 81

I was so transfixed watching Casper execute his part in the battle flawlessly and without showing the tiniest bit of fear that I was almost sad to see him finish. Casper had more work ahead of him; Stephen needed him to do some more scouting, this time to the south.

Too bad he would not get to see phase three.

I signaled to another defender who was patiently— and most likely nervously— waiting for his time to move. At my arm signal, the driver fired up the trash compactor. It was a monstrous machine, a Caterpillar 836H, sporting 523 horsepower and weighing in the neighborhood of 57 tons. It was equipped with a bulldozer type blade on the front and had huge steel tires with spikes for gathering traction while pushing mounds of trash in landfills. It was also almost perfectly designed for crushing mounds of annoying undead.

With a loud roar the diesel engine fired up, shooting a plume of smelly smoke blasting skyward from the exhaust pipes. The ground actually shook as the machine's immense steel tires chewed up the pavement while it charged forward. By now the front lines of the zombies had spilled into our bottleneck, shambling and screaming into our trap. Up on the roadblock and on platforms behind it, our Alpha platoon, with its thirty odd rifles, sat at the ready. Farther back, along barricades of cement and vehicles which separated the southbound lanes from our occupied northbound lanes, a hundred more of our armed personnel acted as bait. They yelled and screamed, waving their arms in an attempt to draw the zombies further south and deeper into our well designed snare.

So intent on getting to their prey, the stupid creatures didn't even look at the steel juggernaut heading their way. I purposely had the driver keep the bulldozer blade about three feet off the ground. I didn't want to push them. I wanted to knock them over and crush them into the pavement. With a sickening crunch, fifty plus tons of steel slammed into the front ranks of the horde. The simplest way to describe what happened to the first ranks was that they just vanished. The large machine didn't even slow down. Deeper and deeper into the unending mass it plowed and churned. The knobby steel tires crushed and maimed and pulped whatever got under its impressive weight as it drove deeper into the enemy. The carnage left behind was amazing, and kind of reminded me of a lawnmower driving through the middle of tall grass leaving a flattened section behind it.

When the compactor passed the bottleneck area, I could see from the fresh burst of exhaust that the driver, while not slowing in the least bit, had to give the machine some more power to press on. Hundreds of undead were forever silenced with every second that it continued its path of destruction. Taking a quick glance around, I saw that I wasn't the only one with my jaw hanging open in astonishment. I didn't have time to stare, however, for once the compactor passed the bottleneck point, the zombies in the northbound lanes now spilled into the bottleneck breach unopposed. At least that is how it appeared.

At my signal, Eddie, who was now in my dump truck with attached V-plow, screamed forward and slammed into the new batch of zombies. He had similarly outfitted trucks on either side of him, and the trio was able to pretty much span the width of the highway. The destruction wasn't nearly as awe inspiring as the compactor, but hundreds were slaughtered in the first pass without us having to fire a single shot. When the trucks made it to the opening of the bottleneck, Eddie and the others quickly reversed back to their starting point. Rifle fire then commenced and thinned out the stragglers while Eddie and the other drivers waited until the area was again filled with infected. Shortly thereafter, Eddie led the charge and accelerated into the howling masses with reckless abandon. After the third pass, a fair amount of twitching bodies covered the roadway. Lowering the blade to ground level, Eddie and the other drivers slammed the big truck into the gooey mash of undead corpse offal and pushed it into the ditch, clearing the roadway for another pass. A team had been set up to immediately begin dumping fuel on the bodies in the ditch to consume them. Gallon milk jugs of fuel were thrown into the heaping mass and lit. It was dangerous work, and our Bravo platoon provided rifle cover while a few brave souls scurried across the road to add precious fuel to the fire, returning after being covered in thick black soot. My heart jumped for a second when I saw one of the men trip and fall. He didn't really trip. His ankle was grabbed by what should have been a lifeless corpse on the ground. I thought I was going to watch him die when the fallen zombie's head snapped back violently from one of our alert sharpshooters on target shots. The man leapt up and practically jumped over our barricades in a single bound.

Up on the roadway, the compactor had passed the turnaround point and was now coming towards to us in the northbound lanes. If Moses parted the Red Sea in the Bible, then our man in the compactor was parting the Undead Sea. Seeing the carnage from the front was something truly awesome to behold. An old farmer put it best.

"It looks like a combine rolling through a cornfield," he said to the guy sitting next to him on the roof of a semi-trailer.

When the Caterpillar tractor made it back to us, an enormous cheer bellowed from every throat amongst us.

We can do this! I thought excitedly. We could beat these flesh eating bastards!

The tractor rolled by my position, and it was time for the driver to head back north to sow more destruction in their midst. The men and women around me from Alpha platoon picked off the few lucky survivors that managed to avoid both the compactor and the V-plow trucks. They had gotten pretty proficient with their rifles, and zombie after zombie fell due to the accurate fire. Discouragingly, even as we killed tens of thousands, with the mangled bodies piled high in the ditch, there seemed to be just as many unharmed ones in sight as before.

My absorption in the battle at hand was interrupted by my radio. Stephen informed me that zombies were starting to filter in from the smaller roads south of the interstate, and things were about to heat up in front of the safe zone as well. He reminded me to make sure that Charlie platoon kept an eye on our exposed flank to the north and west. I assured him that it would be done and that they could be reinforced if necessary by our reserve force, which was basically everyone from the prison that could shoot.

"If the zombies want to keep moving to the north and west, that's fine." Stephen reminded me. "We can't have them collapsing back down on us."

"Roger that. Everything is going smooth so far," I replied. "Keep me informed of any changes on your end."

*

Kleaner was not happy. First off, he was asked to lead a raid, which he had never done before. Then he was told he had to do so with less than desirable troops. The men and women he brought with him were pathetic. Several of the "volunteers" were old enough to be his grandparents. If so many people were not counting on him to acquire those supplies, he would have scrapped the whole mission on account of safety reasons alone. His raid started to go sour as soon as they made it out to the warehouse distribution center in Elwood, which was a small town due south of Joliet, near a train yard shipping center.

When they pulled up to the immense facility, it took them quite some time before they could even open the security gate. It seemed nobody had thought to bring the proper breaching tools. After wasting precious time scavenging through nearby trucks for tools, Kleaner's patience was wearing thin. He managed to find an operable semi-truck that did not have a trailer attached and drove it directly through the front gate. Once inside, Kleaner sent a small team to find one, preferably two more semi-trucks with trailers to load supplies into. The small team drove off in the slightly dented truck he'd used to ram the facility's main gate open. Now all they needed to do was to breach a door to the warehouse itself. Luckily they did manage to locate a maintenance vehicle nearby, and with the tools inside it, they were able to pry open a side door. And that was when the shit hit the fan.

Apparently when the virus broke loose, many of the workers had decided to secure themselves inside the vast warehouse. What those workers must not have known was that they had securely locked themselves inside with an infected person. When the door, after considerable noise, was finally pried open, a group of undead over a dozen strong poured out onto the raiding party. Before anyone knew there was a problem, the man holding a crowbar had his throat torn open by one of the attackers. This, in turn, sent spurting gouts of blood directly into the face of the man holding the door open. Now temporarily blinded, that man was quickly taken down, swarmed over, and set upon by the hungry mouths of more undead. To her credit, an old woman in her late sixties who was holding a shotgun lifted the heavy firearm to her shoulder and cranked off a 12 gauge slug right into the teeth of another lunging undead, ripping away the upper half of its head. However, the elderly woman was woefully unprepared for the recoil of the large caliber weapon.

The recoil launched her off of the top of the stairs she stood on and she landed upon her back, breaking her collar bone and her hip in the fall. She was subsequently swarmed over by the ravenous creatures. The rest of the raid members, at first frozen with shock, quickly ran off screaming. One particular heavyset man was slower to react than the rest and was pulled down from behind within seconds. The zombies tore into his back so savagely that his spine was exposed in mere seconds, all while he was still screaming. Kleaner could only stare dumbfounded at the unbelievable clusterfuck that unfolded before his eyes. He backed up and gave himself some distance as the zombies fed on the fallen raid team members.

Eventually breaking free of the paralysis, he raised his rifle and began slaughtering the attackers one by one. After multiple mag changes, he put down not only the zombies but also walked amongst the fallen members of his team and coldly shot the newly infected before they could change.

The last of the bite victims was the elderly woman with the broken bones.

"You tried, sweetheart," Kleaner said with sorrow. "This is for the best. God bless you, ma'am."

The last shot fired seemed to echo in his very soul. When it was over, he looked in disbelief at the carnage before him. His entire entry team had either run off or remained as a mangled heap on the ground. It was too much to stomach, and Kleaner promptly threw up. His breakfast didn't taste nearly as good the second time around.

Now all alone, his composure regained after his stomach emptied, Kleaner entered the warehouse cautiously and managed to open a few of the empty docking bay doors. Complete subsections were a loss, with the contents spoiled by the lack of refrigeration after the collapse. But this last one held promise. With the additional light from the open bay doors he could see down several rows of stacked pallets of supplies. It was a literal jackpot!

It appeared that some of it had been looted, probably very early on, but much remained. The sounds of truck engines broke him loose from staring, and he returned outside to find his perimeter team had arrived with an additional three trucks. Kleaner helped guide his men in, backing the trucks into the open bay doors.

The first man got out of his truck and noticed Kleaner was alone. Then he saw the bodies. When asked what happened, Kleaner grimly explained the mess that just went down moments ago.

"If any of those cowards that made it out return, they won't be riding back with us," Kleaner angrily stated. "They left me to die, so I'll return the favor of leaving them to fend for themselves. That is, if I don't shoot them myself first!"

He took some of his men, after leaving two pairs of guards at the door, and went in search of both forklifts and the most critically needed supplies. After finding the prime pallets of goods and marking them with chemical light sticks, Kleaner located some hand-pulled floor lifts to move them, and the group began the laborious job of dragging the goods towards the trucks. The score of dry goods was most impressive.

"Mattie will be pleased," Kleaner said to one of the guys with a wink. "I think she is gonna owe me a little more than a hug after this."

"Shit!" the man replied. "You wouldn't know what to do with a fine piece of ass like that."

"True," Kleaner admitted. "But the experimenting would be fun."

While the other men were laughing, Kleaner walked off and checked in a caged off section of the warehouse that held the ammunition marked for delivery to the nearby stores. It was easily breached, the alarm long since dead. Inside he found cases of all of the common calibers of handgun, rifle and shotgun ammunition. Not an overabundance in any one caliber, but a well-rounded score. Pleased at having some good luck for once, Kleaner grabbed some help and made the ammunition a priority.

Even with the extra trucks, it did not take long to fill up all the space. They could not carry as much as they thought and had to prioritize even more. This was made more difficult by the arrival of more zombies who, as always, seemed to come out of nowhere. Some of that new ammo was already locked, loaded and fired, traveling downrange at 2,000 feet per second to ruin some smelly infected bastard's day. The reason for the new influx of undead was that the few cowards who ran off now had returned and brought some undead friends with them. The gunfire lulled. Kleaner took great pleasure screaming at the people who returned. He made each of them look at the old woman he himself had to kill before he reluctantly agreed to let them return to the prison. The raid had been costly in lives, but hopefully lessons could be learned from this, and they could all move on. There was no other choice.

After securing the warehouse doors again when they left in case they had a chance to come back for more, the overloaded trucks made their way back to the prison as fast as they could safely travel. Kleaner knew that Stephen and Mike would be impressed at their haul. The supplies would prove to be invaluable in helping many others. They had paid for it dearly, however, losing a dozen people in the process. As he led the way back to the base, everyone saw the black smoke rising up from the north, ten miles distant, where the battle yet raged.

"I wonder how it's going," the group members asked one another as Kleaner looked on, deep in thought.

He was ripped out of his thoughts by a passenger in his truck.

"Holy shit! Look at that!" the man cried. "They're pouring off the highway."

Looking over at I-80 as it came into view, Kleaner saw an enormous group of zombies milling in their direction from the east. There were so many that it was impossible to distinguish them individually.

He let out an exasperated sigh. "I do believe we should get the fuck out of here!"

39

November 14
Day 81

Stephen clicked his selector from safe to fire and rested his 20" AR-15 rifle with the ACOG on the sandbag directly in front of him. He, along with four hundred fighters from the Bolingbrook and Romeoville safe zones, was lying on the dirt that was piled behind the trench directly in front of them. Everyone was well dressed for the occasion, as there was plenty of warm clothing just lying around. The ground was hard and cold, but Stephen was grateful that it had stayed as warm as it had in the mid-40s. If it had been much colder the crews would probably not have been able to dig the trench at all. Now the four foot pile of dirt and accompanying trench served as a firing position for a motley assortment of men and women from a wide variety of backgrounds and shooting skills. He had talked to several as the action on the highway was heating up and had met schoolteachers, stay-at-home moms, car salesmen and office managers, along with construction workers, cooks, and warehouse workers. He was amazed that what a person did before the crisis had little bearing on whether they were still alive.

Overall, Stephen was happy with the weapons he saw deployed today. This group also outnumbered the three platoons he had brought with him from the prison and hoped they would be able to produce enough carnage downrange to make a difference in the coming fight.

He hurried to his fighting position that also included Dan and Amber, who were already there waiting on him. As he settled in, he took note of the creatures shambling towards them. The undead were just now starting to enter the field of fuel bombs that had been set up in layers in the distance. The bombs were mostly metal trash cans and steel drums with gallons of makeshift napalm inside of them. When the undead flooded the field, Stephen and a few others with tracer ammunition in their rifles would set off the bombs. The seven layers of fuel bombs totaled about two hundred yards in depth, and the hundred yards or so directly in front of the trench was left open for rifle fire.

With the sound of the battle already raging up on the highway, Stephen exhaled and touched off a round, officially starting this portion of the battle. The tracer round flashed a path right through the head of a random zombie, dropping it instantly. The rifle's unexpected report caused Amber to jump and then hit Stephen, yelling at him that she did not have any earplugs in.

"Why the hell didn't you tell me you were going to start shooting?" Amber demanded. "Dan said to wait!"

"That's right, kid," Dan said, puffing on a cigar. "You have the tracer rounds, so quit wasting them."

"Relax, ladies...I'm just a little excited," Stephen shot back. "I'll take care of business."

Stephen's unexpected gunshot had also caused some others along the line to fire in response. Clearly they were all on edge, unnerved by the sight of so many zombies coming at them. Although not as thick as on the highway, a flood of thousands now descended amongst the fuel bombs. Everyone looked on anxiously, hoping that what defensive plans they made would be enough.

Stephen aimed at the farthest row of barrels, which had all been hastily painted bright colors, and fired. A towering fireball erupted and caused a chain reaction, setting off numerous other barrels as well. Everyone saw the flash moments before they heard and felt it. As the others fired at their fuel bomb targets, a wall of flames went up, engulfing the front edges of the enemy. Dozens of undead flailed around as the sticky gas and soap mixture stuck to them and burned mercilessly.

"Get some," Dan said after removing his cigar long enough to let out a low whistle.

"Dear God," Amber whispered, clearly never seeing destruction of this magnitude before.

The inferno continued to burn, sending thick black smoke billowing into the air, minus the few remaining undead torches feebly twitching. Nothing could be seen of the main bulk of zombies.

Slowly, however, from the wall of flames, burning corpses started to emerge before stumbling to the ground. As the inferno died down, scores of undead waded through, undeterred by the sight of their burning comrades. Soon they crossed into range of the next layer of fuel bombs and the cycle was repeated. Again, as the flames from the explosions died, the creatures gained ground, edging a little closer.

"Unbelievable, they just keep coming!" Amber exclaimed as Stephen and the others prepared to light off the third set of bombs.

"I expected no less," Stephen said with a rough sigh.

The next set of pyro bombs decimated the front ranks of zombies, and when the flames died down, Dan passed the word to use the rifles to knock the closer ones down until the kill zone could fill back in. The defenders, four hundred combatants strong, eagerly sent a wall of lead at the encroaching zombies. Within a matter of seconds, nearly a thousand of the decaying bastards were cut down. Unfortunately, several of the remaining fuel bombs were also accidentally hit as a result from the gunfire and exploded early. All too soon, however, the rifle fire slowed due to people reloading weapons and a new wave of undead advanced into the area of the remaining fuel bombs. They hit so fast this time that Stephen and the others were forced to set off two layers at once to stem the tide. This slowed the advance of the undead for a few moments and Stephen wondered if they had wiped the field clean. It wasn't long before a fresh wave of undead put yet another thousand zombies amongst the final layers of fuel bombs.

"Fire at will!" Dan cried as the moans of the undead now filled the air.

An orange fireball erupted a mere hundred feet from their position, causing many of the defenders to duck behind the earthen berm for cover. Stephen wrapped his arm around Amber to shield her from the blast as the heat and smoke reached their position in an instant. After a minute, Stephen raised his head and watched the flames. The burning zombies were now much closer, and Stephen watched in amazement as many continued to crawl towards them while still burning, oblivious to any pain, before finally succumbing to the flames. The smell of burning flesh also started to fill the air, and all too soon the bodies of the fallen infected began to be trampled by a new wave. Several defenders along the front line broke down into tears, overwhelmed by the stress and emotions of the battle. Many from the Bolingbrook crew had never been in combat, and it started to show. Others became disillusioned when, despite all the carnage, the field was once again filling up with undead howling for their flesh and blood.

Stephen's plan from this point on called for sustained rifle fire with the defenders themselves serving as bait, drawing their targets towards the long, fuel-filled trench. Now the entire line opened up and another thousand undead creatures were ripped to shreds within the first minute. With the distance now well inside a hundred feet, the effectiveness of the riflemen increased. Head shots were more common and the zombies fell by the hundreds.

And yet still they came.

The infected paid for every yard they gained, yet the dumb bastards were all too willing to pay that price. The twice killed corpses covered the ground as their rotting brethren stepped onto and over the fallen in order to reach the feast that was in front of them.

Dan stood and slung his rifle over his shoulder. Drawing his pistol, he began to walk up and down the line shouting words of encouragement to the fighters along with curses and disparaging remarks towards the invaders. Some of his comments would make a sailor blush, and despite the seriousness of the situation, Dan received some disgusted looks from a few of the female fighters. They stayed on the line, firing into the enormous wave. Even Amber had gone through nearly a dozen magazines, making every shot count.

Stephen counted down the range markers as he shot and when the horde crossed the twenty-five yard marker, he ran down the line to Kirk Simms' position. He asked the leader of the Bolingbrook safe zone to take the forty assigned men and pull out to the right and light the nearby buildings on fire. The men were set up in teams of four to drive trucks up next to the buildings, light the fires and then move on. They would also thin out the zombies with rifle fire as much as possible before driving on.

"Our right flank's in the air, Kirk," Stephen said. "You have got to slow 'em down and thin them out for us."

The sound of battle, mixed in the smoke, had Kirk a bit rattled. He could actually taste the burnt gunpowder on his lips.

"I'll do my best!" Kirk said, shaking his head. "This is what it's come to. I have to burn down my own fucking town!"

Kirk left to gather the men. Stephen looked farther to the south, anxious to know when Casper would return with news from his scouting trip.

"Not soon enough," he decided.

By the time Stephen returned to Dan and Amber, the zombies had pressed to within a mere fifteen yards. Before the battle this morning, Stephen had made the decision to only have the four hundred defenders bring roughly a third of their ammunition out and the rest was left inside the makeshift wall of vehicles and chain link fence of the safe zone. Rifle ammunition was now running low and many had resorted to their shotguns and handguns. Stephen could now clearly see the distorted and gaunt faces of the zombies as he lined up the front sights of his pistol. Some of the repulsive bastards who had turned in the beginning stages of the outbreak were now so haggard and starved that they were hard to recognize as once being human. Clothing mostly gone, yellow skin stretched tightly over bone, and always the dried blood. Yet they came closer.

The howling became unnerving. And the smell became horrendous.

Some of the people started to break and run on their own back towards safety. Dan grabbed one young man by the back of the neck just as he turned to run and face planted him.

"You're never gonna get any pussy if you run away like one," Dan growled. "Now get back on the line."

More afraid of Dan than the zombies, the would be deserter grabbed his dropped pistol and returned to his position. Shortly thereafter, a woman latched onto Dan in terror when he walked past. He had to peel the sobbing lady off him and reassure her with some gentle massaging. Dan happened to noticed she had an exceptional amount of cleavage showing.

"See kid, what did I tell ya?" Dan said with a wink to the young man who'd tried to flee, and then stared back down at the nice D cups that were pressing into him.

Amazingly, the line held for several additional minutes among the blast of shotguns, curses of the defenders, and moans and shrieks of the undead. As the trench before them rapidly filled from the undead tumbling in naively, the defenders began to shoot the ranks behind those that fell. When the first zombie tried to clamber across the others that filled the trench, Stephen gave the order to light it off, and a sudden wall of flame went up along the entire front. The heat was intense, and thick black smoke again crawled into the sky. Untold hundreds, perhaps thousands of the creatures died in the tightly focused inferno. Stephen, Dan and the others were no longer able to see anything moving on the other side of the flames, and Dan ordered a general retreat back to the safe zone. Stephen hoped that the fuel-filled trench would not only kill a lot of undead but also provide time for an orderly withdraw and the chance for the defenders to rest and refit. The sounds of the moaning undead were now even temporarily masked by the roar of burning fuel.

"I bet we killed over thirty thousand of the moaning fuckers in that field," Dan wheezed to Stephen as they jogged back towards the safe zone.

"Now what do we do?" Amber asked with a tired gaze, seating the last full magazine on her person.

"We're going to have to be stubborn," Stephen said. He swung his full dump pouch over his shoulder. "We're going to kill these fuckers until they decide we aren't worth the effort to eat, and I'm not dying today."

"Don't worry, Amber," Dan said confidently. "I'll exterminate just as many in this very parking lot as we've killed so far. I won't let them touch a hair on your pretty little head."

40

November 14
Day 81

Transfixed by the raging battle to our front and preoccupied by trying to quickly refuel the plow trucks, I was caught off guard when a very dented and blood-splattered Ford Excursion skidded to a stop near our position. It had been honking its horn and flashing its headlights. Behind it was a beat up looking red minivan that also came to a stop. One of the last people I had ever thought to see again, my good friend and workout buddy Chad Evanston, got out of the vehicle and walked up to the nearest guy.

"Take me to the guy in charge!" I heard him yell over the roar of the battle.

I limped my way over to him with a huge grin on my ugly mug and wrapped him in a bear hug. With much laughing and back pounding we greeted one another.

"Holy shit, you're alive! How did you guys find us?" I asked. "I thought you all beat feet for Wisconsin."

Chad first looked at the new scars I sported. "Yeah, we did, but the place wasn't built for the long haul," he answered. "We about got overrun a couple times. We were getting ready to move when we heard your radio transmission, decided to make our way back and give you bitches a hand."

That was when I realized he had two others with him, Terry and Bruce, both former cops like myself, with a lot of experience and talents to draw upon.

After greeting them both as roughly as I had Chad, I let my better looking partner Mattie grab each of them in bear hugs.

"This is fantastic news! Stephen will be stoked to see you guys. In fact, I'll send you down to help him out. He's shorthanded as far as talented trigger men go and will gladly get you into the shit fast. We seem to be holding our own up to this point, as you can see," I said, waving a hand to the heaping piles of undead mush that were now over ten feet high in spots and extended down the road as far as they could see.

"Sounds like a plan, Mike," Chad agreed. "But first you need to hear me out. You've got no clue as to the extent of the zombie infestation you are facing."

He went into great detail about the many times they were forced to detour around huge gatherings of zombies and near the end of the trip, the sheer numbers of the groups heading right to the nice big smoke signal we had burning.

My previously grinning face took a sour and pained turn, then finally one of anger.

"Dammit, we just can't catch a break!" I cursed, throwing my hands in the air.

Turning back to Chad, I again gripped him by the shoulder. "At least you got here in time to warn us," I stated flatly. "It's all we can do to handle the ones we have here now. Go to Stephen's location and fill him in. He should get to be as stressed as I am."

"Who's in the van that was following you guys?" Mattie asked.

"We met them back down the road," Bruce replied. "They were headed towards your smoke signals too. I think they want to help out."

"I'll go say hi," Mattie decided and headed towards the van.

With some more handshakes and farewells, Chad, Bruce and Terry got back into their SUV and tore off down the road to find Stephen at the safe zone, just as the sound of multiple explosions could be heard from that position.

*

The safe zone's defenders were now perched on the vehicle barrier that sat behind the eight foot chain-link fence that surrounded the property. The vehicle barrier had been upgraded as time permitted, and even now additional cars were being stacked along the back wall. The section that Dan, Amber and Stephen called home for the moment was three cars high. Impressive, but by no means impenetrable.

"We can't let them surround us completely," Stephen told Amber as he grabbed her hand and lifted her up into the bed of a truck that sat high along the wall. "I don't want to get trapped in here."

"Me either!" she responded. "Just promise me we will leave before it's too late."

The infected had pushed through the trench after suffering heavy losses and were now entering Dan's private minefield. All the leftover explosives he had packed into junked cars, just like Casper had done on the interstate. In fact, Casper had helped him set and arm the car bombs. He had all the charges wired to a control panel and was now trying to set them off in order.

"Well that was impressive," Stephen remarked drily when the first set of explosives didn't go off when Dan hit the switch.

"Fuck off!" Dan mumbled and quickly hit the next switch.

An enormous set of explosions went off, shredding a big section of zombies.

"See, much better!" Dan said with a smirk.

The incoming undead were close enough that people began firing along the barrier with well-placed rifle shots. Stephen decided he wanted in on the fun and as he lined up his sights on a fat rotting zombie, the disgusting bastard's head exploded into pink mist.

"Looks like you had better pick up the slack," Amber teased, "you're getting outgunned by a girl."

Stephen reply was interrupted by Dan's third set of explosions and then by a tap on his shoulder. He turned to find the glowing end of Dan's cigar in his face and Dan pointing down towards the gate located on the north side of the property.

"Somebody actually wants in this place," Dan said, pointing to a vehicle that was parked in front of the gate.

Stephen immediately recognized Chad, who was yelling at the guards who were not moving the trucks blocking the entrance fast enough.

"Holy shit!" Stephen bellowed after climbing down and meeting Chad just inside the compound. "When did you get here?"

"We'll have time to go over that later," Chad replied. "You have a major shitstorm heading this way from the north."

As Chad filled Stephen in, he realized that plans would have to be changed quickly. Bruce and Terry chimed in as well, painting a dire picture.

" Thanks for the heads up," Stephen said after thinking for a few moments. "We'll need to hold here for a minute so we can get an organized withdraw put together."

It seemed strange to Stephen to be calling the shots with Terry around. Terry had been a high ranking member of the department and handled roll call at work the day everything fell apart.

That seemed like a lifetime ago. Stephen Shrugged. How things had changed.

Chad snapped Stephen from his daydream. "Let's kill some zombies first. Where would you like us?"

Seeing Terry and Bruce unloading Colt M4 rifles from their beat up Expedition, Stephen smiled with satisfaction.

"Out-fucking-standing," Stephen said with a grin. "Take up position on our right flank. It's under pressure from the undead right now, and we could use the firepower."

Pointing to the Tahoe he was using, Stephen told Chad that Mattie had brought him up two extra cases of 5.56 and it was in the back.

"There are also five hundred rounds of .45 in there for that hand cannon of yours," Stephen added.

Now it was Chad's turn to smile.

*

Once the refueling was finished, the trash compactor took off again, tearing through the undead ranks like a scythe cutting wheat at harvest time. We watched in amazement for what seemed like an hour as it continued to make mincemeat of the zombies pressed in tightly together on the highway.

"We could do this all fucking day," I heard someone say behind me.

"It's like shooting fish in a barrel!" another added as the gore poured off the highway, filling the embankments.

I was talking with the two men who had arrived with Chad and his group earlier. They had proved to be a valuable addition. The van was completely loaded down with supplies, and they were both active duty military. They briefly filled Mattie and I in on their exploits. It seemed that they had been part of a failed military quarantine around Louisville and had barely escaped with their lives.

"You would think that Ft. Knox would have been able to handle Louisville," they said, "but politics got in the way, and we were not given the green light to use heavy armor on citizens. It got ugly quick.

Trying to enforce quarantine on an American city that size without the means to do so is not a pretty thing to witness."

After getting out of Louisville, they were making their way northwest to check on family in Minnesota when they first heard our radio broadcast and then saw smoke from the battle. They saw this as a chance to even the score.

"We lost a lot of friends in Louisville," the older with the last name of Green on his BDUs told me, "and have been running ever since. Today we get even."

Their M4s were a perfect addition to Alpha platoon, and both men were skilled in their use.

"Hell, this is gonna be easier than I thought," the younger one said. "They got this well in hand."

"Roger that!" Green answered while walking forward to pick out his first target.

And it was at that very moment that Murphy decided to join in on the fun.

We were unaware of the fact that one of Casper's I.E.D's did not go off. We were informed of that little tidbit of information when on the return trip back down the northbound lanes that the operator of the compactor accidentally struck the vehicle that it was positioned in.

It just happened to be, of course, a gas and shrapnel mixture bomb.

The jarring of the vehicle when the titanic machine struck it set off the I.E.D, which exploded in a giant ball of fire and steel. Chunks of metal filled the air, ripping through the garbage moving machine's glass windows, which added nicely to the shrapnel that tore into the poor, doomed driver. Bits of steel also tore into the machine's engine and hydraulic system. As if that wasn't bad enough, liquid fire splashed over the entire cab section of the compactor as well. It was a good thing the driver was already dead, for the machine banked hard to the right and slammed into the concrete dividers of the interstate and got hung up on it. It was immediately swarmed, with a bunch of them set on fire trying to get at the driver, who was ultimately and violently torn from the cabin.

I stood there feeling like I just got mule kicked in the nuts. The machine jerked and shook while the engine finally stalled, burning from the makeshift napalm that coated it. The sounds of crackling fire were soon replaced by a multitude of hungry voices screaming and howling for our blood. Alpha platoon reacted on queue and opened up, sending a hail of lead into the now advancing horde, dropping hundreds in mere seconds. My next command over the radio was to pull back Bravo and Charlie platoons to cover the immediate area around our location.

"Are we in trouble, Mike?" Mattie asked with a concerned look in her eyes.

"Yes...yes we are."

*

"This is the last of 'em!" Dan bellowed over the gunfire as the control panel he was operating detonated the last series of charges. The explosions rocked the air again and shredded hundreds of additional zombies that were hell bent on tasting human flesh at any cost. Now only the rifles, shotguns and pistols positioned behind a chain link fence and a row of cars stopped the nightmares in flesh from reaching their goal. Sensing the urgency of the situation, the volume of rifle fire increased and no zombie had yet been able to reach the fence. Yet, while seemingly impossible, the undead appeared to also sense that victory was close at hand and pressed the attack. Smoke, sulfur, fire, hissing lead, screams, moans, explosions, gunfire, Molotov cocktails thrown by the hundreds... it overwhelmed the senses.

Glancing down the line, Stephen noticed Kirk running in his direction, and Stephen for the first time observed all the smoke coming from the buildings to the south and east of their location. Arriving out of breath, Kirk informed Stephen that all the buildings nearby had been lit, but zombies were still pouring in from the right.

"Take your men and stack 'em up on the right flank along the southern wall of the safe zone," Stephen commanded. "We need to buy us some time! Look for a redhead with tattoos, his name is Chad. Have him help position the guys. Now move!"

When Kirk left, Stephen was relieved to see Casper tearing up to him on the ATV.

"What do ya have for me, Casper?" "I got zombies pouring off Lockport Road and heading down Collins Street right towards the prison. I got more infected heading down Maple off of I-355 and approaching Briggs Street," Casper relayed with dread. "They're also flooding in off of I-80 near Route 30 and approaching Briggs Street too. We're going to be cut off and the prison surrounded if we don't move quickly. The whole area is infested with 'em. What we see here is just the tip of the spear!"

"That bad, ya say?" Stephen grimaced. "Shit... okay, we need to keep our line hot for a good bit. Go hook up with the men on our north flank and make sure that the zombies don't push between us and our guys up on the interstate.

"I'm on it!" Casper said and tore off before Stephen could ask him what had happened to his scouting partner.

"I'm gonna try and get ahold of Mike on the radio and coordinate a retreat," Dan said, heading off towards the command truck. "Hold here for now at all cost!"

Stephen dumped a full mag from his AR-15 into an advancing zombie and twenty-nine of its friends.

The undead clawed their way to the front of the safe zone, leaving a layer of their fallen comrades in their wake. There were just too many and the reloads were taking longer. With a thud, the first zombie hit the fence, and was shot down immediately. Another reached the fence, and another and another. Now the defenders were firing directly down into the mass. The handguns were out; the defenders were all in. Amber shot Stephen a worried look as the ranks filled in several layers deep around the fence.

"I've seen this before," Stephen said. "The same thing happened back at the high school. We need to keep them from climbing over for a while yet, until Mike and the others get here. We have no other choice."

His pistol barked; he shot yet another zombie through the top of its head. It was the closest one yet.

*

I now had all three of our platoons covering the I-55 from the north and east and had them linked up with the Bolingbrook guys to the south. The number of rounds we brought to the fight was impressive. The training had paid dividends. Zombie after zombie had their heads emptied by a lead projectile, leaving the signature violent jerk and red mist in its wake. The ammunition would not last forever, however, and I was soon faced with three large problems.

First, the undead were starting to arrive from the northwest and were spilling out onto the highway, threatening our rear.

Secondly, my troops were beginning to panic and burning through ammunition way too fast. Casings littered the ground as magazine after magazine was expended to buy us precious minutes.

And lastly, I had just watched two of our three plow trucks crash into our barricade after the drivers panicked, and the zombies surrounded their trucks en masse. Watching the two drivers being pulled kicking and screaming from the cabs before being devoured was very bad for morale. There was just no way to hold them for much longer.

Back at the command truck, Stephen had organized a fancy diagram with vehicle assignments, planned routes of escape and detailed instructions on an orderly withdraw. The command truck had redundant means of communication, HAM, CB, and two-way Motorola radios to facilitate the retreat. I instantly knew there was no way we had time to keep it that organized. I grabbed my radio and screamed for Stephen to sound the alarm for retreat. I was unable to make out any reply, or if he even copied.

"Everybody go!" I screamed into the radio and then put it away. I had my hands full with getting my own folks out of this mess.

I grabbed Mattie and dragged her off the bus rooftop and over to where our V-plow dump truck sat. Eddie, the one driver who had kept his cool, was currently standing outside the truck firing his rifle at zombies who had managed to make it through the hail of gunfire. I grabbed him by the sleeve and told him to ready the remaining tankers to cover our retreat. We had two tankers held in reserve, to use just like we did earlier out to our front. The difference was that this time it wasn't only to kill as many of the infected fuckers as possible, but also to cover our retreat. Eddie ran off frantically to find the other drivers.

"Luckily these infected bastards don't run, or else we would be dead already!" I said to Mattie, who was putting on a brave face, helping several fighters up into the back of the dump truck.

"We need to get everyone off the highway now!" she yelled back. "Start this bitch up, Mike!"

The fuel tankers began to move, and everyone realized the gig was up. They ran south off the highway, racing for their vehicles that were lined up in the median that surrounded the exit ramp. It was like a game of musical chairs, and nobody wanted to be left standing when the music stopped. The undead were now using their combined weight to press through our barricades and enter our fighting position. The trucks were rolling, with their liquid fuel now sloshing off the pavement. The trucks continued south with the drivers letting the rigs roll into the ditch on their own power. From a distance I saw Eddie scramble to safety.

When it looked like our people cleared the road, Eddie set off the fuel tankers. The highway went up in a protective wall of flames. This also detonated fuel bombs that had been pre-positioned in the southbound lanes, south of the barricade. Giant explosions and fireballs filled the sky. Despite the urgency, most of us instinctively paused to see the show. Staring coldly at the devastation and sheer destruction we had left behind, I wondered if we had accomplished anything. We gave the bastards our best shot, and we were still the ones fleeing once more. It wasn't long before I saw our enemy yet again. From out of the inferno and smoke, several figures fully engulfed in flames stumbled on shaky legs and collapsed onto the roadway. It snapped me from my trance.

Grimly, I steered the big truck still dripping with the gore of zombie body fluids and headed south, intent on cutting a path across the Bolingbrook safe zone and back home to the prison. I nearly ran over some of our own guys but managed to make it off the highway and raced towards the safe zone.

"Look at that!" Mattie cried, pointing ahead.

Rt.53 south was covered with twice dead bodies piled in front of the fence that protected the safe zone. The fence itself was now falling under the combined weight of thousands of zombies, who were flooding into the safe zone perimeter. Inside the safe zone, a traffic jam was forming as several hundred people tried leaving in vehicles out of the two small gates.

"Looks like they could use a hand!" I yelled. "Everybody hang on!"

*

Stephen, upon seeing the fuel traps go off on I-55, realized what was happening and gave the orders to retreat towards the prison. Vehicles were already pre-positioned behind the fences, and it quickly became a game of musical chairs to find a seat as the trucks started to peel away at high speeds. Without the sustained rifle fire, the zombies on the fence would soon push it over or be pushed through it out of sheer combined weight. Stephen emptied his handgun into the mass of undead out of spite and then loaded a fresh magazine and holstered the pistol onto his thigh rig. Grabbing Amber, Stephen herded her off the wall and towards the Tahoe. He discovered that Dan and Kirk Simms, along with the radio guy from Bolingbrook, Derrick Booth, had already arrived at the truck.

"Thank God they waited!" Amber cried as she jumped into the back while Stephen made for the driver's seat.

"I'd never leave you guys!" Dan shouted back at her from the front passenger seat. "Not to mention, Stephen has the only set of keys!"

"Let's get the hell out of here already," Derrick chimed in.

Stephen fired up the Tahoe just as the perimeter fence began to fail in the weak spots and zombies poured into the safe zone. Traffic jams were already forming from the bottle necks near the exits and this worried Stephen. Some of the escape vehicles had hungry undead already hitting the glass windows that offered only a small layer of security.

The small group in the Tahoe looked on in amazement at the chaotic scene unfolding when a large blue Joliet city V-plow dump truck tore through the fence and smashed a stack of small import cars out of its way. The plow truck then proceeded to rip a gash into the stream of undead flooding the former sanctuary.

"That must be Mike, and it looks like he has the same idea," Kirk said in amazement."

Stephen gunned the engine of the Tahoe as Mike's plow truck headed for and then crashed through the south fence, clearing an extra escape route for the fleeing vehicles.

"Looks like we might live to fight another day after all," Stephen said, joining the mad dash of vehicles headed south. "Now hang on to your ass everybody, I've gotta try and keep up!"

41

November 14
Day 81

“Well that turned to shit in a hurry,” Chad said. He started the Expedition and threw it into reverse as Bruce, Terry and two others jumped into the truck. Nobody heard him, too busy shooting down the zombies who reached the truck just as they did. Thankfully they weren't smart enough to open the doors. Backing up and swerving to avoid a man running to a different truck, Chad ripped the driver side rear door off the Expedition before the last man in could close it.

"I think we waited too long to leave!" Bruce shouted over the blast of his assault rifle, splitting the head of an emaciated zombie wide open.

The zombie had appeared instantly, as if by magic, in the void left by the missing door.

Chad slammed the gearshift into drive and hit the gas again, maneuvering out of the parking lot. A large tractor, which had been stacking cars along the back wall only an hour before, created an opening along the west wall by smashing through in an attempt at a retreat. Chad took advantage of this gap in the fence to escape from the safe zone. There was no road to the west, however, and Chad lost valuable time making it back to the roadway heading south. The passengers struggled to hang on as the SUV swerved to avoid the vast numbers of undead that were now covering their escape route. There was a flurry of activity all around them as the other survivors struggled to flee to avoid the undead. They saw several accidents, most of which ended badly with the occupants being torn apart by zombies.

Once there was some distance between them and the safe zone, there appeared to be a break in the number of the staggering bastards spilling into the roadway. Chad opened up the accelerator a bit and picked up some speed.

"Just in time. Things are looking nasty here," he said. Up ahead, he could see more infected enter the roadway and look in his direction.

"At this speed I should have just enough room to squeeze through," Chad said to Terry, who was looking wide-eyed from the front passenger seat at the quickly approaching mob.

What he didn't expect was the carload of other fleeing refugees that decided to pass him at that exact time. Their driver did not see the numerous zombies standing in the roadway, and the smaller station wagon obviously would not be able to absorb the impact. The station wagon swerved in front of Chad's SUV and struck the front driver's side quarter panel. Chad was caught off guard, and the unexpected impact knocked the SUV violently to the right.

"Oh shit!" Chad cursed and slammed on the brakes, his momentum taking him on a direct path into the rear of a flatbed tow truck that was abandoned alongside the roadway.

The sound of shattering glass and tearing metal, along with an intense, painful burst of stars filled his vision and hearing as his SUV slammed into the much larger and heavier truck. No one in the Expedition had time to brace themselves as the SUV came to a sudden and violent stop.

Gunfire from the back seat echoed in his head while Chad slowly regained consciousness, coughing from the chemical dust of the airbags deployed in the crash. Blood from his severely broken nose covered the steering wheel. He tried to raise his left arm and screamed in pain. Looking down, he could tell that it was dislocated. Sitting upright and groaning in pain he looked to the right. He could make out Bruce's legs.

Hadn't he been in the back seat?

The rest of him was sticking out of the windshield, and from what Chad could see, Bruce probably had a broken neck. Chad cursed the asshole that ran him into this parked truck and spit out several teeth in the process.

"Goddamn it!"

Coughing, he looked over to the front passenger seat for Terry, and found him. Well, some of him anyways. When he'd struck the back end of the flatbed tow truck, the bed of the truck ripped through the windshield in front of the passenger seat and struck Terry at chest level. All that remained was the twitching lower half.

"Son of a bitch," Chad coughed out in pain.

Still staring in confusion at his fallen comrades, Chad was taken by surprise when hungry hands began pulling at him through the shattered driver's window. Drawing his 1911, Chad shot the zombie through the head with the large .45 slug. Now he could hear that one of his fellow passengers was alive, had crawled up onto the roof, and was firing a rifle at the zombies who were closing in. Firing again and again, Chad and the man took a few down with accurate head shots. Chad heard the man curse when his rifle went dry. This was followed by the sounds of the man jumping off the roof and running away on foot. Chad only caught a glimpse of the man as he fled. Chad also tried to open his door to escape, but it was jammed from the accident. Slowly and painfully, he reloaded his pistol with a fresh magazine with one hand and prepared to defend himself.

Sadly, he was one man. One man with a single handgun, injured and deeply outnumbered. It wasn't long before multiple zombies had managed to pull Bruce's corpse off the hood of the truck and began devouring it. Chad fired vainly to keep the zombies at bay, but he forgot that the totaled SUV was missing a rear door and did not notice that one had managed to climb inside until it latched its teeth into his right shoulder. Screaming in fear and pain, he shot this new adversary in the head, killing it instantly and coating the right side of his own face in brain matter in the process. Rapid breathing overtook Chad as adrenaline coursed through his blood. The gig was up, and he was without a doubt now infected. There was only one way to end this before it was too late. Steeling up the courage for what he must do, he roared in anger.

One of the last truckloads of beaten survivors from the fallen Bolingbrook base raced down the street, and they could only watch in silence, wondering exactly what circumstances had led to so many zombies swarming all over a wrecked and disabled SUV. There must have been two dozen of them. They were well inside the cab and had clearly consumed anyone that may have still been inside. Quickly passing it by, they failed to hear the final gunshot that was muffled under the weight and sound of several zombies already in the process of feeding.

"Must have been fleeing the safe zone," one said to another.

"And look at that," the other man said, pointing at a station wagon that had crashed and had flipped over, experiencing the same fate.

*

Gasoline had been splashed onto the vinyl siding of the houses and the flames quickly spread up the walls of the once expensive homes in the upscale neighborhood of Romeoville. Stephen and a select group of others had tasked themselves with setting the town on fire on their retreat south. In the distance they heard more gunfire; survivors firing from the backs of trucks on any undead that dared to try and weave their way through the fires.

"Last one!" Stephen said as he lit the row of houses on fire. "Let's go, we have done all we can."

"Do you think this is working?" Kirk asked after they had climbed back into the truck.

"Maybe a little," Stephen said. "I hope it buys others a little time."

Thick black smoke hung in the air, and they all coughed slightly from it.

"We got company, fellas," Amber said and pointed to the north where zombies were emerging from the smoke cover.

The last remaining passenger, Derrick Booth, sighed in frustration. "They just keep coming!"

"Dan, get us back to the prison," Stephen said. "There's no point in engaging them. I'm almost out of ammo as it is."

"Roger that," Dan said and hit the gas. "We may be the last ones in tonight."

Stephen got on the CB in the truck and sent out a message to have all of the fire teams head back to the prison. Of the nine other trucks out on the patrol, only five answered, and Stephen was left to wonder to himself how many people were lost in the battle.

And for what...what have we accomplished? he thought. It was going to be a long drive home.

*

When we approached the prison, I couldn't help but repeatedly slam my fist into the steering wheel in frustration, anger, and disappointment. I was not happy. We were running with our tails between our legs from a major ass whooping. It didn't really matter that we took that ass whooping from an unbelievably massive zombie horde. They didn't carry the day by being the smarter or stronger foe. We were just so helplessly outnumbered that once all of our traps and schemes were exhausted, we had no choice but to flee.

I take that back. We did have a choice. Fight and surely die, or retreat and live.

We'd chosen the latter in that regard. I had little intention of becoming one of the undead if I could help it.

"Why are you hitting the steering wheel, Mike? It did nothing to you," Mattie asked.

"I didn't like the way it was eyeballing me," I snapped and hit it again. "Besides, I'm upset that we got our asses handed to us by a bunch of mindless brutes."

"They did have us outnumbered," she replied matter-of-factly. "The option of staying would have been suicidal. Our new Army friends agreed. They decided to stay on with us, I think. I saw them giving Eddie a hand with the tanker trucks, hope they made it out okay."

"I'm sure they're fine," I answered. "The defeat still hurts no matter how you dress it up. A man has his pride, right?"

We pulled up in front of our prison base main gates and sat there in silence, each thinking our own private thoughts. I had no idea what Mattie was thinking when I looked over at her. What man truly knows what women think about anyway?

Hell, I bet *they* don't even know what they are thinking half the time, and they get mad at *us* when we can't figure them out.

My thoughts were simple and primal in nature. I thought of the battle and what I could have done to make it work out in our favor. While we waited there for the gates to open, my eyes drifted over to Mattie and drank in the curves of her body. Damned if my mind didn't go straight into the gutter. She must have felt the heat of my stare or had some "spider sense" because right when my eyes narrowed into what I was sure was a hungry, predatory look, she glanced over at me.

"Really?" she asked, feigning disgust.

"Oh yes...really," I promised.

The clanking of the opening prison doors broke the moment, and we both laughed as I put the big truck into gear and moved into the courtyard. I looked at the thick stone walls.

I'd like to see those bastards try to breach these. But how long did we have until the undead force sealed us in? Not long I suspected.

Backing my V-plow truck up to the inner perimeter where our

campers were, I noticed that Stephen had not yet returned. Mattie noticed this as well.

"I'm worried about them, Mike," she said softly.

"It's Stephen," I replied calmly. "That asshole can fall into a pile of pig shit and come out smelling like roses, he'll be fine."

Mattie reluctantly nodded her head in agreement. Getting out of the truck, we found that all of our human cargo in the back of the truck had survived the bumpy ride home and were eager to get out.

All around us, the prison courtyard was a flurry of activity with so many new arrivals and the rumors of our defeat.

"We need to get to the command center and try to get this place organized," I said. "It's turned into a goddamn zoo in here. Need to find Kleaner and ask him how his raid went. Looks like we are going to need those supplies we sent him after."

"After today I just want to crawl into bed and lick my wounds," Mattie countered. "Can we please?"

I sent her off to the RV, telling her I had to track down Kleaner. I promised I would not be too long, and she said she would wait up for me. Looking at her tired, exhausted face, I doubted she would last ten minutes before falling asleep.

*

Jonas stood looking at the large dump truck entering the prison yard in disbelief. It looked like it had been driving through mounds of bloody raw hamburger. The entire V-plow and a majority of the front end were absolutely covered in a thick, smelly gook. And of course, the unbelieving heretic sinners were not harmed in the least. The big bastard, Mike, looked healthier now than when he left! He was barely limping and had a look of smoldering anger on his face, except when he looked over at the whore Mattie. She seemed to tame the beast inside of the man.

Jonas' eyes narrowed in anger.

What I have in store for all of them will soon make them bow before the Almighty Himself and beg for forgiveness.

Turning away as to not get caught staring, he marched back to his trailer. Once inside, he retrieved his two-way radio and turned it on. It was already set to the correct channel.

"Lewis," he asked quietly into the microphone.

A much stressed, somewhat squeaky voice answered him, "Jonas, I'm here. Is it time?"

"Yes it is. When the next large caravan of vehicles approaches the gates, I want you to fall in behind them. When you reach the courtyard, I'll meet you and show you where we need to park the truck until we can go over the items I had you gather for me. I'm dressed in all black today, you won't be able to miss me. Now hurry! Don't be late and miss your chance to get in."

Jonas then gave Lewis a simple cover story for him to follow if the gate guards asked him any questions as to who he was.

After hearing Lewis state he understood what he had to do, Jonas turned off the radio, stuffed it in his jacket pocket, then left his camper to wait for Lewis just inside of the gate. Standing there in the darkening gloom of the long since setting sun, Jonas lifted the hood of his jacket to ward off the chill of the late fall breeze and vigilantly watched for Lewis' truck to enter the prison grounds.

"Father Kettle, I won't let you down," he whispered. "Your death will be avenged!"

*

Lewis' truck lurched forward and then abruptly skidded to a stop when the vehicle in front of his stopped suddenly. Cursing loudly, he honked his horn impatiently for the vehicle in front of him to get through the prison gates. The gate guard looked back at Lewis and shouted for him to hold his horses.

"Hold my horses? I got something for you to hold, asshole," he muttered to himself, lighting the first cigarette of his third pack of the day.

Sitting there idly, watching the gate guard chat with the driver of the vehicle in front of him was simply too much for Lewis to stomach, so he began hitting the horn again impatiently. The guard's head snapped back to stare daggers at Lewis. After saying a few more quick words he motioned the truck through and stomped back towards Lewis.

"What the hell is your problem, mister?" he said angrily. "We have protocol to follow. We have to be sure nobody that is infected gets in."

Lewis took a deep breath to berate the idiot and then remembered his cover story. "I apologize, sir. It's just that I'm from the Bolingbrook base, and we were completely overrun, and have been on the move all damn day. I'm anxious to feel safe inside your impressive facility," Lewis said with mock sincerity.

The guard leaned into the cab to peer into the back of the bread truck.

"Are you by yourself?" he asked. "And what is all of that stuff in the rear?"

"Yes, I'm alone," Lewis stated. "I did have another guy with me, but he was killed by zombies. He sacrificed himself so that I could make it. The stuff in the rear is some food and farming supplies from the safe zone."

The guard seemed to buy Lewis' story and stepped back. He had already tired of listening to this pipsqueak that he was sure had contributed nothing to the fight.

"Okay," the guard answered tiredly. "Go on inside and find the guy on the main drive wearing the red jacket. He will tell you where to unload the supplies and park your truck. Someone else will help you find quarters."

Lewis put the truck into gear with a wide smile on his face. "Why thank you, kind sir."

When the truck passed through the gate, Lewis visibly relaxed and sighed in relief. It was now dark outside, but a number of lights around the courtyard provided some illumination. Most of the lights, however, were pointed out to provide the guards with a view of any approaching threats. Several yards into the prison yard, he noticed a wiry man in black staring intently at him as the truck entered the courtyard. The man motioned for Lewis to follow then walked off at a quick pace. Lewis paced him slowly with the truck to the southeast section of the premises. After getting the signal to park the vehicle, Lewis did so and got out.

"I take it you're Jonas?" Lewis asked, walking up to the strange man. "I don't think we have actually met face to face. I'm Councilman Lewis, the brother of—"

"No names, asshole," Jonas snarled as he walked past Lewis towards the rear door of the bread truck. He opened the back doors and stood gazing hungrily at the items stored there. "Well done," Jonas smirked, "but do not get comfortable. We cannot have you walking around to be recognized by the men you despise. You will remain hidden at all times. Is that understood?"

Lewis, now realizing that he was the subordinate of this partnership, nodded his head dumbly in agreement.

"Relax; you will not have to hide for long," Jonas said. "This prison and its people are entering their final hours of existence."

"I do hope you have a plan to get us out alive afterwards?" Lewis asked. "I don't want to die in this place."

Jonas just laughed, and Lewis felt a shiver go down his spine.

*

Kleaner groaned when he observed the prison gates open once again to allow another group of survivors inside. The caravan appeared to be five vehicles and was packed with refugees from Bolingbrook. The last truck was Stephen's Tahoe, and Kleaner was glad to see the man jump out of the truck and walk up to him.

"Looks like you guys made it back in one piece," Kleaner said. "It's good to see you."

"Thanks, Kleaner," Stephen said extending his hand. "What's the situation here?"

"Well boss, I don't want to tell you how to run your facility here, but you might want to think about turning some people away," Kleaner replied, looking just as beat as Stephen. "We're running out of room in the dormitory building to house them. The majority of the cell blocks are still too dirty and cold to use. Oh, and I think fresh water and sanitation problems are going to start to emerge."

"I think that problem is going to take care of itself real soon," Stephen said grimly. "The zombies are not too far behind us. The bastards will probably be here in force by morning to seal us in. At that point, nobody else will be able to get in at all. In fact, along those same lines, I need to make an announcement that anyone that wants to leave had better go tonight or risk being stuck in here. This could turn into a long, medieval style siege."

"That's a good idea, and I agree," Kleaner said. "Also, I cannot confirm this, but with this many new people entering, there is no way we are screening all of them properly for the virus. That has me worried big time, boss. If one infected body gets loose in here with it this crowded, we'll have to put down a shitload of people. Could get real messy."

Stephen looked around and for the first time saw the unorganized layout of the new people who had set up camp. People were milling about everywhere and in desperate need of guidance. There were despondent looking souls searching to see if a friend or relative had made it back safely. As if reading his thought, Amber walked up to him.

"I'm going to go check to make sure my uncle is okay," she said, "and I could use a hot shower."

"I'll catch up to you later," Stephen replied. "First I'm gonna find my dog, and then get up to the command center and try to get this place back under some kind of organization."

Kleaner sighed in relief. "Thanks boss!" Kleaner said. "And Buddy is fine. I've been keeping an eye on him. You forgot to mention how much that dog likes to eat. He stole a cookie right out of my hand yesterday! "

Stephen patted Kleaner on the back and chuckled. "We're all in this together. And thanks for looking after my dog."

Stephen began to walk away then spun around and walked back up to Kleaner.

"Before I go, I almost forgot, I need to ask you a couple of things. First, how did the raid go?"

"It went," Kleaner said drily. "I already filled Mike in."

Stephen shrugged and left it alone.

"Also, Mattie explained to me the unusual circumstances of Logan's disappearance, and she wanted me to tell you that she is going to look into it. Please keep me updated if you two find out any news."

"Will do, boss," Kleaner replied, "and that is welcome news."

Kleaner looked back at the traffic jam now clogging the entrance. The open gate made him uncomfortable. The drivers of the vehicles in line were yelling at the vehicles seemingly holding up the process. His guards started yelling back, and now nothing was getting done. Kleaner wished he could just slam the doors shut now and be done with it. Grabbing his pistol from his holster he walked up to the commotion and fired a shot into the air, which quickly gathered everyone's attention.

"Listen up!" Kleaner yelled. "This is how it's gonna go!"

42

November 14
Day 81

With the sun now having set and darkness in full effect, a massive horde spilled down State Street into the town of Lockport, then south across 9th Street. More moaning and howling creatures poured across the 9th Street Bridge from the west side of the river, merging with the group heading south towards Joliet. Even in the moonless night the abominations stumbled and shuffled south. The cries of hunger echoed into the night, howls answered them back as if in response. More shrieks of undying rage came faintly far to the west.

They all seemed to say the same thing.

Living flesh is near! *Sweet, succulent, screaming meat is close*!

Dried, withered tongues licked over cracked and dirty teeth as they anticipated the soon to be ecstasy of rich pulsing blood jetting into their mouths.

The stronger creatures knocked the slower ones out of the way and pushed onwards, pulling ever closer to their time for feeding.

*

I pulled out a couple of cold beers and handed one to Casper. Twisting off the cap, I took a long pull. It was well past midnight now and things were finally winding down for the night. Smacking my lips in pleasure, I had to appreciate the abundance of free booze in this time of societal breakdown.

"Man I needed that," I said, letting a belch rip loudly.

"Cheers then," Casper said as he popped his cap with a hiss.

I tapped my bottle to Casper's. "I just wanted to give you my thanks for the outstanding job you did out there on the interstate, my friend. That was an incredible display of courage you showed in the face of the enemy. I couldn't have done it better."

Casper stared at the ground, clearly embarrassed by the compliments I showered on him.

Nearby was his new girlfriend Holly who, while declining one of my beers, appeared to be happy just being in Casper's presence and had a proud look on her face as I talked highly about him. She had come a long ways herself, from being rescued from a grocery store parking lot, the school, her kidnapping and escape, and finally battling the zombies.

"Thanks boss, but I was only doing my job," he humbly replied. "It wasn't anything special."

"Anything special my ass. You singlehandedly held off hundreds of thousands of zombies for half the afternoon! Most people would have shit themselves in fear. It was fucking amazing!"

Laughing at Casper's attempt to blow off the kickass job he did, I took another long pull from my bottle.

Casper glanced over at Holly, who looked back, expecting him to say something more. He cleared his throat, clearly uncomfortable. "Boss, I need to ask a favor."

I wiped my mouth from my latest noisy expulsion of beer gas. "Sure, buddy, what can I do for you?"

"Would you care if Holly and I cut out of here? You know, before the zombies arrive?" he asked hesitantly.

"You mean leave? Why does it matter what I care? You're a grown man, Casper. You don't need my permission," I replied. "Stephen already put out the call over the intercom. If people want to go, now is the time. Many have already left in fact."

"I know, but I feel like I owe you guys for helping me when I needed a friend," he said. "And you let me into your group, and treated me like I was family."

"Casper, we would rather you stay," I said, "but if you want to leave you have my blessing. Where would you go?"

Casper now had an arm around Holly's shoulders. "I have family in the upper part of Maine. I know it is a long haul, and I'm sure winter has the roads all fucked up by now, but I want to get out and try to check on them while I still can."

"Then let's get you outfitted with whatever gear and supplies you think you two might need," I said with a smile. "You've more than earned whatever you need to take."

Holly moved up and gave me a hug. "You are a good man, Mike," she said. "I'll miss you and Stephen both."

I hugged her back. "Shh... I have an image to keep up, don't let my secret out."

We all chuckled and made our way to go look into what supplies that they would need, but not before I grabbed a few extra cold beers.

*

Lewis stood looking over Jonas' shoulder, breathing noisily, shifting his weight from foot to foot. Jonas stopped what he was doing and looked over his shoulder in irritation at Lewis.

"Do you mind?" Jonas asked. "I really would rather not make a mistake here."

"It would help if I knew exactly what you were doing and what my role in this is," Lewis replied.

Jonas sighed and stood up straight. "Well, if you must know in order to leave me alone, what we have here is all the necessary materials to destroy this complex." Lewis looked confused. "The items I had you acquire were the missing components I needed to make a very powerful explosive. It is called ANFO, more commonly referred to as a fertilizer bomb. The major components are ammonium nitrate and fuel oil, along with the few other ingredients you also collected for me."

Lewis looked closely at the stuff laid out on the bread truck floor. "And you say this will bring down the walls?"

Jonas laughed. "Oh yes, the size of explosion this will make will bring about anything down, remember Oklahoma City?"

Lewis' eyebrows perked up and he whistled lowly. "Wow, that big?"

"Trust me, Lewis, when this bad boy goes off, it will be like the Hand of God hammering these sinful degenerates straight into Hell where they all belong," Jonas said. "Now finish bringing me those materials from the hidden stash; this will be too heavy to assemble and move. We'll build it here in the truck."

Lewis turned off the interior light of the truck and quietly left after making sure the coast was clear.

Once the door was shut, Jonas turned the light back on and

looked at his materials laid out on the floor. He really couldn't start until Lewis brought down three of the large barrels to mix the diesel and fertilizer pellets in. He could work on the bump charge though. ANFO explosive would not detonate without help. It needed a smaller explosive charge to ignite it and explode with its full potential. He set himself to making a container filled with some of the quarry explosive, which was similar in nature only much more refined, that he was able to steal before the base personnel had left to fight up north a few days ago. For a power source, a simple car battery would provide the juice. It was now late into the night, but the excitement of his plan finally coming to fruition had Jonas wired.

After prepping the charge, he set it aside and set to working on the timer mechanism. In this instance he would be using a simple battery-powered kitchen cooking timer. He made short work of breaking it down and hard wiring the proper sequence of wires for the trigger device. He didn't have it fully completed by the time he heard a faint knock on the rear door. Quickly extinguishing the light, he opened the door to find one barrel left at the rear of the vehicle with Lewis nowhere to be found, and he figured Lewis must have gone to fetch the other two barrels.

Trying to muscle the large barrel inside quietly took some doing, but he accomplished it with no major problems.

At least Lewis had shown some initiative; Jonas hadn't had to send him back after the others.

Jonas waited patiently for Lewis to return with the next barrel and helped him load that one as well. Climbing inside, Jonas nearly shook from excitement as he envisioned the destruction his instrument of vengeance would wreak upon the heads of these unsuspecting bastards. Shaking his body hard to steady his hands for the intricate work ahead, he was still a bit surprised that Lewis had actually accumulated everything that he needed.

The project would take him all night, so he got to work. It was too bad that fool Lewis didn't know he was a pawn in this game. He had proven most useful, even if he was annoying.

After a short time, Jonas could hear Lewis return with the last barrel and then climb into the cab exhausted. Lewis was sound asleep, snoring loudly in the front seat of the truck in mere moments.

"Yes, quite annoying indeed," Jonas reminded himself.

*

Casper was anxious to get on the road. It was almost three in the morning and we were all tired. Yet he was adamant that he needed to put some distance between him and the approaching deluge of undead before morning. Finally only teary hugs goodbye stood between him and the open road. Mattie, Dan, Stephen and I insisted on being at the gate to see our friends out.

"Be careful, guys," I cautioned, throwing the last box of provisions into Casper's truck. "I plan on seeing you both again after this is all over. Maybe come visit."

"You're always welcome, Mike," Casper replied. "You all are."

"Wish you'd reconsider," Stephen said, "but I understand the family part and all. Be safe and God's speed."

After a final handshake, the prison door opened and then slammed shut behind him.

"That takes some moxie," I acknowledged as we headed off to bed, "hitting the road alone like that."

"He may end up coming out on top in the end," Stephen conceded, "with us trapped in here like rats on a sinking ship."

43

November 15
Day 82

Like a raging river spilling over its embankment, the ragged beings that were once human with their own families and loved ones flowed down the streets of Joliet. The bloated figure of a career first grade schoolteacher snarled her hunger at what was once a male construction worker. A former hairdresser savagely clawed a school crossing guard, whose uniform was caked in blood and filth. They were eastbound on Ruby Street now and soon met up with another colossal collection of damned creatures pouring south down Route 53. Sluggishly, they merged together and crossed the Ruby Street Bridge. Hundreds were forced off from the main host by sheer numbers and made their way down nearby side streets. The immense numbers crossing both the Ruby Street and Jackson Street bridges spilled across and slowly began infiltrating out into the surrounding neighborhoods as they moved east through town. The hours passed, and the influx of undead moved east through the neighborhoods, growing ever larger as more and more joined the march for food. Hungry, hate-filled eyes turned north up Collins Street and their combined screams shook the very earth upon which they treaded.

Outside the huge stone walls the enormous army of undead arrived and spilled around the prison walls like a stone in a creek, until all four sides were surrounded. So thick and deep were the ranks that the end was not seen in the surrounding distance. The smell of their human prey was so very close, yet unattainable, and this sent the entire horde howling and screaming in rage. And it did not relent, for these beings did not need rest and never tired of the howling, screaming, and moaning. These creatures did not go away once they could not reach the meat on the other side of the infuriating walls, for there was no food anywhere else to pull them away.

As the day went on, the enormity of the situation hit home for everyone inside the prison. Many came up to see for themselves. Quite a few went white with fear, some cried, even more vomited over the edge of the wall. Many were left with the disturbing image of a pair of jumpers who committed suicide, after everything they had been through, by jumping off the wall into the new undead sea.

*

Stretching his arms overhead to relieve the soreness of his back, Kleaner groaned as vertebras popped disturbingly loud in his spine. It had been a long night accompanied by poor sleep. He had finally gotten some rest after speaking briefly with Mattie about Logan's possible whereabouts. Now making his way across the prison yard, he climbed up one of the guard towers, from which a steady stream of rounds had being fired in the past hour. Entering the observation room, he saw five men posted at the windows firing round after round with a pause only to reload their various magazines and rifles. All around the prison now the guard towers were alive with gunfire. The floor of the room was littered with shell casings, and the smell of cordite was as thick as the smoke lingering in there.

"Hey guys, what's with all the shooting?" he asked.

One of the men looked over his shoulder. "The zombies are thick as flies on a piece of dog shit, boss. It has gradually picked up since daybreak and hasn't let up since."

Kleaner stepped up to the window and looked out, which gave him a great view of Collins Street, for which the prison was named.

Down below at street level the area was heavily covered with mounds of twice killed corpses.

"Damn good shooting," he said. They were definitely getting better.

The problem was that even with the huge amount of kills they had racked up, there seemed to be easily three or four times that amount on foot or, in some cases, crawling from lack of feet or legs, towards the prison.

Kleaner leaned far out of the window to look at the base of the wall only to see ranks of undead already wailing and battering their hands in an act of futility against the stone walls. Kleaner leaned back inside.

"Cease fire, men. We don't have the ammunition to kill this many, and it looks like you guys are almost dry up here anyways," he ordered. "I will pass the word to the other guard towers. No sense in exhausting all our long range capabilities when they can't bother us other than their annoying moans. Raise me on the radio if the situation changes but as of right now just watch them."

Stomping heavily down the steps back to ground level, Kleaner did not want to alarm the guards that the numbers they saw were nothing compared to what he knew was soon to reach their doorstep. As bad as it already was, it was only going to get worse.

*

Stephen had seen the videos from the tsunami that hit Japan. In some of the cities, what was a trickle of water on a side street became a violent torrent in mere seconds. That was how the zombie tsunami hit. One last scout vehicle had raced up to the gate and was let in before the zombies closed the gap. Rifle fire bought them the few added seconds they needed to slip back in. The small crew in the vehicle had been out gathering whatever supplies they could find. One last thing that Stephen did before being sealed in was rise early and lead a small team back outside the walls. They placed and rigged dozens of propane tanks in intervals along a path out the west gate of the prison. If worse came to worst, they could blow the tanks and hopefully carve a small path of escape. Dan assisted, and had them prewired with a heavy gauge cord. Stephen left the radio detonator inside the plow truck. Once the first one went, it would start an irreversible chain reaction.

"You'll only get one shot at it," Dan reminded him.

Stephen realized it was a long shot, but would take all the help he could get.

From here on out it would be different. Nobody got in, nobody got out. This was now an old-fashioned siege. The guards, who had not participated in yesterday's battle, saw for themselves the extent of the horde for the first time. The moaning, screaming mass closed in on all sides of the prison as the guards held their fire while the vise close around them. Stephen, Amber and Dan stood with the guards and watched in silence. Buddy growled at the mass of undead.

"This is it," Dan stated to a female guard who was looking out in terror. "There are no more fallback positions. Our stand must be made here."

She was so shocked at what she saw, she didn't notice when Dan finished off his line by placing his good hand directly on her ass.

"We lost too many people yesterday," Stephen lamented. "Lives that the human race itself can no longer afford to lose. And we left valuable supplies out there, now out of reach for the foreseeable future. We didn't move fast enough."

"You did your best," Amber replied, "and you can't blame yourself. Most everyone here owes you and the others their lives, remember that."

"It doesn't bring back the ones who lost their lives though," he sadly replied. The three of them silently stood and looked on with a feeling of helplessness as the prison walls were surrounded by creatures howling madly for their very blood.

He was worried for his friends Chad, Bruce, and Terry, who still hadn't arrived at the prison. Stephen last saw them holding the right flank as the line was caving in; their actions undoubtedly helped many others escape. The radio station updated their broadcast with the message that the prison was unable to accept any more groups of refugees due the tens of thousands of undead outside the prison walls. Over the next few days they needed to begin the daunting task of organizing and rationing supplies to stretch things as long as possible, in hopes that the situation would change in the future. The prison now held over six hundred people and this presented a daunting task. At least eighty additional survivors had fled the prison prior to the doors shutting, preferring to chance it alone rather than be trapped behind the walls.

*

Many other survivors also awoke early, and were sitting around bonfires, talking about yesterday's battle and what the new day might bring. Sitting alone at one such fire was a new refugee, Ben Porter. Ben, a 34 year old former manager of a cell phone store, was now sweating and not from the heat of the nearby blaze. A loner at the Bolingbrook safe zone, Ben never opened up to anyone about his past. Nobody ever asked, and Ben never offered. He had hung back during most of the heavy action, only firing his rifle on a few occasions. It was not his rifle, for he detested firearms, and was given to him prior to the battle. He had pulled the trigger just to show the others next to him that he was pulling his weight. He was not even sure if he hit any zombies. However, the more time that went by, it appeared to him that he may be infected.

He was not sure exactly how it happened. When the order to withdraw was given, he was one of the first guys in a vehicle and ended up in the front passenger seat of a fully loaded Dodge Caravan. While fleeing the safe zone, the driver of the van hit a couple zombies, one of which came through the windshield, landed partially in his lap. The people inside the van managed to push the mangled zombie back through the shattered windshield and off the hood as it thrashed and clacked it yellowed teeth inches from Ben's screaming face. The minivan limped back to the prison and was one of the earlier vehicles to arrive. Only after arriving at the prison did he notice the small scratch on his left arm. The damned zombie's jagged teeth had cut right through his sweatshirt and a small blemish, a scrape really, that had hardly bled at all, was visible. He had cleverly avoided the hastily assembled medical inspection.

"I'll be fine," he told himself. "The shaking is just adrenaline wearing off."

That was late yesterday, and now he stared at the small cut with dread. It was a deep, angry looking red and had dark lines snaking away from it. To make matters worse, he really felt like shit. He quickly looked around and covered up the cut so nobody else would see it. Ben silently stared at the fire and hoped that if he just ignored the problem it would go away.

*

I groggily cracked open my eyes and mumbled out a curse as my sore body voiced its complaints in the form of several body aches. I had slept like shit. Normally you could run a chainsaw next to my head and I would sleep like a baby. But not today. Today I woke up to a bad feeling like I was being watched, like something was going to jump me any second. Glancing at my clock, I realized that it was almost eleven; I had way overslept. There was so much to do, but after yesterday's mess, I deserved to sleep in. Feeling for my radio on my nightstand, I raised Kleaner. He was just finishing up his scheduled rounds.

"Hey, buddy. I really hate to bother you, but let me know when the zombies arrive in force."

The reply was explicative laden followed by a rather long pause. Kleaner's tired voice replied, "You are a tad bit late. They're already here. They have been flowing in all morning. Don't sweat it, not much we can do about it now."

Now it was my turn to curse.

"One other thing before you go," I asked Kleaner. "Any sign of Chad and the guys? Remember I told you to watch for them? They were to be in that police Ford Expedition."

"None of my guards reported seeing them, boss," Kleaner replied. "If I hear anything I'll let you know first thing."

Resigned to the fact we were here for the duration now, I was able to relax and sleep soundly. So much so that not even the bloodthirsty howling of the zombies outside the walls could keep me awake.

*

Mattie woke slowly, and it took a few minutes for her to become fully awake. She was currently unable to move, however. Mike had his large frame half on top of her with his right hand having a death grip on her right breast. It wasn't a painful grip; she was just unable to move his big arm that was draped over her. Glancing at her watch, she saw that it was late morning and was glad for the opportunity to sleep in. They both needed it badly. The stress and physical fighting were bad enough, but add in the afterhours bedroom activities and that was enough to exhaust anyone. She tried to wriggle free and escape the clutches of the sleeping man, very aware of another part of his lower anatomy announcing that it was wide awake, even though he snored into her shoulder.

Good God, she thought. *I've created a monster*!

Giggling quietly, she finally detached herself with quite a bit of effort and tiptoed to the bathroom to clean herself up. She wanted to look into Logan's disappearance. As of yet she had very little hard evidence to go on. Trying to be quiet so Mike could get as much rest as he needed, Mattie slipped out of the RV and set off to start up her investigation. After grabbing a light breakfast in the cafeteria, she sat down and closely looked at her notebook. She was using it to lay out her investigation and had more than a few things written down already. Among them was information she had gotten from the interview with Kleaner last night. He had been tired but cooperative.

The things she wrote down might or might not help her figure out exactly what happened to the big man. She also gathered shift schedules for the men and Logan's last known location. The first place she wanted to look was the guard tower where he and Kleaner had been working on the rifle experiment.

Mattie made her way across the prison yard, amazed at the amount of people milling around.

Stephen wouldn't like seeing so many people sitting around expecting to be taken care of. She wouldn't be surprised to see him handing out shovels for no other reason than to have everyone dig fighting positions around the prison yard.

Mattie chuckled to herself and made her way to the top of the guard tower in question. Once at the top, she looked out the tower windows and observed the unbelievable zombie horde that had descended on them during the night. Gazing for a moment at the sickening sea of lost humanity, she saw the different colored sticks that Kleaner and Logan were using to mark the range and for the rifle effectiveness experiment.

"Plenty of targets now..."

Mattie turned to face the young male guard behind her. "Excuse me, were you working the night of Logan's disappearance?" she asked out of the blue. "If not, when was the last time you saw Logan up here?"

The man's eyes jerked up from staring at her ass to look guiltily at her. "Uh, sorry, I wasn't working that night, ma'am. Last time I saw him was the night before when he made his rounds. It should be in the log book he kept."

Mattie jotted down the information he provided. "I see. And do you know of anyone who might have had a beef with Logan that would seek to do him harm?"

The guard had a shocked look on his face. "You think someone killed Logan?"

Mattie put away her notepad. "I don't know. I need to look around more. Thanks for your help."

At the bottom of the tower she again looked at the new influx of people. Mattie shook her head in frustration. This investigation was going to be a pain in the ass now with all the new folks. She'd have to figure out who was originally here and who wasn't, and there was still so much else to do.

44

November 15
Day 82

Stephen sat in the command center, looking over some updated numbers. A formal headcount had been conducted and it appeared that the prison had five hundred eighty-nine people inside. It seemed more had fled prior to the zombies' arrival than previously thought.

With inmates and staff, the prison had about two thousand people when it was a functioning facility, so there was plenty of room for everyone.

A careful inventory of supplies had been undertaken by the office staff, and it appeared that for the current population of the prison they had enough food to make it into next summer. And that was without the contributions from the livestock. The same with the fuel supply, provided they practiced a little conservation. The generator used a widely varying amount, depending on the load, and several of the RVs had their own smaller generators. That was longer than he would have guessed, on both accounts.

He had a chance to go over his own personal situation as well. The larger RVs, including his and Mike's, had propane generators. Stephen had installed two very large propane tanks in their small inner perimeter and their RVs should have electricity, heat and hot water for a year, if not longer. His RV was also packed with enough food and ammunition to last two people a year. However, Amber pointed out, if the food supply for the other survivors ran out before then, it would become a problem when they saw him eating while they starved. Buddy had his own stash of dog food, but as most beagles do, preferred whatever his master was eating. At any rate, before supplies ran out something would have to give and a way to resupply from outside the prison would have to be discovered.

There was much speculation on that end as well. Mattie figured that the government would have their convoy system up and running by then and they would hear the prison's radio broadcast and send help. Stephen had a more morbid theory that he kept to himself; he figured they would just as easily use the prison as the bait, and jump at the chance to nuke a large group of zombies. Stephen himself was hopeful that maybe the zombies would die off this winter from the extreme cold and everything would be fine by spring. Or maybe they would grow tired of waiting and most would eventually move on. Amber didn't think they had any concept of time and would just sit and wait, and sided with Mattie on outside help. Dan wanted to begin preparing a plan to escape by tunneling out until someone mentioned that if these bastards could smell us all the way from Chicago a few feet of dirt separating us underground probably would not work. After much discussion, it was decided by all that this one particular problem could be dealt with later.

Stephen turned his attention back to the more pressing matters, and wanted to go over some security concerns with Alpha, Bravo and Charlie platoons. With raids outside the prison no longer possible, Stephen wanted to beef up security inside the prison and wanted the platoons on three separate eight hour patrol shifts. With so many people, anything was possible and Stephen felt that any issue needed to be dealt with in a timely fashion. Good old fashioned police work.

He filed the updated numbers with the office clerk and checked in with Dan in the radio room. As he fixed himself and Dan a fresh cup of coffee, Dan told him that the only radio contact he was making was far to the west of Chicago, the suburbs were a total loss. Stephen let out a sigh and told Dan to make an announcement for all squad leaders and the heads of the Bolingbrook and Romeoville safe zones to meet in the conference room downstairs.

It took a while for everyone to show up but finally the meeting got rolling. Stephen gave everyone ample time to express any concerns. After a good hour of debate it was decided that the first shift would start at 0700 and would be handled by Bravo platoon. Alpha would take the afternoon shift starting at 1500, with Charlie handling the graveyard starting at 2300. After conferring with the Bolingbrook guys Stephen mentioned that more platoons could probably be formed over the winter to augment the shifts and provide extra security on the walls. The shifts themselves would entail numerous two man teams with radios patrolling the grounds and two larger reaction teams for quick response. One would be based at the command center and the other on standby at their place of residence. The squad leaders would work out the assignments among their men.

An "after action" report of the highway battle was then conducted and Stephen went over the numbers as far as personnel, ammunition and weapons. Alpha platoon suffered no casualties during the battle, while Bravo and Charlie each had two people missing and presumed dead. Seventeen other workers from the prison also perished while Bolingbrook and Romeoville lost nearly a hundred people, mostly during the retreat. The three platoons had expended nearly 51,000 rounds of ammunition during the battle. The remaining reserves for the main battle rifles were listed at 46,000 rounds of 5.56, 27,000 rounds of 7.62x39, and 52,000 rounds of the 5.45x39. The remaining handgun ammunition was still being counted, but half of their known reserves had been deployed during yesterday's fight. Bolingbrook's four hundred defenders consumed almost 140,000 rounds total of mixed caliber. Their exact remaining round count was unknown but was considered minimal.

As the discussion wound down, additional meetings were planned for that afternoon. Stephen wanted to meet with the squad leaders for the three platoons again to go over a training program to help in the transition from raiding party to police/security force. Kleaner wanted a meeting with his perimeter guards in an attempt to upgrade weapons and personnel from the new pool of bodies. Committees also needed to be formed to handle the more mundane chores around the facility and the heads of cleaning, cooking, maintenance, livestock, and medical among others were all recruiting new people to help out. Everyone headed out, and Stephen went back to his camper for lunch with Amber and Buddy while others grabbed chow in the cafeteria before their afternoon assignments.

*

Ben Porter sat in the corner of a packed room for a communications meeting. The meeting was being conducted in the command center's communication room. He had been roped into the meeting after it was discovered that he managed a cell phone store, and had reluctantly attended. He did not feel good. In fact, he felt like day old dog shit. He did not want the others to know, so he hid his discomfort. Now sitting in the rear of the room, out of sight of the others, he could tell he was burning with fever, and his arm was throbbing. He had never felt pain like this before. The pain kept hammering at him and escalated every few minutes. It was amazing that he managed not to scream in agony.

The damned scratch felt more like a stab wound now, one with a red hot blade twisting in it.

And now Ben began to get mad, irrationally mad. Between the pain and anger he was unable to think coherently.

What the fuck does a cell phone store have to do with radios anyway? he thought, gritting his teeth against the latest wave of agony. *I feel like shit. What the fuck am I even doing here*?

He was having trouble concentrating as his head started to pound, clouding any remaining rational thought. Ben opened his eyes when he felt something wet land on his hand. He didn't know he had clamped them shut from pain. Lifting his hand to see what it was, he recognized that the substance was blood. A single drop had fallen from his nose. Feeling another drop about to fall, he quickly brought his hand up to catch it. Blood smeared across his upper lip when he swiped it away. He had been clenching his teeth and was surprised that his mouth began to salivate. He stared at his blood smeared hand, unknowingly putting it to his mouth, and licked it off. The copper taste exploded in his mouth as if he'd had a bite of a delicious steak. He needed to have more! He *must* have more!

This pissed Ben off even more, and the pain increased in his head. He softly growled, no longer able to comprehend what the man in the front of the room was saying. In fact, Ben wanted to hurt him.

He felt the anger rising. He tried to control the anger, but pain began to slam his body in the worst wave yet. On top of all of this his insides twisted into the worst hunger cramp he had ever felt in his life. Unable to cope with all three at once, Ben gave in.

He suddenly stood up with an inhuman growl of rage and sank his teeth into the neck of the man sitting in front of him. Thick blood sprayed from the horrible bite wound to the man's shoulder, and Ben realized that the sweet taste of blood made the pain and hunger subside slightly. Shoving this screaming man to the side, he turned his blood drenched face to the side. He locked his sights onto his next victim, a young man. Charging forward, he grabbed his newest target and started to feed with a vengeance. Awful screams of pain were the last thing Ben Porter would ever remember.

*

The first victim of Ben Porter's deadly attack was Amber's uncle, Adam Wells, an avid survivalist. Even armed, Adam didn't stand a chance. He had his neck torn open from behind before he knew what happened. The next victim was Tyler Wade, the teenage son of Eddie. He had helped drive the tanker trucks to what was being called "The Battle." Tyler had no time to react to Adam's screams, and now with a gaping wound to his arm, it was mere seconds afterwards that he turned. Now everyone was yelling and moving in total confusion, unsure what had just happened. People tripped over one another, firearms were drawn. Shots fired wildly into the infected and innocents alike.

The sound of gunfire and panicked screams drew the attention of Stephen, who was outside the command center and had just concluded the security meeting with the squad leaders from each platoon. Stephen remembered that a group of prospective HAM and AM radio operators were meeting inside. He a sick feeling in his stomach and recalled the earlier conversation with Kleaner about not being able to screen all of the new intakes fleeing the interstate battle.

Stephen quickly grabbed a nearby guard.

"Get ahold of whoever is on duty and get them here now!" he screeched, then pointed at the others from the meeting. "You guys come with me!"

Inside the command center, the next casualty was Derrick Booth, who had helped set up the prison radio station. Derrick was helping with the meeting and had come up with several great ideas that he would never be able to implement. He was savagely bitten, and blood from a large gash in his neck coated the floor, making it wet and slick. Within less than a minute, the conference room they were using was covered in blood and gore. All the uninjured survivors bolted for the door leading outside, with seven new zombies rising from the floor and following in pursuit. A zombie, drenched in blood, managed to drag the last man to the ground and start to feed. Another survivor ran towards a group of passersby, with three zombies in pursuit. Two were killed by attentive people who recognized what was happening and were armed, but the third managed to infect others before being cut down by rifle fire. Screams and shots erupted from all around the nearby area.

Stephen lowered his carbine after shooting the nearest threat, quickly ordering the squad leaders and others standing around to surround the entire area and try to isolate the spreading infection. If he and the squad leaders had not been meeting nearby, Stephen now felt it was certain most, if not all would have been lost. As the regular platoon troops filtered in and joined in the containment perimeter, tough decisions had to be hastily made, and rifle fire cut down anyone who tried to breach the line. The troops shouted orders for anyone not infected to lie down, pleading that they needed clear shots at any infected. Stephen knew that in the chaotic mess several people, although not infected, probably just panicked and were shot as a result. Unfortunately, the containment perimeter produced a dangerous cross fire and two of Stephen's own men were hit in the exchange. Both of their wounds were ultimately fatal. Two zombies emerged from the doorway of the command center and were cut down from a distance. The office staff in the command center was able to secure themselves behind a locked door, able to wait it out. Stephen and a few others closed in and dispatched the remaining zombies during a room by room clearing of the entire building. It was over in less than ten minutes, but twenty-three former survivors were dead. Stephen had teams sweep the entire yard and found that to the best of their knowledge no infected had been missed.

It took hours for the rumor mill to die down and the identity of the victims to be determined. Eddie was a wreck, having lost his son, and Stephen had to have him detained temporarily for his own safety. Amber also took the loss of her uncle pretty hard, and Stephen did his best to comfort her. The men took the task of putting down their own the best they could, as they had grown to know many of the ones now slain. Nobody knew the quiet man named Ben Porter.

The prison's inhabitants remained on edge after the attack. It was top priority that everyone was to be reexamined medically. Everyone, with the exception of a few cleared guards, had to assemble in the cafeteria and was given a number in line. There seemed to be a slightly longer line in front of Dan's favorite nurse, Shelly. The first exams began immediately and were the best they could put together on short notice. Everyone who passed the examination was given the equivalent of a doctor's note. A hand stamp, along with a red armband was issued to wear upon completion of the exam, so they could be certain nobody was missed. Alpha platoon was cleared first, and then made a full sweep of the prison, looking for victims. Luckily, no others were found to be infected, but several persons were quarantined temporarily out of precaution. Better safe than sorry. The rest of the day and into the evening, everyone was of one another, keeping weapons near at hand while expecting people to start biting one another without warning.

45

November 18
Day 85

Walking from my RV towards the chow hall, I stopped to check out the latest group of refugees that were trying to unpack their meager belongings and settle in to some unused campers. They were the lucky ones; they got a private camper instead of a place in the dorm. One such camper had belonged to Amber's uncle, who had died in yesterday's outbreak. Dan and Kleaner had decided to bunk together. Dan said it was so he could keep an eye on Kleaner, who was distraught over Logan's disappearance, but I think it was because it was easier to drink together. If refugees had kids, they usually got a camper. Most still had looks of despair on their faces; the shock of the infected man that had rampaged through our ranks yesterday was palpable. For all I knew, the adults in front of me weren't even these kids' real parents. Most had probably died at some point during this unending nightmare.

A thin boy about ten years old or so caught my eye standing outside the group of people, looking down at the ground. The poor kid looked like he was half starved and nobody paid him a bit of attention.

I slowed down and headed over to him. "Hey there, bud. What's your name?"

"Max, sir," the kid said, looking up at me then quickly back down.

"Where are your mom and dad at, son?"

"They are both gone, sir," Max said, staring at the dirt.

"Well, Max, I've got some work to do. Would you like to help me?" I asked. "But I hate to work when I'm hungry. Would you care if we got a bite to eat first?"

The small boy's head snapped up at the mention of food.

"Yes sir, I would like that please."

I steered him away from the group that he seemed to be an outcast with. They didn't even notice he was gone.

Max followed me like a lost puppy, eyes filled with wonder and a bit of fear of uncertainty mixed in with it. We entered the cafeteria, and though it was not chow time, I was able to persuade the cooks to fill me a plate of hot food for the little guy. I snagged a can of sliced pears for me to snack on, too. Grabbing a seat at one of the many empty tables, I set the plate down in front of Max and sat in amazement while the little guy packed away enough meat and instant mashed potatoes to easily fill me up. Good food always cheers people up.

Everything smelled good, and the cafeteria was clean, warm and well-lit. A couple of card games were going on in the corner. They were using stacks of worthless cash, just as Chris had, and it made me again think of my lost friend.

While Max inhaled his meal, I raised Mattie, who was trying to find Logan, on the radio.

"Still on it," her voice crackled.

I let her know I was at the chow hall, and going to be splitting some wood out back behind the building later. Mattie said she would come get me in about an hour and would bring refreshments.

Putting the radio back on my belt, I looked up to see Max staring at my untouched can of sliced pears. Chuckling, I pushed the open can towards Max, who snatched it up and downed it in seconds.

"Okay, partner, now that we've had some grub, let's get to work," I said with mixed enthusiasm.

Wiping the sweet pear juice from his face, Max hopped up. "Ready when you are, sir."

"Max, my name is Mike. You don't have to call me sir."

"But my Pa always said to call big people 'sir' or 'ma'am'."

"What happened to your dad, son?" I asked gently.

Max stared at his hands in his lap for a few moments. "He got bitten, sir, and then got really sick," Max said. "My dad attacked my older brother, who told me to run. That was a long time ago. I haven't seen them since."

Damn...the horror these little kids must have gone through. It wasn't fair.

"I'm very sorry, Max," I said, putting a comforting hand on his shoulder. "You ready to give me a hand with some chores? If you do a good job I'll get you a can of peaches when we're done."

"I would like that," he replied, cracking a toothy grin.

I led Max around to the back side of the chow hall to where the pile of wood used to cook the cafeteria food was stacked. Soon we had a fairly good system set up. I would split the wood while Max took the pieces and stacked them nice and neat in a row. Within minutes I was shedding my jacket. Max was getting a good workout too. He never complained and worked hard to impress me. Hell, I wished the new adult refugees worked half as hard as this kid. Every now and then I would let Max take a swing with the axe, both of us cheering whenever a chunk was split in two. The exercise felt good and we hit it hard, both of us getting our money's worth. When it began to get dark, I was looking forward to Mattie showing up with those cold beers to call it a night. Placing another chunk of wood upright, I took aim and slammed the axe home again.

*

Mattie made her way across the prison yard heading over to where Mike was splitting wood. In her left hand were two nicely chilled bottles of Bud Light. In her other hand was her notepad filled with information regarding Logan's status. There was dreadfully little news discovered today regarding that topic, and it was beginning to look more like a criminal matter rather than just a missing person. Logan had simply vanished.

She hoped whoever had caused Logan's disappearance hadn't died in the highway battle, so they could beg for mercy when they found out who did it.

Mattie picked up her pace and transferred one of the beers to her other hand. She was nearing a large bread truck parked near the condemned off limits section of the prison. So intent on looking forward to seeing Mike again, she paid no attention to the truck or the man standing behind it.

*

"For the last time, Lewis, I know you have issues with the people running this place, but they are not your typical run of the mill helpless citizens," Jonas hissed angrily. "They're all battle tested, each with their own strengths and weaknesses. We just cannot run up and attack them and hope to survive. We need to think this through and plan accordingly."

Lewis, who was in the back of the bread truck, argued back. "But you don't understand! Those assholes destroyed everything I had. They demolished my government stocked safe zone, killed my brother and destroyed his compound in the process, physically assaulted me, and had total disrespect for any type of authority I formerly held."

"Trust me, Lewis!" Jonas shot back. "There isn't a day that goes by where I don't want to make them pay for what they did to your saint of a brother. But we're all of what is left to see that his murder is avenged. That's why we must play our cards right."

Lewis noisily blew out a stress-filled breath that he was holding. "It's just so frustrating!" he complained. "What exactly do you have planned to pull this off?"

"The army of Satan's foot soldiers that we hear outside the walls will be fed soon enough. Once the people inside here are fully occupied in their day to day tasks, they will grow complacent. We will take the truck and drive it up alongside the eastern gate, the one they never used, and set off the explosive there. When the gate is breached and the people you hate are overwhelmed by the demonic enemy, we will make our escape in a vehicle when the time is right."

"Well that sounds fantastic the way you say it, but are you positive it will work?" Lewis said with sarcasm. "These fuckers have been most frustratingly hard to kill, as you are well aware."

"Trust me, there is no way they will discover what is happening until it is too late," Jonas stated, tiring of Lewis' whining. "Because all is not what it seems."

Behind him, the sound of glass breaking caused Jonas to whip his head around in surprise. While they argued loudly, someone had walked right past the front of the truck. Jonas cursed under his breath that his heated emotions had caused him to forget to make sure they were completely alone. Focusing on the broken bottles of beer that lay foaming on the ground, Jonas looked up to see the woman that dropped them was Mattie, who was staring wide-eyed at him. Her face was pale white with fear as the look of awful remembrance filled her eyes.

*

Mattie was eagerly looking forward to seeing Mike. She was so distracted that she didn't realize that someone was talking until she passed the front of the truck and then heard a man say those words.

Those words had ripped apart her mental barriers that she had unknowingly erected to protect her mind during that terrible night when Kettle had abducted her...

Those words she made herself unintentionally forget due to the mental trauma she went through.

She now heard that same snarling, hate-filled voice, once again directed at her: "*Because all is not what it seems.*"

And now as she fully remembered who had set her up for kidnapping, she stared into the cold, murderous eyes of the man who now also realized she remembered.

Mattie spun to take off running. Behind her, a shouted curse and running footsteps followed her. Mattie's foot pushed off at a sprint, losing traction in the now wet puddle of beer on the pavement.

Stumbling slightly, Mattie regained her balance and sprinted full out, heading for the closest place of assistance near her.

Mentally cursing at herself for not being armed, she knew that help was just on the other side of the cafeteria next to her.

She neared the corner of the building that she needed to get around to be in view of Mike. She was grabbed roughly by her left arm from behind and jerked to a halt.

"Get back here, you whore," Jonas hissed.

Mattie was not your typical helpless female. She was a police officer and had taken classes on self-defense and combative training, many instructed by Mike himself, who had been one of her department's combative instructors. So when Jonas spun her around to face him, the last thing he expected from the small woman was a right hook smack dab into his teeth.

Mattie also remembered to follow up her advantage and continued to attack. Now that he was momentarily stunned, she tagged him with a two punch combo in the face and a kick to the side of Jonas' left leg, causing him to fall to the ground.

Grunting from the unexpected pain, Jonas lunged forward while on the ground and tripped Mattie up as she again turned to run off for help.

Mattie stumbled forward, her momentum too much to remain on her feet, fell to the ground and slid to a stop with a cry for help escaping from her lips. Jonas scrambled forward on hands and knees, grabbed at her legs and tried to pull himself up along her body as she kicked and screamed at him. Taking a few nasty kicks to the chest and face, Jonas reared away from the pain and managed to end up straddling her chest as she flailed at him with punches and kicks. With her somewhat restrained, Jonas momentarily knocked her senseless with a solid punch to her head, opening a cut over her left eye. Mattie went limp, bleeding and moaning, and Jonas smiled wickedly, reaching for his razor sharp knife.

*

Taking a much needed break, I sank the axe into the stump we were using as a splitting platform and wiped the sweat from my eyes.

"I don't know what is taking Mattie so long. She was supposed to bring us some drinks," I said to Max, who was finishing loading the newly split logs in the neat pile we had made today. "Tell you what, Max, why don't you run back to the chow hall and see if you can get us a couple water bottles? Just tell them I sent you. You shouldn't have any problems."

While Max ran off to get us some water, I was about to put my jacket back on while I waited when I heard a shout for help ahead of me. I jogged ahead, thinking maybe it was another infected person rampaging that we might have missed earlier.

I ran towards the corner of the building, what I saw stopping my heart momentarily. I watched in horror as Mattie's form stumbled from around the corner and fell to the ground with a small, wiry man scrambling along her legs to get on top of her fallen body. She was giving him a run for his money, but he ultimately got the upper hand with a punch to her head. He must have been very focused on her, for he didn't notice me closing in until I heard him snarl something to her. With that, the man raised a large sharp blade up into the air, preparing to stab her.

*

Jonas' blood sang with victory as he yanked his blade free and held it up overhead, ready to plunge it into her chest.

"I should've done this long ago, bitch!" he rasped.

The knife began its downward motion, but Jonas' arm was suddenly grabbed in a vise-like crushing grip.

Before Jonas realized that was a bad thing, something knocked the blade spinning from his much weaker grip. His knife went bouncing across the pavement, and Jonas was physically picked up into the air by that same arm and tossed aside like a child. Skidding to a halt several feet away, Jonas lifted his bleeding face from the pavement where he had struck it to stare at the large muscled man that Lewis detested.

Damn, it's Mike, Jonas thought. *So be it. I'll avenge Father Kettle here and now*!

Mike was sweating heavily, and it was causing steam to rise off of him while he stood over Mattie's still groggy form on the ground. His head turned to face him and with eyes that would have frozen the most ruthless of killers locked onto his, he visibly shook with rage as veins snaked across his bare arms and face.

With a roar of rage Mike rushed at Jonas.

*

I was barely able to reach the man with the knife before he could stab Mattie. Grabbing his arm, I slammed my other hand against the flat of the knife blade, disarming him. I lifted the much smaller man off her and tossed him aside to get him out of range of hurting her anymore. Now standing there panting, my eyes locked onto her beautiful face and my blood boiled with rage at the sight of the cut above her eye. Each drop of blood that pooled from her cut and dripped onto the ground sounded like a thunderclap and shook my very soul.

On the ground before me I saw the man who would take from me all that I had left and held dear in this shithole of a world. The man who was going to die most painfully. The fucking zombies outside the walls were probably jealous of me with the howl of rage that ripped loose. That the little man smiled at me just drove my rage even higher until I went berserk yet again.

My last coherent thought was, *This fucker is going to get some hands on treatment*!

*

As Jonas climbed to his feet, he was brought up short by Mike sidestepping and cutting off his only avenue of escape. Now penned in like cattle and literally backed into a corner, Jonas set himself for combat. He lashed out with his left fist, struck Mike in the jaw, and followed up with a right upper cut. Mike's head jerked to the side and then upward from the impact. His head slowly turned back to face Jonas with a crazed grin on his face, a small trickle of blood leaking from his mouth. Jonas froze momentarily and was hit by a crushing right hook from Mike, which sent him spinning to the ground. Shaking his head feebly, Jonas was grabbed by Mike and pulled up onto his knees. Jonas quickly drew a second blade just as sharp as his other but a little smaller, and rammed it deep into Mike's left thigh.

Jonas had a second to watch. The only reaction given was a slight blink on his opponent's face, which was then twisted into a snarl. That face was then slammed into his own when Mike head-butted him. Jonas' nose cartilage crushed under the impact and his vision swam with stars. Pain began to overcome his body. Jonas knew he must up the ante or it would quickly be over with him most likely dead. With this cold realization sinking home, he started throwing as many punches and strikes as he could towards Mike's head and torso, hoping he could overwhelm him with a barrage of punches.

Jonas' left wrist was grabbed in a crushing grip and then he felt his left arm get slammed into Mike's knee and fold at the elbow in the wrong direction.

He tried to draw in a breath to scream, but the next crushing blow to the face changed Jonas' focal point from his arm to his ruined nose. As blood flowed freely from his shattered nose, holding his shattered arm, he tried to reason with the man.

"Please stop...I giv—" was as far as Jonas got before another heavy punch slammed into his left orbital facial bone with a loud crack that he heard more than felt.

Screaming in pain, Jonas attempted to cover his face with his remaining working arm. It helped somewhat until two ribs were broken from a heavy booted kick. Jonas attempted to draw in a breath and scream at the same time as shattered ribs tore and ripped into his insides. The next round of intense punches to Jonas' face caused blood to splatter in all directions and also knocked him unconscious. If the savage beating would have stopped at that point, Jonas had a very good chance at survival with today's medical knowledge and equipment.

However, that was in a world without zombies.

Unfortunately for Jonas, the beating continued.

*

It felt as if I was being controlled by someone else as I pummeled and crushed the man in front of me. I didn't feel pain, just immense rage.

At some point I felt a sting in my left leg, but it was quickly forgotten with the red veil of rage that I was looking through. Sometime between the breaking of joints and slamming my fists repeatedly into the man's unprotected face, a voice cut through my anger like a knife. The sound of her crying doused my fury like water on a fire. Breathing heavily from the exertion, I stared around confused as to what the hell was going on. I noticed I was holding a bloody mangled man by the front of his shirt. I let go of the man, letting his limp form fall to the ground with a meaty wet splat. Thick coagulating blood covered my fists and arms, and I could plainly see a large bite mark on one of the man's arms. Smacking my lips together, I could taste the coppery blood that probably covered my mouth as well.

"When the fuck did I do that?"

I couldn't tell who the man was. I had crushed his face into a pulp and very little facial structure was left intact. Broken bones protruded at numerous points on his obviously lifeless body.

Then my arms were filled with the sobbing form of Mattie. The more I held her, the more I began to hurt, not mental hurt, but real physical hurt. That little fucker must have worked me over while I was temporarily insane. Mattie reminded me of the pain in my leg by bumping into the hilt of a knife jutting out from my left thigh.

"Hoo-boy!" I winced. "That will leave a mark."

Using her for support, I looked up to see Max standing not too far away with two water bottles, his mouth hanging wide open in shock.

Hawking up a glob of blood-filled spit, I held my hand out to Max.

"A beer would be better, but I will take one of those if you don't mind."

With Mattie and Max's help, I limped over to the medic trailer to stitch up my new wounds and remove this damn knife from my fucking leg.

If it was true that chicks dig scars, I would soon be fucking irresistible.

While Nurse Shelly cursed me for being an idiot, I sent Max off to find Stephen and Kleaner to report the incident. Seeing Mattie get three stitches above her left eye, I thought to myself that she had never looked more beautiful.

When Stephen walked into the trailer behind Max, he sat down and listened to the story, both from mine and Mattie's point of view. When we were done, he first informed me that Kleaner was taking care of the body. Then he took a more serious tone.

"I only see one problem with this story, my friends," Stephen said with a straight face.

"Oh yeah, what's that?" Mattie and I both said at the same time. After the shit we just went through, this better be good.

"Where the hell was your Glock, Mattie?" Stephen asked. He was nearly smiling now, and he was again standing on his Second Amendment pulpit.

"I forgot it at the RV after I changed. I was only going to be gone a minute," Mattie replied meekly.

"We are all supposed to keep our handguns on us at all times. If not for the zombies, then certainly for the five hundred plus people we have running around out here now," Stephen lectured. "We nearly had a full blown outbreak yesterday, and if not for our armed people, we might all be dead right now. If you would have had your gun on you like you should have, you could have put that asshole down, and Mike would have been drinking that beer right now and not having a knife pulled out of his leg."

"You're right," Mattie agreed. "It won't happen again. I promise."

"I hope this teaches you a lesson," Stephen said, giving Mattie a big hug. "Armed citizens are much less likely to become victims. Well, that's enough lecturing. I'm going to go find Amber, and if she is not wearing her pistol right now, she better be in the shower. And hopefully she's doing both."

Stephen walked out of the trailer to a roar of laughter.

46

November 17
Day 84

With their destination finally in sight, Matvei let out a sigh of relief. It had been a long couple of days, and he was beginning to worry that they would not be able to make it in time. Joliet itself was on the outer rim of the Chicago suburbs, and Matvei knew that it would soon be crawling with infected from the city, if it wasn't already. It was a risk that he had to take. He now only had eight men with him thanks to an ambush while trying to cross the Mississippi and an unfortunate accident just outside of Peoria, Illinois. He lost two men to bandits at a makeshift roadblock at a bridge crossing. There had been nearly a dozen men manning that bridge and Matvei killed them all, but not before losing the men and a vehicle that crashed during the gun battle. That loss proved especially painful as that truck had the radio used to make contact with his ranch and it was completely destroyed in the crash. There would be no turning back. His luck had to change, but karma was being a royal bitch.

Matvei was in his Dodge Ram, which was the lead vehicle in the two vehicle convoy. He had Hector, Raul and a third trigger man with him in the truck while the five others rode in the panel van that also contained the last of their meager provisions. As Matvei followed the final direction to the warehouse he got a call over the two-way radio to turn his truck radio to 1320 AM. What Matvei heard was informative and mostly bad news. It appeared that a group of survivors were located nearby and had fortified themselves in an old prison. They had engaged a large group of infected to the north and were now being laid siege by a mammoth group of infected that had spilled out of the Chicago area and was now surrounding the prison. The broadcast was warning survivors that the entire area was about to be overrun.

Matvei slowed the truck in front of the cartel's warehouse and ordered the five men in the van to set up a small perimeter. He had two major concerns. First, that there appeared to be a significant number of infected converging on this location. And second, that if there had been an organized group operating in the area, they may have discovered his cache. Knowing he had little time to waste, Matvei led Hector and Raul up to the fire escape that led to the roof and climbed up the ladder to the rooftop. He made his way to the rooftop entrance he knew existed from seeing the building's layout on a tour several months prior.

"Shit!" Matvei swore in his native language after climbing inside the warehouse.

The building had been looted. Matvei and the others searched the rooms, finding only empty pallets. Matvei opened a locked side door and let a third man inside while the others on the perimeter signaled that they had not yet been discovered. He then began clearing a back room, where the armory was supposed to be located, when he was notified over his 2-way that Hector and Raul had located and secured some prisoners. Hurrying to the front room Matvei found that two men, three women and a child were being held at gunpoint.

"What is going on?" Matvei asked.

"These people are part of the group that stole our shit!" Raul snarled.

The people were all on their knees and were clearly terrified. The men were both trembling, and the women were all crying, along with the small boy who looked to Matvei to be maybe nine or ten. A small pile of guns was lying nearby along with backpacks and sleeping bags. Surveying the room, Matvei also saw that the people had gathered up some remaining supplies from the building and must have stayed the night.

"Let me explain," the oldest of the men asked Matvei, too afraid to make eye contact.

"Proceed," Matvei replied, slinging his rifle on his shoulder.

The man explained how they had been living in a nearby town called Bolingbrook, and when a large horde of zombies moved in, they fled back to Joliet and took shelter at the old prison to the north of town. Their stay was short-lived, however, because the leaders at the prison compound warned that they were probably going to get surrounded and anyone that wanted to escape should do so now. He and the others with him decided to take off and head for a relative's farm in Indiana. Pointing at the third women in line, he said that she had been staying at the prison prior to the rest of them showing up and had been on a supply run to this building led by a man named Casper. The woman spoke then, telling them that the building had been full of supplies when they raided it, and they had stopped by hoping to grab anything remaining for their trip.

"Let's kill them," Hector stated coldly. "They stole our supplies and now have left us as good as dead!"

"Not so fast," Matvei ordered. "They may still be of use to us."

"Sir, you better get up here!" a frantic voice stated. "We got company and lots of it!"

Matvei swore in Russian and ran for the ladder leading for the rooftop. Once up top he ran to where the guard stood near the edge, staring out at what was coming their way. Matvei heard the cursed creatures long before he saw them. They came into view, boiling down the street, thousands in number, heading right to them.

"Damned things are everywhere," he muttered, glancing around for an escape route.

Within minutes, the warehouse structure was completely surrounded on all sides. The horrible howling, coupled with the banging on walls and doors produced an awful racket.

"Looks like we need a diversion to get out of here," Matvei said. "And I have just the thing we need."

Turning for the ladder, he shouted for all the men on the rooftop to grab their gear and be ready to move out. He didn't see the incredulous looks on their faces as he descended down the ladder.

When he reached the warehouse floor he quickly walked up to the prisoners. "Everyone on their feet, now!"

The small group struggled upright, asking what was happening.

Matvei backhanded a woman across the mouth, knocking her to the floor. "I didn't ask you to question me, I said on your feet! Now everyone climb the ladder up to the roof."

The prisoners were herded to the ladder and then up to the roof.

Once topside, the women began wailing in fear at the size of the of undead crowd that now surrounded the building.

Matvei turned to Raul. "Give me three men. The rest I want staged at the door closest to our vehicles. When I give the word, we're going to try to shoot our way out of here."

"You got it, boss," he replied. "You three, stay with Matvei, the rest come with me!"

Raul and the others disappeared into the warehouse, and Matvei turned to his men. "This's what we must do. To escape this we gotta create a diversion, that being this group of volunteers we found trespassing on our property."

Matvei walked up behind a male prisoner, who was currently watching the undead below, and shoved him off the rooftop, screaming down to his death below. The horde bellowed its hunger, and the man was pulled to pieces, still screaming. The remaining prisoners started crying and pleading for mercy.

"Take the others to the far side and try to draw as many as possible away from the front entrance," he ordered. "Make sure they can see them, like dangling a carrot in front of a horse."

At first they didn't want to move. Matvei didn't take well to the disobedience. "If they won't play along we will get some rope and hang the boy off the roof by his feet. Let the infected eat him inch by inch."

As the captives were pushed along, Matvei eyed the carnage below.

"I got a better idea," Matvei said. "One the rest of you should like."

The prisoners were defeated, heads down, and didn't even respond. Matvei pointed to one of his men. "Bring up their weapons."

When the man returned, Matvei tossed them over the roof to the ground below.

"There is the fire escape. We will provide you with enough cover to reach your weapons, then you shoot your own way free. If you make it you live, fair enough?"

The prisoners hesitated only briefly. They had been saying their final prayers and now grasped at the sliver of hope extended. Matvei and his men began to fire, providing cover until the group descended the stairs and reached their weapons.

"Go, go, go!"

Reaching the door, Matvei gave the word. Raul and Hector threw open the door and were immediately engaged with the undead. Their rifles started rocking as their rounds were fired into the faces of the rotting creatures. They made their way out towards their vehicles. As more men exited the building and were able to help, the quicker they moved. Suddenly, the man next to Matvei screamed in pain when a downed infected grabbed the man's legs and pulled him to the ground. The bite to the groin area made him scream even louder. While that poor man tried to dislodge his assailant, he was quickly pulled away from the group to his death.

"Shit!" Matvei swore, spinning to fill the hole his man had left. Firing rapidly, he was forced to kick a zombie away while he reloaded. Just when he was sure they could still make it to their trucks, the main host of zombies began pouring around the corner and joined the battle. There were way too many.

"Back to the warehouse!"

He really didn't remember much of the next sixty seconds, but eventually a much smaller force managed to slam the doors shut and fall to the floor in exhaustion. Lying there gasping for breath, Matvei took a headcount. Raul, Hector and two other men had survived. He was about to close his eyes from fatigue when he heard one of his men growling. He snapped his eyes open, saw that one of them was clearly infected now and was beginning to turn. Whipping out his pistol, he put two rounds into the bloody face of the doomed man. The shots echoed in the large empty warehouse. With that finished, Matvei fished his last cigarette from his pocket and lit it, reflecting on his next move. This appeared to be the end of the line for his once great mercenary army. There were clearly not enough provisions left in the building for the trip to Arizona. Matvei grimaced at the thought of scrounging his way across the continental United States. The silence in the room was broken only by the continuous howling and battering of the doors from outside.

47

November 24
Day 91

Thanksgiving Day... The first two things that come to mind are food and football. As I surveyed the playing field, I had to admit that Stephen did have a good idea this time. The crowd seemed to be happily enjoying the game that was serving as a much needed distraction to the outside world. We had our guards on the wall, but the zombie horde wailing just outside wasn't getting in anytime soon. Beer was served in moderation along with soda, peanuts, and nachos. This whole idea started when Mattie suggested a Thanksgiving feast a few days ago to celebrate the holiday and the fact that we were still alive. Stephen then mentioned that a football game might be a good idea, as a chance to unwind after all we had been through.

When the plans were discussed around the prison, they were met with much enthusiasm. A playing field was set up, to the east of the main RV parking area. It was a little smaller than a regular-sized football field but it would do. Lines were painted, wooden goalposts erected, and spectators lined the sides. Stephen arranged for two teams to be made, the Yankees and the Rebels. Blue and gray clothing was used, along with the corresponding battle flags to serve as logos. It ended up with the Rebels being made up of the original occupants of the prison and the Yankees coming from the Bolingbrook safe zone. This, in turn, led to some good-spirited trash talking leading up to the game. Tryouts were held and both teams ended up with about fifteen players and they even managed to hold a few practices over the last few days. Now, with the sidelines packed and the players on the field, everything had come together for quite a show.

The women in charge of cooking went to great lengths to prepare a feast for all, to be served family style in the cafeteria following the game. Unfortunately, there were not any live turkeys available for the occasion, but we used three butchered hogs instead. This was augmented with cases of different canned vegetables. Not to mention the delicious pumpkin pie for dessert. We made sure to have plenty for everyone. You could smell the food cooking even now from the sidelines. I wondered if Christmas would be as festive.

The feast was for after the game, which still had four seconds left. Dan was the head referee and held up four fingers, marking the time remaining. This was after Stephen's last pass had gotten the Rebels, who were down 27-32, to about the Yankee thirty yard line. As coach of the Rebels, I had just made an impressive show of arguing with Dan after a holding call he made on the prior play cost us ten yards. Dan, of course, was not amused and told me where to stick it. I called my last timeout and walked over to Stephen, the Rebels' quarterback. He was in the huddle kneeling in the mud, sucking wind and complaining of being slammed to the ground by a 250 pound corn fed country boy at the end of the last play.

"Get the sand washed out of your vagina, crybaby," I chided. "Get your head in the game. I've been shot and stabbed and you didn't hear me bitching half this much."

"All I said was it fucking hurt!" Stephen snapped, giving us all a dirty look. "I'll be fine. If anyone wants to block that asshole, feel free. He's been on me all damn game. Now what's the play?" he asked. "I'm up for suggestions."

Making eye contact with a tall Hispanic kid who had good speed, I asked Stephen if he could get the ball to him in stride down the right sideline.

"Just give me a couple seconds," he said, and stared at his lineman, "which means block the other team!"

I jogged to the sidelines and chided Dan, "Nice no-call on that roughing the passer penalty!"

Dan's response was to simply hold up his stump, which I think signified the finger. Stephen broke the huddle and the Hispanic kid went wide right. Now the entire crowd was on their feet cheering. It didn't really matter to them who won. At the snap Stephen ran a play action that nobody bought and then was forced to roll right due to backside pressure from that large country boy. Stephen threw the ball just as Dan shot a flare into the air signaling that time had expired.

Watching Stephen get mauled by the opposing defense yet again, I laughed when he was flattened again by the pass rusher. Laughing at him actually spitting grass out his mouth, I looked downfield to the receiver running at full sprint. It was a well thrown pass to the back of the end zone. The receiver and two defenders jumped up for the ball in stride and as they came down in a pile of bodies, I was unable to see what happened.

As our referees sorted out the mess I waited for the signal from Dan.

Arms up...touchdown!

Everyone took to the field to congratulate one another on a game well played. The country boy that tattooed his helmet into Stephen's ribcage even helped him to his feet. He was then greeted by Amber, who rewarded him with a victory kiss, and soon both were mobbed by the rest of the team. I finally made it over to Stephen and the others and offered my congratulations. Everyone eventually settled down it was off to the cafeteria to eat. A friendly wager had been made and the losing team had to pull guard duty on the towers to let the guards who missed the game eat first. As we headed off to eat I watched the Yankee team members head to their duty stations.

*

Lewis was steaming mad. It had been a week since that nutcase Jonas was killed and again he was on his own. He cursed this fact, for as was usually the case when left to his own devices, Lewis was not faring too well. The fact that Jonas had met an untimely and most brutal death wasn't even the worst of it. The only safe place to hide was in the big bread truck that he drove into the prison. He was forced to share it along with a very large and most likely very powerful explosive that Jonas assembled but never explained how to arm or deploy. Once again he had been forced to stand by helplessly and watch that asshole Mike kill an ally with his bare hands. This time Lewis did not even have a handgun to shoot him in the back with. Like a coward he was forced to stand quietly by and witness yet another murder by the man who killed his brother.

After watching Mike stagger over to the medic's trailer with assistance from Mattie and some scrawny kid, Lewis realized that there might be questions regarding the truck that Jonas was standing next to when Mattie saw him. Once he saw the three of them enter the medic trailer, Lewis quickly started up the truck, moved it to another section of the prison yard, and nervously waited out the next few days. Over those last few stressful days, Lewis refused to come out of the truck during daylight hours for fear of discovery by someone who might recognize him. Only during the nighttime did he feel safe enough to risk it in order to scavenge food and drink from the prison cafeteria and briefly mingle with a few survivors. After it appeared that he was forgotten and things looked to be back to some sort of normalcy, Lewis moved the truck back to near where he had originally parked it, an out of the way area near the administration building and amongst a cluster of other parked vehicles.

Now as he watched the occupants of the prison play a game of football, he sat in the cold truck with only his simmering anger to keep him company. So here he was, cold, hungry, tired, and angry at everyone outside laughing and carrying on as if there were not a hundred thousand zombies outside the prison walls screaming for their blood.

"Laugh while you still can, assholes," Lewis muttered as he watched Mike pass the football to a group of small kids. "We'll see who is laughing when I piss on your cold, dead corpses! Maybe it's high time I get this over with!"

Lewis quit watching the football game as it began to disperse and looked out the driver's side window over to where his other set of wheels was currently parked. Lewis had located an old Dodge Dakota truck that seemed to be ownerless and moved it near where the bread truck was parked. He had managed to steal some supplies for it from the cafeteria. He remembered sweating profusely when he took the truck late at night, expecting someone to confront him the entire time he was moving it. But that was the day before yesterday and as of yet, nobody had come over to take it back. Lewis figured that it must have belonged to someone who had not made it out alive from the battle up north. Which was good, since it was to be his escape vehicle when he set Jonas' plan into motion.

Finally Lewis let his anger drive him to action. He had used the need for an escape vehicle as a reason for delay. That was taken care of, and Lewis knew he had really delayed this long out of fear. Now his jealousy and longing for revenge spurred him to action.

Looking back at the compilation of containers and wires that made up the explosive, he walked up to it, crouched down, and stared at it wondering how the fuck the thing worked.

*

The cafeteria smelled delicious. The pork and other dishes were served up, and the room was as lively as it had ever been. Everyone enjoyed the meal and the company, for once being able to put aside the danger that lurked just outside the walls. At my table shared by Stephen, Dan, Mattie, Amber, little Max and Kleaner, Mattie went over how she had pretty much wrapped up the Logan investigation. She searched Jonas' camper after his death and located the .45 handgun that belonged to Logan.

"That's his alright," Kleaner remarked after Mattie showed him the firearm.

It was now holstered on Kleaner's belt, and he wore it with pride.

Mattie had also discovered handwritten notes that indicated that Jonas had been a Kettle plant from the very beginning. Nothing in the camper indicated that Jonas had anyone else working with him inside the prison. He appeared to be a loner, and Mattie was convinced that he was lying in ambush for her the night she was attacked. His taunt had perhaps saved her life by jogging her memory. A thorough check of the administration building for any additional evidence did not lend to an inside man but revealed an area on the top level that Jonas had been using. Blood located near an open window led Mattie to believe that Logan must have discovered Jonas up there, perhaps talking to someone or running surveillance, and been killed to cover it up.

Kleaner grew quiet at the mention of Logan, and Dan took it upon himself to cheer him up. Dragging him over to a table of shy Latino women who were all giggles and smiles, Dan was able to work through the language barrier with his universal charm. The conversation also shifted to Christmas, with the women wanting to plan some sort of dance. Supposedly a few daring couples inside the walls also wanted to get married, and were making arrangements.

As chow was winding down, I decided to head back to the RV with Mattie and Max, both of whom looked like they could use a nap. A movie projector had been set up in the prison's community room and was playing movies several times a day for the last week. Max heard that a Disney movie was going to be playing tonight and wanted to attend.

We were all stuffed with food and for once it looked like Max had finally eaten his fill. Stephen and Amber were whispering something about a referee outfit, and as they left, Stephen said to swing by the command center in a couple hours. He wanted to go over some long-term security goals and try to get in touch with anyone on the HAM radios who might have news from the government safe zones on the east or west coasts. Before that though, he wanted to hand out some plates of food and pie to the losing team's players who were on guard duty.

Before heading back to the RV, I ran up to the nearest tower just to remind myself not to get complacent and stared out at the colossal zombie army that had been massing at the walls. Stretching as far as the eyes could see, it was certainly a sight to behold. I always tried to not look at them individually anymore if I didn't have to. The churning sea of rotting flesh and bones howled at my very sight and tried in vain to reach me. All the while, others continually tried to batter down the stone walls that kept us alive. They were shredding themselves in the process, yet seemed oblivious to the fact.

"Not yet, you fuckers," I said, "not without a fight!"

48

November 24
Day 91

Matvei finished cleaning his weapons for the second time today. He had all of his remaining .45 ammunition lined up neatly in front of him on the table as he slid the slide back on his USP. 45.

"Twelve rounds," Matvei said aloud, rolling one of the cartridges along the table in front of him.

Finally loading them back into a magazine and seating it into place, Matvei holstered the large .45 and got up from the chair. His rifle was not much better off; he only had twenty-three cartridges remaining.

He was definitely, as the Americans say, up shit creek.

He looked over to where Raul knelt, holding a rosary and mumbling prayer after prayer to whatever God cared to listen.

Hector was faring far worse. He sat in a corner and stared at both him and Raul with suspicion. He talked to himself, and Matvei would be worried except he knew that Hector was out of ammunition.

The other remaining survivor of Matvei's group had gone mad from the incessant howling and while Matvei and the others slept, had opened the door to commit suicide.

He was awoken to gunfire and screaming as he scrambled for his weapons. Infected had already entered through the doorway, and it took most of their remaining ammunition to clear the building. It was nasty work, only made easier by the necessity of the task. Matvei had seated the last full magazine for his G36 and spent seven of the rounds on a group of infected who had managed to meander into a back room. They caught him off guard, and one managed to knock

Matvei to the ground before a 5.56mm round ended the fight with a red mist splattered on the wall.

Only after it was done did he realize that Raul, Hector and himself had all survived, and managed to secure the door. It took most of the day for Matvei and the others to drag the bodies to a back room and seal it off. Matvei then went to great lengths to then make sure that the building was secure, so he wouldn't find any more nasty surprises. He gathered remaining supplies on hand and grasped the fact that they would not be able to hold out for long. They had only enough food and water for little over a week at most.

That was nearly a week ago. The food was running low and they were on their last case of bottled water. Picking the rifle up, Matvei walked upstairs and onto the roof to have yet another look around. It was a clear, cloudless afternoon. Standing in the bright sunlight he listened hard for the gunshots. Sometimes he heard gunfire coming from what must have been the besieged prison, but today they were quiet. Today he only heard the wails of the infected, which increased at the sight of him at the rooftop's edge. Matvei stood on the roof and knew they were running out of options. The horde of infected that blocked them in was already larger than before. He looked down and saw his black Dodge Ram, still parked in the same spot, so close yet so far away. But Matvei knew now that even if he made it to his truck, the mass of infected made it impossible for him to drive off. He knew they needed a miracle, or they would die of thirst in this brick tomb.

49

November 24
Day 91

Looking at the kitchen timer again, Lewis thought he finally had this contraption figured out.

"So I just punch in whatever time I want it to go off and that's that?" he muttered to himself. "Sure, seems simple enough. I just need to wait until the moment is right and get this shit over with once and for all!"

Lewis cracked the rear door to ventilate the accumulated diesel and chemical fumes that were making him lightheaded again.

"Phew, this shit stinks. I'll be really glad to get out of this damn truck for the last time."

Standing by the cracked door, Lewis fished his cigarettes out of his jacket pocket and stopped before lighting one up. Looking over at the homemade explosive device and sniffing the diesel fume heavy air he thought it probably wasn't a good idea to have an open flame right now.

He hoped he got to see the look of amazement on their ugly faces when he destroyed their compound, just like they had destroyed his.

He made his way to the front of the truck to stare out the dirty windshield. He watched the crowd trickling out of the cafeteria, the party winding down. A large portion of the party had dispersed earlier, and most that were left were mainly doing clean up chores. The delicious smell of their feast reached him in the cab and his belly rumbled. He was sure there were plenty of Thanksgiving leftovers inside for the taking, yet he didn't dare. He watched enviously while many of the prison's inhabitants moved lazily with full bellies. Then he had a thought.

Most everyone would be fat and relaxed at this point, he realized. The time to act was indeed at hand!

Crouching down next to his implement of destruction, Lewis tried to warm his hands by blowing on them, and began to think his happy thoughts again as he reached for the timer mechanism.

"I had better throw the keys over the wall so no one can move the truck, just in case they discover what is going on," he muttered aloud. Soon he would be able to carry out his vengeance and leave this cursed city once and for all and head to warmer climates.

*

Stephen was on his way back from the command center after taking some plates loaded with food for Frank and Ed, who were manning the radios. There had been some encouraging news in relation to the government safe zones but it was only rumors at this point. They were going to try to get some confirmation and get back to him later that night.

There was no sense in them going hungry simply because they had a holiday shift to pull, though. Now he just needed to grab some more chow for the poor guys they beat who were working the guard towers.

He checked his watch again. Amber told him to be back in thirty minutes for a surprise and he had a mere ten minutes to go.

He was stuffed but couldn't wait to see what she had cooked up for dessert.

Stephen was in a good mood. The football game today was a hit with the folks, as was the large feast the cooks whipped up for Thanksgiving.

Entering the chow hall, he rounded up some heaping plates of food for the players he had bested.

"A full belly usually takes away some of the sting of defeat," he joked to the ladies who helped fix the plates.

Finding some women who offered to help, Stephen sent them off to the various towers with the plates. He also had one of the ladies fix up a doggy bag for Buddy, who was waiting very impatiently in Stephen's RV. He got "people" food every Thanksgiving, and Buddy didn't think that a small zombie epidemic should change that ritual. With a plate in each hand and a contented whistle, Stephen exited the cafeteria and rounded the building, walking towards the guard tower.

Up ahead, he noticed a large bread truck pull up and stop lengthwise in front of the eastern gates that were obviously not in use.

That was odd. He pondered why the truck was being moved.

Still walking towards the truck, Stephen then noticed Kleaner was approaching and stopped to ask him if he knew what was up. A short man suddenly exited the truck, threw something over the wall and then ran directly at him while looking back over his shoulder. The man passed Kleaner without seeing him and then turned to face the direction he was running, which was right at Stephen. The man suddenly noticed Stephen standing there and slid to a stop.

Stephen's eyes widened in recognition and everything clicked.

"Lewis?!?" Stephen yelled. "What the fuck are you doing here?"

But Stephen already knew the answer.

Lewis had come to a halt a mere ten yards away from Stephen with a terrified look on his face.

"You can't stop me this time, asshole!" he swore at Stephen. "I'll have my vengeance!"

Stephen dropped both plates of food to the ground and drew his pistol. Lewis began to run away towards the southern part of the yard, refusing his command to stop. Stephen had warning sirens going off in his head. He really disliked the little greasy politician anyways, and this certainly didn't help. Stephen fired a single shot, taking Lewis in the back of his right thigh, which sent him tumbling to the ground with a cry of pain. Crawling on his knees, Lewis disappeared around the corner of a building in between the cafeteria and gymnasium, out of sight.

"That little fucker!"

Kleaner noticed the exchange of words and gunfire and came running up to him with his own pistol now drawn.

"What the hell just happened, boss?"

"I don't know, but I feel like we are soon to find out," Stephen replied. "That whining little fuck I just shot was Lewis. I think he was somehow mixed up with Jonas, who must have got him inside before he died."

Stephen glanced back and pointed to the truck. "I saw him get out of that truck parked across the eastern gates. I'm afraid we have been way too lax on security."

"I'll go check it out, boss," Kleaner said. "You go secure the suspect while I handle the truck."

Kleaner jogged back to the truck and Stephen ran quickly to catch up to the wounded man. He found Lewis on the ground giggling madly.

"It's too late fuckers, I win!" Lewis cackled and made an exploding noise followed by more crazy laughter.

Stephen's eyes widened in fear, realizing what the truck's true purpose was, and ran back for Kleaner.

"Kleaner, get the hell away from the truck!" he screamed as he closed the gap.

Kleaner, hearing his name, slowed to a stop at the north corner of the cafeteria. "What did you sa—"

A bright flash filled the air. A colossal fireball erupted and instantly engulfed the spot where the truck used to be. The ensuing shockwave slammed into Kleaner and tossed him into the air like he was hit by a train. Stephen fared somewhat better. He was partially protected from the blast by the nearby building but was flattened by the detonation. The explosion killed everyone who had the misfortune of being assigned to that particular guard tower near the east gate, and a few curious souls who walked up to the truck after seeing a man exit and throw the keys over the wall. The thought that someone would detonate a bomb inside the compound had been inconceivable to them. The shockwave also tore into the back kitchen of the cafeteria, killing or wounding the entire remaining cooking staff that was busy cleaning up after the feast. The gymnasium also suffered damage to its eastern wall, resulting in several dozen wounded. The livestock pen took the brunt of the explosion in the northeastern corner of the yard; all of the animals and their caretakers were killed instantly. Fires broke out all along the blast radius, and the ground literally shook.

Coughing raggedly and severely dazed, Stephen sat up from where he fell many yards distant from where he previously stood. He checked to make sure he had all of his arms and legs, then stood and brushed aside the debris that had landed on him. His ears were ringing, and his head was spinning. He looked frantically around for Kleaner and that rat-faced weasel Lewis. Smoke and debris obscured his vision and he was unable to find either one on the ground. Staggering upright, Stephen turned and stumbled in the direction of the eastern gate, and what he saw when he arrived made his asshole pucker tight.

Where there once was a set of solid steel gates with solid stone walls to either side now was a gaping hole yards wide. The cloud of smoke ascended up into the clear fall sky.

The explosive must have been designed to be somewhat directional, or even at this distance, he would be dead. Whoever designed it knew what they were doing and intentionally wanted to blow out the prison wall.

As Stephen stood staring in disbelief, from the smoke and dust filled air, figures began to slowly emerge. The explosion had killed or maimed every zombie in the vicinity of the gaping hole, but that only lasted so long. Even the zombies were smart enough to recognize what happened and moved to exploit it. The figures that appeared also brought with them the soul cringing screams and howls as the entire monstrous undead horde started pouring into the breach. It was unstoppable in its size and hunger. His hearing coming back, Stephen now heard cries of terror from the living mixed in with the howls of the undead.

*

The camper door slammed open, and Dan stumbled outside with his grandpa's .45 in his good hand, wearing only a scowl and his boxers.

Seeing the remnants of the massive fireball dissipating high in the sky made his scrotum shrivel even more than the cold air.

"Son of a bitch, girl, get me my pants!" Dan yelled to the naked Hispanic woman who stood gaping at the destruction from the doorway of her camper. After a few seconds and seeing that the woman did not move, Dan began cursing again at the lack of her understanding of the English language. He struggled to put on his pants with one hand, and she had begun to yell something to him about her sisters in a Spanish/English mixture.

"Fine," he said, "go find them. I'm going to miss you, girl."

Dan didn't know if she understood or not, but he really didn't care at the moment.

Jogging to the obvious source of the explosion, Dan came across a survivor. He slowed down to check on the man, and saw it was Kleaner. He bent down to help him sit up. The man was obviously stunned and sorely injured from the blast. Kleaner dazedly looked over to the right and saw his boot had been knocked off his foot and was on the ground next to him. Reaching over, he tried to put the boot on and kept wincing in pain. Dan looked closely at Kleaner's boot and winced himself. Kleaner was trying to put on his boot alright, except his foot was still inside it. It had been amputated almost even with the top of the boot!

Kleaner saw it too and shouted in pain.

To make matters worse, zombies stumbled around the corner and made their way towards them. Dan stood and quickly dispatched them each with precise head shots. The pistol's slide locked back and he reloaded as fast as he could manage with one hand.

Granting them a few moments of time, Dan whipped his belt free from his pants and applied it as a makeshift tourniquet to Kleaner's leg.

"Come on, buddy," he said to Kleaner. "We got to get the fuck out of here!"

Dan handed Kleaner his boot and got an arm around him, hoisting Kleaner upright while zombies poured in from the north.

Cut off from getting to the plow truck, Dan swore again. "Shit, this just keeps getting better!"

Knowing that time was short and that the prison evacuation plan would be under way, Dan wove a trail away from the gaping hole in the wall, hoping to come across a vehicle they could use to escape in. Up ahead, partially obscured by smoke and settling dust sat a beat up looking Dodge Dakota. Picking up his pace, Dan dragged his drinking buddy towards it while behind him the howls of the undead mixed with the sound of gunfire. Some of the guards were undoubtedly killed in the explosion, but it was evident to Dan that all of the guards on the wall were now facing inwards, and they had a target rich environment in which to work. A zombie that had wandered dangerously close lost its head to a high-powered rifle round.

"Fuck yeah!" Dan cheered.

*

Inside my RV, I had been looking down at Max, who was napping peacefully on the couch.

"He looks happy," Mattie said quietly from my side, "and that didn't take long."

I put my arm around her and pulled her close. "Yeah, I just wish there was more I could do for others as well. So many have lost entire families and loved ones to these damn zombies. It isn't fair!"

"I think he likes you though, Mike," she replied. "He looks at you like you are his father."

"I hope not. He said his dad tried to eat him once," I chuckled.

Mattie hit me playfully on the arm. "You know what I mean, silly!"

"I know, and that's what scares me. Do we keep him?"

"What, is he a dog or something?" Mattie scowled. "What do you mean 'do we keep him'?"

"What I mean is can we take on that responsibility of caring for him?"

"What do you think we should do?"

"If Max wants to be with us," I replied, actually deciding it as I said it aloud, "I would think that with all the horror this little guy has been through, if I can help with being his new family, I would like that."

Mattie turned me to face her and buried her face into my chest in a big hug. "That's about the most wonderful news I have heard in months."

"What do you mean 'just about' the most wonderful? What's the most wonderful?"

"Well, it was going to be a surprise," she said hesitantly, "but I guess now is a good time to tell you."

I just stared at her dumbly.

"Mike, I'm—"

At that precise time every one of the RVs driver's side windows were blown out from a jolting shockwave and ear deafening explosion that followed.

Luckily I had my back to the window and in doing so shielded Mattie from any harm from the flying glass that pelted my back.

"What the fuck was that?" I screamed.

Max started crying, confused after being woken up from a peaceful sleep covered in broken glass. The RV rocked from side to side, and I looked out the shattered windows at the raging fireball racing skyward and then back to the source of the explosion, where our eastern gate used to be. I also instantly knew what this meant for all of us.

"Fuck me," Mattie said staring at what I also saw.

My head swiveled to look at her. "Hey that's my line."

She started to say something else but the prison's warning siren began to go off. It was that eerie tornado siren wail that managed to unnerve almost everyone that had ever heard it.

"Get Max and your sweet ass to the plow truck now!" I ordered. "This isn't good and it looks like the wall is breached. We're probably going have to make a break for it."

Making sure she understood what I was saying, I continued, "Get it started and be ready!"

I took a few precious moments to grab my M4 carbine and put on my tactical vest, then scrambled from the RV heading to the source of the explosion. Along the way I joined dozens of others that I recognized from the platoons we put together also running towards the blast with weapons drawn. Ahead of me, I saw a growing cloud of smoke and dust clearing from the area where the eastern gate was. I could clearly see the gaping hole where it used to be. A disoriented person was making his way towards me with a shitload of unfriendly figures not far behind him. He stopped and emptied a pistol into the distant mob. As he neared, I saw that the man was Stephen. He was covered in dust, with fragments of rock stuck in his hair and clothing, and he was bleeding from several small shrapnel cuts.

"Stephen, what the fuck just happened?"

Stephen didn't seem to hear me so I grabbed him by the arm as he stumbled past. He jerked from my grasp as if he was surprised to see me.

"What? Oh, it's you. We got big problems, Mike! We have a hole in the wall! It was Lewis, Mike, he did this to us."

He was holding his ears and was most likely momentarily deaf due to the shockwave from the blast. My eyes drifted back to the breached wall and shambling forms of the undead that were streaming into the prison yard unopposed. My anger burned at the thought of that worthless fuck Lewis undoing all of our hard work out of jealousy. But I had no time to deal with it at the present.

"Get back to the plow truck and get ready to evacuate!" I gave him a shove back towards our mini compound.

Stephen nodded groggily and stumbled away while I turned to the rest of our platoons that had stopped along with me, awaiting orders. Everyone looked frightened.

"Okay folks, we need to hold these bastards down for as long as possible so the rest of our people can get to their evacuation vehicles," I shouted while racking a round into my assault rifle. "I want a skirmish line across the front with a secondary line behind them. We'll fire two full magazines then rotate, and the secondary line will fire two full magazines. After that, we'll begin a fighting retreat to our vehicles and make our escape. Remember the plan, folks. We'll convoy south out of town and rendezvous south of town near the NASCAR track. For those of you who don't make it, it's been an honor to fight alongside each of you warriors."

Behind me I heard the snarls and howls of the undead getting closer.

"Now let's give these smelly fuckers a one way ticket to Hell!"

I raised my trusty rifle and placed the reticle of the optic on the skull of a bloated, howling figure and squeezed the trigger. A reddish brown mist sprayed out of the rear of its skull, and it dropped in its tracks. Swinging the barrel minutely to the side I squeezed the trigger again, dropping a female zombie missing the lower part of her jaw. Around me, my guys and gals opened up with their gunfire, tearing into the ranks of undead with a wall of hot lead.

The front lines of the infected went down and stayed down for the most part. These were not shots fired in panic but the steady, controlled firing of now professional zombie slayers. We still were forced to give up ground. The sheer pressure of the zombies to the rear shoved past the fallen, presenting their ugly faces to our skirmish lines as if daring us to take them out. I heard an increase in the gunfire as the rest of our crew now came online. Stephen was right. Sometimes gunfire was music to your ears.

When my weapon ran dry for the second time, I dropped my now empty magazine and slammed home a third. Dropping back for the secondary ranks to move forward to engage the enemy, I took the time to appraise how the non-fighters were doing with the evacuation plans. All around me people ran here and there carrying gear and supplies to vehicles, throwing them inside, then climbing aboard. Many had not taken our advice to have supplies preloaded and ready, and now they were paying for it. Our covering fire was giving them a chance, and that was good. That part of the plan was going along well. I turned back to my guys holding off the undead. Many were now on their second magazine, some done with their second, and patiently waiting for their comrades to finish, even now refusing to leave them behind.

"Okay men, fire at will!" I shouted. "And get your asses to your vehicles as quickly and as organized as possible. Pray to whatever God you follow. We're gonna need it! Godspeed, bitches!"

With that, everyone opened up again in unison. Nearly a hundred rifles responded, buying us all precious seconds.

*

Stephen made his way back to his RV and found that Amber, although no longer in the sexy referee outfit, was prepared to go.

"Oh my God, you're okay!" she cried. "I was getting so worried when I heard the explosion, and you were nowhere to be found."

She planted a wet kiss on his lips as Buddy started jumping at his legs. The dog knew something was wrong.

"I'm glad to see you too," Stephen responded and gave her a quick squeeze. "I'm fine. Now we got to get the hell out of here. Grab Buddy and our go-bags and get to the plow truck. We have to hold there until Mike gets back. I need to grab a few things and will be right behind you."

Amber ran off towards the truck with Buddy in tow. Stephen grabbed his AR-15 carbine from its pegs above the door and chambered a round. Setting his rifle aside, he threw on his battle gear and grabbed a black range bag which contained his two .45 pistols and spare magazines. He was thankful that he did not have to grab much else, as the plow truck had already been loaded with food and ammunition as an escape vehicle. The big truck was to serve that purpose for Mike and himself, along with Mattie, Amber, Dan, Kleaner and now little Max, who he saw in the cab when he ran past it on the way to his RV. He took a second to look around his ever comfortable and now useless RV he had called home.

"What a goddamn shame!" he muttered under his breath as he headed for the door.

Stephen could hear the rapid fire of the men as they tried to hold back the onslaught while he threw his bag and extra rifle into the back of the truck. Amber was in the bed of the dump truck with Buddy and had her rifle at the ready. Mattie also made it to the truck, and was standing on the step near the driver's side door. Taking a second to make sure he had a fresh magazine in the pistol, he placed it back in his holster.

"Okay, ladies," he said calmly amidst the sounds of battle, "the concertina wire perimeter and steel barricades around our RVs should allow us to concentrate on the front opening here by the truck. We need to keep it clear so Mike and the others can get to us."

Zombies were already slipping past the retreating guards and he raised his rifle, setting a fine example by downing three rotting silhouettes in quick fashion. Soon Amber and Mattie were also both firing to keep the front area cleared.

Before long, three panicked Hispanic women ran up to the truck screaming. They did not appear to be hurt, and Stephen quickly decided that they had extra room in the bed of the truck.

"Damnit, I don't speak Spanish!" Stephen yelled. "Get in the back of the truck."

He motioned them up, but they ignored his commands and pointed urgently to the south. Stephen and Amber shot at more zombies as they approached, and the women frantically darted off the way they came.

"Hey, come back!" he shouted at their receding backs. The women didn't stop.

"Oh well, I can't go chasing after them. Hope they got a plan on how to get out."

Turning back to the center of the yard, he stared with agony at the sight of the entire prison yard flooding with undead that would soon overrun their small inner perimeter with ease. Two trucks loaded with fighters drove past, guards firing wildly from the truck beds. Stephen heard zombies hitting the wire all around the small perimeter and knew they would soon be up and over. Their three rifles just could not cover so much territory.

"Where are they?" Amber cried as her rifle ran dry yet again.

Stephen couldn't even hear her over the screams, gunfire and moaning of the undead.

When a mass of rotting figures were about to make it to the perimeter gate, they were mowed down from behind by rifle fire. Weaving his way through the destruction, Mike hobbled up, seating another magazine into his M4.

"Mattie!" Stephen shouted. "Get your ass in the truck now! It's time to go!"

"Are Dan and Kleaner here?" Mike shouted.

"Negative," Stephen answered, scanning past Mike. The only thing he saw was a mass of bodies closing in on them and vehicles on the move in the distance. "If they're not behind you, they must've found another ride."

Mike shook his head in frustration. "Shit! We're out of time. We have to leave *now*!"

50

November 24
Day 91

Lewis clawed himself back to consciousness with great difficulty. Coughing and groaning, he raised his head and noticed that a large portion of a nearby wall had collapsed on him, covering him painfully with bricks and mortar. He gradually worked his way out from under the fallen objects that lay on his chest, the bricks falling into the depression he left in his wake. He was amazed that not only was he alive, it appeared nothing was broken, save for the throbbing bullet wound to his right thigh.

He was going to have to bandage that pretty soon, or he would be in trouble. It was a good thing he found that small med-kit inside his escape truck.

Lewis stood carefully, gingerly testing his bad leg by putting weight in it. He glanced around and saw the devastation brought on by Jonas' fertilizer bomb.

"Holy shit!" he gasped. "I did it!"

Lewis began to laugh loudly and pumped his fists in the air after having something go right for once.

That was when he observed an enormous number of zombies ahead of him, about twenty yards away, moving from right to left. Shortly thereafter, those creatures were met by hundreds of gunshots. He watched row after row of the disgusting creatures die their final death, his pain and victory-fogged brain finally registering that he should get the hell away from the obvious danger. He limped away, whimpering in pain. All too soon Lewis realized he no longer heard any gunfire. The only sound he heard was the labored breaths and cries of pain from his own ragged throat. He rounded the corner of a building, and he could see his getaway truck parked in the same spot he left it. A growling sound from behind made Lewis look over his shoulder. He wished he had not, for behind him were zombies dogging him in hot pursuit, most likely smelling the blood that oozed from his leg injury.

Nearing the truck, Lewis gauged that it would be close, but he would beat the zombie pursuers to it and was just about to sigh in relief when his truck started up and started to pull off!

"Hey that is my truck, wait!" he screamed and limped ahead to cut off the truck.

Whoever was driving must have heard him because it stopped short.

Lewis cried tears of joy as he limped quickly to the passenger door. When he went to grab the door handle, he heard the door locks engage. Pulling frantically on the door handle, he screamed for the driver to unlock it. The passenger window slid partially open, and from inside he heard a voice.

"This is the motherfucker that set off the explosion?" the man growled. "Are you sure?"

Lewis bent to look into the vehicle interior, and his blood ran cold at who he saw inside. In the driver's seat sat the very angry, scowling figure of Dan with a very pale man he recognized as Jeff Kleaner in the passenger seat.

Kleaner croaked weakly, "Yeah, I saw him get out of the truck right before it exploded." Dan looked from Kleaner then back to Lewis. "If I wasn't in a hurry I would beat you to death with my stump, you fucking asshole." Lewis attempted to speak, but Dan cut him off. "Since you will be entertaining company shortly, I'm sure you will not miss my gentle touch, jackass."

Dan slammed his foot on the accelerator and sped off.

"You can't leave me here!" Lewis shouted, chasing the receding truck, but his limp began to get much worse.

Stumbling to a stop, he gasped to no one, "I'll die if you leave me behind. It wasn't supposed to end this way!"

Tears of despair and frustration filled his eyes along with tears of pain when he was grabbed roughly from behind and jagged teeth burrowed into his shoulder. Lewis jerked free, leaving behind a sizable chunk of meat that his undead assailant quickly chewed and then swallowed. Adrenaline blasted into his veins and Lewis clamped a hand to his injured shoulder, frantically hobbling away towards the only safety he could see. Ahead of him sat the medical trailer, an island of refuge in a sea of undead.

Lewis moved to the trailer door and ripped it open. Throwing himself inside, he hurriedly slammed the door shut. Sliding to the floor with the slight moment of safety, he tried to take stock of his injuries. His leg still bled freely from where the bullet had entered and exited his thigh. He could felt the nasty bite wound to his shoulder bleeding profusely as incredible waves of pain radiated from it. The bite wound now felt burning hot. Scrambling over to the medical supplies, Lewis managed to locate some bandages. With trembling hands, he put a pressure bandage around his thigh and then attempted to staunch the flow of blood from his shoulder by holding a gauze pad on it.

Shit, these wounds were going to need stitches.

Shaking from pain and blood loss, it took a few minutes for Lewis to realize he had been bitten.

"Oh sweet merciful God," he gasped aloud.

Outside the trailer, countless hands beat upon the thin walls and door.

"You motherfuckers bit me!"

Anger quickly turned to sorrow as he sank into a chair and cried into his hands. Moments later, the sorrow switched back to intense anger. The howling outside seemed to keep pace with the throbbing pain of his shoulder wound. He began to sweat profusely. His anger soared at the thought of that bastard Stephen who'd shot him, Dan, who'd left him to die, and that asshole Mike who had unwittingly survived every attempt on his life. Most of all, Lewis raged at the thought of dying here trapped like a dog while those he hated with all his fiber escaped!

"Not again!" he cried. "They can't do this to me again!"

If only he could think straight. If only he could focus on a way out.

The trailer started to rock, and the door started to bend and warp from the undead battering the structure. All the commotion was making it impossible to think, and now his mouth was dry. So parched was his mouth that all that mattered now was to find something to drink. Shaking with need, Lewis located a water bottle on a counter and gulped it down.

Lewis bent over at the waist and screamed with the pain that was wracking his guts. God the pain was horrible!

And his thirst was now accompanied by throbbing, agonizing

hunger!

Sinking to the trailer floor, Lewis was delirious with what was happening to him physically. He also began to hallucinate from an extremely high fever. He clenched his teeth as he started to convulse in a seizure of pain, thirst, and ravenous hunger. He soiled himself, but no longer had the dignity to care.

A slight motion to the back of the trailer grabbed his attention. From the rear of the trailer emerged the young, attractive nurse that had been napping when the blast went off. She had obviously been hiding, and even though she was terrified, came out to help Lewis when she heard him crying out in pain.

She smelled divine.

Lewis struggled for air, fighting against the waves of pain that wracked him and managed to gasp, "H-he-help me!"

The woman looked nervous, eyes wide with fear at the door that shook and rattled from the repeated blows of the zombies outside, and edged closer to Lewis, who obviously needed medical attention. She cringed in disgust when she smelled the urine and feces that the man had let loose.

Perhaps this wasn't a good idea, Shelly thought. She decided she should hide, sure that Dan would come for her. And when he saved her, she was going to give him one hell of a reward.

She hesitated too long, however, and was quite surprised when the feeble-looking injured man grabbed her when she turned to retreat back to her hiding spot. With terrible strength he drew her into an embrace, sinking his teeth into her jugular. By the time his fellow undead battered the door aside, Lewis was well on his way of trying to quench his insatiable hunger and thirst with the still warm body of Nurse Shelly.

*

I scrambled into the driver's seat of the giant truck.

Thank God the wailing of the siren had stopped. It was giving me a headache. I climbed aboard alongside Mattie and Max, who were already inside the cab. Stephen stood in the bed of the truck, looking like he was armed for a one man war with all the firearms bristling on his person.

"We're good to go with the exception of Dan and Kleaner," Stephen said. "They know the secondary rendezvous point if they can't make it to the Elwood spot."

"You all better hang on to something. This is going to be one fucking rough ride!" I yelled back, slamming the truck into gear.

Stephen opened up with his AR-15 on a mass of undead to our left. His inner perimeter had done its job, and had allowed us to escape.

His rifle now empty, Stephen shouted for everyone in the back to hunker down as the gates began to inch their way open. Some unknown brave soul had manned his post as ordered and was able to let us escape. I hoped to be able to shake his hand later. The rest of the survivors who managed to make it to vehicles pulled in behind me. The first vehicle was a small foreign car. Not what I would have picked out, but at this point I would have ridden a donkey to escape. With the prison gates slowly sliding open, I gave the truck more throttle and the plow truck ramped up some serious speed. Timing our arrival at the gates compared to speed at which they opened almost perfectly, I yelled for Stephen to trigger the I.E.Ds. Stephen scrambled to locate the detonator as the truck sped at the mass of undead now pouring through the opening western gate. I hoped that the blasting wires were still intact.

My question was answered when our exploding propane tanks carved a large, blood-soaked swath through the thick mass of zombies outside the gates. Propane-fueled fireballs raced skywards, and my V-plow truck slammed into the burning and shredded remnants in my path. I couldn't even feel the first several dozen I hit. Stephen had set the propane tanks out quite a ways, but after we worked past the end of our traps the zombies were thicker in presence, much thicker. So heavy was the zombie presence that I actually had to downshift to keep up speed.

The plow slammed into rotting, bloated bodies and flung them up and off to the left and right of the truck just like a snow-packed road getting cleared. The V-plow worked beautifully, but never as the designers imagined in their wildest dreams. Max was screaming along with Mattie as corpses and body parts fell onto the hood and windshield of the truck. One creature managed to hang onto the hood at the base of the windshield and punched the glass, even though the entire lower half of the repulsive fucker was missing from the impact of the plow blade. I couldn't take the time to try and shake it off since the dump truck wasn't very maneuverable, and while cutting a path of escape through the massive undead it was less so. The problem took care of itself when the stupid creature let go of the hood to work on the windshield with both hands. A few moments later another animated corpse flew across the hood and knocked it loose, dragging them both off the hood. I swear its evil bloodshot eyes stared at me unblinking the entire time it slid off the hood into the mass of doomed souls on the ground. From the rear of the truck I heard Stephen's and Amber's rifles going to work as well.

I would've given them a thumbs up, but I kind of needed both hands to steer.

When we neared the back edges of the undead mob, we saw that the road beyond was packed with many hundreds, maybe even thousands more making their slow, methodical journey to our doomed base. Glancing quickly in my rearview mirror, I couldn't tell if we still had the dozens of vehicles from our convoy with me. The situation was just too chaotic to take my eyes off my mission, and Stephen couldn't hear me yelling for him to check. I hoped that Dan and Kleaner, along with most of our other people, were with us or at least made it out of the prison before it was too late.

*

The foreign car that Kevin Jackson was driving shook repeatedly from the impacts of undead striking it, and the little car jerked erratically from side-to-side. He was focused on the bumper of a truck directly in front of him, trying to keep up. The truck had a bumper sticker that read "Forward" with an easily recognizable logo imbedded. Kevin had to chuckle.

That ended up going about as well as this clusterfuck. We fell for that hope and change bullshit twice. Lotta good it did us.

Currently, in a situation that was growing worse by the second, his wife was bitching at him about what a terrible choice of a vehicle he'd chose to escape in and had to give him a play-by-play announcement of his bad decisions while he frantically tried to keep up with the truck.

"Watch where you're going," she screeched into his ear. "I swear to God you're such an idiot to have picked this piece of shit for our escape!"

"It was the only one left," Kevin said hotly. "It wasn't like I had much choice when the fucking wall blew up!"

The little car slammed into a zombie that flew up into the windshield then bounced up and over the roof, but not before denting it soundly and spider webbing the windshield.

"What the fuck are you trying to do? Kill us?" she screamed, punching Kevin in the arm.

"I'm trying to follow the truck the best I can. Will you shut the hell up?"

"Well your 'best' leaves a lot to be desired, you dumb bastard!" she spat. "I swear if we make it out of this we are through! My mother was right about you. I never should have married your sorry ass, let alone stayed with you all these years. Everything you have done in your life has been a failure! Now I just hope your dumb ass doesn't drag me down with it!"

Kevin's blood pressure skyrocketed, his knuckles turning white from gripping the steering wheel so hard.

"That's it!" Kevin screamed back. "Since you want to leave me, I guess it's ok to say that you are a nagging bitch, whose shit I've put up with for far too long! And you know what? I fucked your sister last spring at our Memorial Day barbeque after you passed out drunk."

For the very first time in years, Kevin's wife was at loss for words. And for a few precious moments of blessed silence, Kevin was able to concentrate on keeping up with the large blue dump truck ahead of him. With a shriek of rage, Kevin's wife backhanded him right in the nose. Stars and pain blinded him as his wife began to claw at his face with both hands. The two of them struggled with one another, failing to keep the little things in perspective. Little things, like keeping both hands on the wheel. The car swerved off the track the plow truck had made and slewed sideways, coming to an abrupt stop in the road after hitting a seething mass of zombies. The vehicle immediately behind Kevin slammed into the driver's side, which broke his left arm. The impact also broke the passenger side window from his wife's head striking it. Kevin groaned in pain. He could hear other loud crashes as the next dozen trucks slammed into one another, causing a huge blockage. The entire convoy of fleeing vehicles behind them was forced to a halt, either by wrecking or quickly applying the brakes.

He watched with dread as the trail that the plow truck made slowly filled in with ravenously hungry zombies. His wife screamed for him to help her. Looking over, Kevin calmly watched dozens of clawing hands grab hold of her and pull her through the broken window. After his wife disappeared into the masses, others climbed onto the hood while more reached in through the broken windows. Kevin pulled out a small revolver.

"Well, at least I won't have to hear her damned bitching

anymore," he said and promptly shot himself in the head.

Behind Kevin's mangled car, most of the other fleeing survivors were not so lucky.

A couple of the trucks tried to throw it into reverse and move around the accident but were unable to gain the necessary amount of speed to plow through the increasing mass and weight of the zombies. One by one they ground to a halt, trapped by the frenzied crush of decomposing bodies. Gunfire flared here and there, punctuated by the sounds of breaking glass and screams of terror. Some were able to climb onto the roofs of their vehicles and fire futilely into the mass before either being tripped or dragged from the vehicle rooftops. One large truck, also equipped with a snowplow, managed to break down a side street and cut a small path for a few of the lucky ones to follow.

*

The old Dodge Dakota rocked from the severe impacts as it rammed into the undead trying to get at Dan and Kleaner, who was currently passed out next to him. Dan was glad he was able to wrap his belt around Kleaner's leg where his foot had been amputated or else he would probably have bled out by now. His unconscious passenger was absolutely no help as he frantically maneuvered the battered truck through and around the quickly closing in groups of undead. He was pretty sure he was the last vehicle to attempt to leave, and as a result, was barely able to make it out of the prison gates. The zombies were swarming worse than welfare recipients at a housing voucher sign up promotion. His truck slammed into yet another creature, and fluid gushed into a geyser from under the crumpled hood. He'd obviously ruptured the radiator or a hose.

Up ahead he saw a mound of zombies swarming over a blockage of vehicles that apparently had wrecked upon exiting the prison. The smell of fresh meat and blood was sending them into a killing frenzy and they fought one another to get a taste.

"Son of a bitch, the entire roadway is blocked by this mess!"

Dan's adrenaline was amped up, making everything appear in slow motion. To the west were the railroad tracks that ran north and south, cutting through the east side of Joliet. Dan remembered that with a lot of luck and prayer, if he could make it to the other side of the tracks, that the Ruby Street Bridge was very close and hopefully a way out of this death trap. Gunning the engine, Dan steered the shuddering pickup through several dozen more zombies and cut across the landscape towards the railroad tracks where the undead presence was much lighter.

Smashing into the last few remaining stinking corpses in his path, Dan's truck then hit the first sets of tracks. The truck jerked as if it had struck a tree. Up and over the first set of rails it rocked, and when it hit the second set of rails, the truck lurched to a stop.

"Oh fuck, this is not good," Dan cursed when he saw that the engine temperature gauge was now edging into the red.

He slammed the truck into reverse, gunning the engine to back off the rail. With much screeching of tortured metal, the truck moved back a few feet. When Dan put the truck back into drive, his driver's side door window exploded inward. He ducked to the side away from the shower of glass, evading the clutching hands of a rotting corpse. Unable to draw his pistol, Dan looked for something to distract the zombie. Not seeing any weapons, his heart fell until his eyes latched onto an object on the floor board in front of him.

Kleaner's bloody amputated right foot!

"Sorry, buddy," Dan grunted, "but I need this more than you do right now!"

Quickly grabbing it, Dan sat up and shoved the bloody meat into the clacking teeth of the creature. The zombie bit down on the morsel and quickly forgot about him, munching on the fresh meal. Seeing his attacker occupied momentarily, Dan stomped hard on the accelerator and screamed curses at the truck. He whooped in joy when it popped loose with a shower of gravel and tearing metal. Looking in the rearview mirror, he scowled at the sight of a thousand zombies in pursuit behind him. Up ahead loomed the massive steel drawbridge, and as he drew near he cursed. There was a steady stream of zombies making their way east over the bridge. And to make a bad situation worse, his truck was shuddering and shaking, way beyond the overheating stage.

Not seeing any other option, Dan gunned the truck towards the bridge, hoping to get to the other side. Just before the top of the bridge, the engine locked up tight, and the truck screeched to a halt at the peak. Dan didn't pause for a second. He threw open the door, exited the disabled vehicle and began emptying his pistol at all the undead now heading at him. He needed to buy a few seconds to think. After downing all the nearby threats, he looked at the west end of the bridge and his blood ran cold. At the bottom there was a bottleneck where what looked like several thousand undead were clawing and shoving each other, trying to get through to get at him. Back where he came from wasn't any better, for there were hundreds of others closing off the east end of the bridge. The noose was set, and now it was about to choke the fuck out of him.

Dan reached inside, grabbed Kleaner, and with a heave dragged his unconscious form across the driver's seat and out onto the bridge surface. With their doom closing in rapidly, Dan hurriedly dragged Kleaner to the bridge pedestrian walkway. Shoving his limp body over the steel girder support frame and onto the walkway, Dan scrambled across.

"Sorry, bro, but I don't see any other way off this bridge," Dan said softly to Kleaner, "and the water's gonna be a bit cold."

He scooped Kleaner up and heaved him over the railing into the dark waters below. Not wasting any time, which was quickly running out, Dan threw his legs over the railing. As the nearest zombie grabbed at him with clawing fingers scratching at his back, he leaped far out into air and made a most spectacular splash when he belly flopped into the frigid water below.

When he surfaced, Dan knew he only had a few minutes in this cold water to act. He found Kleaner floating face up nearby and struggled to reach him. About a hundred yards farther downstream, he spotted a couple of houseboats that were parked next to the river's retaining wall. The river never froze over due to the barge traffic and swift current, therefore, many boats were usually parked there year round. Dan used the swift current to his advantage and with much flailing of arms and kicking of legs, slammed into the back of the first boat. Coughing up mouthfuls of the dirty water, he heaved himself out of the frigid river onto the deck of the boat. He reached down and grabbed Kleaner before the unconscious man drifted away.

"Come on, buddy. I got you," he gasped to his friend.

Kleaner's head lolled from side to side as Dan grunted from pulling his dead weight out of the dark water. He was successful but he had no time to rest; he had to find dry clothes and shelter before they both froze to death.

*

"This is not looking good, Frank," Eddie said, looking out the second story window of the command center building. "They're hounding us worse than my ex-wife's divorce lawyers, and I'm guessing they're not after child support money."

Frank cursed over at the HAM radio console. He'd just been talking with a contact far to the west that had relayed some startling news regarding the safe zone on the West Coast, which was confirmed by a second contact. Frank wanted to get the information to Mike, Stephen and Dan, but current circumstances made that impossible. The only local radio traffic he was getting was garbled screams for help. They were on their own now. Of that he was certain.

"The way they're stacked up deep outside the door, it won't be long before they make it inside," Eddie said with a knowing dread.

"Boy, aren't you just full of good news today?" Frank quipped.

Both men chuckled drily at his sarcasm.

"Well, we can make 'em work for their meals, eh?"

"I hear you, friend," Eddie said. He pulled his hefty .45 pistol, dropped the magazine and checked to see how many rounds he had remaining. "Let's see how they like a little hot lead for an appetizer."

"Man I wish I had a shot of whiskey," Frank grunted while loading fresh shells into his shotgun before checking his pistol. It had been Officer Sherman's duty pistol, and Mike had given it to him on the first day of the outbreak.

"That I can do," Eddie replied, surprising Frank by pulling a pint bottle of Jim Beam from his back pocket.

Downstairs, the howls of the zombies increased and so did the repeated blows against the outside door.

*

The blood-drenched figure stood up from feeding on the mangled corpse of the nurse. Nothing but bones remained and those were now noisily being cracked open to reach the sweet, tender marrow inside by others just like him. He turned and exited the trailer through the shattered door and walked against the tide of the countless others trying to get into the trailer. He screamed in anger at those before him as they screamed back. His wounds no longer hurt but were replaced instead by a mindless ache in his soul. They would all now continue their relentless, mindless search for food, never quenching their urges. Even though he could taste the rich blood on his lips, he needed more. His hunger had not diminished in the slightest.

He almost made it to fresh kills where others like him feasted on mouthwatering sustenance. Each time he howled in rage when it was consumed before he could get some for himself. He caught a scent of more food nearby. Turning to face where that most succulent odor came from, he lurched forward, grateful for his newfound sense of smell.

He must have more!

He clawed at those in his way, howling his anger at those who would slow his progress. Reaching a small structure, he shoved and clawed his way to the front and added his newfound strength to breaching the barricaded door. With the combined might of dozens of others as hungry and hate-filled as he was, the heavy wooden door began to splinter from the repeated blows.

Soon, the portal was torn asunder, and he was among the first to gain entry into the building, snarling his ravenous hate. Smelling the sweet meat above him, he located the stairwell and started to climb. The need for more food made him moan and howl as he neared the source of the delicious smelling morsels. Near the top of the stairs, his mouth began to drool in anticipation of the feast ahead. Lines of thick, bloody spittle hung from his open mouth, which howled his hunger as he entered the room. Standing in the far corner before him was his meal. Roaring with anger, he lurched forward to claim his reward first as his prey before him raised their arms, holding small objects. The shiny chrome object that was pointed at him had a large opening on the end facing his chest. Both of his meals started to scream at him, which made his anger burn.

The shiny objects thundered in reply to his howls. His torso jerked backwards as some unknown force punched him. Many of his brothers snapped backwards and fell away from the noisy, delicious smelling meals. He fell to his knees and quickly scrambled upright and forward undeterred. He opened his blood-covered mouth. He roared his undying hunger again, needing to sink his teeth into his screaming prey. The meal directly in front of him raised the shiny object one more time at his howling face.

The last thing that the poor creature formerly known as Councilman Lewis saw was the bright flash from the muzzle of the handgun that was pointed inches from his forehead.

*

Similar scenes played out all over the prison as those refugees that couldn't escape became trapped in outbuildings and small campers. Even barricading the doors, they were unable to stop the combined weight of the creatures outside. The door to the dormitories was one of the first doors breached and everyone left inside died when their shotguns ran dry. Some elected to kill themselves while others did not have the time to choose. Screams of terror and gunshots filled the air. In a panic, a survivor failed to properly close the door to the church behind him, and a large group of zombies poured into the building. Within minutes the doomed refugees were torn to shreds while in prayer in front of the altar.

In the RV parking area, a small perimeter was held around a group of campers that were hastily assembled in a circle, similar to a wagon train in an old Western movie. At least twenty people were firing into the horde that surrounded them and were able to hold their ground for a short time. The last man to join the small circle was the gatekeeper who had made a break for his truck after opening the gate. He had been too late, and there would be no escape for him. As the population of zombies in the prison yard swelled, their fate was sealed. There were just more targets than they had bullets. Ammunition ran low, and the fighting soon turned to hand-to-hand and the survivors were pulled down into the group of undead, screaming their pain and fear. Mere moments went by before many of the recently deceased rose again to join their new brethren in the feast.

A few survivors managed to make it into the cell blocks and locked themselves in. Zombies screamed at them, reaching through the rust-covered bars. Having no food or water, the survivors would soon have some tough decisions to make. Most of the guards on perimeter duty found themselves trapped in the guard towers. They had a great view of the destruction going on in the yard. They used their position to aid the escape convoy and then the small circle of RVs with suppressive fire, but after it fell, they lost hope. Several committed suicide, and it would be a good two weeks before the last one died of thirst. For now, with the hundreds of zombies that tried to get through to the cell blocks and towers, the remaining men simply watched in stunned silence. The thousands of zombies packing the prison grounds screamed their hunger and fury skyward.

*

Mattie had the radio in the plow truck set to 1320AM and

listened in horror to a live broadcast of the radio station being breached. The sounds of screams and gunshots filled the cab as tears streamed down her face. I turned off the radio and gave Mattie a squeeze on the leg before being forced to again grab the wheel and rev the engine to break through another thick section of zombies that blocked our escape. They were all heading towards the prison in search of food. It now seemed the streets farther to the south held a lighter number of animated corpses walking in the roadway.

Stephen started banging on the roof of the cab while looking behind us as we drove.

"Shit, shit, shit, shit!" He leaned up to my window. "We've lost everyone that followed us out of the prison!"

"All of them?" I yelled back. "What the fuck happened?"

"All of them," he replied. "The last truck in line stalled out and got swarmed like fucking locusts."

"Not much we can do now, bro. We can't go back for anyone. They knew the risks."

'I know," Stephen replied angrily. "It's just we have been getting our ass kicked way too much lately, and it's been costing good people their lives."

"Don't worry, I'm sure you will get your chance to smoke some more of these fuckers before too long."

We crossed underneath a railroad viaduct and got a good look ahead, where there were thousands of undead spilling over into the east side of the river.

"Don't even try it, Mike!" Stephen shouted.

I cranked the steering wheel hard and took out an abandoned car in a shower of shredded car parts as the truck made a wide left turn and surged forward.

The truck picked up speed, and I was glad for the extra momentum. Yet another monstrous-sized undead horde clogged the roadway ahead. It appeared they were more focused on the warehouses across the road rather than us.

"Hang on back there!"

I only had seconds until the first ranks were disintegrated by the sheer weight and force of the dump truck. I temporarily lost sight when what seemed like buckets of ground beef and blood were splattered onto the windshield. Keeping my foot to the floor while Max and Mattie screamed in terror, I tried to get the windshield wipers going.

I downshifted to lower gears as the wipers got the zombie goo removed enough just in time for my sphincter to clench very tight. I only had a split second of warning then I hit an abandoned van almost broadside with the V-plow. Everyone inside the truck cab hit the windshield or dashboard from the impact. I could only hope Stephen and Amber had remained inside. The van, impaled on the V-plow, correspondingly slammed into the rear passenger side of a disabled truck. That second vehicle was shoved to the side as we sped past. Luckily I had enough mind to keep my foot to the floor as the truck continued to shove the van right through the hundreds of other zombies clogging the road in a shower of sparks and mangled limbs. The van finally dislodged, falling off the plow on the driver's side. It crushed a few zombies in the process, and we got an immediate boost in speed and power. I could now make out the circus of noise coming from the back. Stephen was shouting, Amber was crying, and Buddy was howling, so I know they made it through.

Eventually we broke free of the mob around the warehouse and plodded our way south to McDonough Street. Unfortunately, I could see that all the metal shrapnel thrown from these impacts must have hit something vital on the big truck.

"Don't get too comfortable, gang," I said. "It looks like we are losing oil pressure. Something must have gotten punctured."

"Do you think you can fix it, Mike?" Mattie asked, already knowing the answer.

"Maybe, if I had a garage to work in and the correct parts to swap out," I responded, "but I don't think the zombies will calmly stand by for that to happen."

In fact, the path to the south looked less promising by the second. Zombies seemed to be pouring off the interstate and into our path.

"We'll never make the rendezvous point," I called back to Stephen. "Truck's about had it."

"Not sure there's anyone to meet anyways," Stephen conceded. "Let's try for my place and create some distance before we're on foot."

We made our way up and over the desolate McDonough Street Bridge to the west side of the river. Hopefully the hard part was done and we could stay ahead of the zombies until we found a place of safety. A short two miles later the truck stalled for good. We coasted to a stop, and Stephen called for everyone to grab their rucksacks and weapons and form a perimeter.

"Suppressed rifles only," he ordered. "We're gonna be walking from here, and we can't afford to draw a crowd."

Stephen and I made sure all the ammo that could be carried was taken. Food and water was also important, but since that wasn't our primary need at the moment, I just made sure everyone had a few days' worth.

"I hope you two have comfortable walking shoes on," I said, looking down at Mattie and Amber. "We got a good hike in front of us to get to Stephen's house."

Stephen was looking around for the ever present undead threat, and had already downed a few persistent followers.

"Come on gang; let's get moving before more show up," he urged. "With all the noise we made, we are bound to have a lot more company soon."

Stephen took point, followed by Mattie and Amber, who had Stephen's beagle, Buddy, on a leash. The tail of our little formation was ended with Max and me pulling rear guard.

We were a motley crew of five survivors and a dog. As I limped at top speed, I kept cursing at Stephen to slow the fuck down.

"Hurry your crippled ass up!" he hollered back to me. "Even my fat dog is keeping up!"

I was also occupied with answering Max's questions as to what the new curse words he was hearing meant. As if that wasn't bad enough, Mattie was saying something quietly to Amber. They both looked back over their shoulder at me silently for a few moments and started giggling and talking quietly to one another.

I was about to say something when Max cut in with, "Why do you always stare at Mattie's butt?"

"I don't always look at her butt," I snapped. "I look at other women's butts too."

Max looked confused. "But why do you look at butts? Butts are ugly."

I coughed a few times, and I handed Max my trusty aluminum bat and shield to keep him occupied. "Because I like her butt, that's why," I said as the giggling in front of me got louder. "Here you go kid, now carry this and be quiet."

"Quit staring at my ass and hurry up old man!" Stephen yelled from the front.

For the love of God, this was going to be a long walk.

51

November 24
Day 91

Matvei heard the explosion and raced back up to the roof. Sure enough, the evidence of a massive explosion was rising into the air from the north.

"Looks like trouble in paradise," he mumbled.

A short time later, it became obvious by the behavior of his ever present adversary that someone was coming. Soon Matvei spotted a large V-plow truck headed his direction. It was carving a gash through the waiting undead, and he saw an opportunity.

"My luck is about to change!" Matvei cried while racing down off the roof to gather his gear.

Once he reached the warehouse floor, Raul approached him and asked what was happening.

“A truck is driving past here any second!” Matvei cried. “Grab your gear. Where the hell is Hector?”

“He’s taking another shit, boss,” Raul replied. “That old can of potted meat was bad, and he has been shitting non-stop all day.”

“He’d better hurry up if he wants to go with us. We can’t delay,” Matvei stated, swinging his pack over his shoulders.

Hector emerged from the back room, “I’m ready, assholes. You were going to leave me here to die all along, but I’m on to your plans.”

This guy is losing it, Matvei thought. If he didn’t need to leave right now, he thought he might have to kill him before he tried something stupid.

He kept his thoughts to himself for now, however. “Good, we are all ready. Let's move!"

Matvei peered out the small six-inch wide window of reinforced glass that was in the side metal door. Sure enough, the plow truck was cutting a path right by his truck. Matvei grimaced when the plow smashed into the van, which then struck his Dodge Ram. As a bit of luck would have it, the truck stayed intact, and the plow drew the majority of the infected away in its wake. He knew they only had seconds to act and threw open the door and raced for the truck.

Several undead noticed his presence and turned to attack. Matvei downed five with headshots delivered from his rifle and missed the others. The plow truck had hit his Dodge hard enough to spin it around like a top, forcing him to fight his way around the damaged cargo van to the driver's door. Reaching the truck, they opened the doors and climbed in. Just as Raul was going to shut his passenger door, one of the infected wedged its way into the gap. Raul was trapped, with teeth gnashing less than an inch from his face. Matvei drew his pistol and placed it against the hideous creature's forehead, pulling the trigger. He then redirected his pistol towards, firing at two more that were at his open door. Hector was forced to use his empty rifle as a club, and managed to beat back several attackers. Slamming the doors shut as more slammed into his driver's window, the men breathed a sigh of relief. Matvei was thankful that the keys were in the ignition, and that the truck started immediately.

They were not out of the woods yet. Matvei threw the truck into reverse and drew away from the van. The truck shifted hard back into drive, protesting before the transmission grabbed. He stepped on the accelerator and tried to follow the best he could through the dwindling path that the large plow truck had made. Finally, he was able to reach the point that the horde started to thin in numbers. Just in time. Nearly every warning light on his dashboard lit up. The truck had suffered major damage, being spun around by a plow truck and directly into a parked van.

"We got lucky," Hector said from the back seat, making the sign of the cross.

"The boss makes his own luck, Hector," Raul replied. "You should know that by now."

Matvei only smiled.

52

November 24
Day 91

We were all relieved when we reached Stephen's subdivision and found that it had not burned to the ground. Everyone was exhausted from the multi-hour walk, not just from the walking, but from the constant harassment from zombies. Our four suppressed rifles were the only thing that kept us alive during the long hike. It looked as if the majority of the zombies that had been roaming his neighborhood when we left had moved on in search of food. Finding his hidden house key, Stephen opened the front door, and we piled inside. Buddy, happy to be home and scratching at the door was the first one inside.

"Don't get too comfortable, Buddy," Stephen joked. "The power and water are both out. There's no heat, and we're not going to be able to stay here long."

"You had a nice place," Amber said admiringly. "I should've spent some time here."

"That would have been nice," Stephen replied with a tired smile.

We all gathered in the living room, and Stephen filled us in on everything that had transpired prior to the explosion that wrecked our world. Obviously we had a lapse in security that nearly cost us everything. I took some solace in the fact that Stephen had shot Lewis and there was really no way he had made it out alive. Yet with no body, I would never really know for sure. With our home gone, we turned towards the future, and discussed where to go from here.

I stated the obvious. "We have maybe a day or two before the horde we met today makes it this far west."

"I agree," Stephen replied. "We're going to have to secure some extra wheels in the morning. My truck is not going to be able to fit us all."

"I'm just glad we made it," Mattie said while patting young Max on the shoulder.

"We all did a good job today considering the circumstances. Now let's get unpacked and get some rest. I think we still have some of Stephen's stuff in the basement."

"Mattie," Stephen said, "help the others get unpacked and organized down here. I'm going to show Amber the upstairs and then take first watch from the office."

"I'll come relieve you in a few hours," I said. "I hope Dan and Kleaner show up! This was the only plan B we had."

"I'm hungry," Max chimed.

"I hope you like dehydrated meat patties."

*

It was well past midnight, and Stephen was starting to get tired. Amber kept him company for a while, but he insisted that she get some rest, and he promised to join her shortly. He again rehashed the day's events and lamented that Dan and Kleaner were missing in action.

"You did alright today, Stephen. We made it out alive when others didn't," she reminded him. "You really can't blame yourself for everything bad that happened."

"Thanks," Stephen answered, "but I'm just doing my job. And if I would've paid better attention, rather than playing football, maybe I coulda stopped that fucker."

"Knock it off already," Amber said, getting irritated now. "Enough with the pity party, we got work to do. And you gotta figure out a safe place to go. I'm going to bed."

"Keep the bed warm for me."

"Don't be too long!"

Then he only had Buddy and the horrors that transpired at the prison to keep him awake. He had started the day in a warm and cozy RV, won a football game and enjoyed a Thanksgiving feast. Now, so many had died horribly, Dan and Kleaner were missing, and he was standing watch in his cold former residence. They lost a lot today, and his mind was racing, trying to figure their next move.

"Do we head west towards the government safe zone?" he asked himself, "Or south where it's warmer? Or north for that matter, maybe the zombies will die off in the cold?"

Buddy was suddenly on his feet and looked to the south. Stephen wondered if there was a problem when he noticed the headlights of an approaching vehicle. Slowing to a stop in front of his residence was a large black Yukon sport utility pulling a small enclosed trailer. Stephen thought maybe Dan had shown up after all.

"Are you sure this's the place?" a male voice asked as the driver's door opened. "I've never been to Stephen's house."

"I'm pretty sure this is it," a female voice responded. "They brought me here after they rescued me from my car. That seems so long ago, though."

"Well, we'll see. There aren't any radio transmissions coming from the prison and 1320AM is offline. Something must have happened. If they're not here, we'll have to just head out alone again."

At that remark, Stephen hit the powerful Surefire light on his carbine. To his surprise he lit up Holly and Casper, who suddenly stopped in their tracks.

"Holy shit!" Stephen yelled out the upstairs window. "I didn't think I would see you two again. Hang on. I'm coming down to let you in. I know there's going to be some people happy to see you!"

*

I was awakened by Mattie yelling with joy and soon found out that Casper and Holly were here. Mattie still hadn't stopped hugging Holly, and they were both crying. She kept going on and on about how part of her new family had just returned, when things were looking their worst. I had to admit my spirits were lifted.

"Good to see you, brother!" I said, getting up to shake Casper's hand. "What happened?"

"I was going to ask you guys the same thing," Casper replied.

"Well it's been a long day," I sighed. "Where do I begin?"

"How about with why you are all here," Holly asked, "instead of at the prison."

After filling Casper and Holly in on what happened during the final week at the prison and its eventual downfall, Casper told us the tale of his travels. He and Holly made it well into southern Indiana and managed to avoid any major zombie concentrations along the way. They spent a couple of days securing their new transportation and outfitting it with supplies for the trip east. During this time, Holly began to worry more and more about their friends that they had left behind. She missed us all, and Casper admitted that he felt the same way. Holly finally convinced Casper to head back and see if there was any way they could help. When they reached radio range just today, they could not raise anyone, and 1320AM was no longer broadcasting. When they reached Joliet, they saw the large horde of undead and feared the worst. Holly knew where Stephen's place was and insisted that they check the house before trying again for Maine.

"And here we are," Casper said, finishing his story and pointing his thumb over his shoulder, "and I got a lot of shit in that trailer out there."

"Good news. Good news," I replied. "We sure need it."

Eventually all the excitement died down and everyone was tucked back in. Mattie sat up with me in the office on guard duty. We wrapped ourselves in a blanket and talked about Casper's arrival, how lucky we were, and what would happen from here.

"I sure hope Dan and Kleaner show up," I said wistfully. "We can only afford to wait a day or two for them."

"Me too," Mattie whispered before leaning in close, "but I do know of one other person who will be making the trip with us."

"Oh yeah, who's that?" "Our baby," Mattie said softly and simply. When I stared dumbly at her, she said, "I'm pregnant."

I managed a smile on the outside.

On the inside, one famous phrase came to mind. "Fuck me...."

53

November 28
Day 95

Matvei cursed and punched the steering wheel in frustration when the truck finally died on him. He was actually surprised it had made it this far. Too bad, however, that it decided to quit on him out in the middle of nowhere. There was nothing, save a snarled mass of abandoned cars, but damn cornfields as far as he could see. Matvei ordered his men out to check the other vehicles. As he expected, none of them ran.

"Well, my friends, it looks like we walk from here," he said to Raul and Hector.

"I need to stretch my legs anyways, boss," Raul replied. "I'm sure some new wheels will pop up. At least we cleared the city. There's no infected in sight."

"And it's a good thing. I'm going to have to take another shit soon," Hector groaned, holding his midsection. "And I won't be able to carry much, I feel weak as fuck."

"Look on the bright side, Hector," Raul said. "We don't have much to carry."

That much was true. They had nothing to eat and hardly any ammo.

Matvei had one .45 pistol round left and seven rounds for his rifle. Raul had only nine rounds for his pistol, and Hector was completely out. Matvei figured he was okay with that for now, as Hector was growing increasingly unstable. He gave Hector an aluminum baseball bat from the truck as a weapon, and slung Hector's empty rifle over his shoulder. Grabbing their meager gear, the three ragged former mercenaries began marching westward.

54

November 28
Day 95

The over-packed black Chevy Colorado rocketed westbound down the I-88 toll road.

"You had better slow the fuck down," I suggested. "It's not like the zombies are right on our ass."

Stephen was calmly weaving in and out around the occasional stalled, wrecked, and abandoned vehicles that dotted the roadway. We were now west of DeKalb, Illinois, and out of any immediate danger. Stephen's house had provided two days of sanctuary before a large chunk of the same horde of zombies reached the far west side of Joliet. When we left, we had been forced to take back roads until reaching I-88.

"I'm just trying to keep up," Stephen said. "Talk to the asshole driving point."

"Mattie," I said, turning to face her. "Tell him to slow down."

Dan had arrived at Stephen's house the morning after Casper's arrival, driving a green Jeep Wrangler. He'd gotten lucky and found it near the river, downstream from Joliet. Our group sat transfixed, listening to Dan's tale of his escape from the prison and desperate plunge into the frigid water. After dragging Kleaner onto the boat, Dan was forced to watch his friend succumb to his injuries. The shock of his severed foot, blood loss and the freezing water was just too much. If Dan hadn't found a change of clothes for himself in the small houseboat, he too would have died of hypothermia. He'd cut the mooring lines and let the boat drift downstream until he was clear of the horde. After making it to shore, he found the Jeep and made his way to us.

Mattie was sitting in the back seat of the crew cab truck with Amber, and had been trying to teach Max and Dan in Spanish via the two-way radio.

"*Tiene lindos ojos*," Mattie was saying. "You have pretty eyes. And by the way, Mike wants you to slow it down a bit."

Up ahead in the scout vehicle, Dan scowled as he listened to the radio Max was holding.

"Nice, but who cares. Now I would like to know how to say 'You have a nice ass' or 'Let me see your tits' in Spanish. That might help me out in the short term, in case we happen by some lonely senoritas. And tell Mike that we're barely moving up here!"

"Mattie," Max said, "Uncle Dan wants to know how to say 'tits and ass' in Spanish."

"Put Uncle Dan on the radio!" Mattie shrieked.

"Dan!" Mattie yelled. "He's just a boy! You have to watch your lang—"

"I hate to cut you off, Mattie," Dan said abruptly. "But it looks like you're gonna get your wish on slowing down, I see something in the road up ahead. Looks like a big mess of cars."

Slowing down to a crawl as they drove by, Dan counted seven vehicles in the jam. One stuck out above the rest. Parked directly in the middle of the road was a black Dodge truck that was beat to hell, hood up and doors open. What made this one different was the pool of oil dripping on the roadway and remnants of steam coming from the radiator. This one was new, clearly not involved in the long ago accident.

"Looks like someone has been here recently," Dan said into the radio, "but I don't see anyone around."

"It's not worth stopping," Stephen replied. "We need to find a place to hole up before it gets dark. Keep going, I'll look around for a second."

Stephen stopped for a few minutes and checked out the wreckage. Not seeing anything noteworthy they were again on their way.

A short time later Dan was back on the radio.

"Holy shit. You've got to see this."

When we caught up to Dan it became quite apparent what all the fuss was about. Directly in their path was a commercial airliner. It had landed on this long, straight stretch of highway. The emergency inflatable escape ramps had been deployed but had long since deflated and now flapped lazily in the wind. Off to the side was another plane that didn't have as smooth of a landing. It had veered off the interstate and ended up in a nearby cornfield. The plane left a trail of destruction and had broken up as it crashed. It had literally broken in half, with luggage and parts of the plane scattered all over. A huge swath of the field had caught on fire and surrounded the area with a blackened region of ash and debris.

Dan was already out of the Jeep when we rolled up. Stephen pulled off to the right, stopping the truck safely behind the wreckage. The Yukon, which was driven by Casper along with Holly, bringing up the rear of our little convoy, pulled off to the left well in front of us. I had Mattie run up and get Max, telling her to take him over to the Yukon with Holly.

"What do you make of that?" Dan asked as we walked up.

"Well they had to land somewhere," Stephen replied. "Once they heard the airports were out of commission, they must have tried to put down outside of the cities. I am surprised we have not seen more of this. Kind of like the stalled trains I ran across last month." I shouldered my M4 carbine and set off. "Let's check it out. There might be something we could use. At the least, we can load up on peanuts and soda pop."

Stephen already had his rifle in hand. I swear that guy liked his guns more than women.

Except maybe for Amber, I thought as I watched her walk up behind us.

We decided that Dan, Casper, Stephen and I would move up to check out the aircraft.

"Be careful, guys," Amber cautioned before walking back to the Yukon to sit with the others. "I don't like this."

"Tell Casper to get his ass up here," Stephen said, giving Amber a gentle smack on her behind.

After Casper came running up, the four of us made our way towards the tail end of the jet that had landed on the highway and took cover behind one of the landing gear's tires.

"How do you think we should clear this plane?" Stephen whispered.

"I'm not sure," I answered. "I don't even know how we are going to get inside the damn thing. The door hatch has to be twenty feet off the ground. We might be able to pull one of our trucks up to the door, but I would hate to run into anything hostile inside it while doing so. We would be sitting ducks."

Just as it looked like Stephen was going to say something, a loud banging sound came from the wreckage of the other plane. We spun to face the possible threat and with our rifles ready for action, gave each other quizzical looks.

Stephen took point; the rest of us followed. We cautiously crossed the open lanes of the interstate and continued onward down into the burnt wreckage of the plane. Glancing at the tail, I saw that it was a United Airlines plane from the logo. The tail end was surprisingly intact, but the wings and forward section were a twisted, melted shell. Gradually, we closed the gap and walked the length of the tail end out of view from all the plane's windows. From inside we could hear more banging, followed by a man's voice growling words that I took to be swearing.

I was sure it was swearing, but it wasn't in a language I recognized. I could tell he was cursing from the frustration and anger I heard in his voice.

We turned the corner and looked into the open inside of the broken half of the plane. Inside, we observed two men. An average-sized Hispanic holding a pistol and a bigger man wearing some sort of camouflage fatigues. The large man was currently banging away at a refreshment cart that was lodged under some of the wreckage. He was also using what was left of an AK-47 as a hammer.

"That's no way to use an assault rifle," Stephen said out loud.

*

Hector felt like hell and was in a very bad mood. His feet ached along with his gut. For the last three days he had had to shit almost every couple of hours, was feverish and weak from dehydration.

Food poisoning really sucked.

When the three of them had come across the plane wreck, he had been unable to hold it any longer, and had run into the cornfield holding his belly. Matvei and Raul went on to search the planes. He really hoped that they found some medications for his sickness inside somewhere. On his return to the road, as he neared the edge of the cornfield, he heard female voices and quickly stopped in his tracks. Easing forward, Hector looked out and saw three beautiful women and some brat standing near a large truck with their backs to him. They were staring at the two planes in the distance while the redhead was preparing snacks of some sort.

"Today's my lucky day," he whispered. "I haven't had pussy in weeks, and now there are three here for the taking. I'm sure the boss has something for whoever they're with."

Hector was still angry at Matvei for sending those women off the roof back at the warehouse before he could sample their fruit. He had no weapon. His rifle was out of ammunition, and last he knew Matvei was using it as a hammer. The women seemed distracted by what was going on up ahead, along with whatever else they had to gossip about during an apocalypse. They seemed lost in conversation when he slipped onto the roadway well behind them. As he made his approach, he passed the smaller black truck that he was using as concealment.

"Jackpot!"

In the truck was a Polish AK-47 underfolder. He no longer needed his stupid bat. He grinned when he checked the magazine and found it loaded. He knew how to handle one of these. He was back in business.

Hector cautiously approached the Yukon, wanting the element of surprise. He was almost upon them when a small dog spotted him and barked loudly. The women jumped and two of them reached for pistols.

"Sorry, ladies, don't do that unless you want to die!" he ordered, swinging the barrel back and forth between them. "And I'll kill the kid. I'm only after your food, and mean you no harm. Drop your guns and kick them towards me!"

The two women hesitated.

"Fucking do it now!"

Mattie glanced from side to side and tossed her pistol to the ground. "Do it, Amber."

Amber complied, staring in defiance at her attacker the entire time.

A predatory grin grew on Hector's face as he snatched the closest woman by the arm and spun her around facing the others.

"What is your name, sweetheart?"

"H-Holly," the woman replied, trembling in fear. "We did as you asked, please don't hurt us."

Max started to cry.

"Well now, Holly. I truly want to apologize for this, but I need to do this to keep the others in line." He reached up with both hands and wrenched Holly's neck sharply and roughly around, breaking the woman's neck. As Holly's lifeless corpse fell to the ground, the others began to scream.

"Shut up! Shut the fuck up!" Hector roared. "I will kill you all right now unless you all shut up, and I will start with the boy!"

They quickly quieted, and Hector continued. "So now that you know I am serious, I want you to do exactly as I say or I kill the boy as your next warning."

The two women grew quiet.

Hector looked at the two fine looking women and decided to get on with it. "You two. Take off your clothes, now."

Mattie and Amber looked at each other and slowly started undressing. The look of pure lust coming from the stranger horrified them both.

Mattie acted as if she was having trouble with the buttons on her shirt as a stall tactic.

This can't be happening again! her mind raced. *I refuse to be a victim again*!

Next to her, Amber had now undressed down to her undergarments. The man looked as if he could no longer wait, stepped forward and grabbed Amber to him, while roughly shoving Mattie to the side near the open door of the Yukon.

She glanced inside and saw Casper's old revolver sitting on top of the center console. She looked back to see that the man had ripped at Amber's bra and was going to work on her panties.

Mattie decided it was now or never and lunged inside the truck grabbing the revolver. Outside the truck, the man cursed in anger and shoved Amber to the ground as he stared right at Mattie.

Mattie swung the handgun out towards her assailant, who in turn brought his rifle up to fire.

The sudden, deafening sounds of gunfire shattered the silent afternoon day.

*

The man in the plane spun faster than I had expected and reached for a fancy looking rifle that was draped over a row of seats by its sling. The Hispanic man also spun around at us.

"Not so fast, friends," Stephen said, lifting his rifle up to his firing position. "If we wanted you dead you would have been on your way to meet your maker by now."

The first man stopped his movement towards his weapon and raised his hands in surrender, motioning to his partner to do the same. After the Hispanic man holstered his pistol and surrendered, the first man spoke.

"I apologize," he said in a deep voice that was thick with an unknown accent. "You men took me by surprise is all, something that doesn't happen often for me."

Stephen lowered his rifle to a ready position and looked hard at the man. "Those look like Russian Para Brown VSR fatigues," Stephen said with a puzzled look on his face.

The man's eyes widened briefly at the comment. "Yes they are. How did you know? I was in the Russian military attached to our embassy when this disaster went down. Again, I'm sorry for my aggressive behavior. We haven't seen too many living people lately and the ones we have run across were the bandit type."

"I don't blame you for your reaction, guy," Stephen replied. "These are rather unusual times we live in."

I motioned for Dan and Casper to cover the rear, in case there were more men around.

"Where are you heading?" I asked.

Matvei's mind raced. He couldn't believe he let someone get the drop on him! These men before him did not look like they would be fooled easily. Better to tell them mostly truth and try to get their assistance on his journey west, or kill them all when the opportunity arose and take their gear.

"You may call me Matvei, and I'm heading west. I have some comrades that own a sizable ranch in Arizona. I was going to see if any of them were still alive."

"We were heading west as well," Stephen said. "Do you have transportation?"

Matvei grimaced slightly. "Alas, I do not. My truck parked out on the road blew a radiator hose and seized up where it sits now. We were in here scavenging for supplies before we set out on foot. Would you mind if we rode along with you?"

"I guess we could always use an experienced trigger man," Stephen said. "Don't see any reason why you couldn't hitch a ride with us."

"Thank you, comrades. The ranch I was heading to in Arizona is well supplied and fortified. If you help me reach it, I will make it worth your while."

"Grab your rifle and let's get back to our trucks so you can meet the others," Stephen said and then looked curiously at what Matvei picked up.

"You have a select fire G36?" he asked. "Damn."

"Sure do. By the way, don't bother checking the other plane," Matvei said. "I already did. The survivors cleaned it out."

"I'm not surprised," I replied. "By the way, I'm Mike and this is Stephen, Dan, and Casper."

Matvei paused slightly in thought. These were the men who had emptied out the cartel's warehouse!

At the mention of our names, the Hispanic man tensed up. I was about to ask what the hell I said wrong when gunshots broke the silence from outside the plane.

"Look out, boss!" the Hispanic man cried, drawing his pistol. "It's a trap!"

The next few seconds turned the tail end of the wrecked aircraft into a mini version of the OK Corral. Casper and I were in the midst of turning to run outside to see what the problem was, thinking of our ladies outside, when Dan sent multiple bullets into the torso of the Hispanic man. At the same time, Matvei's hands blurred into action, whipping his rifle up. However, as fast as he was, Stephen was faster. Round after round punched through Matvei. Blood sprayed from his chest and out his back as the projectiles ripped chunks of meat from the man, sending him lifeless to the floor of the plane.

"Goddamn was he fast!" Stephen exclaimed, moving forward to make sure the man was down for good.

"You and Dan stay here," I said. "Something's happened to the girls!"

I sprinted outside and around the blind side of the plane wreck, then ran past Dan's Jeep. Before me lay a sight that will haunt me for the rest of my life.

I could see the lifeless form of Max lying face down in the roadway in a pool of blood. Amber was lying semi-nude next to him. She had attempted to use her body to shield the child and had paid for it with her life. She had been shot several times, her right hand mere inches from her pistol. Up ahead I could see a man standing in the open door of the Yukon as he grabbed the body of Mattie and threw her to the ground. She was covered in blood and did not move when she hit the pavement. In an instant he saw me, raised his rifle and fired.

Screaming in rage I raised my own rifle and sent an entire thirty round magazine his way. The man, as well as the Yukon, was peppered by my assault and the wild shooting by Casper.

The man slumped to the ground in a bloody heap as I ran towards Max. When I saw he was dead, I sprinted over to where

Mattie fell.

"Oh no, no, please be okay."

Turning her gently and cradling her head and shoulders, it was clear that I was too late, she was gone.

"Don't leave me," I whispered, brushing her hair from her face. "I need you."

Casper let out a cry of anguish. I glanced over to see him holding Holly. From the angle of her neck I could tell it was broken. I couldn't say a word. Moments later I dimly heard Stephen's cry of grief behind me. I was surrounded by slaughtered loved ones, and their blood and pain burned what was left of my soul to ashes.

EPILOGUE

November 29
Day 96

We stood there staring at the four shallow graves that each held a part of us. Nobody said a word, for none were needed. A strong breeze pushed at us from the north, sending the corn fields around us rustling in the wind. Tears had been shed by all. None of us wanted to say goodbye, but all of us knew we had to.

"They deserved better than this," I said. "This isn't right. They shouldn't be dead."

Dan spun away and marched for Stephen's truck. It was his way of not showing us his tears. Buddy was whining, unsure of why his master and the others were so upset.

Stephen put a hand on my shoulder. "I know, Mike. I miss them too. Come on."

I looked him in the eye for a few moments, and then nodded.

We walked past the bullet-riddled Yukon. It was stained dark red with both the blood of our loved ones and their killer. I was so sick of seeing blood. We were forced to transfer over from it some of our meager provisions. We worked in silence, struggling to ignore the crimson reminder of our loss.

After loading the truck, Casper and Dan strode wordlessly into the jeep. I was worried about Casper. He had come so far, but now looked like he might break for good.

"You got point," I hollered up to Dan, who didn't bother to reply.

Sliding into the front seat of the truck, I sat there and stared out the passenger window.

Stephen got in with his dog, closed his door and sighed. A few moments later he asked, “I got the trailer hooked up. You still wanna head west?”

I shrugged my shoulders.

“Where we headed again?” Dan asked over the radio. “I vote as far west of here as we can get.”

“West it is then,” Stephen mumbled back, and started his truck.

As he put it into gear and drove away from the one thing in this world that mattered to me, his iPod turned on.

I thought I’d cried all the tears I had left, but found I was wrong when the music brought back haunting memories of the past.

It was Metallica. The song: “Turn the Page.”

"No free man shall ever be debarred the use of arms. The strongest reason for the people to retain the right to keep and bear arms is, as a last resort, to protect themselves against tyranny in government."

-Thomas Jefferson, Proposed Virginia Constitution, 1776.

14

BY PETER CLINES

Padlocked doors. Strange light fixtures. Mutant cockroaches. There are some odd things about Nate's new apartment. Every room in this old brownstone has a mystery. Mysteries that stretch back over a hundred years. Some of them are in plain sight. Some are behind locked doors. And all together these mysteries could mean the end of Nate and his friends. Or the end of everything...

DAY BY DAY ARMAGEDDON

GREY FOX

BY J.L. BOURNE

Time is a very fluid thing, no one really has a grasp on it other than maybe how to measure it. As the maestro of the Day by Day Armageddon Universe, I have the latitude of being in control of that time. You have again stumbled upon a ticket with service through the apocalyptic wastes, but this time the train is a little bit older, a little more beat up, and maybe a little wiser.

DEAD TIDE

BY STEPHEN A. NORTH

THE WORLD IS ENDING. BUT THERE ARE SURVIVORS. Nick Talaski is a hard-bitten, angry cop. Graham is a newly divorced cab driver. Bronte is a Gulf War veteran hunting his brother's killer. Janicea is a woman consumed by unflinching hate. Trish is a gentleman's club dancer. Morgan is a morgue janitor. The dead have risen and the citizens of St. Petersburg and Pinellas Park are trapped. The survivors are scattered, and options are few. And not all monsters are created by a bite. Some still have a mind of their own...

PERMUTEDPRESS.COM

DEAD TIDE RISING

BY STEPHEN A. NORTH

The sequel to Dead Tide continues the carnage in Pinellas Park near St. Pete, Florida. Follow all of the characters from the first book, Dead Tide, as they fight for survival in a world destroyed by the zombie apocalypse.

PERMUTED PRESS

THE ROAD TO NOWHERE
BY BILL BRADDOCK

Welcome to the city of Las Vegas. Gone are the days of tourist filled streets. After waking up alone in a hospital bed, everyone seems to have fled, leaving me behind. Survival becomes my only driving force. Nothing was as it should have been. Things seemed to lurk in the buildings and darkest shadows. I didn't know what they were, but I could always feel their eyes on me.

PERMUTEDPRESS.COM

ZOMBIE ATTACK: RISE OF THE HORDE
BY DEVAN SAGLIANI

Voted best Zombie/ Horror E-books of 2012 on Goodreads. When 16 year old Xander's older brother Moto left him at Vandenberg Airforce Base he only had one request - don't leave no matter what. But there was no way he could have known that one day zombies would gather into groups big enough to knock down walls and take out entire buildings full of people. That was before the rise of the horde!

PERMUTED PRESS

THE INFECTION
BY CRAIG DiLOUIE

The world is rocked as one in five people collapse screaming before falling into a coma. Three days later, the Infected awake with a single purpose: spread the Infection. A small group—a cop, teacher, student, reverend—team up with a military crew to survive. But at a refugee camp what's left of the government will ask them to accept a dangerous mission back into the very heart of Infection.

THE KILLING FLOOR
BY CRAIG DiLOUIE

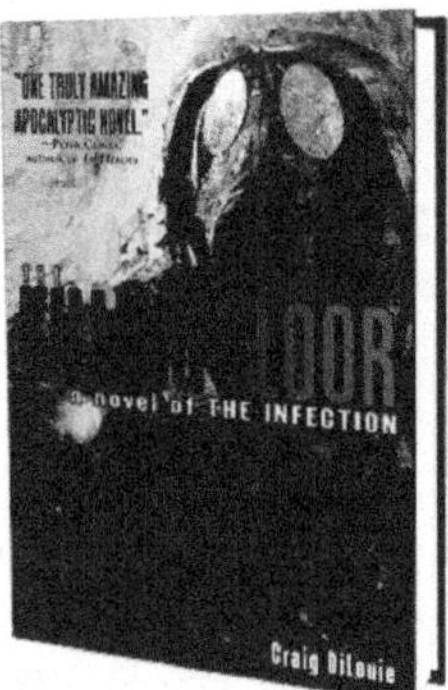

The mystery virus struck down millions. Three days later, its victims awoke with a single violent purpose: spread the Infection. Ray Young, survivor of a fight to save a refugee camp from hordes of Infected, awakes from a coma to learn he has also survived Infection. Ray is not immune. Instead, he has been transformed into a superweapon that could end the world ... or save it.

THE INFECTION BOX SET
BY CRAIG DiLOUIE

Two full #1 bestselling apocalyptic thrillers for one low price! Includes the full novels THE INFECTION and THE KILLING FLOOR. A mysterious virus suddenly strikes down millions. Three days later, its victims awake with a single purpose: spread the Infection. As the world lurches toward the apocalypse, some of the Infected continue to change, transforming into horrific monsters.

PERMUTED PRESS

THE BECOMING

BY JESSICA MEIGS

The Michaluk Virus has escaped the CDC, and its effects are widespread and devastating. Most of the population of the southeastern United States have become homicidal cannibals. As society rapidly crumbles under the hordes of infected, three people--Ethan, a Memphis police officer; Cade, his best friend; and Brandt, a lieutenant in the US Marines--band together against the oncoming crush of death.

PERMUTEDPRESS.COM

THE BECOMING: GROUND ZERO (BOOK 2)

BY JESSICA MEIGS

After the Michaluk Virus decimated the southeast, Ethan and his companions became like family. But the arrival of a mysterious woman forces them to flee from the infected, and the cohesion the group cultivated is shattered. As members of the group succumb to the escalating dangers on their path, new alliances form, new loves develop, and old friendships crumble.

PERMUTEDPRESS.COM

THE BECOMING: REVELATIONS (BOOK 3)

BY JESSICA MEIGS

In a world ruled by the dead, Brandt Evans is floundering. Leadership of their dysfunctional group wasn't something he asked for or wanted. Their problems are numerous: Remy Angellette is grief-stricken and suicidal, Gray Carter is distant and reclusive, and Cade Alton is near death. And things only get worse.

PERMUTED PRESS

ROADS LESS TRAVELED: THE PLAN

BY C. DULANEY

Ask yourself this: If the dead rise tomorrow, are you ready? Do you have a plan? Kasey, a strong-willed loner, has something she calls The Zombie Plan. But every plan has its weaknesses, and a freight train of tragedy is bearing down on Kasey and her friends. In the darkness that follows, Kasey's Plan slowly unravels: friends lost, family taken, their stronghold reduced to ashes.

PERMUTEDPRESS.COM

MURPHY'S LAW (ROADS LESS TRAVELED BOOK 2)

BY C. DULANEY

Kasey and the gang were held together by a set of rules, their Zombie Plan. It kept them alive through the beginning of the End. But when the chaos faded, they became careless, and Murphy's Law decided to pay a long-overdue visit. Now the group is broken and scattered with no refuge in sight. Those remaining must make their way across West Virginia in search of those who were stolen from them.

PERMUTEDPRESS.COM

SHADES OF GRAY (ROADS LESS TRAVELED BOOK 3)

BY C. DULANEY

Kasey and the gang have come full circle through the crumbling world. Working for the National Guard, they realize old friends and fellow survivors are disappearing. When the missing start to reappear as walking corpses, the group sets out on another journey to discover the truth. Their answers wait in the West Virginia Command Center.

PERMUTED PRESS

PAVLOV'S DOGS

BY D.L. SNELL & THOM BRANNAN

WEREWOLVES Dr. Crispin has engineered the saviors of mankind: soldiers capable of transforming into beasts. ZOMBIES Ken and Jorge get caught in a traffic jam on their way home from work. It's the first sign of a major outbreak. ARMAGEDDON Should Dr. Crisping send the Dogs out into the zombie apocalypse to rescue survivors? Or should they hoard their resources and post the Dogs as island guards?

THE OMEGA DOG

BY D.L. SNELL & THOM BRANNAN

Twisting and turning through hordes of zombies, cartel territory, Mayan ruins, and the things that now inhabit them, a group of survivors must travel to save one man's family from a nightmarish third world gone to hell. But this time, even best friends have deadly secrets, and even allies can't be trusted - as a father's only hope of getting his kids out alive is the very thing that's hunting him down.

PERMUTED PRESS

DEAD LIVING
BY GLENN BULLION

It didn't take long for the world to die. And it didn't take long, either, for the dead to rise. Aaron was born on the day the world ended. Kept in seclusion, his family teaches him the basics. How to read and write. How to survive. Then Aaron makes a shocking discovery. The undead, who desire nothing but flesh, ignore him. It's as if he's invisible to them.

PERMUTEDPRESS.COM

AUTOBIOGRAPHY of a WEREWOLF HUNTER
BY BRIAN P. EASTON

After his mother is butchered by a werewolf, Sylvester James is taken in by a Cheyenne mystic. The boy trains to be a werewolf hunter, learning to block out pain, stalk, fight, and kill. As Sylvester sacrifices himself to the hunt, his hatred has become a monster all its own. As he follows his vendetta into the outlands of the occult, he learns it takes more than silver bullets to kill a werewolf.

PERMUTED PRESS

PALE GODS
BY KIM PAFFENROTH

In a world where the undead rule the continents and the few remaining survivors inhabit only island outposts, six men make the dangerous journey to the mainland to hunt for supplies amid the ruins. But on this trip, the dead act stranger and smarter than ever before and the living must adjust or die.

THE JUNKIE QUATRAIN
BY PETER CLINES

Six months ago, the world ended. The Baugh Contagion swept across the planet. Its victims were left twitching, adrenalized cannibals that quickly became know as Junkies. THE JUNKIE QUATRAIN is four tales of survival, and four types of post-apocalypse story. Because the end of the world means different things for different people. Loss. Opportunity. Hope. Or maybe just another day on the job.

BLOOD SOAKED & CONTAGIOUS
BY JAMES CRAWFORD

I am not going to complain to you about my life.

We've got zombies. They are not the brainless, rotting creatures we'd been led to expect. Unfortunately for us, they're just as smart as they were before they died, very fast, much stronger than you or me, and possess no internal editor at all.

Claws. Did I mention claws?

BLOOD SOAKED & INVADED
BY JAMES CRAWFORD

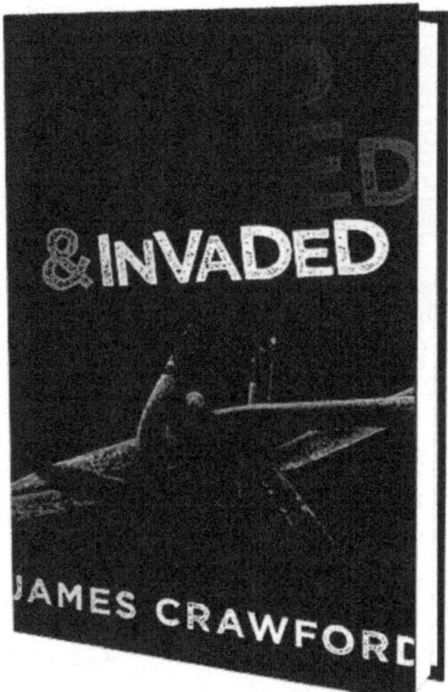

Zombies were bad enough, but now we're being invaded from all sides. Up to our necks in blood, body parts, and unanswerable questions...

...As soon as the realization hit me, I lost my cool. I curled into the fetal position in a pile of blood, offal, and body parts, and froze there. What in the Hell was I becoming that killing was entertaining and satisfying?

PERMUTED PRESS

INFECTION:
ALASKAN UNDEAD APOCALYPSE
BY SEAN SCHUBERT

Anchorage, Alaska: gateway to serene wilderness of The Last Frontier. No stranger to struggle, the city on the edge of the world is about to become even more isolated. When a plague strikes, Anchorage becomes a deadly trap for its citizens. The only two land routes out of the city are cut, forcing people to fight or die as the infection spreads.

CONTAINMENT
(ALASKAN UNDEAD APOCALYPSE BOOK 2)
BY SEAN SCHUBERT

Running. Hiding. Surviving. Anchorage, once Alaska's largest city, has fallen. Now a threatening maze of death, the city is firmly in the cold grip of a growing zombie horde. Neil Jordan and Dr. Caldwell lead a small band of desperate survivors through the maelstrom. The group has one last hope: that this nightmare has been contained, and there still exists a sane world free of infection.

THE UNDEAD SITUATION

BY ELOISE J. KNAPP

The dead are rising. People are dying. Civilization is collapsing. But Cyrus V. Sinclair couldn't care less; he's a sociopath. Amidst the chaos, Cyrus sits with little more emotion than one of the walking corpses… until he meets up with other inconvenient survivors who cramp his style and force him to re-evaluate his outlook on life. It's Armageddon, and things will definitely get messy.

THE UNDEAD HAZE

(THE UNDEAD SITUATION BOOK 2)

BY ELOISE J. KNAPP

When remorse drives Cyrus to abandon his hidden compound he doesn't realize what new dangers lurk in the undead world. He knows he must wade through the vilest remains of humanity and hordes of zombies to settle scores and find the one person who might understand him. But this time, it won't be so easy. Zombies and unpleasant survivors aren't the only thing Cyrus has to worry about.

MAD SWINE: THE BEGINNING
BY STEVEN PAJAK

People refer to the infected as "zombies," but that's not what they really are. Zombie implies the infected have died and reanimated. The thing is, they didn't die. They're just not human anymore. As the infection spreads and crazed hordes--dubbed "Mad Swine"--take over the cities, the residents of Randall Oaks find themselves locked in a desperate struggle to survive in the new world.

PERMUTEDPRESS.COM

MAD SWINE: DEAD WINTER
BY STEVEN PAJAK

Three months after the beginning of the Mad Swine outbreak, the residents of Randall Oaks have reached their breaking point. After surviving the initial outbreak and a war waged with their neighboring community, Providence, their supplies are severely close to depletion. With hostile neighbors at their flanks and hordes of infected outside their walls, they have become prisoners within their own community.

RISE

BY GARETH WOOD

Within hours of succumbing to a plague, millions of dead rise to attack the living. Brian Williams flees the city with his sister Sarah. Banded with other survivors, the group remains desperately outnumbered and under-armed. With no food and little fuel, they must fight their way to safety. RISE is the story of the extreme measures a family will take to survive a trek across a country gone mad.

AGE OF THE DEAD

BY GARETH WOOD

A year has passed since the dead rose, and the citizens of Cold Lake are out of hope. Food and weapons are nearly impossible to find, and the dead are everywhere. In desperation Brian Williams leads a salvage team into the mountains. But outside the small safe zones the world is a foreign place. Williams and his team must use all of their skills to survive in the wilderness ruled by the dead.

DEAD MEAT

BY PATRICK & CHRIS WILLIAMS

The city of River's Edge has been quarantined due to a rodent borne rabies outbreak. But it quickly becomes clear to the citizens that the infection is something much, much worse than rabies... The townsfolk are attacked and fed upon by packs of the living dead. Gavin and Benny attempt to survive the chaos in River's Edge while making their way north in search of sanctuary.

ROTTER WORLD

BY SCOTT M. BAKER

Eight months ago vampires released the Revenant Virus on humanity. Both species were nearly wiped out. The creator of the virus claims there is a vaccine that will make humans and vampires immune to the virus, but it's located in a secure underground facility five hundred miles away. To retrieve the vaccine, a raiding party of humans and vampires must travel down the devastated East Coast.

PERMUTED PRESS

AMONG THE LIVING
BY TIMOTHY W. LONG

The dead walk. Now the real battle for Seattle has begun. Lester has a new clientele, the kind that requires him to deal lead instead of drugs. Mike suspects a conspiracy lies behind the chaos. Kate has a dark secret: she's a budding young serial killer. These survivors, along with others, are drawn together in their quest to find the truth behind the spreading apocalypse.

PERMUTEDPRESS.COM

AMONG THE DEAD
BY TIMOTHY W. LONG

Seattle is under siege by masses of living dead, and the military struggles to prevent the virus from spreading outside the city. Kate is tired of sitting around. When she learns that a rescue mission is heading back into the chaos, she jumps at the chance to tag along and put her unique skill set and, more importantly, swords to use.

PERMUTED PRESS

Made in United States
Orlando, FL
11 March 2022